Oswald Crawfurd

Beyond the Seas

being the surprising adventures and ingenious opinions of Ralph, Lord St. Keyne,

told and set forth by his cousin, Humphrey St. Keyne. Third Edition

Oswald Crawfurd

Beyond the Seas
being the surprising adventures and ingenious opinions of Ralph, Lord St. Keyne, told and set forth by his cousin, Humphrey St. Keyne. Third Edition

ISBN/EAN: 9783337179038

Printed in Europe, USA, Canada, Australia, Japan

Cover: Foto ©Andreas Hilbeck / pixelio.de

More available books at **www.hansebooks.com**

BEYOND THE SEAS.

BEYOND THE SEAS.

BEING

THE SURPRISING ADVENTURES AND INGENIOUS
OPINIONS OF RALPH LORD ST. KEYNE,
TOLD AND SET FORTH BY HIS COUSIN,
HUMPHREY ST. KEYNE.

BY

OSWALD CRAWFURD,

Author of "The World We Live In,"
"Portugal: Old and New," &c.

THIRD EDITION.

LONDON: CHAPMAN AND HALL,
LIMITED.
1888.

RICHARD CLAY AND SONS,
LONDON AND BUNGAY.

BEYOND THE SEAS.

CHAPTER I.

IN the year of Our Lord one thousand six hundred and fifty-two (1652), only one year and four months after His Sacred Majesty King Charles, the Second of that name (my dread Sovereign and the best of Kings), had been crowned at Scone, and but eight months after the fatal fight at Worcester, disastrous to the King's cause, we—that is to say, my young kinsman and master and myself—reached the city of Genoa in our wanderings. After Worcester rout we had taken ship at Rye and run to Scheveningen in Holland. Thence, after long journeying through the Low Countries and Germany, we crossed the Tyrolean Alps into Tuscany, and passing across Italy to Genoa, embarked upon the Spanish trading galleon *Esperanza*, in English *The Hope* (happy omen ! not altogether to be frustrated), bound for Barcelona in Spain, but with intention to touch at the Port of Palermo, in

B

Sicily, that fair and fertile island being then an appurtenance of the King of Spain.

It happened that on the 2nd day of May, at a little before seven o'clock in the morning, we lay becalmed some three sea leagues or thereabouts off the Sicilian coast; a light, south-easterly breeze having died away with the dawn, and the high lands on either side of the city of Palermo being now and again seen and unseen through the mists of early morning.

I am thus particular, for it was in the idleness and leisure of this morning time that I formed the resolution to begin to set down in writing the true history of the adventures which had befallen my young kinsman (and former pupil in war and letters) and myself since the fight at Worcester. Not indeed opining that there had happened to us at this time any greater dangers or more moving and wonderful incidents, perils, and adventures than to perhaps some other worthy and loyal gentlemen in these melancholy times; but that I did then wish, and do now still more urgently desire, to recount the circumstances of our fugitive and exiled life, in order that I may the more particularly set forth and blazon and expatiate upon the singular learning, gravity, courage, and wisdom, *rebus in arduis*, in trial and adversity, of the young gentleman, my companion in these misfortunes, who was the head of our family, *præsidium et dulce decus*, the guide and ornament of our house, now alas! fallen from its pride and magnificence, of which I, a poor scholar and soldier-adventurer, am but an unhonoured member (and who must needs bear the bar sinister on my escutcheon), and, so to speak, allowed to name myself one of the family but on sufferance and by condescension.

So forming this aforesaid resolution, little did I reckon and forecast that this very day, then so newly dawned, would be the turning-point of our lives, and that henceforward my kinsman's fortune would be, though still varied and most strange, indeed to the point of marvellous and astounding, higher and greater than that of any Englishman of the times who has sought and counted upon the favour of the fickle goddess Fortune beyond the seas.

Thus have I, as my shrewd and gentle Reader has already perceived, got at a stroke *in medias res*, into the middle of my subject (a method which H. Flaccus commends to the teller of history in prose or verse) before I have so much as told my own name (which is no great matter) or my Lord's (which is), or what was the purpose of our taking ship for Spain from Genoa, or why we touched at the Sicilian port of Palermo, which was indeed, as the reader will have gathered, no business of ours, for we purposed not even to land there, but the ship's own and its masters'.

Know then that upon the final defeat at all points of our forces in England and Scotland, and the triumph of the Sectaries at Worcester, there was no place in the land for us King's men who had fought and laboured for the true cause. We gentlemen of the army especially were hunted like hares and foxes, and needed, and indeed did most cautiously and wakefully use, the subtlety and cunning of these beasts to fly from and elude the packs of our enemies ; for if captured we were mercilessly imprisoned, starved, maltreated ; the common sort shot without trial, by decimation, one man in ten, to fright the rest ; the leading men tried for disobeying the usurper, and many of them barbarously executed for that loyalty to their King and country, which in all nations and times has been acknowledged the chiefest virtue of a good citizen. My young Lord's estates, we had but good enough cause to apprehend, would be shortly confiscated and seized by the usurper Cromwell, who then had gathered all government into his own hands, and was as absolute with our lives and estates as a very grand Sultan of the Turks.

Notwithstanding the manifest peril in which he stood, my Lord was for making his way to his own house in Somersetshire as soon as the battle and the rout of our side that followed it were over. It was against my will that we rode thither, but, "It will be safe enough from the Roundheads," said he, "till the rumour reaches the Castle how the fight has gone against us, but we must ride faster than rumour, for I have my business to do there." And we rode hard, and by the second day in the morning had reached the gates of St. Keyne Castle.

I questioned him not as to his business here, concluding it was some matter of heirloom, of jewels, or plate, or muniments, or of moneys, that he would secure against the spoiling of his estate ; but his business was to provide for the safety of his cousin and ward, the Lady Geraldine Scudamour, a child of but fifteen years, his sole near relative save myself (who am indeed, as I have hinted, no legitimate kinsman of his or hers) : this young lady's wardship having, upon his father's demise, so quick and strangely were matters jumbled in these jumbled times, devolved upon him, a youth, though grave beyond his years, of but twenty-three. The Lady Geraldine resided at St. Keyne Castle with a religious lady from the convent of the Ursulines at Poitiers, and when my Lord and I alighted from our horses, 'twas the child who greeted us.

"Geraldine !" cried my Lord, after he had saluted her upon the cheek, "Geraldine, my dear," says he very gently but sadly, "the King's cause is lost."

The child went very pale.

"Lost !" she called out, "then will they murder us all ?"

"Nay," said his Lordship, "thou wilt be spared, and madame here. The lady came up at this moment, very much frightened.

"But you, Ralph !" and the child clung to him weeping, "what will become of you ?" for the two had been in a manner playfellows together.

"Our kinsman Humphrey and I," quoth he, looking at me confidently, "will pass easily through our enemies and embark for Spain. The king of that country lacks soldiers of fortune, and we intend to offer him our swords."

" Then will I go with you too," cried out Lady Geraldine. " I will be your page, as Bellario was to Philaster in the play."

The French religious lady, catching something of the child's meaning, shook her head reprovingly.

But the child cried to her kinsman to let her come too, and he for peace's sake humoured her fancy a while.

" But," asked he, " how shall we manage, my dear, in war time, when fighting is on hand ? 'Tis then no place or time for young maidens."

" Oh," said Lady Geraldine, " see how tall I am, and slim of my figure.   I will so dress, as Bellario did or Imogen in the plays, that no man, or woman either, but shall say I am a man ; " and indeed the maiden was slim and tall and upright, being then, I think, a month or so past her fifteenth birthday, and quick and strong in her carriage, and rather wan of face, so that in man's dress she might easily have passed for one between boy and youth.

My Lord laughed a little, and looking upon me, " What say you, cousin, to this ? " quoth he.

Now, I have never failed to inculcate upon my young Lord the evil ways and evil example of women, and put him in remembrance of all that the learning of both ancients and moderns has discovered and expounded in discommendation of women and their ways ; to wit, their vanity, and their lightness, and their leading of men's thoughts away from learning and gravity and wisdom into folly and levity. How that, in ancient times, the wisest nations—that is to say, the Greeks and Indians—saw right to include and seclude them in dwellings apart from men; how the civilest people of the moderns have done the same, to wit, in Convents and Nunneries, and the cunningest and most advancing, and in war the most terrible of modern peoples, namely the Turks, have built their Harems and Seraglios (*teste Busbecquio*) for the utter obclusion of the weaker sex, to the inestimable peace, comfort, ease, and freedom of the rest of mankind. I likewise did not fail to strengthen and support my argument with innumerable instances from the Christian Fathers, as Jerome, Cyprian, and Chrysostom; from the philosophers, as Seneca; from the satirist Juvenal; and from the lighter poets, as Propertius, Martialis, and above all Ovidius Naso (*vide* his *Ars Amoris*, passim).

But on this occasion courtesy and good manners forbade me to be too convincing, and I therefore forewent any response to my kinsman's invitation; contenting myself with remarking that women's constitutions were too nice and delicate for the rough usages of a campaign or to look upon blood and wounds, and their bodies too weak to bear its fatigues, too weak even to sustain the mere weight of a soldier's arms; nay, even to hold out a soldier's sword in their hands.

"Look, Humphrey," cried my girl cousin, "I am

stronger than you think," and the child, going to the
trophies of ancient armour that stood in the hall like
armed knights all arow, snatched up a morion from
one figure, took a great battle-axe from another,
and fixing the first upon her head with a look
between laughing and terrible, she raised the axe
in both hands, pretending a swashing blow. "Now
look to it, Humphrey," cried she, smiling on me,
"for I will kill you dead for your hard words of
women."

But the weapon was too heavy for her puny strength
and fell forward upon the paved floor.

Her cousin laughed a little, overlooking the unreason of the child, then turning to the nun,
"Madame," said he, "there is, I fear, no longer safety
for you or my kinswoman in this castle's walls.   In
an hour you and she must ride forth towards Bristol.
I pray you to prepare yourself and the Lady Geraldine; and do you, madame, cloak your religious habit
with a riding dress, for no doubt the road will be
infested with Sectaries.   You will travel to Bristol,
where I have provided a gentleman of my friends to
meet you, and a house for your due lodging. So soon
as things have quieted down, a passage will be taken
for you both to Havre-de-Grace, where I have
provided friends to receive you, and whence you will
be carried by ship to The Groyne in Galicia of Spain,
near which is the great Benedictine Nunnery of St.
Scholastica, of which our aunt Lady Priscilla Scudamour is Abbess, and where my cousin will continue

her education ; and I desire that you accompany her and still have immediate charge over her person."

We did not attend the ladies on their journey, which they made in company with several of the trustier of Lord St. Keyne's servants, but after staying a while for some necessary correspondence and having set his affairs hastily in order, my Lord and I rode fast in their track, for though we feared to be seen in their company, justly deeming that our cavalier dress, arms, and appearance might provoke molestation to them, we hung on their traces for two days, unknown to them, that we might make sure that no hurt befell them, and ready, if aught happened amiss, for a bold stroke of help or rescue. But nothing took place worthy of note, for the countryside was not yet aroused nor the Sectaries drunken (as they afterwards were) with the news of their great victory, of which indeed only unconfirmed rumours were as yet flying along the roads, insomuch that men were still doubtful on which side to incline. Note likewise, that about the environs of Bristol and along the main road from London in the east and this, the greatest and richest city of the west, were to be found as many King's men as Roundheads, and as we rode by many spoke out their minds, to the effect that they had it in their hearts to wish good luck to us and to the King (perceiving clearly enough to which party we belonged).

Seeing how matters went, my Lord spoke openly to some along the road who had served on our side and who knew him by sight or rumour, saying, "Friends, the King's cause is ended for the time, and they who love it and me will serve both by taking arms abroad where I intend, namely with the King of Spain."

This was bold speaking, and I feared for the speaker that it might get bruited in a wrong quarter, but its very boldness won it good acceptance with the honest yeomen and farmers' sons with whom my kinsman spoke, and many were minded at once to bring their swords, their horses, and themselves into a company to serve him; but, "Weigh the matter well," said he, "and in a day or two I will return along this road, when as many of you as will can join our troop," and to some he appointed one place of meeting and to others another, as the case might be, upon the road. Sure enough, when we had got as far as the gates of Bristol, where we knew our ladies and their servants to be in safety, and had turned back, we met several of these said farmers and yeomen, all good fellows, and stout and valiant men, a-horseback, armed some better, some worse, one with sword and pistols, another with a pike, or a musquetoon, ready to side with my kinsman and myself. For they were all loyal men disappointed with the issues of things, hating the tyranny of the Fanatics and not yet (by a good deal) sick of fighting for their King and for their liberties.

We rode on, making south, with design to embark at Poole in Dorset, always riding forward very quickly and cautiously, increasing in numbers as we went along, and avoiding the towns where troops were posted. At this time, however, the Parliamentary forces were mostly gathered in the west (with the arch usurper Cromwell) or in the northerly parts of England, and we found the town garrisons weak and the country side more bare of troops than we had either expected or hoped. We employed a circuit to avoid Bath, where was a strong troop of horse, and made pretty straight through Devizes towards Salisbury, wherein was a strongish garrison too, but mostly foot, militia men, as we had heard, and, as indeed proved to be the case, for there were barely three-score horse soldiers in the city.

Now by this time we feared no such force, for our own troop numbered nearly a hundred men, so many had fallen in on our passage through Somerset and Wiltshire, and, though our business was for the present rather flying than fighting, we were not like to run from equal or nearly equal numbers of the enemy upon a direct challenge given. We had hopes, so fast had we ridden, that no news of us had gone on before, but as fast as we had come it appeared that treason had travelled still faster, which happened in this wise, that as we passed through Pottern, a small township a little north of Market Lavington in Wiltshire, and lodging that night in the hay-barn of an honest gentleman and a Royalist, some three miles beyond the town, when the troop was in motion at dawn next day, three fellows on good horses overtook us. I was riding with my Lord at the head of the men and doubtless seeing me to be the graver looking of the two, my hair grizzled, and my face somewhat furrowed and careworn (though less with years than with trouble and long service) and my Lord having a very young face and at the moment turning his head to laugh and jest with the men, as was ever his wont to do on the march, the newcomers mistook me for the chief in command and accosted me: "We would crave to join your honour's troop," said their spokesman, very civilly, "and fare with you, being loyal King's men, as we perceive you to be."

I will note here that at this period the Puritans and Sectaries had mostly ceased to wear their hair long, and they dressed in very sober clothes, while we, their enemies, went to a contrary extreme both in hair and dress. These fellows, however, were betwixt and between, distinguishable in look or dress neither one way nor the other.

"Address yourselves, sir," said I, "to this gentleman" (purposely not naming him), "for I am but the lieutenant of this troop, and his Worship is in command."

On this my Lord questioned them a little, and they answering readily enough, he bade them fall in with the men. "And do you," said his Lordship to me in French (for he spake all the tongues), "disperse them separately among our men, for I rather misdoubt their honesty."

This was wisely devised, for the men were, as it

afterwards turned out, nothing less than vile Parliamentarians come on purpose to spy upon us.

The next morning we had come to the edge of a huge plain that lies north of Salisbury, and advancing a little way into it where there were neither woods nor hedges to incommode us, nor a hill within many miles round, and we were safe from observation and surprise, we deployed the troop and performed some necessary drill and preparation for battle, having as yet hardly had time in our hasty march to do more than appoint two lieutenants, four cornets, and sundry under officers.

This manœuvring and drill was over at a little past noon, and when we got into marching line again and struck across the plain or common, one Cornet Brown, a Somersetshire man well known to me, he having fought by my side many years ago in the Low Countries, came up to me as if upon necessary business of the march.

"Captain St. Keyne," says he under his breath, "these three new recruits are, an' it please you, no true men at all; they are soldiers sure enough, but they have never fought on our side."

I asked him how he knew that.

"They are drilled soldiers, sir, I can see, because they turn, and back, and keep their horses in line, and draw their swords, and make the cuts, and follow the word, like well-trained men, but when I have questioned them as to the war and with whom they have served, they give no straight answers, and their

talk is too sober for men of our side. If there were
ever a . . . tree on this . . . common," said the
cornet, looking about him, and swearing a couple of
hearty oaths into the sentence (which I need not
record), "it would be well to string up the three
rogues as a warning to any others who may be
following on our track."

"By the laws of war, Cornet," said I, "we should
be justified on this testimony of yours alone, and I
will report the matter to our commander."

Note, that the mark of a Roundhead fanatic was a
demure habit of speech and a superstitious sobriety
and softness in the use of words, as of conscience-
smitten men fearing to awaken the wrath of Heaven
upon their hypocrisy, while our poor fellows were all
innocently free and bold of utterance, and very
outspoken.

I laid the matter immediately before his Lordship.

"I imagined it might be so," said he, "and I conceive we should wisely alter our course, lest these
fellows have either prepared the garrison at Salisbury
to oppose our way, or are but in the van of others
following on our track from the west."

CHAPTER II.

WE marched still onward till past sunset, when coming to a shepherd's hut or croft on the plain, my kinsman called a halt, and ordering the troop into a half circle round about him, commanded the three recruits to advance, then bidding them dismount and causing them to be disarmed, he spoke as follows to the ranks of his troopers :

"Comrades ! we have here three men in our midst who are traitors to our cause and to us, and who must know themselves by every law of God and man to be worthy of death. They have plotted our undoing, and if we do not put them to immediate death, it is rather lack of time to give them a soldier's trial and such justice as comports even with haste and exigency of war, rather, I say, this haste that we are in than any foolish and futile desire to show them mercy. Therefore I order that as their lives might justly be forfeited to us, so their arms and horses be taken from them in the name and for the service of our rightful King, and that they be bound and cast into this hut, the door made fast, and a guard set." He then turned to me. "Captain St. Keyne," said he, "I desire that you see to

the due execution of this order.   We encamp here for
the night," said he to the men, "and when the bugles
sound the *reveille* to-morrow morning we will up-saddle
quickly and away."

Thus did we, picketing our horses and eating and
sleeping in their midst, with a strong patrol to watch
and guard over our prisoners ; and in the night, about
two hours before dawn, while it was still very dark,
the bugles sounded, and we saddled up and rode
away, but examining into our gaol house, namely, the
little hut, we found one of our birds flown ; how, we
never knew, but probably by the help and confederacy
of the others.   He had got out and off in the darkness,
and, what was more amiss, had stolen away upon
one of the troop horses and ridden we knew not
whither, though we guessed to Salisbury ; but this
mattered little to us, as we had already determined to
leave that city well alone, and trend to the south, and
pass eastward, and then to the south again to some
Kentish port, my Lord having already got news by the
road that the road to Poole was blocked by its garrison
under Colonel Prideaux, who held there some 2,000
militia men.   Therefore my Lord decided to make
eastward almost to Middlesex, where we had intelligence that Major-General Skippon, commanding the
militia regiments of London, had sent out parties of
horse to hold the lanes and roads in hopes to pick up
returning stragglers from Worcester rout ; thence we
proposed to pass suddenly due south by roads leading
to small ungarrisoned or but weakly garrisoned towns,

reach one of the Cinque Ports in Kent or Sussex, now certainly abandoned by the usurping troops, and there take ship for Spain.

This, then, was the plan of our march, but it had like to have been frustrated by the escape of our prisoner, for certainly he or some other spy had alarmed the garrison of Salisbury ; and the horsemen therein, to the number of some seventy, had sallied forth to meet us, and were then nearer to us than we had any notion of, for as one of them who fell into our hands afterwards informed us, their scouts viewed us that morning from a wooded hill-top to the north of Salisbury city. Here they espied us passing along the road making eastward, some mile and a half or two miles below them ; but seeing that we outnumbered them and marched in very regular order, they thought it more discreet to let us go upon our way than to hinder us. So, descending the opposite side of the hill into the Winchester road, which runs in that valley from Salisbury in a pretty straight line, they marched in all haste to the former city (which would have lain on our road too had we not gone about to the north to avoid it), and there being reinforced by some fifty or sixty sabres of the garrison, they retreated before us towards London, feeling us, as our soldiers have it, with their scouts and outposts, but never letting their main body be seen by us till we had got off the open down country hereabouts, into the woods and waste land of Surrey, about Leith Hill and Dorking ; nor, indeed, did we see them then, for a time, nor should have known of their being there, but for an odd and happy occurrence.

We held our march along the Downs, and, in the main, on high land, for there is a very long ridge of hill before you reach Guildford town, lying east and west, on which is good travelling, and whence a good view is to be had on either side and a long way ahead. Here, then, we marched boldly onward, being assured of no ambushes, but so soon as we viewed Leith Hill, a tall, well-wooded eminence, rising abruptly to a goodish height, some thirty miles from London, we struck to the south to touch its foot, not unwilling to lose ourselves among the woodlands in these parts from the observation of the forces of the Fanatics under Skippon, which, as I have said, we guessed were waiting and watching for such as ourselves in the neighbourhood of London. Had it not been, as I have said above, for a most fortunate occurrence at this aforesaid hill, we had run right upon an ambush, cunningly laid for us by our enemies from Salisbury and Winchester. We had, as I have said, entered the forest, which lies pretty thick here, but interspersed with open glades, when we perceived a gentleman on a fine stone horse galloping hastily to us down the hill and along one of these said glades.

"Hold!" cried he, raising his hand, and without waiting to bestow on us more ceremonious address, "hold, gentlemen, and proceed no further, or you are dead men!"

This person being questioned of us, for at first we

were inclined to suspect such hasty and officious intervention in our business, named himself to be surrogate and estate bailiff to one Squire Evelyn of Wootton, a well-known King's man, upon whose lands we then it seems were riding. The squire, he told us, was living abroad away from the troubles, and Mr. Legge, his surrogate, knew that in warning us of our imminent danger he did but what his master would wish him to do.

"And what," demanded my Lord, "is this danger?"

Mr. Legge informed us that a troop of well-mounted horse soldiers, 145 in number, for he had counted them as they defiled below him, had entered the woods some six miles to the south, and were posted on either side of a wooded valley through which we needs must presently pass. Though concealed by the trees, these were not set so thick but that he had looked down upon and espied them from the neighbouring Hill of Leith.

We called a halt, and sending scouts on foot up the hill, which is a very rugged and steep one, could spy down upon the armed men lying in ambush a league or more along the road we were about to follow.

When it was made plain to us how things stood, my Lord called us about him and said:

"Gentlemen, your enemies and the King's have set a trap for us, not content with the chances of an open fight, though they outnumber us by over two score, and are lurking yonder to fall upon us unawares. Now," said he, smiling a little upon the stout fellows around him, " I have it in my heart not altogether to baulk them. What say you, gentlemen ? "

The men sent up a cheer, and crying out that they were ready to follow their leader at any time and any whither, gathered up their bridle reins, and some loosened their swords in scabbard or dropped fresh firing in their carbine locks, looking up to my kinsman for the word to ride up and engage the enemy.

" Softly ! gentlemen," said he, " my leading shall not be direct into the ambush set for you. This honest friend here tells me of a path that keeps to the shoulder of the hill and leaves the enemy to the right. I will take you along it, and thither shall the Sectaries follow us and, if they choose, engage us on more equal terms."

Herein, I conceive, my Lord most prudently resolved, though there seems at first sight some slight flavour of rashness in the project, for though as I have said we were but poor fugitives from the rage of the Fanatics, yet often in warfare *in medio tutissimus ibis* (to give a new interpretation to the maxim), it is at times politic to escape by going into the very midst of our enemies, and certain it is that if we had not then and there engaged with this force they would have hung upon our steps ever afterwards, hampered and hindered us of our purpose, and prevented us in our escape.

Our troop, then, marched along certain paths shown to us by Mr. Legge in the thickness of the wood, always keeping on the shoulder of the hill, till we had travelled some league and a half, and were then got to a long ridge of steep hill well overgrown with trees, which is a spur of Leith Hill that runs to the north. Here on the acclivity of this ridge we halted, having given the go-by to the enemy. My Lord now went from man to man, counselling and encouraging each in turn ; he advised them how to use their carbines or pistols, namely, to discharge the fire-arm only when an enemy was at the very point of it, " for otherwise a wild shot that hits nothing, the loading and ramming home of charges and priming your piece, will keep you out of the fight and at a disadvantage from the enemy, but," holding out his drawn sword to the men, " this will be our best weapon to-day ; trust to this, friends, and the day is ours ; never stop to feint or parry or guard, but strike quick, point or edge, and strike home."

Thus did he speak, showing himself to be most wise in war and skilful in the art of cavalry, though still but young, for he had in all fought but once in a set fight at Worcester with the Scotch army, and, before that, only in that running and victorious campaign of forays and skirmishing begun in Cornwall, and that ended in our victory under General Hopton at Lansdown Hill near Bath, and the death of that great and brave commander Sir Bevil Greenvil ; my Lord being then but a lad of fifteen, he winning his spurs that day, but getting a wounded foot from which he did not recover till long afterwards.

We had now got, as I have said, to a woody ridge called Redland Hill, and we looked down below on a broadish plain pretty thickly interspersed with oak trees and with great holms or holly trees, the ground beneath being free from underwood, and hard, sound turf. This wooded plain is known as Holmwood. Presently we could hear, and then plainly see, six or seven scouts of the enemy galloping here and there, searching the woodland for signs of our troop, as the foremost hounds of a pack scurry hither and thither when the scent of the hare is lost and they are at fault and casting to recover it. So soon as the scouts caught sight of us, for we were at halt and in their full view, they galloped back, and in a few minutes had led the main body up at a round trot.

Presently we saw that Mr. Legge's information was correct. We learnt afterwards that the garrison at Winchester and some men from Dorking having joined the Salisbury party, it reached in number to 145, all told, being just fifty more than we had.

They too, like us, halted in line, and there we stood, both troops, not 500 paces between us; they, though in force, not daring to ride up to us, standing as we did on the steeply rising ground broken by trees and much above their heads. Presently some of the enemy began to call out to us, jeering and mocking us. One fellow cried loudly that we were men of sin given over and predestined to the burning, and bade us come down, an we dared, and reap the reward (so did he say) of our evil doing. Others called us rogues and bloody-minded malignants, others cowards, whereat some of our fellows earnestly besought to be led against them. Two or three of the Sectaries fired their pieces at us and the bullets whistled overhead and cut the boughs and branches behind our ranks, and one bullet struck the sword hilt of a trooper and jangled it, but did the wearer no hurt.

My Lord then directed six of our men to return the enemy's fire, "but not more than six of you," said he, "as you love me, for I want but to draw their fire, and then we will charge down before they can load again."

Some of our troopers thereupon fired a volley, with good aim, for two of the Sectaries' horses lost their riders and galloped off. This provoked the enemy, and there came a general volley from them with such good aim that four of our fellows rolled from the saddle wounded and one dying. Then, before the smoke of their firing had cleared off in the misty air, my Lord, drawing his sword, bid the bugler sound the charge and led his men down the hill through the trees, first at a slow walk, then at a trot, then quickening his pace to a fast hand-gallop as we drew within 100 yards of their position. Then he cried out very loudly, " God save King Charles !" and, with a terrible answering shout, our fellows in a moment were upon the Rebels.

In affairs of this kind with cavalry, every man fights his own battle, and it is hit or miss, sink or swim, winning or losing, before he has drawn fifty breaths; then he wakes as from a strange, eager dream, where he has seen pistols belching fire, sword-blades sweeping through the air, horses rearing up amid smoke and shouting and the noise of shots, and brave fellows—friends or enemies—falling from their saddles and rolling on the ground bleeding and wounded and dying. He awakes, I say, from a sort of confused swound and his party is beaten and in flight, or he himself with his friends is pursuing and cutting down a defeated enemy.

In this skirmish the enemy numbered 145 to our 95, but we had this advantage that we made the onset not without some help of sloping ground; and note, that in all cavalry fighting the best side to be on is the charging side. Nevertheless, outnumbering us as they did, they stood up against our onset without flinching, which again is a rare thing in warfare, for the one or the other of two bodies of horse mostly gives way before it comes to an actual shock of man against man. We had charged in line, and clave our way easily through the enemy, emptying many saddles; then, turning our horses some twenty or thirty yards beyond, at the bugler's call we engaged them again, and we should certainly have overborne them altogether but for two things—one, that we were so greatly outnumbered that their flank men, who had never been engaged at the first charge, now spurred up and joined the medley, so that both parties were rabbled up together, and went at it helter-skelter, pell-mell, every man singling out an enemy to fight with to the death, for in these affairs we seldom took or gave quarter. The other thing against us was that there had joined the enemy a detachment of horse from Dorking under the famous Colonel Messenger, numbering some twenty-five or thirty veteran troops of Hollis's dragoons, all wearing Lord Essex's orange scarf over their uniforms of red. These sturdy and valiant soldiers came fresh upon us who were already outnumbered, and fought as I never could wish to see men fight better. Whether by design or accident, but I suspect by design of that good soldier Colonel Messenger, who had taken the chief command, his dragoons were placed some fifteen on each flank with orders to close in after the charge. As for the rest of the enemy, they were raw men of the militia, brave fellows, but unused to the shifts, noise, and confusion of battle, and we had, as I say, speedily overcome and put them to flight but for Hollis's dragoons. On this account the fight was long and obstinate and bloody, and we had no leisure to pursue and utterly rout the militiamen until we had put to the sword the whole of Colonel Messenger's troopers ; they, like brave men, neither asking nor giving quarter.

CHAPTER III.

COMING to my reasonable senses, as it were, after the heat and madness of the fight, I perceived how things had gone. The enemy were vanquished and our men were in pursuit and scattered far and wide through the wood, and I was alone, and my horse, wounded to the death, was staggering beneath me to a fall.

Now, I would have my readers to know that I, who have written so far as a soldier, and have shown, it may be, tokens of affection for the sword, the carbine, the great horse, and all the various circumstance of war, am in my heart a peace-loving man. Yea, for all my long training to arms from a boy upwards, in the Low Countries and Germany, and for these last troublous years of civil war in England, I could wish almost never to hear again the trumpet's call or a shot fired in anger. I am indeed not one in whom, as Virgil has it, " *Sævit amor ferri et scelerata insania belli,*" who is maddened by the cruel lust of war. My true delight is in books and in philosophy :—

> " How charming is divine Philosophy,
>   Not harsh and crabbed as dull fools suppose,
>   But musical as is Apollo's lute,"

as that sweet poet and bitter Sectary, Mr. John Milton, has lately sung, and I have at times longed with a very earnest longing, and especially when my duty has called me to strike down brothers of my own blood and race in these cruel wars, to put aside the contentious spirit of soldiering and wholly give myself to retirement and a scholar's labours.

So much have I to say in excuse and extenuation of what I did at the close of this fight. Of a truth, many a man, if he would tell all, has grievous sins of commission and omission (as the theologians use to say) upon his conscience, and of the latter kind of sins none have so much oppressed me in memory as that which, as I have said, I did or failed to do after this very skirmish at Holmwood.

It happened in this wise. I had dismounted from my wounded horse and caught a loose one that ran by. Looking to him more closely as I was girthing him anew, I perceived it was our bugler's, and his horn was still lying in its case or holster. I took it in my hand, and, considering a little, blew our private signal of rappel or recall.

So soon as I had done this I began to repent of my doing it, and have continued ever since to repent though I endeavoured then, and do still at times vainly try, to salve over my conscience with various sophistries, as that the day was won already ; for

those only who had been stubborn in the fight,
Messenger's dragoons, lay on the ground, poor
fellows! around me; that our men were scattered
and at any moment liable to be fallen upon by some
new enemy; that we were a flying and not a fighting
force, and our business was retreat not pursuit.   Say
and argue how I would, I still greatly fear that, as
a soldier and a Christian man, I did shamefully amiss
in at all this day sparing the enemies of England
and our King.

However this may be, I blew the signal of recall
upon the bugle with a loud and warning note, and
presently the contention, the shouting and the trample
of horses, and the clash of sword against sword, the
sounds of battle which still I could hear all round me
but could see nothing thereof for the thickness of the
trees—presently, I say, these sounds ceased, and the
troopers answering the call began to centre towards
me one by one and in twos and threes, coming
through the glades of the wood; tired men on tired
horses, and many of them wounded and faint with
battle.

Our men had suffered heavily in this fight, and
though thrice I sounded the rappel only twenty-seven
of our troop answered the roll call out of ninety-five
strong men who had ridden into the woods that
morning.   Some few more came in after a while on
foot, having parted with their horses, but there was
no lack of mounts, for over two score horses ran up
to the bugle riderless, mostly unhurt horses of the

enemy, and with these we could make a good general remounting of our men. Of our officers were killed both our lieutenants, a cornet, and three corporals. My dear kinsman was wounded in three places, but all happily light flesh wounds, and being bound up they incommoded him but little. Cornet Brown, a valiant gentleman of great strength and activity, and a most skilful swordsman, had killed Colonel Messenger with his own hand, and three of his dragoons, and received from one of them a thrust with a sword in the side. It was a bad wound, and I doubted if we could carry him to the coast, but we managed to do it. I also had got a pistol ball lodged in the left shoulder, and a little slash of a sword had laid open my left cheek, but 'twas no great matter. Many of our troopers were wounded, but all carried things with a brave face. We had got but one prisoner (so keen and unmerciful had been the fighting), a young fellow, a townsman of Salisbury, who begged for and got quarter from myself when he lay at my sword's point ; and fearing that if we set him free he would tell of our route we were fain to carry him some thirty miles with us, and then we gave him his liberty at Ashurst in Kent.

My Lord was pleased to approve of my having sounded the recall, for, said he, we have now given the alarm, and shall be followed from all sides. His first care was to send a scout up to the top of the hill whence we had just descended, with orders to look about him and note the approach of any force, and, seeing any, to come to us at once. In less than half an hour the fellow returned with news that on the bare Downs to the north, beyond Dorking, was a strong body of horse travelling westward. This, we could not doubt, was a part of Skippon's command from London, purposing to cut us off on the road, which doubtless they considered we should take to the north. So soon as their line of march would be struck by the enemy we had dispersed, they would no doubt alter their course towards us, and seeing that this fresh enemy was but ten miles away as the crow flies, it behoved us therefore immediately to force our march southwards to the coast, where we had news of a Dutch Snow lying in the Downs and ready to carry us away.

We girthed up our horses therefore, and with as forced marching as our condition would allow travelled due east to the coast; but learning by the way that there were large garrisons at Maidstone and Rochester, and a larger still at Canterbury, all which places lay near to but not upon our road, we abandoned our first intention to seek issue from the kingdom by a Kentish port, and travelling eastward only for a time, suddenly altered our course to due south for the port of Rye, in Sussex, which we reached without further adventure on the third day from Holmwood; but our swift marching cost us many men left by the way, for when we got within sight of the sea we had but sixteen men, all told, and all of us were dismounted.

I will here observe that all through this part of the

country from Dorking south and east there was more of disaffection to the usurper than to the King, and that we could find help and counsel and supplies all along the way, and, what was of more account, a sure messenger to carry our letters to the shipmaster, who was waiting for us, and bid him meet us at Rye.

Our horses we had disposed of at very good prices to one honest gentleman or another along the road, and thus each of the troop, besides what private means he enjoyed, had certain ready moneys of his own, as beseems gentlemen soldiers of fortune travelling to the wars. Before reaching Rye the whole troop was, as I have said, afoot, and we marched through the streets of the town with no concealment and no concern, perceiving that the people were altogether on our side, the garrison of less than a dozen men being too weak to molest us, and keeping to their barracks.

From the cliffs near the port we saw our ship, a Snow of some 150 tons, standing on and off in the offing, and we lay that night in the barn of one Farmer Jumper. He, though with us in heart, for he sent to offer us this accommodation of his barn, begged that in policy we would use some pretended violence in taking possession thereof. Here, then, we lay that day and night in great comfort and content- ment, being visited after nightfall by many gentlemen and others of the neighbourhood, all of them bringing presents for our entertainment, as kilderkins of old ale, strong waters, pies of meat and fruit, loaves of bread, great cheeses, and the like ; so that we could make a soldier's feast and a carouse, and afterwards lie soft and warm in the farmer's hay, taking full rest after our labours, knowing well that we had good friends outside who had set watch and ward and would warn us should our enemies endeavour at molesting us.

Betimes next morning we embarked in two boats for the Dutch ship, a great concourse of people standing on the quays, and very sadly, many men and women in tears, watching our going off. My kinsman, sitting in the stern sheets of the last boat to go, took off his hat, and, giving it a wave, called out, " God save King Charles, and send him a speedy return !" (we had all then thought the King was got away from England, but he did not, in truth, till later) and we all, waving our hats in like manner, joined in this prayer, which hearing, the people on shore, numbering perhaps some three or four hundred, took up the cry with a mighty voice ; and thus, leaving England, the last thing we saw was the weeping faces of our countrymen, and, mingling with the noise of winds and waves, we heard their shout of " God save the King, and send him a speedy return ! " —a good omen, but, alas ! not for many years to be accomplished.

I have been thus particular in my account of this affair at Holmwood, because, though admitted to be a grievous defeat of themselves by the Parliamentarians, the difference in numbers on the two sides, and the great advantage had therein by Cromwell's people, have never yet, that I am sensible, been acknowledged by them. On the other hand, our leader and ourselves have been much reprehended for that we fought at all when we must well have known that our cause was lost ; but I have never yet learned that a man is blamable who strikes in his own defence ; and if a man, then why not a body of men ? Had we been let alone, be sure we had never fought. It has ever been held right policy to help a retreating enemy ; yea, to go so far as (in the words of the adage) to build him a golden bridge to escape away upon. But these fellows stood in our way, pursued us hotly, would have hemmed us in, laid a cunning trap to take our lives ; yet all their fury and their cunning we frustrated. Are we, then, to blame or they, if they reaped the reward of their rashness ?

So far contentiously ; but I have desired too, in the recounting of this long retreat—or rather this long flight—of so considerable a body across nearly the greatest breadth of England, this fight at Holmwood and the safe embarking of the remnant, to evidence the genius for war of my young kinsman, for to him alone is the credit, and, indeed, the glory of it due. He needed no advice of me and his other lieutenants, though we were all of us men long practised in arms, and the youngest nearly double his years. He called no councils of war in straits and extremities, necessities sometimes, but evils always, as serving to divide and distract judgment

D

and to set envious or foolish men to cavil and contend, and often greatly to discourage the soldiers, who follow the less readily when they perceive their chief hardly to know his own mind. But my Lord ever resolved quickly and well, as was evidenced in changing our course and throwing out our pursuers near Salisbury, in avoiding the ambush at Leith Hill, not by ignoble flight but by bold outwittal of the enemies' device; and again, by that sudden fierce onset at Holmwood against odds, followed by the utter rout and discomfiture of our foes. Yet that which chiefly recommends him to me, *rei militaris perito*, who have closely studied the art of war, is that love and confidence which he had the art to inspire in those about him—a high virtue which many famous commanders have lacked, but the greatest of all, Julius Cæsar, Scipio the African, Alexander the Great, and Hannibal, with some others of less note, never have wanted.

Touching the retreat and the Holmwood skirmish, I would have it noted that, in the earlier cavalry affairs of the civil wars, in which we gained many successes and some renown, the Parliamentary forces were far less apt for war than ourselves; not that our side was much to boast of, except in willingness to fight at any moment and against any odds; but the armies of the rebels were for the most part a very sorry set of pitiful rogues and ragamuffins, and we, though often overnumbered, did most easily over-match them in all else than numbers, such as discipline, swordsmanship, and the use of fire-arms. Of great guns I speak not, neither side having much to boast of on this score, neither having any cunning in artillery, nor many great pieces to show it with. Nor, indeed, was either side much given to general-ship at the first going off, for, after some form of manœuvring, our lesser officers would confuse their orders or forget they had any, and let all go, horse and foot, artillery and small arms, till we would get all rabbled up together, we and the enemy, and then it was man to man ; and perhaps this was the best manœuvring for our people, they being stout and strong and nimble in the use of arms, gentlemen's sons or at least gentlemen's dependents, or farmers, mostly out of the north country, hearty fellows trained to cudgel-play and quarter-staff ; and the enemy's army but riff-raff and tail-corn fellows from the towns—tapsters, drawers, runaway apprentices, and the like. Good lack! how our men would con-quer and overbear them and wound or slay, or put them to terror and flight and utter rout and ruin ; till but for the natural pleasure a soldier must ever take in killing and diminishing the King's enemies, I had forborne many a time from striking and slaying the poor rogues from very pity of them.

In these latter days, however, the tables had been turned upon us, for so soon as the Parliamentarians had got some sort of settled government they began a reformation of their armies, and drafted into them men of character and substance, yeomen and farmers

and farmers' sons, sober fellows under strict discipline
and training; such men as with their English blood
and spirit would face and master double or treble
their numbers of any troops I have encountered
anywhere abroad (though this perhaps is but parti-
ality in me), while it was we who had to take the
riff-raff of the towns into our ranks, whence our later
defeats at the rebels' hands; though I am by no means
averse to testify to the generalship and management
of that great (though misled and misleading) soldier,
the Usurper Cromwell. He it was mainly who effected
that great reformation of the army which went then
by the name of the *New Model:* a name all but
forgotten in these latter years, but then a word of
great import and terror, it being rather a congregation than an army, of well-ordered and staunch
soldiery, as to whose discipline and bravery and
loyalty to their mistaken cause no honest soldier
should speak but with abiding respect.

It was because there were nearly thirty of the
New Model soldiers, to wit, Colonel Messenger's
dragoons, among our enemies at Holmwood, whom
we yet overthrew, that I contend for our victory being
a great and signal one.

CHAPTER IV.

ENOUGH for a time of war and fighting : I have, I trust, in hand pleasanter and more edifying themes wherewith to entertain my readers.

So soon as we were landed with our sixteen troopers at Scheveningen, in Holland (for it was thither our ship was bound) it had been our intention to travel without loss of time across France and over the Pyrenees into Spain. But we discovered that this was not easily to be accomplished, seeing that the Kings of France and Spain were now at war, and that we and our men could neither hope to obtain free passage through the first country nor entrance into the second from that of its enemies. It was resolved, therefore, for our party to travel into Italy, and take ship from some Italian port to the King of Spain's dominions. In the meantime my Lord proposed to himself to obtain, through the Spanish Ambassador in the United Provinces, confirmation of his Catholic Majesty's already expressed desire that my Lord and his troop should enlist into his Majesty's service. He proposed to await the answer in

Holland. For this purpose my cousin obtained an interview of Don Narciso Gusman, the then Envoy of the Spanish King, at which his Excellency, who was already aware of my Lord's exploits in first defeating the Fanatics and thereafter escaping from their rage, and was a nobleman of courtly demeanour and of very ceremonious and gracious sentences, highly extolled my Lord's prowess and success.

His Excellency took upon himself to promise that his Majesty, his August Master, would welcome him into his armies with a very lively satisfaction, and begged him the more certainly to count upon speedy promotion and the continued favour of the King, his Master, inasmuch as he perceived that his Lordship conversed with great ease and correctness in the Castilian tongue. His Excellency, furthermore, proposed to my Lord that, during the considerable interval that must necessarily elapse between the sending to Madrid and obtaining of a reply, the direct route being interrupted, his troopers might find temporary employment, high pay, and some of the good chances of war in the armies of the Emperor, the close ally of his Sovereign Lord. In the meantime we, to wit, my kinsman and I, might remain in the Low Countries, whereby the King, his master, would be certain of not being disappointed of the services of two excellent officers (he was pleased thus to couple my name with my kinsman's), "and I myself," continued the Ambassador, smiling upon us and bowing, "will enjoy the opportunity of further cultivating the acquaintance of two most distinguished and estimable gentlemen."

Thus far the Ambassador, using the courtly and complimentary phrases of his nation and his employment, which phrases and method are, to speak sooth, not very easy for me, a rough soldier, to convey into our homely English speech.

My Lord accepted the offer of the Ambassador very gladly ; and this of itself might be esteemed a sufficient answer to those pestilent and slanderous polemics who, overlooking my Lord's many titles to fame and glory, have for this long time past ignorantly narrowed him down to a mere soldier-adventurer, whose many exploits are referable solely to that Good Fortune which, they will have it, mostly favours the reckless and daring who rush into action without taking thought for the future or having any wise prevision for the event of their adventures miscarrying. I say this resolve of my kinsman might sufficiently answer these deniers of his fame, as showing that his mind was not merely set upon warlike adventure, but loved and adorned the civil life as well. Indeed, he was apt in scholarship and in learning, and longed to help to reap that great harvest of philosophy which at this period, in every nation of the world (save our own, now so sorely oppressed and stifled of her free breathing) was, so to say, ripe, or ripening, for the sickle.

Had he been, as so maliciously has been alleged, a mere soldier, basely seeking only after war fame,

would he not, the opportunity now offering, have run
incontinently into this chance of serving with the
Emperor? But not so ; my kinsman never loved
fighting for fighting's sake, though, thank God for it,
he has never feared to strike a blow and stake his
life when the cause was good and his heart has been
in it. The greedier and baser kind of hawks, train
and mew them as we will, when they are whistled
off the fist, will pursue their quarry straight and
direct, seeking only to feast upon its blood and flesh ;
but the long-winged falcon is of a nobler race, and,
being released, flies upwards, soaring to the extremest
altitudes of light, and casting here and there with
her strong wings, rejoicing in her expanding vision
and command of the firmament : so did my kinsman,
newly released, not care to follow greedily after the
camp and the battle, but would try his flight amid
the wide learning and deep philosophy which then
were chiefly to be found in the United Provinces and
its towns, to wit, Leyden, Amsterdam, Dort, Haarlem,
and the Hague. To feel the strength of his own
wings amidst those of strongest flight was indeed to
him a new and perpetual delight. I shall have many
occasions hereafter of showing to my readers how
worthy were my cousin, had he enjoyed fuller leisure,
to have held a place in name (as he did in fact)
among the great philosophers as well as the great
commanders of the time, and how, though silent
in the world of printed letters, he had advanced
in the deeper learning as far as, and indeed, as I

shall contend, in some matters farther than the very foremost of them all.

But alack! what a task have I set myself to perform, and whence am I, a poor witless soldier doubled with a poorer scholar, to derive courage for such an undertaking? I know my unfitness for this work but too well. I know I am no accomplished writer in the modern manner, for I can use no neat-filed phrases in the present approved style. If I am a scholar, my breeding has been, I fear, too much of the camp and barrack. Therefore, let the reader not look here for the new modish way of writing. I am content to go forward in the older method, and to be called Pedant by the levity of an unlearned generation. It shall call me, however, by what hard names it please, before I will follow the new fashions. I will not imitate our modern masters when they do up their poor hasty snatches of sense into paltry packets, as a needy apothecary will tie up his drugs into the smallest compass, and I must presume for the same reason, that as one is poor in drugs so is the other in matter ; and if it be not lack of matter, then sure is it that they impute dulness to their reader, and fear to breathe him with too long a stretch of his understanding. Maybe it is that they have forgot the art, or never learnt it, to use a more sustained division of their utterance (an art not so hard but that patient study, more modesty, and less haste to be on familiar terms with their readers might teach it to them). Be it how it may, they disdain, or have forgot, or never knew how to marshal and array a long, well-sounding phrase, compact of harmony of thought and harmony of sound.

Well! I have admitted my shortcomings, and for all this vapouring of mine I am somewhat abashed on account of them in the gay company of modern readers and writers; but, Gentle Reader, you know now the worst my enemies can say of me. I pray you therefore to make your choice, and either take me for the good matter I have to indite, or leave me at once for my old-fangled manner of telling it. Only you are hereby warned that having made a beginning of tasting me, you are to please eat the whole dish. I am modest as to myself, as you see, but I am nothing of the kind as to the story I have to tell. I know I have good stuff to give you, and weighty, and most wonderful and unheard-of adventures to relate, and so I will not have you throw down my book hereafter with a " Pish, here is a Pedant for you ! " or a " Hang him for his formality ! "

CHAPTER V

I WILL remind the reader of this narration that at this time was just ended that long and cruel war that had held all the Powers of Europe for more than thirty years, whence it has since been named the Thirty Years' War, as if the authors of and actors in it had feared to give it its true name, or to hint at the true causes of why it was begun and why so long continued; which were nothing else than, at the beginning, hate of Princes and Priests, which afterwards but cloaked the lusts of Kings for power and territory. Not but what some of the chief actors and agents in this long fighting were among the greatest of mortal men; among whom I need but mention that great commander Wallenstein, Duke of Friedland, on the Imperialist side (my own first master in the art of war), and on the other, that incomparable King and Heroic General, Gustavus Adolphus, King of the Swedes, Goths, and Vandals, though but a heretic in religion;—but where am I got? I had meant but to say that this great war was just ended, and ended too the much longer and more cruel war in which our present hosts, the Dutch, had striven for eighty years against the oppression of foreign tyrants.

Now, it is very observable that when the spirits of men are suddenly relieved from the oppression of long warfare, they are rendered especially lively and eager and apt for new labours, as a man's limbs and body might be from whose back a burden is taken ; and they run freely at these times into new enterprize and adventure with a most surprizing nimbleness. Their wits which have worked in the dull mill-work round of sieges and defences and sallies, surprises and marches, now go abroad seeking still to conquer, but not in the vulgar domain of their neighbours' cities and provinces ; they seek to attack and to kill still, it is true, but it is error and folly they would attack and destroy ; and to defend, but it is no longer their cities' walls and their goods and their own lives, but Sacred Truth herself they would now protect from ignorance and from prejudice.

Now such a time was come upon the world, and there were signs and wonders all round about us to those who had the understanding to see them. I mean not such monsters seen in the heavens as the vulgar love to marvel at, and which possibly, did we but know their motions, are after all no more harmful to us than the commoner stars of the sky. I intend not such superstitious wonders and signs as these, but signs that men were now at last permitted by the Divine Ruler of the world to perceive the secrets of His Rulership—I mean the secret laws of nature—

and to predominate by the mere gift of Philosophy
(God-given or it were naught) over the void and the
darkness and mystery of Nature. These things are
the signs and wonders I speak of; and truly, was it
not wonder enough that mere helpless men had looked
upon such things as I shall presently string together,
and should have made them plain to their fellows?
As, for example, that Signor Galileo Galilei had
reasoned out the Copernican doctrine of the circum-
ambient orbs; though this was a seed earlier
garnered, but it had fallen among the rocks and
stones of superstition and for a time prospered not;
and again Signor Torricelli had weighed the immaterial air and shown that the very *vacuum* (hitherto
so called) hath a body and a being; and again Mr.
Hervey had perceived that the valves in men's veins,
discovered by Sylvius and Fabricius, could betoken
no less than some constant fluid movement therein,
whence he derived the notion of that continual flux
and reflux of the blood which is governed by the
force and influence of the heart, as that is by the soul;
just as the flux and reflux of the tides is governed by
the influence of the Moon, as Herr Kepler has lately
demonstrated. And again, the same Kepler has in-
geniously conjectured, or as some believe, established
that the starry and moony influences do in some
similar way govern and turn men's lives; and this
same philosopher has furthermore expounded how
the planes of the moving stars (which some call
planets) pass through the Sun (as to which, however,

though I am far from denying, I humbly admit, after
such a study of the matter as I am able to bestow
upon it, the matter is as yet not quite so apparent to
me as I could desire, and perhaps it may turn out on
fuller knowledge that their planes do not so pass).
But to resume ; it was now a pregnant period and
the birth of some philosophic matters of great moment was seemingly at hand.

All these great discoveries touched indeed but the
material and mechanical nature, and my kinsman
esteemed them chiefly as helps and presages in reaching more essential and spiritual things still hid.
Therefore was it that he, in whose apprehension
already lay the seed of what should presently turn to
strange and marvellous fruit, and who would afterwards conquer some of the darkest secrets of life, and
death itself, and perceive and prevail upon the powers
of so-called supernatural things more effectually than
many who have practised the black, forbidden art of
Magic, calling the images of the living before him at
his will, and other the like marvels ; all this too not
magically and by incantation of any Evil Powers, but
by Divine Philosophy and to the greater glory of God ;
all which things I shall hereafter have occasion to
recount to the astonishment and delight of my
readers; therefore was it, I say, that he, though he
loved to question the learned men and philosophers
around him, and to drink in their opinions, himself modestly refrained (as one too young and
green as yet to mingle in the controversies of veteran

polemics) from putting forward his own conceipts and plerophorics.

Only at times did he speak out, though as yet but obscurely, what lay in his soul, and it was to be observed that in his case *fecit indignatio orationem*, to misquote and mis-scan the poet : it was when some presumptuous person, trusting to the revelations of the new material Philosophy, would deny the pos-sibility of a higher revelation, or of a life beyond the laws of the material world, that my cousin would denounce such narrowness very critically, though temperately. He would then endeavour to show that a higher revelation is still to come and will display laws not contrary to known laws, but beyond them. Then sometimes would he touch too upon the strange matter which (as I have hinted) afterwards his learn-ing and researches carried so far; and those that heard him were often astounded, and even I marvelled somewhat, saying to myself, "He preluded some-thing of this before, but whence got he these high, strong notes, this division in his descant and full diapason of eloquence ? "

I remember one such occasion when a gentleman of some fame then, and of much greater thereafter, for his fantastic reasoning and philosophy of the government of the world (but whom I will not further name in this place) strove to set down the ordering of the world to very material causes, that my Lord stood up to him, contending with him not sharply but civilly, and somewhat in the

Socratic manner of shrewd questions forcing consonant replies.

This philosopher having held forth very learnedly as to how our bodies being confessedly material, and all thought in us, all feeling, will, understanding, and fancy, being but emanations and attributes of our material bodies, the life therein must, like it, be material too—must come with it and go with it into nothingness. "Life therefore," says he, "beyond the grave, is nought and impossible—a vain dream."

My Kinsman—" And the soul, what is that ?"

Philosophus—" Why, my Lord, it is nothing more nor less than the sum total of our thoughts, our wills, and our emotions."

My Kinsman—" Has it had no before, and will it have no after life, think you, Sir ?"

Philosophus—" Why no ; the seat thereof is certainly the brain, which is a mysterious but yet a very corporeal body, and this same soul is the machinery and clockwork of the body, as the weights and pendulum are the main machinery of a clock. Put your finger on the pendulum and the clock will stop ; destroy the brain and you kill the man, and his soul too ; hurt the brain and you hurt the so-called soul ; stun it and the soul is stunned. Let but a tiny drop of blood press upon this brain of yours, and the soul—that so wrongly supposed spiritual essence—lies in abeyance ; thought. feeling, and all faculty of emotion cease too ; remove the pressure and it lives again, and thinks and feels anew. Is it then to be

supposed that a material thing will survive the catastrophe of real death, which so small a circumstance
can benumb into temporary death? Not so; and
eternal life for man born of woman is but a vain
expectation."

My Kinsman—"Born of woman. In that, Sir, lies
your answer. Pray what is born? What passes from
a woman to her child?"

Philosophus—"Why, my Lord, nothing but a
renewed life."

My Kinsman—"Well, Sir, I would not have you
answer yourself more aptly. It is life that comes
from the parents, and their life from their parents,
and so back, and thence again, without a break in
the chain, from Him Who is the Giver of Life. And
in this life is comprehended, by admission of all the
philosophers, an essence, an *energueia*, a force, an
incomprehensible something, impalpable, but yet
existing in us: it is not emotion, will, consciousness,
or thought, but it is that which causes all these things:
it is never born anew, but passes; and as it never was
entirely born or initiated, so surely it would be very
rash to conclude it shall ever entirely die and end."

Philosophus—"I maintain that it is benumbed with
a blow, that it slumbers with sleep, lies senseless in a
swoon, and will assuredly die with that which is
greater still than a swoon, or sleep, or wounds—
namely, Death."

My Kinsman—"Sir, I would have you know that
the soul is more wakeful in sleep than when we are

E

up and about, and in a trance travels afield as it
cannot do when the grosser body lives its life beside
it ; and 'tis most certain that the souls of mortals are
never so near to be divine—for assuredly the very
grossest of them are part of the spirit of God Himself—
as when they lose touch of their carnal embodiment ;
and this we see in men's visions, and even in common
dreams, and very plainly in the ecstasy of the higher
passion falsely called love (I say falsely, as likening
it to a baser emotion, but it is indeed and of a truth a
part of the Divine glory), so that many times we see
one lying in a deep reverie or trance, his body inert,
motionless and dull, whose soul meanwhile, taking
upon itself a simulacrum or adumbrated image of its
earthly body, shall travel, released from natural law,
disregarding space and all material obstacles, and
shall appear to those it loves, to warn, to counsel, or
to comfort them."

Philosophus—" And this wonderful thing has
happened, my Lord ? "

My Kinsman—" Why, Sir, to my private knowledge
it has happened, and happens continually ; but I am
young in years and raw in experience and wisdom,
and it behoves not me therefore to seek to convince
you out of my own authority, but I will only remind
you of the innumerable instances which your great
learning, Sir, will immediately recall to your memory ;
as how Tully himself was intimately persuaded,
no doubt from experience, that the spirits of the
dead may haunt the living, as sufficiently appears

in his expressed wish to kill himself for no other purpose than that his ghost might act as *alastor*—or
avenger—to the tyrant Emperor Augustus. Plutarch
also relates that the ghost or simulacrum of great Cæsar
appeared to Marcus Junius Brutus. These instances,
indeed, are of the soul released and made free to travel
by death, but that it is equally released by trance you
may read in Cardan (*De Subtilitate Rerum*), who
gives numberless instances of those who have had the
will to visit in seeming, but unreal, bodily presentment,
even at great distances, their friends, their children,
their parents, or their lovers, sometimes visibly to
them, oftener not, but yet the visitants always
adumbrated and felt as a comforting neighbourhood.
Camerarius in his lost tractate, entitled *Mysteria
Naturæ*, quoted by S. Scheretzius, has noted many
such examples, and the learned Scribanius (in his *De
Liberatione Animæ*) mentions the case of a gentleman
of Pavia, of great gravity and accomplishment, who
could not only at his pleasure convey his own spirit
elsewhere, but who could at times, and by a rare
bending of his will thereto, draw to him the liberated
spirits of others, over whom he was able to exercise a
particular influence ; not, be it noted (for they lay at
home inert and senseless), over the persons themselves, but upon the shadowy embodiment of their
spirits. Such *simulacra*, I take it, are similar to those
seen at times near graveyards at night : not harmful
ghosts, as the ignorant imagine, but the poor spirits
of dead men and women revisiting their ancient

haunts, clothed in mortal shape no doubt rather by the projection of the seers' imagination than having any actual and material existence of their own, these seers' desire to behold them acting in sympathy with the spirits' own strong desire for visible embodiment. The same Scribanius too cites the aforesaid tractate of Camerarius (extant in his time, but now lost) for instances of men above the ordinary run in strength of understanding and of will, who have been enabled to invoke or convoke, by no magical incantations, but only by using freely and powerfully the secret processes of Nature herself, the souls of living men and women into their presence ; these sometimes coming invisibly, yet have they been able to give evidence of their presence (as by low sounds like words uttered); sometimes, though thinly and in shadowy form, showing themselves clad in their true bodily lineaments and appearances."

He stopped a little abruptly, as modestly refraining from talking too freely in so learned a company, and, as his voice ended, there fell an admiring silence upon the company, none seeming to wish to follow him who had spoken with such gravity and so convincing a flow of utterance.   I did indeed myself not a little marvel at the grace and beauty of his discourse, as much discoverable in its manner as its matter.   His adversary himself, a very worthy gentleman and disputant, and one ever more eager to get at truth than to silence his opponent, bowed his head and spoke not for a space, as willing to express that what had been so well and learnedly set forth gave him cause for further thought and inquiry.

Some there were present, both men and ladies, for it was a large mixed company, that had not yet much regarded my Lord but as a young gentleman of goodly looks and gentle birth and manners, who had gained some glory in the wars, and whose name was, as truth is to be exactly told, somewhat noised at the moment on account of a duel lately happened (of which more anon). These then, I say, having hitherto set no greater regard upon my kinsman than for these exploits, were exceedingly amazed to hear him speak on such grave matter so sweetly and so well, and now looked upon him and scanned him with much curiosity.

At this time my Lord was in his twenty-fourth year, though at times his face, which was of a palish, thoughtful cast and thinnish, gave him the look of having some years more of age. His hair he wore in the cavalier fashion, long and waving to his shoulders; it was of a darkish brown colour and pretty abundant; his beard he trimmed as was then and still is the fashion, in long mustachios and with a point or tag to the chin. He was tall and slight of figure and very active, an excellent horseman and an exceedingly pretty swordsman both with the light French rapier and with the long Italian sword. He was likewise well trained in the play of sword and dagger, after the fashion of our forefathers, the which when it comes to medley fighting is the most useful method of fence a man can have practised. Of his looks I will not speak, for in truth being but a rough soldier and scholar, I am little given to consider such things either in man or woman. But I well remember on this occasion the saying of a gentleman who was in our company, and was himself a scholar of Cambridge and fellow student of Mr. Henry Moore, and, like him, of the new Platonist school, who consider inner moral beauty and excellence to be figured in the outer man. This gentleman whispered me, as my Lord ended, and, after a little silence, there went a buzz of amazement round the company.

"Truly," said he, "we might have guessed this by the young Lord's face; he tells of matter that an angel might speak with a voice like an angel's too, and, sure, it was all prefigured in his face, which has certainly a most uncommon radiancy and beauty in it."

As for me, I frankly say that I like not these refinements of Philosophy; and as for this Platonic doctrine that virtue goes with good looks, it must very wrongfully condemn some homely-faced men with good hearts, and sanctify and acquit as unjustly many a ruffian that I have known with the heart of a wolf and the face of a cherub.

I will admit, however, that the lad was comely, and, to speak truth, I had often wished him otherwise, for I easily foresaw in it a lure and a snare to idle and foolish women, of a sort that abound everywhere, and nowhere more than among the Royalist English who

had now shelter in France and the Low Countries.
I feared in this beauty of his a possible temptation
to him to depart from the wholesome practice of
despising and avoiding the perfidious female sex, and
I could have wished his features cast in a mould as
homely as my own, who have in truth never, at any
period of my life, suffered from the aforesaid temptations and consequent perils. I determined therefore
to continue to use all my efforts to temper the true
metal of his nature with my counsel, and to determine
him with such sound discourse as my own experience
of this too often weak and wayward portion of the
human kind should furnish, reinforced by the wisdom
of the learned in all ages. Not but that his Lordship,
what with his own wide reading of the ancients, his
soldier's life, and therefore constant listening in the
camp and at the mess to the just defamation of the
sex by honest fellows by it cajoled, and as an effect
of my own constant hortations in season and out,
had arrived at such a misesteem and despisal of
womankind as even I could scarce wish made stronger.
Note, too, that in our age the ancient estimate of
women held by our formal grandfathers has passed
away, who had it by tradition from knightly times,
when men knew no better than, in the darkness of
their ignorance, to over-prize, to over-rate, and almost
deify silly and reprehensible women ; but now we of
this wiser age know better, and, being forewarned of
their true natures, are the better forearmed against
their doles and their furberies.

CHAPTER VI.

I SPOKE just now of a duel engaged in by my Lord that had caused some little talk at this time.

It happened thus : there were now, as I have said, many English gentlemen of quality come over after the troubles at home, and as they had no affairs or business of their own to engage them, either of peace or war, there was among them much dicing, drinking, and worse employment. It happened that one day my Lord and I were gathered after a pretty heavy carouse in a tavern with some friends and acquaintances of ours in the city of Amsterdam, and were throwing a main together. When some few scores of pistoles had changed hands, the talk turned, amid the rattle of the dice box, upon the ladies, the estimation of whom expressed by the honest gentlemen present was no higher than it is usual to find expressed (and certain to be deserved by the subjects thereof) among gentlemen of ease and leisure.

Among the ladies touched upon was a certain Lady Penelope . . . . (I omit the surname for good reason) a young lady of a very comely presence, who, it had become pretty notorious, had turned her attention and regard wholly and somewhat suddenly upon my Lord, while he, I will not seek to deny it, had encountered her civility with no marked repugnance. Being, however, a new comer, he was unaware that the lady had previously distinguished my Lord Bulleyn in similar fashion. It is not to be supposed that this young lord, who had fought with reputation under Prince Rupert, and was in all respects an accomplished gentleman and soldier, entertained any serious regard for the lady, whom he nevertheless allowed the world to consider as the then object of his affections, having publicly complimented her twice or thrice with music before her house, and treated her with an entertainment of masques, as well as sent her sundry rich presents, my Lord Bulleyn being a nobleman of vast estates in Yorkshire.

This lady's name and manners it was that some of the gentlemen present began to reflect upon with some freedom, none reprehending their doing so, not even my Lord Bulleyn, who was, as ill luck would have it, of the company, and he was rallied very freely by his friends present upon his loss of the lady's affection. So little did he seem to resent their banter that he himself joined in the laugh. My kinsman, who had a liking and friendship for this nobleman, hardly, indeed, gathered that he was touched by the levity of the young lady, till his neighbour at the table whispered him how matters stood ; nor could he then, seeing how lightly his friend took the matter, suppose that he was sensibly offended either by the lady's conduct or the gentlemen's taunts, in which I need hardly say my kinsman had in nowise joined.

I have no doubt things would never have gone to the bloody issue they did, had the gentlemen present been less indiscreet, for in truth there was no real reason for the umbrage which my Lord Bulleyn took. But Fate willed it otherwise, and Lord Bulleyn chose a very light circumstance to fix upon for his *casus belli*, or excuse for the duello.

My kinsman (who had a most merry and gracious humour in company, as I have before hinted) thinking, so soon as he heard of Lord Bulleyn's inclination for the lady, to turn off the matter with a jest, took out his tablets and wrote quickly a quatrain impromptu in the nature of an epigram ; then rolling up the leaf into a little pellet he flicked it across the table to Lord Bulleyn. All he meant was to show the elder lover how little he, as the new favourite, regarded the favour he had received, and how he gave his friend joy at getting quit of his flame.

Lord Bulleyn, taking the paper and unfolding it, could not forbear smiling at its pleasantry, and in certain token of his having taken my kinsman's act in good part, he nodded his head pleasantly towards him. There the matter was ending but for the gentlemen present, who, hoping to get more food for merriment at the poor young jilted Lord's expense, clamoured to have the paper read out to them ; but Lord Bulleyn crumpled it up and threw it on the floor, and only upon the gentlemen insisting he picked it up, and, amid much laughing and jesting, he read out with something of a wry face the four lines, which ran as follows :—

> "When Celia her inconstant eyes
>   Did kindly turn on me,
>   I less esteemed the favour done
>   Than welcomed Strephon free."

—Strephon, I need hardly say, standing for my Lord Bulleyn.

Soon after this the company broke up, and it was not till next day that my old friend Colonel Salter (formerly of Hopton's) waited upon my Lord in our lodgings on behalf of Lord Bulleyn, and very formally demanded amends for the slight that had been put upon him by my Lord's lampoon, as he was pleased to call it.

There is a convenient and retired bit of ground for these encounters about a quarter of a mile outside the ramparts of the city of Amsterdam, and thither we repaired within an hour of Colonel Salter's visit. He and young Mr. Percival, my Lord Bulleyn's cousin, a very fierce and hasty gentleman, and a very pretty swordsman, but who had never fought in the wars, were this nobleman's seconds, and we picked up on the way to the field an Irish captain of horse, to serve as second friend on our side. This gentleman readily agreed to oblige us, on which I requested to be informed if he were well acquainted with the use of the small-sword, inasmuch as I expected that the duel would extend to the seconds, and the other side were all noted swordsmen.

"Faith, Sir," says he, somewhat confusing the matter, " for backsword or cudgel-play I could boldly answer that I was, but of your sharps and points I know very little."

I had guessed as much, for the Irish gentlemen, though as brave men as exist upon this earth, are seldom trained to the rapier. Therefore I answered that I heartily thanked him for his obligingness, but would not risk his life in our quarrel and would seek another second. The Irishman however would on no account be put off.

"I thank you humbly, Sir," says he, drawing himself up, "but if you decline my services, now that I have offered them, I shall take it to be an affront to my honour."

"But, my dear Sir," quoth I, laying my hand upon his arm, "I love you too well" (for I had met this honest gentleman before) "to invite you to such peril of your life against some of the finest swordsmen of the day."

"I may not be a finished fencer, Captain St. Keyne," says he, "but never fear, Sir, that I shall flinch from my man or discredit your duel."

So I bowed, sorry for his obstinacy, but not without admiring the humour of this Irish gentleman's courage.

So soon as the two adversaries had faced each other, the whole six of us fell to, so sharp set were we

all for sword-work in those idle days. I had leisure
but to glance at my kinsman, as I got to my guard,
and to see that he was taking Lord Bulleyn's passes
very coolly, without ripost, which made me a little
fearful of the result ; for if a man constantly receives
the point, and is content to parry only, 'tis evident he
must be reached at last.

I found the chances of the duel had brought Colonel
Salter opposite my point, and considering him to be
altogether as good as, or perhaps a better man than
myself, I fought very warily, but I did not then know
that the Colonel had received a wound at Dunbar in
the right ankle, which, though it did not make him
limp, stiffened the joint a little, so that it hindered
him of the necessary quickness in replying to my
assault. Pressing upon him somewhat, after we had
quickly exchanged a dozen passes, I found him to flag
a little, and presently perceived I had more control of
his weapon than I had expected. Very soon my lunge
was rewarded ; the sword-point, entering the fleshy
portion of his arm above his sword-wrist, passed
through some five or six inches of the muscle of the
arm, spitting it, as it were, in a very singular manner,
and came out below the elbow—a curious wound and
a disabling one, for the colonel's arm was entirely
paralysed, and his sword dropped from his hand.

Turning to my Lord, I perceived to my inexpressible relief and joy that he had overmastered his
antagonist, having himself received only two flesh
wounds in the neck, from which he was not bleeding

very much. He had at last, so he afterwards told
me, on being very hotly pressed, riposted in earnest,
and as I looked he was passing his sword clean
through his adversary's shoulder. The wound, as my
kinsman withdrew his sword, caused Lord Bulleyn to
grow dizzy, but such was the young nobleman's
courage that he would not acknowledge his defeat,
but stood up still crossing swords, though staggering
a bit on his feet. My kinsman seeing how things
were and that Lord Bulleyn was at his mercy, weighed
upon his opponent's sword in *quarte*, ready to parry,
but making no thrust himself.   On this, young Mr.
Percival who had already very quickly disposed of
his adversary, the Irishman, by running him through
the body and laying him upon his back bleeding
and senseless, now seeing his cousin and principal
getting the worst of it, in plain truth utterly defeated,
and owing the continuance of his life to my Lord's
forbearance, lost all command of his temper, and indeed of his senses, and running round to his cousin's
side, against all rule and principle of the duello,
assailed Lord St. Keyne furiously outside the other
gentleman's sword ; and had I not, seeing what the
mad fellow was about, run in and struck Mr. Percival's
sword up, most assuredly he would have murdered my
cousin while Lord Bulleyn engaged his sword.

So soon as my kinsman perceived that he had a
fresh antagonist, he leaped back with incredible swiftness to disengage his sword from Lord Bulleyn, and
lunged fiercely at the new man, who in his turn would

most certainly have been whipped through the body
(for I had succeeded in lifting away Mr. Percival's
guard in that very moment) but that my cousin in
the very act of lunging perceived that he was oppos-
ing an unguarded man, and though too late to stop
his lunge, dropped his point with an up turn of the
wrist as he came forward, and so did the gentleman
no hurt. In the meantime I still held up Mr.
Percival's sword, and turning the blade of it downwards by a simple movement in *seconde*, and bearing it
against Lord Bulleyn's blade, still held by him
en garde, I held it thus imprisoned, thus rendering
this young gentleman, who had been proceeding
against all rule and honour, harmless.

The whole thing had passed in three clicks of a
sword-blade, one, two, three, and no word was
spoken by any of us till Colonel Salter, standing by,
raised his unwounded hand and cried out very sternly,
"Mr. Percival! What are you about? Drop your
sword at once, Sir!"

This seemed to call the young gentleman to his
senses : he drew back like one dazed, and released his
sword point.

"Put your swords up, gentlemen," cried the Colonel,
standing by with his wounded right arm hanging
down, "Honour is satisfied."

We did his bidding. "Sir," he cried, speaking very
stiffly to the young gentleman who had been his
fellow second, "you had like to have committed
murder upon a man who had not his weapon free to

defend himself, and I call upon you humbly to beg his pardon, or by . . . ." says he, "you shall answer your crime, for it is nothing else, to me!"

". . . . me! Harry," cried Lord Bulleyn, very angry, though he was badly hurt, "do you want to disgrace us all with your folly? If you ha'n't murdered the gentleman, 'tis none of your doing. Ask my Lord's pardon, or . . . . me, Sir! but I'll whip my sword through your vitals!"

Mr. Percival hung his head and went very white, being overwhelmed with shame and mortification. Then he spoke, in a broken voice, "Gentlemen, I acknowledge my fault, I knew not what I was doing. I humbly crave your pardon, and," turning to my cousin, "chiefly yours, my Lord."

"Come, Sir," said Ralph, taking him by the hand, "enough is said. You are a brave man, if a rash one. Let us not hear another word on the matter."

In the meantime the Irish gentleman was lying upon the turf, and was like to have bled to death while we stood thus discoursing upon the point of honour. He was pretty badly hurt, for Mr. Percival's sword had passed through and through him. We carried him insensible into a little tavern by the river side, and, staunching the blood as well as we could, presently got a Dutch surgeon to him, who gave us some hopes of his life; which indeed were not disappointed, for in a fortnight this brave gentleman was afoot, and in a week after almost recovered, the blade having touched no very important part. ˉ ⸒" But," said he to me afterwards, " I got no satisfaction at all out of the fighting, for the second pass from Mr. Percival was through my body, and I saw no more of the business." Lord Bulleyn was laid up with a fever from the hurt in his shoulder, which all but carried him off, and my Lord too had lost more blood than he imagined.

Thus did a duel end very pleasantly and honourably for all concerned (for I consider Mr. Percival's repentance and apologies to have condoned his rashness) which might easily have had a very unfortunate termination. Lord Bulleyn's blood-letting and the other distractions to his mind caused him to forego all thoughts of the lady who was the primal cause of all this pother, and to revert to his former love and esteem for my cousin. Moreover, Lord Bulleyn's conduct of his sword in the duello (seeing that he had bestowed two not inconsiderable wounds on his adversary and still stood up to fight, after himself receiving a very bad one) procured him much applause from his acquaintances. This duel was indeed a nine days' wonder ; all condemned Mr. Percival's headstrong behaviour, yet not without finding in it some redeeming touch of loyalty to his cousin ; all commended my Lord Bulleyn's stoutness ; but most of all did they approve and praise the forbearance, generosity, and valour of my dear kinsman, which indeed were beyond all laudation.

We sojourned after this some weeks in different

F

towns of the United Provinces, waiting for letters from the King of Spain, seeing much learned, edifying company, and more that was neither learned nor edifying.

Many ingenious gentlemen inquired of me curiously in regard to my Lord's opinions on various philosophical matters, and particularly as to his views and perceptions as to immaterial and essential things, which views being once expressed by him had occasioned much comment and interest among them· It is partly for this reason that I have reported, somewhat exactly, his above discourse upon this point, as defining what he then held, and shadowing forth some further discoveries which he afterwards made. I have been thus particular too for another reason, which is this : the vulgar, men and women (but chiefly, as may be imagined, women) had carried away an altogether warped and exaggerated notion of what my Lord had then put forward, and the thing being hacked from one to another of these foolish bearers soon came to be stretched into a wholly absurd and monstrous doctrine, insomuch that I have been seriously asked if my young Lord had not received some terrible supernatural revelation or another ; whether it were not true that he possessed influence over the Powers of Darkness ? Could he call the spirits of the dead into his presence ? Had he not an attendant familiar ? and so forth.

"Why, madam," I cried to one lady who had questioned me thus, "if the hundredth part of all you suggest be true, my Lord would as richly deserve death as the two witches who were burnt at the stake last week!"

During this period my kinsman, being one who, in Tully's phrase, was an *omnis homo*, who loved all forms of life, and could equally touch the highest as entertain himself with the most lowly affairs, having been somewhat wearied with the hardships of war on the one hand, and on the other with the long vigils and the aridities and disappointments of study, and as *neque semper arcum tendit Apollo*—the diligent should not keep for ever on the full stretch—so my cousin, I say, now sought (as he highly deserved) some salutary rest and relaxation. He mingled therefore very pleasantly with the light humours of the ladies and gentlemen round about him, native and foreign, but chiefly English, who then greatly resorted to these Provinces. As he still touched great revenues of his estates, for the pinch of those holding lands at home did not come till later, he lived, for the few months we waited in expectation of news from Spain, in no little magnificence of lodging and dress, and with entertainments of various kinds, such as of music, or dancing, or else of masques in some retired and rustic pleasance in the neighbourhood, to which he would freely bid great concourses of his friends and acquaintances; whereby he obtained great reputation and glory (in that kind, and among the vulgar). My Lord was ever of a gay and kindly disposition, and those that served him loved him for

his sweetness to them as well as did those that had
fought by his side in the wars (as I have already
shown) ; and he loved music, and singing, and
dancing, and all the several pastimes that idle persons
of quality follow.   In music indeed he did not himself excel, nor was he versed, as he had had little
time to practise the art, though I remember when he
was a young boy he both sang and played upon the
theorbo-lute with some promise of excellence; but of
his own accord he abandoned this diversion as he
grew older, and though he was always free in praising
the excellent performance of his friends, and chary of
disapproval, he conceived, in private and to me, that
music was somewhat of a snare and a temptation
from its very pleasurableness, and tended to absorb
all the faculties and affections of the mind into itself
and to withdraw them from more arduous and important pursuits; therefore he opined that both singing and the touching of instruments of music should
be accomplishments abandoned to women, or to those
men who happen to be crippled, or weaklings from
birth, or wanting in vigour of mind and manly courage, and so (poor souls!) unfit and unapt for the
handling of the sword or the management of the
great horse in battle line.   Yet he willingly fell into
the prevailing mode of this day in verse-writing
(which is but a sister muse of music) and he was of a
most facile and happy humour in the inditing of
songs and epigrams.   Indeed, his fame in this respect
went so high that some verses were commonly

ascribed to his pen that belonged of right to other authors; as, for instance, that gracious and pleasant song against the foolishness of love, beginning;

> " Never believe me if I love,
>   Or know what 'tis, or mean to prove."

These lines were very obstinately set down to him, perhaps as smacking somewhat of his expressed opinions on this trivial and tedious subject, though they were certainly written by another hand several years before,—I believe by that of Sir John Suckling, in whose book, printed since this incomparable poet's death, they are at any rate included.

On the other hand, a song written by my Lord, and which enjoyed at the time a very great vogue, and had for its first lines ;

> " Like to the changing Lunar Star,
>   Or water for inconstancie,"

was commonly ascribed to the famous Lord Rochester, but was in truth composed by my kinsman at this time of our residence in the Low Countries, and by him given to a lady of his acquaintance, one Mrs. Cecil Courthope. This lady did in fact sing it very prettily to her lute (with a setting of Mr. Henry Lawes), the lady being then at the Hague, while we were there, with her brother Sir Edward Courthope, of Courthope Hall in Yorkshire, at a time when my Lord Rochester, since noted for his

verse, was plain John Wilmot and a little child of
five, or at most six years of age.[1]

[1] I have given but the first two lines of this song because I
am not certain of rightly remembering the whole at this distance of time.   Should I find a true copy of it before this book is
ended, either one on paper or in the memory of a friend, I will
set it down entire in this place for the diversion of the curious
reader.

CHAPTER VII

AFTER we had waited several months in the United Provinces—it may have been five or six, but my memory for dates is not exact—we at last got our reply from the Spanish King, delayed on the route, the messenger said, by the chase of the vessel which bore him from Cadiz to Leghorn by a Rover from Algiers, one of that pestilent and piratical nation who set at defiance all the Powers of Christendom, be they and their Ottoman Suzerain at peace with them or at war.

When we came to have the letters read to us by the Ambassador of his Majesty, we saw that we had wasted our time in awaiting them, as even his Excellency was bound to confess, for the letters, with a profusion of civil phrases, promised and undertook neither one thing nor the other. The great officer of state who wrote was indeed, so he stated, "intimately persuaded" (this was his exact phrase) "of the glory of our past achievements and of the reflected illustration which the presence of such eminent cavaliers would bring upon the armies of Spain; but, on

the other hand, these forces were already, and had
ever proved themselves to be, invincible in every
battle-field " (they had to be sure, for all these fine
words, been latterly very signally defeated by the
French under Condé at Rocroy, and again by the
great Turenne in Roussillon, to say nothing of their
having repeatedly been worsted by the Dutch : but
this by the way); " and were therefore," the letter
continued, " independent of all foreign assistance ;
nevertheless, the esteemed honour of our presence in
Spain was so great as to overcome all considerations
of mere necessity, and he" (the high officer in question) " made sure that his Majesty would highly
value and cheerfully welcome our offer to join his
armies."

This was but a cold offer for our services, and but
that he hoped to find more of adventure and surer
paths to glory among the Spaniards than among the
Imperialists, who then seemed, after their long wars,
not a little tired of campaigning, my Lord would have
hesitated to depart upon so doubtful an invitation.
Cold as it was, we were yet rejoiced to leave this life
of idleness and ease.

On the second day after we got our news, therefore,
and after setting our business in order, we began our
journey, with no greater retinue than a servant apiece
and two followers on horseback, leading each a
sumpter mule. As to letters, we burdened ourselves
with none, and with papers none either, save a pass-
port from the Spanish Ambassador declaring our

intention of taking arms with the King of Spain, and calling upon all Powers and Rulers by the way to further and forward us upon this our destination.

As we were in no haste to join an army where we seemed not to be expected with any impatience, so we journeyed at some leisure to Italy. Having another reason not to make too great speed, which was that we desired on our arrival at Genoa to find our men released from their engagements in the Imperial service and able to join themselves to us: we having had letters from Cornet Brown that he and those under him had joined the army near Vienna on what, in the cant phrase of the day, was called "*Novices' Terms*," which was half pay but with privilege to discharge themselves, in case no campaign was going forward, at very short notice, three weeks' or a month's, I think. The men, said the Cornet, did not love their employment nor the company they found themselves among; there was no fighting or prospect of any, and all they hoped for was to join his Lordship and share his fortunes wherever he might choose to lead them. This letter, I think, determined my kinsman to haste away more than aught else.

"They are all good fellows, Humphrey," he said to me ; "and I long to be at their head once more," and he named several of them to me, recalling some deed each had done or endurance he had shown. "Come! cousin," cried he, "let us get to horse at once and on the road to join these good, stout fellows again, who in truth are no more able to do without us than we without them."

By the way we often fell awondering as to what chances had happened to our friends, for as such we loved to speak of them, though many of our troop were ignorant men of rustic manners and lowly birth ; and readers of these pages who are proud and conceited of their own rank and quality may perchance think it unmeet and an improper condescension, in one of my Lord's birth and fortune, to have placed himself on terms of amity and comity with men of such low degree. If so, I will tell them roundly that they know nothing of the soldier's trade, which is in some sort a republic of a nobler kind, where the brave man and worthy soldier is the equal of any; not but what discipline goes before all, but a good officer knows how to exact it without losing his men's love, and a good soldier knows how to render it without any touch of slavishness, seeing that both are persuaded that without discipline an army is nought, and will fall away before an enemy in battle like a rain cloud before the sun. Then, as a commander loves and esteems his men for their stoutness in fight and their heartiness and brave endurance in cold and rain and wind and scorching heat and fatigue, in sickness and in pain of wounds, so do they too love him for the like qualities. And let me tell these cavilling gentlemen who live at home in sluggish ease and safety, and have never seen a company drawn up in battalia, a sword flashed in anger, or a

gun fired with intent to kill a man, that a good
soldier, be his private condition what it will, is
equalled with the highest when they two have marched
together, shoulder to shoulder, over rough and smooth,
by day and night, in storm and sunshine, tended
each other when sick and weak, fought side by side
and mayhap warded off imminent death from the
other, risking to get a mortal stroke themselves to
save a comrade's life. Why, gentlemen, think you
that we who have undergone these things together
are not so much even as friends? I tell you we are
not friends only, but brothers, for life and till death!

But where am I got to? I had only in my mind to
say a good word for all honest soldiers against the
many bad ones the world will ever be giving them,
and to justify my Lord's calling up with me, as we
rode along our way, the memories of the brave
fellows who had been so tried with us in adversity.
Now these sixteen men, which were all that were left
to us of our little army, if I may so call it, of ninety-
five, with which we had marched through Somerset
and Wiltshire, were all proved men. Many of the
elder ones I had known, or at least they had known
me, as an officer in former campaigns; some had
fought with the Scotch against the rebels at
Worcester and knew his Lordship there by sight
or reputation; several were his own tenants or
near neighbours, and every one we could call by
his name and Christian name, knowing too each
his disposition and what service each was best fitted

for ; in short, no sergeant could know each man of his guard or no priest his parishioners better than we knew those in our little wasted troop.   What wonder, then, if my cousin was eager and impatient to have under his orders again such men as these, so tried, so worthy, though alas ! so few.

CHAPTER VIII.

I WILL make a very short story of our journey to Italy, though it was a long and weary one, yet with no perils or adventures very worthy of remembrance, but many delays and contrarieties. We followed in the track which Dutch trade has made to Italy, that is, through Westphalia to the cities of Frankfort-on-the-Main and Nuremberg and Munich in Bavaria, and thence due south by Innsbrug into that strange region of tall mountains called Tyrol, thence along the valley of the Inn and over the great rugged peaks of snow, where, steep and awful as is the country, the passage is yet said to be easier than to the east or to the west. Nature has indeed seemed to wish to set up here an impassable barrier between the cold north and the rich and fertile south which only the strange unconquerable restlessness of men has enabled them to force.

Through all this country till we had come into the very mountains of Tyrol, we saw such traces of the long war, ended but three years before, as were enough to make a man weep for pity. It is commonly said that out of every thousand inhabitants of these fair countries not a hundred were left alive, what with famine, and the pestilence thence ensuing, and the many cruelties and violences of the great armies on either side ; hordes, by all accounts, of hungry ruffians, for the most part knowing nothing of right discipline, regarding no calls of humanity, and caring for nothing but rapine and wrong and murder of the defenceless inhabitants, and plunder of their goods.

Of the unhappy condition of the country we met with abundant evidence, for the fields were everywhere untilled, the roads unkept ; in whole leagues of fertile land often was no man or woman or child to be encountered, though plain signs of their former abiding were to be seen in fences now decayed, bridges broken down, and cottages roofless, with their walls blackened with smoke. In the cities it was no better ; the grass was growing in the streets, every second house was a ruin, and of the people many went half naked, having wan faces pinched with hunger and misery. The once thriving Free Cities of the Empire—I speak of Frankfort, Nuremberg, and Augsburg, so famous for their advancement in learning, scholarship, science, and all the arts—were now decayed through the violence and corrupted by the grossness of war, or altogether dead and ruined. Even in that ingenious and civil city of Nuremberg, eminent once for wealth and ease and all the arts of peace, was naught now heard but sighs and lamentations for departed prosperity. There had

lived here, over one hundred years before, that great
master in graving upon copper, Albrecht or Albert
Dürer, whose fame is not even yet passed away,
though the Dutchman Mynheer Rembrandt Van Rijn
is thought by many to have surpassed him, as he
certainly has surpassed all others, in the intricate
cutting of designs upon plates of copper, to be thence
printed upon paper, and in the apposition thereon of
light against the darkness of shadow ; an art for its
ingenuity and as spreading abroad the knowledge of
pictures in distant regions, comparable only to that
greater discovery of printing.

My Lord has at all times possessed a very lively
observation and delight in pictures, painting, and the
arts of engraving, sculpture, and building, and during
our stay in the United Provinces had diverted himself greatly with these matters ; having at my instance
allowed his portrait to be limned by the aforesaid
Heer Rembrandt, which that worthy gentleman accomplished very faithfully ; and this is that great
picture which now hangs over the chimney in the
chief dining hall at St. Keyne Castle, showing my
Lord at full length, standing against a very dark
field of battle, with smoke of artillery and so forth.
His face has somewhat more of a ruddy colour than
it bore at this time; the dress too is more fantastic
in colour and cut than was ever usual with my Lord
(except perhaps once or twice and in these early days,
for afterwards my Lord dressed ever in dark and
sober clothes, though composed of very rich silks,

satins or velvets), but in this great picture, though
his jerkin is of black velvet, he wears a green scarf, and
his short cloak and breeches are of a reddish brown,
but more red than brown, with tall buff leather boots
and great spurs. The face is indeed admirably limned,
and I find upon it a look such only as I have seen at
very rare times and then in moments of battle, surprises, sudden assaults, and the like ; and it is surely
a sign of insight in this noble painter that without
the possibility of having seen my Lord so moved, he
should have so contrived this very eager and militant
expression, this frowning of the brows and setting of
the lips which the countenance wears in the picture,
which indeed is suitable to the attitude of my Lord
therein, for his hand is on his sword to draw it and
his foot is advanced as against a coming enemy.

My kinsman and I often entertained ourselves while
we were in the Low Countries with the sight of many
fine pictures, Italian and others, which the rich and
civil burghers of the chief cities have procured for
themselves ; they showing them freely to curious
strangers, and having themselves great pleasure not
only in pictures and other curiosities of the arts, as
for instance, in copper-plate prints, whether graven
with a tool and bitten in with acids, in which last art
this aforesaid Rembrandt is the chief master ; and
these same burghers, even in this time of great im-
poverishment, were nothing less than mad in their
extravagant seeking after such works, and other
curiosities of a much lower rating, going so far as

to give 1,000 florins or more for the bulb of a tulip, a thing which almost passes belief.

It is to be supposed that a people so lavish about a flower that a snail might eat in a night, or a merle scratch up with its claws, are not less so with regard to works that with care are imperishable, and the like of which had never been seen before and might never be again while the world lasts. Accordingly the richer of them sought after these before-mentioned prints with such fanatic eagerness that no rich citizen with pretension to taste thought his house furnished if he did not possess certain of the more famous of these works of the great master ; and I myself over-hearing two worthy gentlemen discoursing each of his possessions in this kind, have laughed in my sleeve to hear one mock and banter the other, because forsooth he had failed to buy a particular print while it was still to be had : " What!" he cried, " does Mynheer So-and-So really assert that he has neither a root of tulip *Semper Augustus* in his garden, nor a single copy in his house of *The Marriage of Creusa* or the *Little Juno with the Crown* " (both prints of Mr. Rembrandt's). Upon such frivolities will men's conversation turn !

Arriving at Nuremberg, which we did through a most piteously war-wasted country, for war had raged all around this once so rich and happy city, and it had itself been held by the Swedish King, and stood a siege by the Imperialists, my Lord inquired after the works of the great master Dürer, but to our surprise we found

G

little knowledge of and no pride among the people in
him who had raised their city to such a pinnacle in the
arts. After a time came one to us who having heard
of our repeated asking, very civilly said, " Sirs, my
great grandfather, by name Pirkheimer, was a friend
of the painter you are curious about, and I have many
engraved works by his hand, heirlooms in my family,
which you are very welcome to see in my poor house."
We repaired thither with pleasure, and the gentleman
unfolding his portfolios exhibited to us perhaps
sixty or seventy different engravings of this famous
master.

Never before were my eyes so ravished by man's
handiwork, nor could I have believed that it was in
the power of a man's fingers to trace out upon paper
so delicately the utterance of his inner spirit, the
workings of his fancy and of a most subtle imagination ; and Lord ! how far is the German artist above
Heer Rembrandt Van Rijn, not perhaps in the rendering of lights and shadows, or the curls and twists of
men's hair and beards, and the curiosities of their
raiment, but how greatly does he better him in truth
and dignity ; for the Dutchman, when he sets himself
to paint a sacred piece, can often rise no higher than
to fill his picture with gross fat Dutch burghers, or
mean fellows in dirty rags from the Jews' Quarter of
Amsterdam, with hungry, scoundrel faces ; but Herr
Dürer having to draw the Blessed Virgin, though it be
on a bit of paper not greater than the breadth of a
man's hand, will limn her with such a high, pure look

on her face as testifies to all beholders that she is indeed worthy to be chosen out and blessed among all women upon earth ; and though she be depicted but as adjusting her Babe's dress, there is an awe and love mingled together upon her face as Christians dream and indeed know that there must be in it, but could not hope ever to see set forth in a picture.

Of all Herr Dürer's works there were two which chiefly ravished us. One of a Knight riding through a dark and horrid valley and being followed and mocked by a terrible Shape of a Goblin : at the Knight's side is the grim form of Death, riding on a poor lame jade of a horse, with shambling gait and down-hanging head. The Figure of Death holds up to the Knight an hourglass and a timepiece, to warn him that his last hour is at hand. But the Knight, though his face is not defiant, is steadfast to keep onward upon his path, and his horse is of a like courage to his own, though the way is beset with skulls and foul reptiles, and though the Knight's hound is terrified by all these ghastly, spectral forms. A true allegory of life which the most cursory may read as in a book.

There was a print among those of Herr Dürer that moved my kinsman and me yet more strongly than this, for it seemed so apposite to the miserable circumstances of all this great, war-wasted country ; and that was one which showed forth and interpreted all the blessings and virtues which follow upon Peace, who is represented in the likeness of a stately dame crowned

with the peace-auguring olive, and round about her
are those blessed circumstances that follow in the train
of peace, all expressed in signs and tokens, such as the
squared stone and the workman's tools, and the globe,
and the burning furnace with crucible therein; each
to signify that the arts of architecture and carpentry,
and the smelting of metals, flourish only in peace
time ; so too Justice now reigns supreme, as typified
in the drawing of the equal poised balances, since
inter arma silent leges (in war time equity may go
hang) and mathematics prosper, as shown in the
Magic Square (so-called) drawn upon the wall ; and
religion is shown not to be troubled, for there is the
quiet convent bell in its place, with its rope to toll it
by ; and the flourishing of commerce is expressed by
the distant view of a busy sea-port with ships entering and going forth upon a gently moving sea ; and
Winged Love himself is drawing upon a tablet, to
typify the love that springs from leisure and contentment.   The central figure of Peace herself is winged,
to prove that her origin is heavenly, and at her girdle
are keys implying that she alone can unlock the
mysteries of nature, and also, depending from her
girdle, is a wallet full of money, meaning that Peace
brings wealth in her train.   At the woman's feet lies,
crouching and asleep, the form of War itself, in likeness
of a gaunt and wolfish hound.   The sun has newly
risen in the firmament, and his light is falling on hill
and valley, while flying away before this new-come
light of contentment and joy, is a winged dragon form

with its horrid jaws opened in act to howl, as it bears away a placard marked *Melancholy*. A most noble allegory, and like the other most plain to be understood.[1]

We passed through the territories of the Elector of Bavaria and the cities of Augsburg, Munich, and others of lesser note till we entered the region of the great mountains at Innsbrug, and here the poverty of the inhabitants and the asperities of the country and its bitter cold were very great and sore. Though it was now midspring, yet even the valleys were snow clad.

I could tell the reader many strange things of this country, such as of the many powerful witches and warlocks that dwell in the mountains, who are reputed, whether superstitiously or not I shall not here stop to

---

[1] Many years after this, being entertained at a college in the University of Oxford, I happened to mention this engraving and discoursed briefly to the learned company about me upon its happy signification. "Sir," said one of my hosts, a very ingenious Doctor of Arts, "you mistake this thing altogether. This pictured print I know well, having procured myself a copy from the Hague, and as to its interpretation, you are, by your leave, altogether mistaken, for the artist certainly intended only to represent the *Melancholy Temperament* in the guise of a very sorrowful female." I could not forbear smiling in my sleeve at my host's fancy, but let him not perceive my merriment, nor did I argue the point with him, considering it one of those matters that are too plain, and the truth too apparent, for discussion; but if this gentleman's interpretation were true (as most certainly it is not) what a sad reduction to a pitiful performance would there be of Herr Dürer's noble allegory of War and Peace !

inquire, to be very potential in the affairs of the dwellers in the mountains.

In these awful mountains we met with many delays and sundry small crosses and adventures, but none of any moment; and I will not dwell upon them, being impatient to relate the much stranger things which came to pass later on. Nor will I expatiate upon how, coming from the inhospitable, snowy north, and treading ever upon ground that sloped to the south, and the air growing daily more balmy, and passing many famous cities, as Botzen, Trent, and Roveredo, we at length, as we neared Verona, saw spread out beneath us like a great wide map, the warm, sunny champaign country of Lombardy, rich and green with growing crops of rye and wheat, and white with the blossom of countless fruit trees.

It was at Genoa that we had agreed to unite with the men of our troop who, having been in the service of the Emperor, had, as I have said, discharged themselves therefrom, and travelling through Venetia had reached Genoa some fortnight before our arrival. There we met the whole sixteen of our friends, no mishap of sickness or accident having, for a wonder, happened to any of them, and they all being sound in wind and limb when my Lord and I reviewed them in Genoa; and such a set of goodly, stout, brawny fellows as did a man's heart good to look upon.

Their dress was new, for, having put off the livery of the Emperor with their service to his Majesty, and that we might not go ragged to our new employ, the troop had, at my Lord's orders from Holland, equipped themselves in such uniform apparel as was purchasable at Genoa, as near as possible to represent the colours of the King of Spain. This new livery of theirs was a plain dark-buff jerkin, red breeches with green points, tall jack boots, and a sword-belt over the shoulder of a brightish yellow, and each man had green feathers in his gold-laced hat. Every trooper carried a brace of horse pistols in his girdle and a good carbine on his shoulder. So we marched down to the quays, two and two, his Lordship at our head, to embark in the Spanish merchant ship that was to give us passage to Barcelona in Spain.

As to the servants we brought with us, we were loath to part with them, they having proved themselves very honest and faithful ; serviceable and stout, too, as they had shown in a little brush or skirmish we had with certain robbers who had come out upon us from the forest in passing along the Brenner mountain road. These four men were as loath to part from us as we from them. Two were soldiers, one a Spaniard, the other a Frisian, and these two volunteered to serve in our troop, into which we readily drafted them. The two others who had charge of the sumpter mules we proposed to continue as our servants, but they also were desirous to take service in the troop. Both were Dutchmen and both sailors. One had, he told us, served as cabin boy in the flag ship of their famous admiral, Piet Heyn, at Tholen, in the great fight against the Spaniards

twenty years before. " Why then, Jan, my good
fellow," said I (the Dutchman's name was Jan Loots),
"you and I have fought against each other before
now, for I myself was in Count John's ship on that
day, that had your admiral yard-arm to yard-arm for
three hours : 'tis but fair you should serve on my side
for a change." So we carried both men with us, and
I truly think it was by God's direct Providence that
we did so, for it happened that before a week was
over this same Jan Loots was the means of pre-
serving our lives and liberties in as great a strait and
peril as ever I was in.

It thus came to be then that our little army was
swelled to twenty-three, thus told : officers, three, my
Lord, myself, and Cornet Brown ; rank and file,
twenty, including the four new recruits, twenty-three
men in all.

Thus equipped and ordered, and a couple of dozen
native porters to bring up the rear with our baggage
and spare arms and ammunition, we marched down
to the place of embarkation through a pretty thick
crowd of the townspeople come to see the English
troop go off to the wars in Spain. Our fellows had
been in Genoa, as I have said, a fortnight before we had
arrived, and though in difficulties with the language,
had made friends among the people, who are here
very civil. When our own servants came in our
small retinue, I imagine they must have talked something over-enough of what the troop had done in
England under my Lord's command, for when he and

I soon after our coming at Genoa paid our respects
to the General Commanding in Chief of the Forces
there, we found him as well aware of our doings as
the people of the United Provinces had been; and
this officer was pleased to address us a set compliment upon what he called our "glorious services" to
our Master and King. On our going off to our ship,
the general courteously sent a company of musque-
teers, with a bass-drum, a horn, and a couple of
hautboys, so that we had music at our parting, which
our fellows liked well; and they went down to the
waterside laughing and jesting with the citizens,
keeping step to the music, but swinging in their gait
and swaggering a bit (as is the way of us English);
and the people seeing these tall, comely fellows, their
long swords clattering along the pavement, their
carbines carried jauntily on their shoulders, and
themselves so gay and *debonair*, were greatly pleased
with them, and shouted out in Italian, "*Evviva!*"
and "*Bravi!*" which was their Italian way of wishing
us God speed and good luck; all which we took for a
very good omen.

Note, that we soldiers, being simple folk, are mightily
taken with kind looks and cheering words, particularly
of our own people, at going upon service or returning
therefrom, and we bear such last words and cheers in
our mind often through the long watches and fatigues
of the campaigns; and in our fighting and troubles
we ever look to the prospect of a kind welcome home
again, which things I beg my fellow countrymen will

remember, and not be too chary either of their God speeds to us at our going, or of their welcomes when we come home, for I think it is very politic of our people to remember how their homes and hearths and liberties are guarded for them by us soldiers; and we, too, should ever bear in mind that we are to march forth and suffer and fight, not for our own pleasure and profit (as so many think and do), but for the honour and safety of their King and for the good of those they leave at home—fathers, mothers, brothers and sisters, sweethearts, or friends, among which latter I am willing they should number all good citizens who love their country and honour the King.

CHAPTER IX.

WE met with a contrary wind, though not a strong one, on standing out from Genoa Harbour, and for three days and nights were tacking, and had not made three score of leagues on our way to the Port of Palermo in Sicily, the first at which we were to touch. Then we got a light slant of wind from nearly east and went along merrily, this being our ship's best sailing point, she being tubby in build, and but a very slow sailer at best. It was on the fifth day at sea, being the 2nd of May, 1652, that we sighted land, and this not Sicily, but an island called Ustica lying a few leagues to the north of it. Then it fell to a calm, or almost one, with light airs from the eastward now and again, which just helped us on at times; and by daybreak on the sixth day we lay quite becalmed, the heights on either side of Palermo Harbour being in sight some two or three leagues off, though the morning was a little misty.

The attentive, courteous Reader who has followed me thus far (if indeed such an attentive Reader there has been) will doubtless remember that it was to this point I had brought this narrative almost at first starting. Now, then, that he knows (as I hope) so much of the preliminaries as imports him to be acquainted with, I can proceed to the recounting of more important particulars.

Our men had just got their breakfast on deck, for the morning was warm and fine and the sea very calm, when we heard a gun fired from a small fort on the hill to the west of the city, whose towers and houses we could already discern. We looked and saw a flag run up in the same fort, presently there came a report of a second gun, whereupon the crew of the vessel began immediately to hurry up from below amid much talk and noise, and some ran up into the rigging, and every man began to peer and spy anxiously here and there upon the horizon ; then came a third gun from the fort, and immediately there was visible a still greater consternation among all on board. In a little while this signal by the three gun shots and the flag was repeated from the city fortifications, and again almost immediately the same signal came from a sea fort on a hill some four or five miles east of the Port ; again it was repeated along the coast, for we could plainly hear the shots and see the smoke of the gun, though the place of firing was out of our sight, and once more the sound came, but much further off, from the east.

Seeing how the crew of the ship were affected by this gun-fire signalling, we enquired its meaning and learnt that it betokened nothing less than that sundry Barbary Rovers, or Pirate vessels, had been sighted from the direction in which the sound was first heard. This, it seemed, is the warning always given along these coasts for all the inhabitants to fly into the woods and mountains, and all boats and ships at sea to run to the nearest port, for shelter from these bloody robbers and cruel scourges of sea and shore. One gun and the flag means, it seems, that a single vessel of the Rovers has been seen; two guns, two of their ships or galleys; and three guns, as now, a squadron or fleet of three or more. "The worst of it is" said the Captain to us, "that we know not how near or how far off the Pirates may be, or if the signal has come from round the island, out of our hearing, or has begun where we heard it first, showing that the Pirates are newly come from the open sea, and even now may be upon us at any moment. If it is not so," said he, "it is strange that we have heard no signal guns to westward of Cape Gallo."

Even while he spoke to us the Captain's doubts were resolved, for we saw, over the tops of a low ridge of rocks beyond the fortress on the hill in the west, the peaked tops of two lateen sails travelling against the sky very fast towards us. The Italian sailors who had gathered in a crowd in the fore part of the vessel gave a shout; "And," said the Captain, "we are lost men, unless by a miracle the wind should arise and blow us into Port before the Pirates can reach us."

"Why," I said, "there is no more wind for them than for you."

"What!" cried he, "did you not notice the gun-smoke carried eastward by the long-shore wind? It is blowing from the west along the coast line and for nearly a mile out to sea, though it is calm here. These fellows in a trice will cut us off from the shore; then, even if they have no slaves to row them, as I suspect by their rig they have not, they will at any rate man their sweeps, for they carry three times the crew we have, and their ships are narrow and swift, and ours very slow, and be upon us in an hour or two at furthest."

He was right about the shore wind, for looking, I could see the line of wind-ripples extending out from the shore about a mile but no further.

I asked what was to be done?

"Why," said he, "if there were but one of them, though these Rover galleys are crowded with men, three to one of our crew, I would propose to fight. We have two guns, plenty of small arms, and the men would fight for their liberty even against odds; but against a squadron what can we do? And look!" cries he, pointing to the ridge of low rocks, "here come the Pirate's consorts," and we now could see above the ridge the mast heads and peaked sails of two more large galleys.

"Will the people on shore not put out to our help?"

"Not they!" cried the Captain; "these Spaniards of

Sicily are not what they are at home :—they are sneaks and curs, Signor Capitano, they care only to enrich themselves, and they will do anything but strike a blow for honour. They have three fine War ships there in Palermo Harbour,—I see their masts at this moment—but they will cower behind their guns while these kites are swooping down upon us at their very threshhold."

My cousin was standing by as the Captain and his officers were thus in conversation with me.

"Gentlemen," said he, "it seems to me that with so many stout fellows as I see about me, and armed as we are, we could make at least some kind of a stand for our lives and liberties. Your countrymen were ever noted fighters by sea and by land."

"Sir," said the Captain, "you little know what these African brigands are; how trained and disciplined in attack, how strong their ships are in artillery, what skilful marksmen they are, how great the crowd of armed men on board, and what terrible Devils (for I can call them little else) they are at fighting. Did you, Sir, know but a tenth part of what I do of their fierceness and barbarity, you would abstain from counselling resistance which will but whet their native ferocity, and make our lot the harder to bear. At least, surrendering at discretion, we shall escape with our lives, though I know we may not escape bonds and hardships and even the scourge."

By this time not the officers only, but the crew of the Italian ship were gathered about us, and our fellows too came up, but inasmuch as the Englishmen could make out little or nothing of the talk, and knew nothing of the imminent peril we were in, so they were laughing and jesting, while the poor Italian sailors forecasting the fate before them, looked woebegone indeed. The Italian Captain went on, and presently I began to hope that there was something in his speech beyond its apparent meaning of a counsel to bare submission, and soon I had reason to alter my opinion of him from a pitiful cur to a brave and very cunning fellow. Thus it always is with Italians, who even while they seek to persuade others and themselves to right issues and brave action, will ever be doing it by guile and tortuous courses.

"Sir," he said to my Lord, and pointing to the troop, "I would prevail upon you to let these honest gentlemen of yours know that their lives are probably safe if they will consent to go down upon their knees and beg these Barbary ruffians for mercy, who will then bind them, as they will our men too, and carry them captive into their infamous dens: there got, some will be fettered to the oar for their lives, others will be sent into mines and never see the light of the sun again, others will be chained in gangs and set to scavenge the streets, and all will be starved and ill used, and live under constant dread of the whips of savage and cruel masters. But is not this better than to fight with no chance of victory and every certainty of death, though to be sure it would be a glorious and happy death against these enemies of our faith, who, when they have got us, will never rest till, by scourging and starving and torturing us, they have caused us to blaspheme against our blessed religion and curse the Holy Cross itself, and so they will cause our immortal souls to perish when they have at length tormented our bodies into the grave."

We now saw the Italian captain's drift clearly, and his men began to be moved by his subtle rhetoric, muttering among themselves, clenching their hands, and presently, breaking out, they besought the captain to show them the way to make the best resistance that was possible.

Our own fellows needed no such roundabout eloquence. " Look you ! " cried my Lord, " here are three scoundrelly Sea Rovers coming to take us ; we must make the best fight we can." The men gave a cheer and went for their arms.

We had come so very quickly to our decision to offer resistance that the Pirate vessels were still beyond the rocks in the west and their hulls yet under the horizon, when we began to make our pre-parations. The *Esperanza*, which was our ship's name, was a square-rigged, two-masted vessel, short and broad, and a slow sailer, and standing pretty high out of the water, for though she carried cargo it was not a very heavy one.

The crew was fortunately pretty numerous, con-sisting of forty-nine men, all told, and all of them Genoese, who are I think the stoutest and most valiant of the Italians, as they have proved at all times by gloriously maintaining their independence for so long by sea and land against all its assailants. About half of these men had served in the navy of Genoa. Besides them we had three young Spanish gentlemen on board, passengers to Spain, each with his two servants. These gallant gentlemen were all for fighting, but they looked little used to serious work in that way, and I did not count much upon them. This then brought our number up to fifty-eight, all good men, the six Spanish servants being stout, likely-looking fellows, natives of Galicia. Add to this our own troop, which now came up to twenty-three, and our fighting strength was eighty-one, all told.

While we were all consulting together and advising, some one thing, some another, my Lord, who had hitherto held his peace, said : " Gentlemen, if we are to make anything of this business, it will only be by our deputing all authority to our captain, who is in sole rightful command on this deck, and by obeying his directions, with no distraction to him by any word of objection, or cavil, or advice offered."

The captain considered a little, and addressing himself to his officers and men, said : " The English cavalier's advice is good, but I would have him and you to know that I am but a seafaring man, with no knowledge of war, and therefore claim no experience in the ordering of such a matter as we now have in hand ; and as I know this English gentleman is a captain of war who has done great things in his own country, and is accustomed to command in battle, and moreover as he speaks well in the Tuscan tongue, which we Genoese can all fairly understand, I do hereby transfer to him the government and ordering of this ship and all who are in it, and call upon you all to obey him, as I will myself, in everything he may be pleased to command."

" I accept this charge," said his Lordship; and immediately, having already considered what was best to be done, he began to give his orders.

The cargo was chiefly bales of woollen cloth, of velvet and of silk. These he commanded to be brought up from the hold and built up in a sort of bulwark all round the gunwale to the height of a man, with loopholes between every three or four bales for the men to fire through. My kinsman left to me to inquire into the state of the ship's cannon and to distribute among the men small arms of all kinds, this being a department of warfare of which I have made some careful study. I found the ship furnished with two 18-lb. guns, as fine pieces of Italian ordnance as ever I saw, and I believed we should make very pretty practice with them : there was abundance of powder, which I found to be good and dry, but unfortunately there were in all but thirteen cannon balls. These I set in open boxes by the sides of the guns, and got powder, rammers, linstocks, and all in readiness. To remedy the deficiency of iron balls I had some cartouches or cartridges made up with bullets, pistol balls, and slugs, and laid half of them by each gun ; and by my Lord's order, who had

already designed his method for the coming battle,
each gun was loaded at the first with a cartridge of
this small shot. To each man of the sailors, and to
the Spaniards (for our own men had their arms), I
served out one pistol or a brace, according as I
judged of their skill in using them, for there were not
enough pairs to go round, and each man had either a
cutlass or a short pole-axe, at his choice. I ordered
the muskets to be carried on deck, and caused to be
laid down by each loophole three or four of these
arms ready loaded, for we had many more muskets
than men to use them.

Coming up on the quarter-deck after I had got
through this work, I found that the three Pirates
were now in full view rounding the point, the wind
aft for them, but light. We perceived that they were
not rowing galleys—that is, not rowed by slaves, but
wholly sailing ships, lateen rigged. This was better
for us, and yet worse : they would not reach us so
soon in a calm, not being moved by a great crowd of
men ; but, on the other hand, the room of unarmed
slaves chained to the rowlocks would be filled by
fighting men, and we might, we believed, now count
upon having 140 to 180 enemies in each of their ships.

Another thing I discovered on coming up on deck,
which before I was ignorant of ; this was that a
current was setting us to westward, that is, in the
direction of the fort from which the first signal guns
had been fired, though parallel to it and carrying us
past it. We had in the morning been opposite the

city, now we were west of it half a league. This, too was against us, for till now if the wind had got up it would have driven us in ; but now if it came we must pass by the Pirate ships first, for they already stood nearly betwixt us and the entrance.

The men had worked hard, and now had raised a very fair bulwark, lashed and made fast with ropes to the gunwale railing all round ; and my cousin had caused to be built up another similar bulwark, well secured and loopholed, across the poop of the ship from side to side. This poop was high, raised some four feet above the quarter-deck, there being a round house below it. The tiller came up to the poop, and the bulwark of bales had now converted it into a little citadel which, if the deck were rushed and cleared by boarders, might still afford a refuge to a remnant of us.

" 'Tis a thousand pities," said I, " we have no piece of ordnance to mount here that should command the deck below."

The captain remembered that he had in the hold a disused rusty sort of a cannon, which, being old-fashioned and having no carriage belonging to it, had, since he had commanded the ship, done no other duty than to serve as ballast. I asked to have it shown me, and thinking I saw some fight still left in the old piece, we got it up. It was a strange kind of a gun, perhaps a hundred years old, a short piece, that would carry a four or five pound shot, and bound round with rings of iron ; and it had seen much service in its day, for the touch-hole was so large that I feared to charge the gun till I had *bushed* it with splints of hard wood driven in : then we made a rammer and cleaned out the piece, and mounted it on a makeshift carriage of a strong wooden box, laying the gun with wedges and making it fast with rope, so that its fire from its station on the poop would rake our own deck from end to end. We had no ammunition proper for it, and I imagine it was never constructed to carry a ball, for it had something of a bell mouth, like a blunderbuss, and as we were out of slugs and bullets the captain brought me a barrel of various sized nails, with which I loaded the gun nearly to the mouth, and tying up half a dozen loads more of this irregular shot in woollen bags, I laid them and the powder in an open box by its side. The Italians called this piece, the like of which I had never seen before, a *Pederero*, or *Pederara*, as being, I suppose, contrived for the shooting of small stones or gravel.

New we were ready, and could look about us a bit and see our enemy's movements. The three Rovers might now be about two leagues from us, and still within the influence of the light westerly breeze and sailing very gently along, with their lateen sails out over the sides. They kept close in to hold the wind, sailing, as we could see by the line of ripples, just within the outer edge of it; and now we very unexpectedly found we had a friend where we least expected one, and that was on shore.

The three Rovers were now in single file, with four or five cables' length between them, passing in front of the Fort whence we had first heard the signalling, and we noticed that they kept edging away as far from it as they could, but still not so far as to get into calm water. As the Pirates came nearer we could see that the last vessel of the line was the smallest of the three, carrying but one gun in her bows, and the vessel that sailed in the middle place was the largest, carrying four cannon, and a chase gun in her bows.

The Fort stands on a tongue or ridge of rocky land somewhat advanced into the sea, and the Pirates could remove themselves from its guns no further, still to keep the shore wind, than about a quarter of a mile. As the first of them got abreast of the fort the gunners there fired upon her two shots. It is true the first missed its aim, going too high and striking the water many hundred yards beyond the ship ; the second shot struck nearly as far too short ; so the Rover got off scot free. We could see embrasures for ten guns, and hoped for more firing from our friends, but there were apparently but two sound guns to fire with, and they seemingly had to be loaded again, for the second ship of the Pirates passed unharmed, and it was only when the third Rover came by that the two guns were ready to be fired again, which took place almost at the same moment. By this time the gunners had got their range, and the shots were marvellously true, for the first brought the foremast of the third galley by the board, and the second did

better work still, for it cut down the great single yard
of the mainmast, and brought yard, sail, and all
tumbling down upon deck. Our men set up a shout,
and the air and sea were so still and calm that we
could hear it plainly answered from the quays and
housetops of the city, whither the citizens of Palermo
had crowded to see out our capture by the Pirates.

The Rover was disabled and in disorder for the time,
but presently they got out their sweeps and began to
endeavour to row beyond the reach of the guns, but
not before the fort had again fired twice upon them,
striking both times, but with what effect we could
not discern. The second Pirate immediately hove to
in order to help her consort, but the first ship kept
on her course towards us, and it was to her only that
we now looked.

So soon as she had got into calm water she hauled
down her sails, and manning six great sweeps on
either side, she advanced towards us very swiftly over
the water. My Lord commanded our people to lie
quiet behind the bulwark of bales. Presently the
Rover, being got within three or four hundred yards of
us, a person on board of her hailed us in the Italian
language. At my Lord's direction the captain
answered, asking what the other's business with
them might be. "Send a boat to us with all your
officers in it," cried the spokesman, "and you shall
discover our business."

The captain, at my Lord's order, made answer that
he could not, seeing that his only boat was not

sea-worthy (which was the case), and he again demanded to know what the Pirate's business was.

The Pirates, never, it may be supposed, apprehending that a single merchant vessel intended serious resistance to three powerful Corsairs, though they may have wondered a little at our deck defences, took no precautions to ascertain our strength and intentions, and looking on our ship and us as already their prey and delivered over to their mercy, forbore to injure what they considered their own property by firing upon our ship. They accordingly came near and within easy talking distance ; so when our captain asked what their business with us was, he who was their spokesman, thinking he had got hold of a very simple fellow, began to jeer and mock : " Why," said he in very good Italian, " you must know you have had the good fortune to fall into the hands of true believers, who will speedily convert you into the right faith by such persuasive arguments as the scourge and the bastinado, and to such as are very obstinate we will administer the argument of impalement and other convincing reasons of the like kind." The pirates laughed at their spokesman's merriment, who, to judge by his cruelty and also his Italian speech, must have been one of those villainous Christian Renegados who, having denied their own faith, have falsely pretended to that of the Pagans.

By this the Pirate had come up nearly alongside, and peering on them through the loopholes of our

fortification of bales we perceived that there could
not be fewer than 140 of these bloodthirsty ruffians
crowded upon the deck of the Rover, swarthy,
bearded villains, each with a scimetar by his side and
three or four pistols thrust into his girdle.   Then they
stopped rowing, their ship being not above twenty-five
or thirty yards off, the way on their vessel still
carrying them onward towards us.

This was the moment my Lord had determined
upon : "Fire!" he called out, and at the word our
starboard gun was fired, loaded to the muzzle with
small bullets, while our crew let fly with all the
muskets we had got ready.   The men were crowded
so thick in the forepart of the vessel, all eager to be
the first to board us, and they were so near, that I do
not think one single bullet of the scores in the cannon
charge could have missed of its aim.   There rose up
a most terrible cry of rage and surprise from them,
and before they had recovered of their confusion we
had run the larboard gun over to the enemy's side and
fired her with equal aim and still better effect among
the crowd.   Then the Pirates rallied a little and ran
to their cannon, which all lay on the spar, or upper
deck.   While they did so, our fellows fired some fifty
or sixty more shots with their muskets loaded with
slugs, doing great destruction among them, for the
ships were now fouled and entangled together.   Still
so great was the enemy's resolution that they got one
gun laid and were about to have fired it but that my
Lord, seeing what they were about, jumped on the

gunwale and waving his sword called out very loud in
English for his own men to board, and climbed down
into the Pirate ship without waiting to see who
followed him. We leaped down after him so quickly
that we all twenty-three of us stood on the Pirate's
deck before we had received half a dozen pistol shots.
The Turks seeing, amid the clouds of smoke which
now covered everything, that they were boarded by
men in uniform, perhaps magnified their numbers, and
certainly discovered to their cost that they were not
merely pouncing upon a defenceless prey. Then we
rushed the decks, fighting very strenuously with sword
and pistol for three or four minutes till we found the
Turks begin to give way a little, and by this time
some two dozen or more of the Italians and the nine
Spaniards had followed our board, and we overcame
the Pirates; and as they sought no quarter, we killed
or disabled all but some score or so who fled below, and
whom we did not care to follow.

Now all this, from the first gun fired to the end of
the fighting, did not occupy five full minutes, but
then no quarter-minute of that time but was taken up
with a hard struggle for life or for death. It was a
thing wholly in the nature of a surprise, and had it not
been so it would clearly have been impossible for
some forty or forty-five men, however stout and nimble,
to overcome over treble that number as we had done;
but it is to be remembered we must have killed or
badly wounded with the two shots of our cannon at
close quarters, and with our musketry fire immediately

after, a large number—perhaps a third—of the enemy ;
and what is most extraordinary is the little hurt our
men took, for not one of the Italians was even touched
(this I ascribe to the scanty and hasty firing of the
enemy) and only two of our own fellows were wounded :
one got a cut from a scimetar on the left arm, but
when it was bound up he said he felt none the worse
or weaker : another had a pistol shot graze him above
the knee, but it did not so much as lame the man.

So soon as the Pirates' resistance was overcome my
Lord ordered those who carried axes to break up the
tiller, cut the sheets, halyards, and shrouds, and break
to pieces the rowlocks in which the great oars or
sweeps were worked ; while I myself, at my Lord's
orders, quickly spiked the four guns with some great
nails, breaking off the heads short, so that the guns
were useless for a day at the least.

When we looked about us we perceived that we had
had the misfortune to drift a cable's length or thereabouts from our own ship, the fellows on board the
Esperanza not having had the common wit to lash
the two ships together when we boarded.   The Rovers
carry boats enough in their ships to convey the whole
of their crews, and to make their piratical adventures
on shore, and there were two great launches lying
amidships ready with oars and sails complete, either
of which would easily have held our boarders, but my
Lord had his reasons for having both the boats lowered,
which in a few minutes we had accomplished, on the
side away from and out of sight of the other two

Pirate Galleys, and dividing our company in them, we rowed back to our ship.

We now saw that the second Rover, and the largest of the three, after standing by for a while to aid the stricken ship, was rowing up with all haste through the calm water to come to the help of her consort whom we had engaged. It was certain that she knew not, what with the distance and the heavy smoke that still hung over us, all that had happened to her sister ship and how complete her discomfiture had been at our hands; but seeing as she came up the two launches set forth on our return from the Rover, it is likely the new-comer supposed they were filled with boarders from her consort, and therefore she would forbear, as she did forbear, from firing her guns into the merchantman, whom she must have conceived to be now full of her own men; which fell out luckily for us, for had she cannonaded us it is certain she could not have failed, and in no long time, to have sent us to the bottom.

So it was that when we had got back to the *Esperanza* the first thing we saw was this new and terrible enemy some 500 yards only from us and still coming near, but slowly and, as the boatmen say, "easing" her sweeps. My Lord resolved to begin the ball, so waiting till she was within twenty-five yards, and stem on to our starboard gun, he gave the order to fire first one and then our second gun (both loaded with round shot), which was still trained on our starboard side. My Lord had called to Jan Loots and

said, "Do you, Jan, lay this gun and fire it," having
observed this fellow's knowledge of great guns, and
his incredible Dutch phlegm and coolness ; so the
Dutchman, while we all watched him, never hurrying
himself a jot, laid his piece, twisted and turned it to
his content till he had got his aim, and just waiting
the rise of the sea-swell, laid the linstock to the touch-
hole.   The shot was so truly aimed that he raked the
enemy's deck, as we could plainly see, from stem to
stern, laying low half a score of our enemy.   "Now the
other!" cries my Lord, and Jan in the same leisurely
fashion fired the second piece.   The aim was not
quite so true as the first, yet it did us better service,
for it struck to the one side of amidships and passing
fore and aft as the first had done, cut down and broke
to pieces all the sweeps on that side.   By this accident
to them the Pirate for the time could neither near us
to board, nor keep in a good position for firing his
guns to advantage.   Nevertheless he began at once
to return our fire with great and small pieces, which
we endeavoured to answer as well as we could with
the disadvantage of having but two cannon, against
the enemy's five, and but sixty or fifty musketeers
against his 150 or more.   However we did him a good
deal more mischief than he us, for our men were protected from shot and splinters by the bulwark of
bales, while his deck lay quite open to us ; and we,
being higher and firing down, had. the better and
bigger target for our shots, and his having to fire
upwards was no doubt the reason that most of his

round shot struck our masts and rigging, pretty soon encumbering the deck with a hamper of spars and ropes, while not above three or four came into our hull. Seeing which, the Pirate made up his mind to use what sweeps he had left and come to closer quarters, and to board us by means of his boats, relying no doubt upon being able to put on our decks two men to one of ours. So getting his two large boats into the water and putting some sixty men into each, over the side furthest from us, they rowed towards us very fast.

As soon as my Lord perceived how critical was our predicament he ran among the men, directing them to load their pieces with slugs and reserve their fire till the Corsair's boats were got into the water; the cannon he ordered to be loaded with bullets and the muzzles to be lowered to the utmost.

Presently the two boats of boarders were upon us we peppering them hotly with small shot in the short space of time we had to fire, and getting off our two cannon upon them. The first gun fired—it was manned and aimed by Italians—took no effect; but the second was aimed by Jan Loots, and he waited and waited till I feared the boat would be got under his muzzle. At last he let fly, and with so pretty an aim that positively I believe he accounted for about half the crew : certain I am I saw over a score of the Miscreants roll to the bottom of the boat, and she herself was so riddled with bullets through her sides and bottom that she began to fill with water However, she held on till the crew of her laid hold of our vessel's side and scrambled up with the other boat's crew. My Lord, willing to spare our small numbers to the utmost for what they had still to do, had quickly retired all his men to the little citadel before mentioned on the poop; and thence we fired at our will and ease upon the Turks, who were running to and fro in search of us upon our wreck-hampered deck, disappointed no doubt at finding, after their pains to come at us, that we were still out of their reach. At last, seeing our game, they got together in a crowd before the mainmast to prepare, as we believed, for a storm of our position.

So soon as they were in a bunch, Jan Loots, whom my Lord had now put in charge of the old wide-mouthed piece, or *Pederera*, inside our citadel, discharged it among them; and though the gun scattered its shot of great nails, and wasted them to right and left, yet at least five of these queer bullets reached the group of Turks, for there were knocked over as many of the villains. Its effects, however, were less to terrify than to anger and inspirit them, and under the cover of the smoke, which in the hazy air hung very thick over us, they charged up to our position on the poop, and with such fierce determination that, though a dozen fell by our pistols, or hangers, or pole-axes, some six or seven scrambled up and were killed by us inside the bulwarks. The rest ran back, but presently came again to the charge, so very bravely do these Infidels fight. At last they were discouraged beyond hope of rally, for while they were so charging us, the men kept firing on them with musket and pistol whenever they could catch sight of a man through the smoke; and as quickly as she could be loaded the old *Pederera* never ceased her fire at large into the darkness of the smoke, and no doubt accounted for a good many of the villains.

When presently there came no more shots from them, and we could no longer hear their scuffling over the deck, we stopped too, and perceived that under cover of the smoke they had got into their one boat—the other had sunk—and were making off to their ship. We counted fifty men in the boat, many hurt, out of the 110 or 120 that had come at us, and as we plied them pretty freely with shot on their way to their friends, it is to be supposed that they took home with them even less than this number.

As soon as we began to shoot from our ship with our big guns, so did our enemy do the same very furiously. While this was going on, the enemy, re-solving again to close with us, was using the sweeps he still had unbroken by our second shot, and was coming slowly up to us through the firing.

It was now that my Lord proceeded to execute a stratagem which for boldness, cunning, and novelty exceeds all I ever heard of in naval battle. First, he told off all the men in twos and threes to enter the boats he had brought from the first Pirate and which still lay alongside, fastened by their painters. They were to discharge their firelocks before they entered

them, and before all the crew were got in them the
cannon were fired again a last time; and finally,
when nearly all were aboard the launches, he bade
set light to a barrel of damped powder, which raised
so thick a smoke as covered up ship and all, and lay
like a thick mist on the water all about her. In this
cloud we rowed away, having at the very last spiked
our own two guns; but the little old *Pedcrera* we
carried with us, and two or three charges for her, and
at my Lord's order we fixed her, on her makeshift
carriage, in the bows of the boat, pointing her muzzle
upwards with a slant, and loaded her. Then we
pulled away gently from our ship, and lying upon
our oars some few boats' length away, and the fog of
smoke still hiding us, bided our time.

Presently we could hear (for we could see nothing
now in the thickness of the smoke cloud) the Pirate
vessel come bump up against our ship, the noise of
their musketry fire still continuing, and some of our
light-hearted fellows could not forbear laughing to
think the enemy was so busily firing through the
smoke into an empty ship, and we now within a
stone's throw of them. Then my Lord ordered us to
give way with a will, and with his own hand on the
tiller he ran us right alongside of the Corsair. He
had justly supposed that most of her crew would be
out of her, boarding the *Esperanza*, but there were
about forty men left, and some of these catching
sight of our boat as we got near, the whole of them
ran together to the side of their vessel, as if taken

aback at the sight of us whom they had so little reason to expect. Before they had much time to think of it, my Lord gave orders to fire both our muskets and the *Pederera*, which we did in the very act before scrambling up the low side of the Corsair galley.

We very easily and very quickly overmastered them ; but the moment after, the rest of the crew—those namely who had invaded our empty ship, the two vessels being now lashed together—hearing the affray, began to jump down and back into their own vessel to attack us. Here came some very stiff fighting, for we were pretty evenly matched in numbers, the Pirates rather, I suppose, the larger force, though we had already done so much to kill and disable a very large number of them. It was mostly sword work, for as we had fired off our pistols, so too had the others ; and the combat was very long and very sore, and there were great shouting and noise on both sides—of the Turks crying upon Mahomet their false Prophet to help them, of the Italians calling upon the Saints, and both fighting bravely ; but the English kept their breath, saying no word, good or bad, but fought on very stiffly indeed.

I will not deny that we had the advantage that but very few of us as yet were wounded so badly but that we could fight, while over a score of the Pirates bore our marks ; and then again we had the surprise and our boldness in our favour, and that they were fighting they hardly knew how, with whom, or why,

or wherefore. There must be some magic, sure, they
must have thought, about this empty ship of ours,
and our coming at them so strangely, and the bodies
of their own men lying on the deck : and all this had
happened in a flash, as it were, and by what cantrip
or enchantment they must have been hard put to it
to conjecture, and perhaps they felt they were fighting against some more than mortal enemy. So, as I
say, we had an advantage; and presently, and through
our good cause, and by the mercy of the Almighty
we began to prevail against them, and we drove the
Pirates slowly into the corners and slew them, and
some of them leapt overboard in the despair of defeat
and were drowned ; and the deck was slippery with
men's blood, and the air full of their groans.

Then at last we had conquered and overcome our
cruel enemies who had so triumphed in the thought
of our captivity. But this last victory had cost us
very dear, and our side, which had as yet so miraculously escaped with so few and such slight wounds,
had now lost a dozen men killed. Two of our own
troop lay dead on the deck, and six were wounded,
but none very badly. All three of the young Spanish
gentlemen and one of their servants had fallen,
fighting bravely, and of the Italians six were killed
outright and either eleven or twelve wounded.

We had but a few minutes' rest to attend to the
wounded when we heard the noise of great oars in
their rowlocks, and saw the third Pirate closing upon
us. A light breeze had now sprung up, and was

blowing shorewards, and against this the Corsair could advance but slowly. Seeing his own men so tired and weakened by their morning's work, my Lord determined to employ other tactics against our third enemy. He therefore ordered all hands to set the foresail of the Pirates' ship, we not being a strong enough crew to hoist the great yard of the mainsail. He ordered the captain himself to take the helm, and had the Pirate's own cannon loaded, and directing the ship to be laid broadside on to the enemy as he advanced, he gave the word to fire the two guns. Then presently began between us and the enemy a pretty lively cannonade ; but at this work we had a very signal advantage, for as the Pirate's only gun was a chaser fixed in his bows, he could not fire it without exposing his deck to be raked by our two broadside cannon. The fight was then a very unequal one, and but for a chance disabling shot we were pretty sure to get the better of it, as indeed very soon happened ; for seeing that every shot of ours did most terrible execution all along their decks, and that their gunners too were flurried by our two shots to their one, they began to lose heart. Then came a lucky shot from Jan Loots, which struck their only cannon and overset it, killing and wounding the gunners. At this they quite lost heart, and betook themselves to their boats, we still assailing them briskly the while with cannon and musketry shot. We knew not whether they intended boarding, being still some sixty or seventy in number, though many hurt ; but they had seemingly no mind to attempt this forlorn hope, and had no wish left but to fly from a ship wherein they could hope for nothing for themselves but death and destruction. So we saw them row away in their two great boats, and immediately my Lord gave orders to stop firing.

The Italian captain and his officers very earnestly entreated that my Lord would pursue them in the ship, and that our gunners might pick off the boats and sink them; but my Lord would not. Said he: "I will allow no firing upon unresisting men." The captain urged that these Pirates were the scourge and terror of the seas, and as they would have shown no mercy or forbearance to us, so we were not bound to use any with them. "They may be all you say, and worse," said my Lord smiling, "but they have fought like brave men while there was a chance left for them. No," said he, "they shall go their ways in peace for me;" and he would not be moved.

We had now leisure to look about us and count the fruits of our victory, and to thank our God (which I believe each of us did in his heart most devoutly) for our so marvellous escape from this great and terrible strait we had been in. We had overcome, partly by lawful guile and partly by boldness, an enemy number-ing fourfold our own force, and with arms, discipline, and swiftness much exceeding our own. I cannot forbear here to note down for the admiration of my readers the behaviour of that "poor fellow," Jan Loots—so do I call him now in a sort of irony, and

somewhat to reproach myself for my wrong judgment
of him, for it was so we in the troop had been used
to name him ; and when I urged upon my Lord that
he should be admitted of our number, and my kinsman was nothing loth, Cornet Brown objected a little.
" This Dutch fellow," said he, " an' it please your
worship, is altogether too soft and ease-loving for a
trooper, though I grant he is a good-natured fellow ;
but he will ever care for his pipe and his pot better
than for fighting, and will do the troop no credit
at all."

"Well," said I, " Cornet, we can but try him, and
if he runs away, poor wretch! he will never corrupt
the troop to do the same."

The truth was, I had got to love the fellow, he was
so gentle and obliging. Jan was a round-faced Dutchman, a simple fellow, very quiet, who spoke but little
(indeed he had but little English to speak with), and
was civil to every one about him ; and, as I have said,
when we had that little trouble with some robbers in
the mountains he seemed not to lose heart ; so, a little
doubting his sufficiency, we clad him in our livery
like the others and gave him his arms.

On the morning of the sea-fight, as I was serving
out the ship's hangers and pole-axes to the crew, he
begged to be let have one of the latter weapons, and
this though he carried his own trooper's sword and
pistols. I gave him his choice of several, and he
picked out the longest and heaviest axe he could find.
He was indeed, as we afterwards found, a fellow of

prodigious strength and activity, as well as courage,
when once he had woke up a little. When he
went with us to board the greatest ship of the three
Corsairs, he whipped off his coat in the boat, put
away his pistols and sword and sword-belt, and
turned up his shirt sleeves, having nothing but this
great pole-axe in his hand, and in our worst strait,
when the returning boarders came upon us and had
like to overwhelm us utterly, Jan ran furiously among
the thick of them, whirling his axe round his head,
and bringing it down with such right aim and force
on the turbans and shoulders of the Unbelievers that
they could make nothing of him, and I profess that I
myself with my own eyes saw him slay no fewer than
four of them in succession with this terrible weapon;
and he did all through the engagement mighty execution with his great axe, insomuch that afterwards,
when our troopers wanted to magnify some great
swashing blow, they would liken it to one from Jan
Loots's pole-axe, and "Jan's axe" after this got to be
a byword among us.

But this is by no means all; for it is undoubted
that but for Jan's shot at the Pirates' boat with the
boarders, and the great discouragement to them that
followed it, I do verily believe we should have been
hard put to it to win, in the very beginning of the
fight, for all my Lord's strategy and valour. Then
again, but for his two shots at the second Rover, one
raking their deck and the other breaking half their
oars, we should have gone near to be undone; so

that to Jan Loots, whom we had so meanly thought of, we all owed our lives and safety.

The breeze had now got up a little, and we steered for the other vessels—our own and the other two Pirates, all now empty, drifting about at large—and putting half a dozen men in each to man a pair of sweeps, and so help to keep her course and to work the mended tiller, we set all sail on the *Esperanza*, and, taking advantage of the slight favouring breeze, towed the other three towards the harbour of Palermo.

As our ship, drawing her great prizes after her, came slowly in, an immense multitude of citizens who, all through, had watched the progress of the fight, despairing for us at first, then fearing and doubting of our escape, then hoping a little, and at last, when we came towing the three great ships of the enemy, confounded with amazement at our triumph, and hardly believing their own eyes—the citizens, I say, now ran down to the piers and quays, while others looked from every window that gave a view of the harbour, and some were crowded even upon the house-tops; and all this vast multitude began to fill the air with resounding shouts of welcome and gladness. Looking upward upon a lofty mountain that in a horseshoe shape girds the city some way off (for there is a goodly plain between), we saw people there too in crowds, and the cry of the townspeople was taken up and echoed by the countrymen far and near among the hills.

We learnt afterwards that upon the signal guns giving token of an approaching Corsair, the people from all the coast, even those four or five miles away from the sea, would fly terror-stricken to the mountains or to the strong cities, and there abide and watch the doings of their enemies. It was these poor people who were now beside themselves with joy at our victory and their deliverance ; for it is almost impossible for us who are Englishmen, and are mostly not averse to striking a blow for our liberties, to understand the submission and fear these inhabitants of the Island had come to be in on account of the Barbary Rovers ; not even the ships of war in the harbours, though armed and manned, daring to leave the safety of their moorings to go forth to encounter them ; nor would the soldiery in the garrisons suffer themselves to be led to meet them, when they landed from their ships to raid the villages. A fear and slavishness which in defenceless peasants may be excused, but in men trained to arms and wearing the livery of war, is, to be sure, a most mean and pitiful circumstance.

CHAPTER X.

So soon as we had come to our moorings in the Harbour, we gave over in charge of the Port Constables our prisoners, of whom we had some fifty, mostly wounded, but some unhurt, who had run below when our boarders cleared the decks. These and our own wounded we sent ashore, and the dead we gave in charge of them also for burial. Then we asked for a guard of Sicilian soldiers to be set in each vessel, seeing we were like now to be boarded and overrun by our friends, as in the morning we had so nearly been by our enemies ; for no sooner were we in the still water of the smaller harbour of the two which together make up the Port of Palermo, than some hundred of rowing and sailing boats came up, full of townspeople eager to see the captive Turks and the prizes and us who had so miraculously (as they thought) conquered and captured them ; and they rowed round about our ship laughing with pleasure, singing some of them to the music of their mandolines and guitars, clapping their hands, both men and women, if they but caught sight of one of our fellows, and throwing flowers and garlands on to our decks, calling out we were their deliverers and preservers, and I know not what ; behaving in short more like children at play than serious grown-up men and women.

Presently came off to us in his gilt barge, in great state, the Governor of the city with a company of his musketeers, to compliment my Lord upon our victory and to bring a civil communication to the same effect from the Viceroy, or Vice Regent of the King of Spain ; this little King of the Island of Sicily having his Court with no small pomp and magnificence at Palermo itself. His Grace the Viceroy was graciously pleased to command my Lord's presence before him with as little delay as might be accordant with his convenience, in order that his Grace might learn from his Lordship's own lips the tidings of his glorious achievement.

It was too late that night to comply with the Viceroy's desire, therefore my Lord signified through the Governor, that on the morrow he would have the honour of obeying the august command, and of waiting upon his Grace.

The next morning therefore, after the refreshment of sleep and rest, for the troop was in truth quite worn and weary with this long day's work and fighting, we took boat for the nearest quay. My Lord and I and so many of the troop as were fit to carry arms and to march, which were as many as eighteen all told, for of our six wounded men, only three were so hurt that they could not move; the rest must needs fall in. The two killed of our troop, the Governor had promised should have a soldier's funeral, with full honours, that evening; so here do I take my leave of these my companions, *sociorum et sodalium fidelium*, of these most true and trusty comrades and friends. One was Dick Spooner, an honest Gloucestershire man, a yeoman soldier, whom we could but ill spare; he had followed us from the very first; the other was Jack Page, a Kentish man, a young gentleman who joined us after the fight at Holmwood, on the recommendation of Mr. Farleigh of Chevening. He had never the chance, poor fellow, of striking a blow for the cause of his King and country; but 'twas his misfortune, not his fault, for he was lusty, strong and loyal, and died fighting nobly against the Pirates. He was a man of most pleasant life. *Requiescant in pace:* may these brave and faithful soldiers rest in peace!

When we reached the Harbour Stairs, we found in waiting for my Lord and myself, two most noble Barbary chargers sent by the Governor and very bravely caparisoned, and at the head of our troop we rode through the streets to the Viceroy's palace, which is set on a hill in the outskirts of the city.

If the joy and exultation of the people had been great the evening before, what shall I say of their behaviour to-day?

The noise of our exploit had spread far and near, and the city was invaded by multitudes of country-

men willing to be assured of the good news through
their own hearing. It was well that the Governor had
had the forethought of lining the streets with his
troops, and sending two companies of musketeers to
clear the way before us, and another to keep them off
us in our rear, for otherwise we could not have passed
through the crowd, so thickly did they press upon us
in their wonder and admiration. There was a great
band of music, drums, horns, hautboys, bassoons and
cymbals, ready for us to march to, and much display
of banners and pendants and flags borne in procession
before us, flowers flung upon us from windows and
balconies, and gay-coloured scarfs and kerchiefs
waved by the women; and yet we were but a sorry
set of fellows for such bravery, for though as I have
said but six of our whole troop were badly wounded,
hardly any of us had escaped some little mark or
token of the Pirates' swords or pistols. Some of us
limped, some had an arm bandaged, some their cheek
laid open or their head tied up, and we who rode at
their head on our fine Barbary horses, had come no
better off for looks than our followers, for my Lord
had a bullet through the fleshy part of his right arm
and carried it in a sling, and I wore a great black
patch across my left eye. Homely as we were,
however, the people seemed never tired of cheering us
on our way to the Royal Palace.

In the great Piazza in front thereof we left the
people behind, and there followed in through the
gateway into the courtyard only our escort of soldiers

and the music. The Chamberlain then conducted my
Lord and me through many courts and corridors and
lofty halls till we came to the Throne Room, bedight
with rich Flemish tapestries and hangings and rare
carpets from the East, where his Grace Don Roderigo
Mendoza Roscas y Sandoval, Duke of Infantado,
Viceroy and Captain-General of Sicily, sat enthroned
and wearing the Order and Red Cross of Calatrava,
encompassed with his courtiers and great Officers
of State.

We kissed the Viceroy's hands, tendering to him
our homage, fealty, and obeisance, as to a Sovereign
Lord, which in deed, though not in name, he is. Don
Roderigo was a gentleman of fine bearing and courtly
manners, a tall and handsome personage, and in years
between fifty and sixty, perhaps inclining to the
greater age. He asked us many questions of our
encounter with the Corsairs, and expatiated greatly
upon my Lord's ingenuity in stratagem and singular
audacity in applying that stratagem to action.

His courtiers being a little removed to the one side
and the other, his Grace spoke very freely to us as to
the military condition of the island ; as to how all the
picked forces were drawn to serve in the campaign
against France and he had but the riff-raff fellows for
his regiments, and how the coasts were daily swept
by the Rovers from Africa, the farmers and their
families carried into captivity, commerce impaired,
and the prosperity of the country ruined. Don
Roderigo was very particular in asking my Lord as

to military affairs in England and as to our share in them, and questioned him closely too as to his separate command of the small body of horse which had passed in retreat and safety through the midst of England after the battle of Worcester, and of which his Grace had heard but confused accounts; and he enquired likewise as to the terms of my Lord's engagement with the King of Spain, his master. By his discourse I perceived his Grace to be no thoroughly informed soldier, he having indeed served but one campaign thirty years before with the great Spinola in the United Provinces, and since then being more versed in civil than in military affairs; yet he spoke shrewdly enough, if in general terms, of the main issues of the art and practice of War.

After a conference of some duration, during which the Duke had treated us with particular condescension, his Grace commanded the Lord High Chamberlain to present us to the several great Officers of State and of the Court, who were then standing in the Presence Chamber, "as cavaliers of high renown," said his Grace in our hearing, "and as guests in our island, whom it is my special care and delight to respect and to honour." The High Chamberlain accordingly presented us to the Generalissimo of the Viceroy's forces (but subordinate to his Grace) by sea and land, Don Diego de Camporeal, a young man and a nephew of the Duke, and to the Archbishop of Palermo, who is likewise President of the Viceregal Council. Then we were saluted by Don Pasquale Truxillo, whose title in Spanish is Consejero de la Contaduria Mayor ; in English, Lord High Treasurer of Sicily. Apart from these high officers to whom we were duly presented, and coming in respect of importance in the affairs of this Island next to the Viceroy himself, is the Italian Jesuit Priest, Monsignore Distori, Head of the Holy Office in Sicily and Grand Inquisitor.

With all these high officials and some lesser Officers of State we were duly made acquainted, and by them most courteously entreated ; but I observed that no one of the personages of State entertained us with any serious discourse touching the affairs of Sicily itself, saving only the Italian Churchman and Grand Inquisitor, a most devout and zealous priest, who asked us of the condition of the Faith in England, and complained of the slackness and licence in religious affairs of the Christian world at large.

Don Diego de Camporeal, the Generalissimo, was a young gentleman of great dignity, good manners and courteous speech, much favoured of the ladies of the Court both of Palermo and Madrid, and lately removed from the latter city, to his very great discontent. This nobleman was from the first greatly affected to my kinsman.

K

CHAPTER XI.

THE Genoese captain of the *Esperanza* having received a pretty severe wound, and having partly to re-man his ship, to fill up the losses by death and of men down with hurts received in the fight, and the ship herself requiring to be re-sparred and re-rigged, it was a month before all was ready to put to sea again. During this time we frequently attended at the Court of the Viceroy, and my Lord was by his Grace received into especial favour ; insomuch that I call to mind that an entertainment of a Court party of pleasure for the sport of wolf-hunting having been projected to the Viceregal hunting-lodge in the mountains of Madonia, ten or twelve leagues from the city, which my Lord and I were invited to join, my Lord, being still at that time suffering from his wound, happened in the Viceroy's hearing to mention his disability on this account to be a party to a diversion of which he had never yet partaken (wolves being at the present day unknown in the County of Somerset, or, to speak by the book, certainly not so abound-

ing there or elsewhere as to make common sport
for hunters), his Grace immediately was so com-
plaisant as to defer the hunting until such time as
his Lordship should be able to take his share
therein.

It might have been some five days before the time
of the *Esperanza's* sailing for Barcelona that the
wolf-hunt took place, and the gentlemen of the Court
repaired to the hunting-lodge aforesaid—a fair house,
set in the heart of the mountains and forest.

It was on the second day of this pleasuring that
the Viceroy, taking the occasion of my Lord and
myself riding with him through a glade of the forest,
and it happening that we were separated from the
other gentlemen, his Excellency suddenly asked my
Lord if he were still fully resolved to proceed with
the Genoese ship to Spain.

"Yes, your Grace," says my Lord, civilly, "such is
my intention, unless my longer stay in this Island
should conduce to your Grace's service."

The speech was but a complimentary one, struck
upon that anvil of fine courtesy which it is usual for
Spaniards to beat out their phrases upon, but the
Viceroy was pleased to take my Lord at his word.

"Why," says his Grace, "if it were but to please
myself and for the service of the King my Sovereign,
I would fain keep your Lordship in Sicily for as long
as I stay in it myself."

My Lord bowed, thinking he was answered in his
own coin, and for a space neither gentleman spoke.

In that interval there fell upon our ears the distant
sound of a cannon fired from the direction of the
coast, then another, then a third; and as we were on
very high ground and overlooking the great plain
round Palermo, we could view the waters of the sea
beyond the bay, and we could see very plainly the
rising of the smoke as the guns were fired from that
very fort wherein we first had heard this dread signal
of the Corsairs' advent.

Don Roderigo looking very gravely upon us—" In
that," says he presently, " in that signal, my Lord
Baron, you have the reason for my wish to keep you
with me." And when we were silent, seeming to him
perchance to muse and wonder at the unexpectedness
of his speech, he began—" Think ! gentlemen," growing as he spoke to a sort of crescendo of indignation,
" think, that I, who have myself been a soldier, who
am a gentleman of unsullied lineage and a Grandee
of Spain, who am the Ruler of Provinces fairer and
richer than any other in the world, peopled with a
race of men as brave as live, am doomed to see them
daily spoiled and my people insulted by the Unbelievers. Remember, gentlemen, that my precursor
on the throne I fill, Don Garcia of Toledo, once saved
the honour of Christendom with his Sicilian galleys
in the great fight against the heathen at Malta.
Think," he went on " that I, who wear the badge of
the proudest Order in the world " (the Duke was
invested with the Order of the Golden Fleece as well
as with that of Calatrava), " whose motto is that its

knights are to strike with the sword before ever they speak with the tongue—put it before you, gentlemen, that I should command armies whose generals dare not march afield, and war ships that skulk in harbour when the enemy draws near!

"You will not wonder, my Lord," said the Viceroy in a less majestic tone (for truly his Grace's rhetoric had been nothing short of majestic and fit for a King to use, but now he lowered his voice to a more persuasive note), "you will not wonder, my Lord, that when two brave cavaliers like yourselves come to my Island with the glory of a great achievement fresh upon you, I ask myself if there is not here work as worthy of your swords as any you will find in Spain. Pray might I inquire what especial end your Lordship sets before yourself in seeking service with my Master the King of Spain?"

My kinsman told him plainly how the matter stood. " I am not, may it please your Excellency," said he, "a soldier of fortune by profession, and the accident of my birth would have forbidden my giving myself wholly to this noble service, but the circumstances of our unfortunate country, and the necessity that my august Master the King has lately stood in for the sword of every loyal man able to use one, forced me not unwillingly to take service with the King's armies ; and if I have fought not without some small favouring of fortune, and consequent repute, I will frankly declare this happiness of achievement in me is far less due to myself than that I have been able

to profit by the teaching of one who has studied all
the art and mystery of war, both abroad and at
home, and is skilled and learned in it with a mastery
unequalled. Yet he cares for no advancement and
seeks for no glory, and for no laurel, though he has
deserved all three, unless they fall to me who am his
pupil. And this my master, your Grace, and my
tutor in all learning, military and civil, is my dear
cousin here, Captain St. Keyne."

So far my kinsman, and I have recorded this
speech of his at full; not, as the mocking reader may
suppose, in that it sets me up for admiration, for I
declare formally, and on my conscience, that I deserve not one-tenth of this praise. There are many
of my fellow soldiers who still live and can remember
me in the wars, and know me well for a rough soldier
of fortune; and these my friends will, I am persuaded, readily bear me out in saying that I never
ran after a higher fame than to be an honest soldier
and faithful comrade; and if I am justifying myself
at this moment, it is not to convince the world of my
own prowess. That I have studied the art of war
deeply in many countries is true; that I have lived
through many long campaigns, through privations of
war, through sickness and wounds, is true also; and
that I have imparted all I have learnt to my pupil
and kinsman, who has joined his genius to my learning, that is true also. But where is the praise to have
been diligent in teaching one who was even as a son
to me for the love I bore him? Or that I little re-

garded honour and advancement except they fell to
him, nor even desired the laurel itself, that fair object
and end of all true soldiers' endeavours, but if it
flourished on his brows—*tam caro capite*—on his whom
I hold so dear?

I have recorded my kinsman's speech to the
Viceroy in full, that it may be patent how great not
only was his own modesty, but how infinitely great
and noble his generosity, who at this very moment of
his triumph wished to shift the wreath from his own
to another's head. So did Pompeius Magnus in the
zenith of his fame, when having newly overcome the
parties of Marius in Spain and of Spartacus in Italy,
and one said to him, marvelling, "Surely, Pompey,
thou hast a divine genius for war." "Not so," replied
he, "but I owe it to my father, who early taught me
the division of a battle and all the secret arts of war."
Now Strabo, Pompey's father, was, by all seeming,
but an ordinarily faithful and well-trained soldier, no
genius at all, and perhaps, to compare the great with
the small, but such a plain, unpretending fellow as I
am myself. But to pass on.

His Grace the Viceroy bowed to me as my Lord
spoke, and smiled, as no doubt implying, "I understand this magnanimity, which confirms me in my
high estimate of your young Lord."

My kinsman then proceeded thus: "It is not unknown to your Grace that, though our party in the
State is conquered for the time and lies now in
abeyance, as much perhaps through our own debase-

ment and disorder as through the valiance of our
enemies, we are yet persuaded that a time will soon
arise when the people of England will grow sick of
the violent and fanatic methods of her present unrati-
fied governors, and that then they will be willing to
throw off the yoke of their present tyranny, just as
they have been lately stirred, not perhaps altogether
unrighteously, to break the yoke of their former
rulers. It is certain that as the kingdom was lost by
the sword, so will it have to be won by the sword;
and therefore has it behoved all true and loyal men,
during this period of their country's servitude, to
avoid even lip-service to their oppressers; to quit
their native land and go abroad, and perfect themselves in that art of war by which they can hope in
time to replace their lawful King on the throne of his
ancestors. Now, therefore, your Excellency will perceive my reason and my cousin's for taking service
with the King of Spain, and for carrying thither in
our company as many tried and trusty Englishmen as
would follow us. We look to gain knowledge and
experience of war. I hope for myself to obtain
advancement to high command, and to gather some
fame in the Spanish war with France, knowing that
being thus signalized I shall be the better able in due
time on returning home to render worthy service to
my King and to my Country."

The Viceroy listened with great attention to my
kinsman's words, and seemed to ponder them deeply
" I could suppose," said he, "nothing less from your

Lordship's prudence, loyalty, and valour than this high resolve, of which I would crave permission to express my most profound approval; but," his Grace went on, with a courteous smile upon his lips, "has your Lordship ever heard an old French saying to the effect that there are many castles in Spain, but never a one of them is well furnished within?"

My Lord bowed, but spoke nothing, in his courtesy, as not willing to confirm any current ill report of his Grace's fatherland.

"Yes," said the Viceroy, "Spain is a land of great promise and poor performance, and it is in truth no exception to the rule of most kingdoms, that office, whether it be military or civil, goes by favour and not by merit. Were it not so, and were the best leaders of our armies to be advanced to the highest posts, I am confident that our present war with France would end in our favour in a year. Now, could I conjecture that so eminent a Captain as your Lordship would obtain that advancement which you deserve, I would, in my country's interest, do nothing to detain you here; but I fear that your Lordship and your cousin will languish in subordinate posts; that neither you nor your men will be sent forward to the front, but may perhaps find yourselves doomed to remain in some small, retired, provincial garrison, away, it is true, from danger, but away likewise from all chance of service and renown."

His Grace had employed a very powerful argument with us, and he continued:

"Therefore I would put it to you, gentlemen, that you might still do great service to the King, my Master, without departing from this Island, seeing that if you will consent to take service with me, I will immediately put the three sailing galleys you have captured into commission and set you in command over them, and I will add to this squadron three powerful, fast-sailing, square-rigged corvettos, each carrying twelve fine guns of Venetian make, two of which ships now lie here, and one at Messina, but not one of the three has ever fired a shot at an enemy; and you shall have charge of my coasts and six miles inland, and of their protection from the Corsairs of Tunis, Tripoli, Algiers, and Morocco; and all the coast fortresses of the Island shall be under your command, and you shall have detailed for your service ten strong troops of horse, of over a hundred sabres to each troop, to scour the coast, as to whose disposition in various parts of the Island you shall yourself advise me; and your command over these forces by land and by sea shall be answerable and subordinate to no one but to myself."

So spake the Viceroy, who had already well considered this scheme of his, and had, as we afterwards learned, fully debated it in Council and carried it there, but not without some considerable opposition from certain members thereof.

My kinsman was surprised by this offer of the Viceroy, and was, it may be conceived, mightily taken with the greatness of the prospect it offered;

but he perceived also how it could not fail to raise up as many enemies and opponents as there were high Officers of State engaged in the government of the Island.

"Consider of it well, my Lord," said the Viceroy "before you give me an answer, and take your kinsman and counsellor into your conference. I have ittle doubt his wisdom and experience will discover and set forth any objections which my proposal may carry with it."

My Lord thanked the Viceroy heartily for the great honour he had done him, and said he, "I will obey you, my Lord Duke, in conferring upon it with my cousin, and together we will bring you an answer, no later than to-morrow."

On our ride homewards from the hunt, which was that evening, my cousin fell by the way in a deep muse upon this proposition of the Viceroy: at last he broke forth:

"Is it not, cousin Humphrey," said he, "the most fortunate circumstance in the world, and almost beyond hope or expectation, that two soldiers like ourselves, bent upon the pursuing of Fortune, should suddenly find opened before them such opportunity and anticipation of worthy employment as this?"

I smiled to think how the Viceroy's advice had been forgotten, that I was to be conferred with, whose experience could point out and suggest any difficulties to the undertaking.

"For, look you, cousin, this project of fighting for

Spain against France was beginning to sit somewhat
uneasily on my conscience; for how are we to be
sure that Spain is in the right of it? And should
honest men give their sword to an unjust cause?
Why not with France against Spain? Faugh!
Humphrey, it is, when you look at it, an ill deed,
even with a righteous cause (unless indeed to save a
man's own people or the throne of his King) to lay
desolate a country, as we lately saw all those leagues
of land laid desolate; to widow countless wives and
make countless children orphans; to help to stifle
the arts of peace and to silence and confuse all
learning, in the senseless clash of arms and the
damnable rattle of drums. I will declare to you,
Humphrey, that since I looked upon that so eloquent
allegory of Peace and War by the painter Dürer,
the matter has come to me in a new light, and my
steps war-ward have grown heavy and have dragged."

"It is to regard the thing very curiously, Ralph," I
answered, "but I will not deny that my own conscience has at times somewhat twinged me on this
very account."

"Now here," says he, "all will be different. Of
hard fighting we shall have enough and to spare, yet
not a stroke but will be to save this fair Island and
these poor peasants, to whom my breast warms, from
foul injustice and rapine. Did you not notice when
we passed through those wasted lands of Germany
how everywhere the people standing by their ruined
hovels looked on us askance, with hungry, unfriendly

eyes, perceiving we were soldiers, and of the felon tribe who had ravished and murdered their kith and kin, and left their houses flaming, and their silly granaries and gardens wrecked and ruined. And now we have seen (in contrast to this) the gratitude of these Islanders, their extravagant show of joy and love to us when we, though only by a side-wind in saving ourselves from the Rovers, saved them too and avenged some of their many wrongs."

I saw my cousin so set upon undertaking this work that I urged nothing against it but its greatness, and the insufficiency of the means at his disposal, " For," said I, "you will have for your enemies all the Barbary Rovers from Tripoli in the east to Tangiers in the west, who have had their wicked will of this poor Island now for a generation."

" You have taught me, Humphrey," said my cousin Ralph, "that the true art of war is to suddenly bring against the enemy all the forces we have, and to break him with the swiftness and weight and unexpectedness of our blow. That will we do against these Corsairs."

But to speak honestly, I saw not how this might be effected, we being dispersed in a mountainous Island and they free to choose time and place of attack.

But this consideration was not enough to distract him from following his bent ; nor, in plain truth, was I much less inclined than himself to the undertaking and accordingly, after much conversation together upon the ways and means of carrying out the Viceroy's

wishes, we betook ourselves at an early hour the
following morning to the Palace and kissed his
Grace's hands upon our acceptance of the new offices
he had bestowed upon us ; my Lord as General
of his active land and sea forces, and I as his
Aide de Camp, as the French call it, and second in
command.

CHAPTER XII.

IMMEDIATELY there commenced a very busy time for us. My Lord resolved upon two things from the very first, and he had the Viceroy's ready consent thereto; first as to re-manning of the three corvettos and the new manning of the captured galleys with picked men of any *provenance,* whether Spaniards, Italians, or native Sicilians; and secondly, that before any naval or military achievement was entered upon, the ships should be thoroughly re-fitted, and the men trained to the use of their arms, whether the cannon, the firelock, or the sword, and drilled for service by sea or by land. For the navigation of the ships he would employ Genoese and Venetian sailors only, who are beyond all others skilful and bold in danger. The rest would be a kind of naval soldiery, to board, and fight and serve the guns, and to bear a hand with the sails in case of need. The ships were to carry large crews, the corvettos 280 men apiece, the galleys 170; and there was besides this to be a land force under my Lord's command of 1,100

troopers, to meet the continual raids of Corsairs by
land ; they being so bold and cunning in their enter-
prises as to sail round the coasts with their galleys
to alarm the natives, while another unsuspected ship
of the Pirates would then appear suddenly, after the
alarm was past and the peasants returned to their
homes, and invade the country, even though it were
some four or five miles inland, and capture perhaps
some forty or fifty (men, women, youths, and maidens)
carrying all alike into cruel captivity ; or else they
would creep up to the coast under shelter of night,
land, and gather up the people by the houseful, asleep,
the father and mother, with their innocent children ;
or surround some remote country church at early mass
and capture a whole God-honouring congregation at
one swoop.

Now, to meet this cunning and malignant warfare
of the bloody-minded Miscreants, there was in the
Island no provision whatever, excepting the coast
fortified towers with ten or a dozen soldiers in each,
who could do no more when the Pirates landed than
shut their gates, draw in the ladders to their upper
stories and windows, and sit coy and trembling and
hoping the Pirates would pass them by, bent on more
profitable harvest ; who would sometimes in their
anger if baffled of easier prey, besiege the forts,
dragging ashore their ship cannon to batter down the
walls with, or heaping up faggots in the battery ditch
level with the parapets, run in upon the weak garrison
and cut their throats, or if they had more leisure

would leave them impaled round about their own fort, half in sport, half in cruelty, and to terrify the peasantry.

These being the methods of the enemy, it was incumbent upon us to contrive some scheme to frustrate their devices, and my Lord's imagination to this end was a masterly one.

In order that our stratagem may be understood by those who are curious in the noble art of war, and I desire for readers none who are not, making as I do no pretence (as will already have been perceived) of addressing myself to the idle and unlearned, and especially willing to avoid the discredit of furnishing entertainment (as so many in this wanton age affect to do) to weak and wayward women ; but to resume ; I say, that in order that our design in this defensive war against the Pirates may be the better understood, I give the reader a little rude cut or print of the contours of the Island of Sicily, in which are set down roughly and without use of compass or other instrument, the chief ports, mountains, and a few chief rivers, showing also, by lines of navigation in the seas round about, the nearness of the haunts of the different Pirate nations, as the Tunisians, Moroccans, Algerines, Tripolitans and the like, together with such general topical information as beseems the Reader to be acquainted with. If he cavil at the rudeness of this map or chart, it is good he know that it is a copy (only smaller and not so full) of the map I drew up by the order of my Lord General (for so I must now

L

call him) to enable him to proceed to the disposition of his sea and land forces.

The Island of Sicilia is, as I take it, of the bigness, or nearly the bigness, of Ireland (though an honest Irish gentleman of our company denies its being even half so great), but in richness and civility far exceeding that remote and barbarous Island. Sicily greatly exceeds the Northern Isle in all natural commodities and productions, to wit, in rare fruits, as oranges, granados, mulberries, figs, and lemons ; and in possessing most fertile vineyards and olive groves, and fields of wheat, of barley, and of rye, and of that rare Turkey corn which is indeed a marvel to behold for its height and the size of its ear, and for its lush and prolific growth. There is here moreover that great reed or cane whence sugar is made, and which thrives here as well as in the Indies of Asia or America. Moreover the Island excels all other lands I ever knew or heard of for its sweet and constant air, never too hot in summer time or cold in winter. Again there are marvels here such as no other land can boast, mountains which hide abundant stores of sulphur, that most strange and mysterious mineral, which mayhap will turn out, as some learned alchemists allege, but gold itself in disguise, and that requires but to be alloyed and smelted in a crucible to take its golden, metal shape, when every Sicilian peasant will command wealth like another Crœsus. In the seas around is found great wealth of the precious red coral, which would be fished up, to the notable enrichment of the

people, but for the harrying of the Corsairs. To continue (for of the wonders of this Island there is no end)
there is Ætna Mons, higher than the tallest Alpine
cliff, which many times shoots forth flames and
fire and ashes, but not maleficently as does the
terrible Volcano of Vesuvius, which after stifling the
elder Pliny (that most learned scholar) buried the cities
of Herculaneum and Pompeii under its ashes. But
Ætna is a kinder monster, though fabled to have been
the prison house of the Giant Typhon, of the hundred
hands, whose groans beneath the mountain mass used
to shake the heavens (as the poet Theocritus fables),
and his moving quake all the solid earth. Ætna is
nevertheless no longer hurtful, seeing that the fire and
ashes that rise from his jaws fall in a gentle beneficent
enriching shower on the vineyards and orchards below
his hill, and many times with this rain of fertilizing
ashes will fall precious stones, gems of price, so that
(as I am told in the Island) many a farmer walking
on to his fields after a fall of this dry volcanic rain,
and looking but to see his young crops helped with
the enrichment spread over them, will find sparkling
in the dust at his feet some precious Garnet, or
Chrysophrase, or Tourmaline, that will outvalue all
that his granaries can hold. No wonder therefore is
it that the peasants on the mountain's side, which they
populate very thickly (and their little terraced wheat
plots and orchards and vineyards are of an incredible
fertility and beauty), call Ætna their father, and themselves his children, who inherit largely of their father's

bounty. So would they be rich and happy too, but for the wicked encroachments and invasions of the ravenous Turks, who are brought about their fat and fertile fields and farmsteads, enticed by their richness, like wolves by the smell of the sheepfold, to pillage and steal their flocks and fruits, and to kidnap, or, failing surrender, to wound and maim and kill their owners.

On the opposite page is my map of the Island, which I pray the Reader will study a while.

It will be noticed that there are a good many mountains in the Island, but, if truth were to be fully depicted in my map, there would appear still more, but I have lacked the skill to draw them; for after passing to and fro over the Island, at my Lord's order, I do verily believe that there is hardly a scrap of plain ground in all of it saving three; to wit, one biggish plain round the sea port of Catania, another about the Port of Trapani in the other extremity of the Island, and a third, a horseshoe shaped one at the back of Palermo, between it and the hills. The mountains in the north side of the Island are prodigious in their height, their anfractuosities and their wildness, and they branch out into all the corners of this triangular Island. On the southern coast they slope down to a lower level and a lesser wildness; and, note, that in the length of this southern shore there is not a single decent harbour, for Girgenti has but a miserably unsafe anchorage, and Licata, another puny place, has still less; but of this latter port more anon.

Now, my Lord's plan of campaign against the Corsairs was fourfold ; first he would establish posts of observation on various high points on the Island, from which to give early notice by beacon fires or otherwise to his cavalry, or to his sea forces, of the approach of the enemy ; secondly, he would build wooden huts or barracks along the coast, in which to house and stable his troopers and horses in detachments, which barracks should be in full view and correspondence with the beacons aforesaid, and each about twenty miles apart and set some few miles back from the coast ; by this means he would be able to concentrate a force of about 100 troopers, in three hours' time at furthest, at any point invaded by the Corsairs ; thirdly, he would establish fresh, unsuspected batteries and gunners on the coast lines, and to this end use some of the guns in the already existing fortified huts or towers along the coast, which numbered at this time twenty-one, at intervals and on salient points, each containing five, six, or seven guns, and of gunners some twelve to twenty ; but of these guns hardly two in each fort were in order. Now my Lord rightly considered that except for the giving warning of the Corsair's approach these forts were now useless, seeing that the enemy had long ago taken their measure, and long ago had learned to give them a wide berth ; but as the gunners were, as he discovered, expert marksmen, and the guns fine Italian pieces wanting but a little repair, he petitioned the Viceroy in Council to allow him both to repair all the guns and to remove

men and materials from these forts to some new
masked batteries which he proposed to construct.
This was his third proposal. His fourth was to keep
the six ships of his little squadron continually cruising
round the Island, whenever wind and weather permitted, not together, but one following after another
at a distance of five to ten leagues ; in such wise that
if any one of them came upon and got into action
with an enemy, whether a single ship or in force, the
consorts of our ship would presently one after the
other be at hand to support her.

Of these separate items in my Lord's plan each
was dependent upon all the others, seeing that without
them all together a fair fight against such over-
whelming forces as the Pirates could bring against us
was not possible. Nevertheless, though the Rulers of
the Island ardently desired to see the discomfiture of
the Turks, and the peace of the Island secured, if for
no better reason than because their own individual
revenues were sensibly diminished by the ruin of so
large an extent of territory, and the embargo so
constantly laid by the Pirates' doings upon foreign
trade, yet my Lord found it very difficult to have his
way with them in these excellent reforms of his,
seeing that the most of the Councillors were men
stantes super antiquas vias, who had long worked under
the yoke of rigid custom, and were lovers of the
ancient methods for no better reason than that they
had not vigour of imagination enough to foresee and
forecast the advantage of new and better ones. They
then, being men of little genius for affairs, could no

resist the temptation, which so constantly assails their like, to take up only to deface, the designs of those abler than themselves (they having no projective power of their own) and to warp them into some confused new shape, and so claim these disfigured bastard bantlings for their own legitimate children, not seeing that such mutilated creatures can never live and prosper. Of which I will relate a curious instance.

When my Lord's project was first laid before the Council of State, which is a necessary and usual course in the government of this Island, it met with much objection and disparagement from several Lords of the Council ; indeed, none but the Viceroy himself and his nephew, Don Diego de Camporeal, General of the Forces (who, knowing little of military or State affairs, cared still less for either), had a good word to say for it. After one meeting of the Council held, the Viceroy called upon my Lord and me to attend before the Councillors with our plans and particulars, and to expound and explain them. We found, as we expected, that the most strenuous objector was the Lord High Treasurer. We expected this, for Don Pasquale Truxillo was a gentleman who had filled this post under successive Viceroys, and was one of those who can never see that new emergencies in a State require a new policy to meet them.

" Well," said he, " your Grace and my Lords, I will not deny that the English General's scheme shows considerable ingenuity, but I would have him and you to know that there are those who have had more experience of Sicilian affairs than he has. Now I have filled my present office for twelve years, and before that I was, as your Lordships know, Comptroller of the Exchequer for seven ; and during all those years things have certainly been no worse than they are now. I do not say that the incursions of the Corsairs are not an abominable, a shameful, and indeed a ruinous circumstance; the Island is impoverished by them, I admit ; not a week, as I am aware, passes but a Sicilian ship or half a dozen fishing boats, or a few families of peasants, are captured and lost to us ; but at least we know where we are ; it is very bad, but it might be worse. Now where may we be landed if the designs of this most ingenious gentleman (whose exploits in these seas I am the last to impugn) are accepted ? Why, if his plans are defeated, we are worse off than ever, and that too after a very large expenditure of money ; and the Rovers made bolder than before. Even if he is successful and beats off the Pirate ships, what will happen ? Why a fleet will sail from Algiers or Tunis or Salee, and lay Palermo and Messina and Syracuse in ashes."

The Viceroy very temperately contended that the chief cities of the Island were so defended by fortifications, and these so well manned by gunners and garnished with artillery, and the harbour filled with war ships (which last were so extraordinarily bent upon protecting the citizens that they never ventured into the open sea), that he believed they might set aside all fears of the African Pirates assailing their cities, who it was well known regarded plunder as far above honour, and were very loath to run into mere fighting without a prospect of booty.

My Lord Treasurer would bow to the superior wisdom of his Excellency in a question of policy, but he could not forego his opinion that for the outlay now proposed to be made there was no precedent whatever ; and particularly he would protest against any vote for the building of new fortresses when there were a score or more of them already in existence on the coast, which buildings it was now proposed to dismantle.

The Viceroy called upon my Lord to explain the necessity of this portion of his scheme, which he did by showing that he trusted to the new batteries almost wholly to resist such a general attack by a piratical fleet as the Treasurer had forecast, with the small squadron at his service. This he proposed to effect by manœuvring to draw the enemy, should they happen to greatly outnumber him, to fight him under the guns of his batteries, which would be masked from their observation by trees and bushes ; "and your Lordships of the Council," said he, "will be pleased to observe that on the map I submit to you the batteries are placed in couples near together round the Island, so that a ship of ours coming in shore at a point between any two of them would be reinforced by no less than twenty great guns firing from a steady land platform."

The Lord High Treasurer considered the scheme too ingenious and imaginative to be workable in practice, for he would appeal to his brother Councillors, many of them versed in campaigns, if such a stratagem had ever before been used in warfare, and would it not have been hit upon by some great Commander or another had it been practicable? He then argued against the scheme of the new forts on the score of their great and ruinous expense, which the resources of the Island could ill afford.

My Lord being requested again to speak, observed that they were not forts he proposed to build, but batteries only, and such batteries would be built on projecting headlands with earthworks on their sea faces, a ditch all round, and on the land side a stockade to save them from a sudden attack in the rear, and his forts manned and armed at no expense, with guns from the fortresses already existing, and which for a generation had done little service but as signalling stations. These rough defences would cost but the labour of his soldiers, and the help of a few peasants.

The Lord High Treasurer now shifted his ground, and said the history of the loss by capture of several forts on the Island was doubtless unknown to the authors of this scheme. If the Pirates could assault and take stone-built towers, what defence could be expected from such naked batteries as were now proposed? He foretold that every one of them would be captured in detail by the Pirates within a month of their building, and their defenders butchered.

My Lord would not deny but that his batteries lay under some risk of capture, but then all war was a perpetual risk and danger. He submitted however that there would be less risk to the new batteries than to the old ones, on account that these had been isolated, and any attack upon them safe from interruption, but in future his scheme would provide for an immediate convergence of troops by land and of ships by sea upon any threatened point.

These assuredly were most convincing arguments; but those who know the ways of men in whom power and authority have swelled the native perversity of their understandings, and strengthened their inherent obstinacy and stiff-neckedness, know well that such men having but once put forth their opinion, perhaps in idleness only and not to lie under the reproach of having no judgment at all of their own on a proposition, will cling to that opinion right or wrong, through thick or thin, ay, even though an angel from Heaven should come to reason against them for the contrary with logic and with rhetoric divine.

So was his Lordship, Don Pasquale, Grandee of Spain, and twelve years Lord High Treasurer of Sicily, implacable and inexorable on this most simple and necessary point of the new batteries : on the rest of the scheme he was ready to concede to the gracious wishes of the Viceroy, but bowing to the Duke sitting at the head of the table, "your Grace must permit me, in the best interests of this Island and of our Gracious Sovereign and Most Catholic Majesty, to protest against this innovation of the sea batteries, fraught, as I have endeavoured to show them to be, with innumerable dangers to the Island and difficulties to the State."

The Count, by reason perhaps of his holding the purse strings of the Island, carried with him whenever he expressed his conviction a large following. Although in the government of this Island the Council is but a consulting body, professing but a formal and seldom used privilege of appeal to the Government at Madrid, and the Viceroy is as absolute a ruler as the Grand Seignor or the Czar of Muscovy, and it was open to him at his choice to override the vote of his Council and carry out his single rule, yet it will be readily understood by those who are used to affairs of State, that a wise Governor, however absolute he may be, does not care at every step to be an absolute Dictator. It thus came to pass that his Excellency, unconvinced by the arguments of the Treasurer, and indeed very fully convinced of their unwisdom, was nevertheless content to let this matter of the new batteries lie by, while the rest of my Lord's scheme was carried at once into effect.

I have dwelt a little fully, and I fear the Reader will think not a little wearisomely, on this point of the batteries, first to make evident to the curious Reader the constitution of the Council and Government of the Island in those days (and I am not aware that they are altered in these), but chiefly because this hitch in my kinsman's scheme and the pertinacity in the wrong of my Lord High Treasurer, did at a later date all but wreck the prosperity, nay, even the very existence of the Island of Sicilia as a Christian State.

CHAPTER XIII

My kinsman and I, acting under his orders, used all diligence for the recruiting of our new forces, and then to get our little squadron of ships fitted, armed and manned, the body of 1,100 troopers horsed and drilled, and the beacon huts built on the hills, and the barracks on the shore. We now found that a circumstance which we had almost forgotten, on the occasion of our taking of the three Corsairs, had inclined every man of any mettle or hardihood among the sea-going people in Sicily to offer eagerly to engage with us. The circumstance was this; when we had got our three prizes safely into Port, we heard of an old disused law, made for the encouragement of captures from the Turks, that ships and prisoners, by whomsoever taken, should be sold to the State at a fair assessment, one half of the proceeds to be the prize of the chief in command of the captors, one quarter to his lieutenant, and the residuary quarter to be apportioned among the rest of the crew. Hearing of this law, my Lord, who being in sole command of the *Esperanza*, had been legally recognized as the conqueror and capturer of the Pirates, declared at once it was not becoming for him as an English gentleman and servant of his King to be dividing prize-money with poor sailors and soldiers, and taking such a lion's share to boot ; and so forewent his share. I was of the same mind as my cousin, and so our troopers and the crew of the *Esperanza* divided the whole of this prize-money, which for the three ships alone, with their guns and gear, was valued at not less than 2,500 great doubloons of gold, while the forty-five surviving prisoners being mostly stout strong fellows, went into the State galleys at 120 dollars, or pieces of eight, each (and dog cheap too), which made in all something like £8,800 of our English money, or about £120 apiece for each man engaged—a very pretty windfall.

Now the news of this magnificence of my Lord's was very quickly noised abroad, and created an incredible admiration among the people, and a very ardent desire among them to enlist with a leader of so noble and generous a character.

The beacons which I have mentioned above were but snug wooden huts fit for a couple of men to live in, and the barracks were of wood too, each to accommodate from forty to fifty men, with stables hard by ; and so carefully did we post the beacons on the sea-coast acclivities of the Island, that it required but twenty-three in all to guard and watch the whole of Sicily, for in the circuit round the larger towns none were needed. Beside each hut were in readiness

about twelve tall narrow piles of resin-bearing wood
thatched with rushes to keep them dry, and the same
number of planks of wood, painted white on one side
and black on the other, each plank turning on a pivot
in the ground. Every beacon hut was in full view
from at least two barracks; there being twenty-three
barracks as there were twenty-three beacons. Now
the method of signalling was this: the sea-shore to be
watched from the beacon was to be divided into
twelve fairly equal portions, and delimited off and
bounded by some natural mark, as a cliff, a tree,
a stream, a reef of rock, or a tongue of sand. These
twelve portions of coast were to be plainly set down
in a chart or plan kept in each beacon, with the said
portions or districts marked one, two, three, and so on
up to twelve, counting from the east, and a counter-
part thereof was to be posted on the inner walls of
any barracks in view therefrom. It will be evident,
then, how this signalling would work. So soon as a
Pirate ship or a Squadron was observed off the coast,
and her presence was announced by the signal guns of
the fortresses, the troopers were required to saddle
up their horses and watch the beacon huts for their
signal, which, by the men there, would be given at the
moment the Corsairs landed. As soon as ever they
touched the shore in a particular district, the number
of that district was to be notified to the two barracks,
if by day by turning the white sides of so many of
the planks towards the sea, so that the look-out men
in the two adjoining barracks should see them, if by

night, by lighting the right number of beacon fires. The instant the signal was up, some forty-five to fifty or more troopers from each barrack would start at their best pace towards the same point on the coast; so that in two or three hours at the outside, oftentimes much sooner, ninety to a hundred armed horse soldiers would be drawn up at the water side ready to cut off the raiding party before it could return with booty and prisoners.

In the meantime our ships would be forewarned as well, and would be hastening up to endeavour to catch the Pirate vessels while their crews were still on shore.

This was my Lord's plan, stated shortly. There were in it other contrivances, by which, in cases of great emergency, such as the appearance of a fleet of Pirates on the coast, or a landing by them in great force, messengers could be sent across the Island, and men could be brought up from a distance, and ships warned to come up or keep off as the case might require.

Two months or more we gave to the drill and discipline of sailors and troopers, and it was but a very little time for the business. This matter gave us incredible trouble, for the men being of every sort and nation, and mostly of a bold and reckless temper, attracted by our pay which was liberal, being no less than a half dollar for troopers and a quarter dollar for sailors, with rich prospects of plunder and prizes for both : the men, I say, were exceedingly wild and ruffianly, and we had all the pains in the world to teach these licentious fellows civility, obedience, and good discipline. I think in the first fortnight we had flogged a score of both kinds, namely sailors and soldiers, and then drummed them out of the ranks, shot some half dozen of the worst of the troopers, and strung up to the yardarms of our ships as many of the more obstinate sailors, before their manners mended at all. After this matters sensibly improved, and in time our discipline came to be very good indeed, but it was long before we could venture to relax a jot in our stern treatment of the men.

One little circumstance I will mention here, though indeed it hardly deserves record in so grave a chronicle as mine, but it may serve to provoke a little merriment from some of my old companions in arms, who, having fought their campaigns on the grand scale in Germany and the Low Countries, may a little despise such a small business as this soldiering and sailoring of ours in Sicily. It was this, that having recruited somewhat hastily for both services, the fellows, seeing the high pay offered and the good chances of the service, were so eager to come in that they stayed not to choose between the sea and land services, but got in where they could, so that we often found that we had carried to sea the makings of a very good trooper, a bold, dashing fellow enough, but who thought the end of the world was at hand when the ship began to roll or the sea to come over the deck. So too we recruited into our cavalry some excellent sailors, to whom a trotting horse was far more terrible than a tempest on a lee shore, who would haul at their bridles as they would at a rope, and part company with their saddles pretty well as soon as they had embarked upon them. Yet we had established such good discipline by this time, that neither the wrong-placed sailor nor soldier dared for his life utter a murmur of remonstrance. It was pleasant to see these poor fellows when, after watching them a bit with as stern a countenance as I could muster up, I would come up to them as if to reprove them and then put it to them that they had my leave to exchange,—the sailor to a horse, the soldier to a ship. It is well to note that these transferred men were afterwards among the cheerfullest and most trustworthy men we had.

The state of discipline and cheerfulness and hope-fulness to which we had brought both our ships' crews and our cavalry was indeed exemplary. By his word "hopefulness," my soldier readers will know what I mean, but others mayhap not, so I will say it is the condition a fighting body should ever be in of expecting and desiring soon to meet the enemy, and of feeling pretty confident to give a good account of him when they do. But this hopefulness and this good discipline had perhaps never been attained but for the fine bearing and good example of our own English troops. They were now constituted by my Lord his personal body-guard, and wore, in addition, to the uniform of the regiment (as I must call it) which was of the Spanish colours, a kind of baldrick, or sword-carrier, of gold lace over the right shoulder. When we marched through the streets afoot, as we did at times till the regiment was fitly mounted, our fellows following close upon my Lord and myself, marching very steadily and firmly together (for they had greatly improved their drill with their few months' service in the Imperial armies) the townspeople could never forbear admiring and cheering them as they passed, seeing these handsome, clear-skinned fellows, with their honest English faces, towering a head and shoulders above the rest of the regiment, and remembering too how bravely they had fought against the Pirates in the sight of the whole city.

Jan Loots the Dutchman, and his brother Dutchman Piet Potgeiter, though sailors, were not without some knowledge of a horse, Jan especially, he being handy at most things, and having been bred a farmer's son in his youth. He carried himself fairly well on horseback from the first, and though he had got to be very well liked among the troopers and was ill to be spared from them, being a fellow of excellent temper, patience, and resource, yet my Lord was fain to destine him to a special kind of employment, so approved was Jan in gunnery and so skilled in the rigging of ships and the like. Therefore at times he was serving with my Lord on the ships, at others he was my right hand man on shore, in my business of the barracks and beacons.

At last we got things in some order, and the ships

put to sea under my Lord's captainship, and made their first cruise round the coasts. I stayed behind to get the beacon huts and barracks finished and in order. We could only gradually establish ourselves along the coast. At first we had the three which lie, as the map will show, in the easterly corner of the Island, then two more to the south, and so on; and we garrisoned the barracks as quickly as we could get trained men and horses to fill them. While these preparations were going on, nearly three months were, I will not say wasted, but at least spent, and all the time the Corsairs were raiding our coasts and pillaging our ships. Never before had they been so bold or so cruel to the people.

My Lord had made several cruises of a few hours with his squadron from Palermo, less to meet with the Pirates than to get his men accustomed to the sea and to their ships; but now at last he set forth in earnest in search of the African Rovers, sailing from the port of Messina with all his six ships. It was on the morning of the Feast of Saint Bartholomew that he set forth, with a good breeze from the westward: as this wind was favourable from the African coast, it was pretty certain to bring up one or more of the Corsair ships, so the occasion for coming to quarters with the enemy was very good. I did not myself see the starting of the squadron from Messina, being then busy with the beacon hut which we called No. 4, for we could not be troubled with the names of the places where they were set up, and so numbered them

in the order they were built; and the Reader will find
No. 4 on the map, among the hills and some way
inland of the Port of Syracuse, on the south coast.
Being then at work with the building of this
hut and the two barracks in correspondence with
it, we only saw the squadron pass. My Lord, having
then hoisted his ancient in the largest Corvetto, was
leading in her. The six vessels were still in company,
but it was my Lord's intention, for the reasons I have
before set forth, to cruise in single file, and with a
distance of some leagues between the vessels.

It was a very brave sight to see our squadron sailing by, and to know that every ship was fully manned
and armed, and intent upon searching out and punishing these iniquitous despoilers and ravishers of innocent men and women. Being where our hut was
building on a high mountain which overtops all
others about it, and is about ten miles from
the sea, we could look down upon a vast extent of
sea coast in a horseshoe shape beneath, with Syracuse in the east, its white towers and houses
encompassed with evergreen groves of orange and
lemon trees, and its quays and wharves spread out
beneath our feet. A marvellous fine sight, the whole
coast line that was in our view being, I verily believe,
not less than a hundred miles in length, so great
was the prospect and so clear the air; and everywhere we could observe the sea beating upon the
stones and jutting cliffs and sandy linguets, but very
gently, showing a white line of foam and little break-

ing waves along all the windings of the shore; the
sea so blue as I had never seen it before, and calm,
and spread out so vastly that verily it begot a sort
of awe in me, for its very width and greatness. Yet it
was most serene all the while, with countless little
ripples or curls of sea foam far and near under the
light wind; just such, I did suppose, as the Poet
Homer once saw and noted, standing perhaps on just
such an eminence as this in Tenedos or Samos of
the Ægean Sea, when he called these tiny breakers
the uncountable smiles on Ocean's face, which indeed
they are, as if Nature herself were glad and smiling,
conscious of her own beauty.

While we were still looking upon this great spread
of sea, upon which never a ship was to be seen, there
swam into our view all our squadron; the three
galleys, with the breeze abeam, heeling over under
the weight of their great fore and aft sails; the square-
rigged ships bearing themselves more stiffly and as if
proudly.

Then of a sudden—filled with this great view of
land and sea and cities, and on the entrance into the
prospect of our ships—my heart was gladdened
within me, to think that my Lord and I, who had so
lately been cast forth by the afflictions of our own
country; despairing of her for the time, and setting
forth to seek our fortunes in the wide world, should
so quickly, in these few months only, have been thus
befriended by favouring Fortune, so safely conducted
by a kindly Providence through such great dangers

and perils to this high destiny of having already won honour and fame, the favour of the Regent of a great Island, and being now entrusted by him and his people with command of war ships and land forces, and the conduct of a holy war of defence and protection against the accursed nations of Pirates.

While we still looked, a gun was fired from the flag ship, and at this signal all the others hauled their wind and presently after hove to. Then followed some exchange of signals, and the Admiral then held his course alone (the wind being now a little north of west) towards Cape Passaro, which makes one angle of this three-cornered Island, and from which cape they were now distant some fifteen or twenty miles. We watched my Lord's ship rounding the cape with a very wide berth, and then, altering her course, she stood about due west, sailing nearly close hauled to the wind, and making, as we could see, very good weather in the freshening breeze.

My Lord had purposely chosen to sail to windward along the southern coast, which, as it is the richest and most populated, so is it likewise, from its lack of harbours and the dangers of its navigation, the most undefended and remote from chance of interference with the Pirates. Therefore is it the part of the Island to which they most frequently betake themselves not scrupling, in the knowledge of their impunity, to carry their raids five, six, or even seven miles inland from the sea shore. It will be readily understood that the Rover galleys, though by the nature of

their great fore and aft lateen sails, they had a
superiority of speed in going to windward, close-
hauled, and in ordinary reaching if the sea was calm
would in sailing with the wind abeam in rough
water, or in going before the wind, be quickly overhauled by our full-canvassed square-rigged Corvettos,
with their fine and shapely hulls, that yet had a goodish breadth of beam. Unless, therefore, the Rovers
were strong enough to fight and beat us, or quick
enough to bring their vessels up into the wind again
before they were disabled by our shot, they ran a
very good chance of capture if once we could get the
weather-gauge of them.

Having noted these things, I set the men again to
their work of building the hut, leaving only one to
watch the ships and coast batteries and report on any
signs of approaching Corsairs.

Here I will observe that our method of building
both huts and barracks, wherein we wished to use as
much speed as possible, was to take with us a body
of some forty peasants from one point to another,
with a dozen sumpter mules to carry tools, food,
cooking pots, and other necessaries. Our own company consisted of twenty or thirty of our troopers,
fully armed and riding their horses. These fellows,
having their hearts in the work, would picket their
horses, pile their arms, strip to the shirt, and set to at
cutting down trees, digging trenches, and building up
the beacon fires ; so that in an incredibly short time
we had established in each place a decent wooden

house, a shelter box for a watchman, laid the twelve
beacon fires before mentioned, set up the twelve signal
boards in their places, and built up a huge thatched
stack of split pine for fuel.   In addition to this were
left two little three-pounder guns of brass, with which
to exchange signals with our ships at sea.

CHAPTER XIV.

WE had been but an hour at our work when the look-out man called to us that he had seen two puffs of smoke away in the far west ; this we knew was from a coast fort too far off for the sound of the gun to reach us, and presently the signal and this time the sound of the gun came from the nearer batteries, and were again repeated along the coast to the east of us. Although we guessed that this notification of the coming of two Rovers would advise the rest of the squadron to move forward, we judged it not amiss to jog their memory, and therefore, running up a flag, we fired our guns thrice, and lowered our flag and raised it once, which was agreed to signify that the squadron was to proceed to the assistance of their consort. By this time the two Rovers were in our sight, scudding down the coast before the wind with great swiftness, their sails goose-winged, as sailors use to say; that is, with one great peaked sail boomed out to either side, looking for all the world like two great white herons or gannets flying across the waters.

So soon as they perceived my Lord, which was not

for a little time yet, we having the advantage in prospect from our height, they bore down upon him,
thinking no doubt he was a merchantman, and yet
they must have wondered a little too that at the sound
of the warning guns on the coast he had not turned
and fled, and still more that he still carried on when
they steered for him.   But in truth these Pirates of
the Barbary Coast had set up such a terror in all these
seas by their fierceness and inhumanity, that the last
thing they ever expected was that any ship, however
great or strong, would dare to show any fight against
them.   Perhaps too they were taken in by a little
manœuvre which my Lord, evidently to beget or confirm this belief of his fear of them, now executed.
When he first sighted the Pirates he was beating to
windward, close hauled, on the starboard tack ; but
presently, as if he was suspicious of the strange sail,
he put his helm down and came about upon the larboard tack, the ship's head then pointing to the little
Port of Terranova, which lay some leagues to the
west, but which he might hope to reach upon this
tack.   True there is no harbour there, except for
small boats, but on the hill near the town is a
small fortress carrying several guns, and no doubt the
Pirates imagined he was running thither for the protection of its guns, or perhaps, if very hard pressed,
was preparing to beach his vessel on the coast, which
is low and sandy thereabouts.   So soon therefore as
they saw what my Lord was about, one of the Rovers
altered his course so as to cut him off from the shore,

while the other held on full towards the Corvetto, and presently, as we could see, was nearly at close quarters with our flag ship.

We looked down upon the two ships, being perhaps ten or twelve miles away, but the air so clear that their rigging and tackle, seen against the sea, seemed as if drawn with thin lines of a pen dipped in ink upon a blue paper ; and their decks lay open before us, but appearing no wider than a man's finger nail, on the which we could see numbers of men moving, who looked like so many little grains of sand.

Now while we stood wondering what would happen next, and the troopers by me on the hill could hardly draw their breath for their solicitude and eagerness, and while the two vessels were coming head on towards each other, my Lord suddenly put his helm hard a-weather and bore up ; or, to state it more plainly for such as know not the sea, he turned his ship's head from the wind, and so laid himself broadside on towards the Pirate, and before the fellow had recovered from his surprise, and while the galley was still coming end on, the whole broadside of the Corvetto had been poured into him with a raking fire at less than 100 yards' distance; first one gun, then a second, then a third, very deliberately, to the number of seven, which was all she had, her full complement being thirteen, one of them in the bows. Our fellows on the hill shouted for joy, and there was a great laugh from them too ; though why they should have laughed puzzles me, only that when we are much wrought and

in great expectation and anxiety, we know not well
what we do ; and perhaps they laughed to see the
rogues so suddenly taken in by the honest men, which
in truth is always a most delectable sight.

We did not observe however that much harm was
done by the Corvetto's broadside, for at least four of
the shots missed or hit lightly and glanced, and we
saw them skipping over the sea beyond; moreover we
perceived none of the Rover's top hamper or yards
to come down ; but frightened they certainly were, for
they seemed less busy to serve their own guns than to
give the Corvetto a wide berth, which they did by putting their helm hard a-larboard, and to enhance the
swiftness of their flight they got their sweeps out. My
Lord luffed and stood close hauled again, so keeping
his broadside still opposed to them, and we could see
his gunners reloading ; but so quickly did the rogues
get away down the wind and with their sweeps, our
ship too moving the while away from them, that my
Lord must have judged the galley too far to waste
powder and shot upon, for he fired no more at her
that time.

Now, so soon as the Corvetto had shown her teeth,
the second Rover, that had been so industrious to cut
off the poor silly merchantman from her harbour of
safety, immediately altered his course and bore down
right upon the Corvetto, and my Lord still holding on
the larboard tack to meet him, was seemingly preparing
to treat him with the same compliment wherewith he
had saluted his consort ; but the Rover was wary, and

coming nearly within gunshot, having previously got out his sweeps, with their help travelled so quickly that he was about to cross the Corvetto's bows before my Lord could get his ship round on the starboard tack. While the Corvetto was still in stays and her sails all shaking in the wind, the Rover fired his broadside of three very powerful guns, with such good aim, though high, that two of the shots passed (as we afterwards learned) close over the Corvetto's deck, and one struck her bows, but at such an angle that the shot glanced off into the water.

Seeing that the Corvetto lingered somewhat in stays, not coming about so quickly as she should, I feared that some of her upper tackle was shot away, and she hindered thereby of her quickness, but when we could make out nothing coming by the board, I put another construction upon her slowness, and guessed she might be waiting to fire her bow gun.

" Be sure," cried I to the men about me, " my Lord has a mind to let Jan Loots have a throw at the fellow, and is keeping her hove in stays till his shot is made."

But my Lord was playing a very different game, for presently the Corvetto having come round forged ahead to windward, going very fast through the water. By this time the wind had freshened a good deal, still my Lord kept all his canvas up, and now the ships seemed to be racing apart, the two Rovers going together down the wind, and my Lord forging ahead to windward close hauled, which puzzled us exceedingly, for presently there was a mile or two between the Corvetto and the Rovers. In a little while however we perceived my Lord's design, for, so soon as he had fully got the weather-gauge of the others he kept his ship away before the wind, and having all his canvas up, though the wind was now strong, bore down upon the Pirates with exceeding swiftness. Though he could venture, with the Corvetto's breadth of beam, thus to come at them with such a spread of sail, the Pirates with their huge sails and in their cranker ships were forced, with the wind that blew, to reduce their canvas ; this gave the Corvetto so greatly the advantage that she overhauled the galleys hand over hand.   Perceiving this, the hindmost of the two, which was the one that had fired at the Corvetto, ran up into the wind again, to recover her advantage and get past her enemy and so avoid being overtaken on her worst sailing point ; but she resolved on this manœuvre too late, or performed it too slowly, for as she got on the wind again, she had to pass my Lord so close that the two exchanged broadsides, the Corvetto receiving but one shot in the hull, and our fire, to our inexpressible joy, bringing the Pirate's fore mast by the board and so breaking her wing, as it were, disabled her.

As soon as ever the vessels had crossed, my Lord put his helm over again, and bringing the Corvetto quickly up into the wind, shot ahead, and in a few moments he was half a mile away from the stricken ship, which with her remaining sails still made some

way toward the shore. He took no further notice of
her at all, and we perceived he was manœuvring to
get at the other vessel, which seeing her consort's
mischance had gone about, and was now on the
larboard tack, pointing to land, while my Lord was on
a long board with the Corvetto's head toward the
open sea. There was a simple fellow among our troop,
a Spaniard and a landsman, knowing nothing of
sailing and ships and but little of aught else—" Why!"
he calls out, "our ship and the Rover are running
away from each other!"

"Hush! you silly fellow," cried I, "and wait a little."

Presently my Lord went about, and though the
Pirate could sail closer to the wind and so as we could
see was travelling faster than my Lord could, over the
sea to the westward, our ship had at starting the
weather-gauge of him by about two miles, and so
could afford to lose a little lee way, well knowing that
the Turk would have to tack again at the shoreward
end of his board, which presently happened, and then
the two travelling on opposite tacks with their bows
pointing to each other were bound to cross, each ever
nearing the other, though still a good way apart. Just
before they crossed, my Lord as we expected turned
from the wind to make his swoop upon the second
Pirate, as he had upon the first, but the rogue was too
cunning to wait the encounter and, turning too, ran
before the wind, not so soon however but what a shot
reached him from the gun in the bows of the Corvetto,
with what effect we knew not, except that it did not

N

miss. Immediately afterwards the Corvetto, not caring
to make a long stern chase of it, put her head about
again and went to windward. The Pirate followed
her enemy's example a few moments after, but in
these manœuvres the Corvetto was more smartly
handled than the Pirate, or with her shorter hull was
quicker in turning, for the Rovers' galleys and feluccas
are, as I have said, very narrow and long, and mainly
built for swiftness upon a wind, or for rowing in calm
waters, not for scudding or for any quick manœuvring
in rough weather ; so that there was now a longer
distance between them than before and so much more
advantage of the wind for the Corvetto.

I protest that never yet have I seen a braver sight
or nobler sport than this chase of the Corsair, with
the doubles and tricks of the cunning scoundrel Sea-
Robber and the skill and patience of his pursuer. Not
otherwise have I seen in the marshes of Lincolnshire a
great-winged crane or heron circling and mounting to
the sky, to find refuge in the upper air from some
noble falcon in pursuit. Each bird for a time is busy
to raise himself above the other, the one to make her
stoop, the other to prevent it, till at last the falcon,
gaining the upper gauge, turns downward upon her
quarry and swoops upon him like a thunderbolt ; but
the crane twists and turns in his flight to avoid his
enemy, and so the aim is missed, and immediately
both birds turn and circle upwards and mount the air
again, the one seeking for safety, the other to gain
vantage for another stoop.

So was it between the Pirate and the Corvetto; my Lord never leaving him at rest, but swooping again and again upon him, sometimes getting a shot at him by swift moving, never giving him time to get the weather-gauge of the Corvetto. At last my Lord either made a swifter swoop than before from the windward, or the Pirate fumbled in the turning of his ship for the fourth or fifth time to avoid the stroke, and my Lord caught him in the act and got near enough to fire a broadside into him, with the good effect of bringing the enemy's yards and guys and stay ropes down by the board. Then our people in the Corvetto, having her under good command, manœuvred to rake the galley's deck, and hardly getting a scratch themselves in half an hour's firing had all but wrecked the Pirate, shooting away two of his three masts, and not desisting till the rogue made signs of surrender and distress by showing some sort of an ancient upon his remaining mast and lowering it, for these fellows as a rule carry no pendant or flag of any kind, as Christian nations use. Then my Lord, leaving his conquered enemy a helpless log on the water, went for the other lamed Pirate, who had all this time been creeping away towards the shore, still being distant from it some four or five miles, so slowly was she travelling and so quickly had the fight passed between the Corvetto and the Pirate's consort. It was clear there was no fight in the first vanquished Pirate though we saw his decks crowded with men; indeed there was no chance for him but in

boarding, and on account of the high sea and the
inutility of his sweeps, that course was no longer
possible to him.

Suddenly it came upon me to understand what he
would be at, and I called out to the troopers about
me, " Get to your arms, men, and to horse !   We shall
be in the fight yet ! "

The distance to the sea, though no greater than
about ten miles as the crow flies, is no less than
sixteen or eighteen miles by such roads as there are,
but except at first over the mountains the travelling is
fairly good.   In a quarter of an hour the troop was
on its way, twenty-two in number, all good men,
fourteen of our own English fellows and the rest
Spaniards and Italians from the mainland, but all
seasoned soldiers.   For a time as we rid we lost sight
of the sea and ships in the valleys, being behind the
woody ridges of the hills ; after more than an hour's
fast travelling when I called a halt of two or three
minutes to breathe our horses, on a little hill-side
overlooking the plain which still intervened between
us and the shore, we caught sight of the ships again,
the Pirate now not more than a mile from shore and
still coming in very slowly, it being evident that his
purpose was to beach his vessel and for the crew to
save themselves from the Corvetto, though they should
deem it hopeless to save their ship.

My Lord was in chase of them, and no doubt
perceiving their design, was carrying on a running
fight with the Pirate ; but the sea on the coast here

shoals fast, and with the Corvetto's deeper draught of
water our people were cautious in pressing on too
boldly. The Rover, in spite of the high sea, had got
out three sweeps on his lee side, and so often as he
perceived the Corvetto coming into position to fire,
he would quickly, with the help of his rudder and
these great oars, turn his broadside to his enemy and
fire, thereby seeking to confuse our people's aim, if
not to do some mortal damage to them or their ship ;
so infinite is the subtlety and so great the daring of
these Infidels, more like those of incarnate devils than
of honest Christian men !

Perceiving that the Pirates were aiming to bring in
their vessel upon a little sandy cove at about an
hour's ride from us, where they would be arrived
before we could be, and that a wooded dell or valley
led to it from the higher ground, I shaped our
course to enter the head of the valley unperceived
by them.

We rode on, plainly hearing, ever and anon, the
noise of the cannonade of the two ships, and catching
a glimpse now and then, through the trees which
encumber this part of the land, of the Corvetto and
the Pirate galley, now half a mile apart, and the smoke
of their cannon rolling away over the waves to the
east. I gave the order to slacken our pace so as to
freshen up our horses and men and to give the
scoundrels time to land, and also to afford myself a
little leisure to mature my plans, for, said I to myself
these fellows will certainly beach their vessel here,

and when she is high and dry on the sand they will
land without having so much as to wet their feet.
Perhaps they will scatter and fly at once, but their
numbers are so great (for I reckoned the galley,
which was a very large one, might hold over 200
men) that they will seek to defy my Lord's landing
to get at them.   Probably, thought I, they will
endeavour to land some of their cannon and mount
them on the sea shore, and firing from *terra firma*
against ship fire or upon boats attempting to land,
will easily, with their superior numbers, hold their
own against the worst our people can do.

So considering we reached the valley head, and
there I halted the men at some quarter of a mile
from the cove, in a place where they were hidden by
the trees.   Going a little forward myself to recon-
noitre I found the Pirate galley already beached and
lying upon her beam ends in the sand.   In the
shelter from her hull were over 250 of the Turks
very busily engaged handing out arms and stores.
They had landed one gun with her carriage, and
they were getting out a second piece, and had set
the first behind a little ledge of shore rock, man-high,
which served their gunners for a sort of natural
parapet.

It was pretty clear to me that a landing in the
face of nearly 300 armed men and with a couple
of guns in strong position would be very tough work
for the Corvetto.   I made no doubt that my Lord
was fully aware what the Miscreants were about, and

was resolved to get upon them before their defence
was fully established. He was now firing upon the
Pirates to distract and delay them, but from the
shelter they had with their ship and the motion of the
sea the cannonade did them little hurt. The Corvetto
was then some half a mile from land, and was coming
slowly in shore, feeling her way with the lead. The
boats were already lowered, and I made no doubt
but that my Lord intended a desperate attack with
all the men he could spare. I imagined he was not
aware of our being at hand, and I could think of no
way of letting him know without apprizing the enemy
as well. Indeed, the neighing of our horses made me
already fear we should be discovered by the pirates,
but there was such a noise of the waves breaking on
the shore, the shouting of the Turks, and the
musketry and cannon of the ship, keeping up a
hot fire all the time, that I soon concluded I need
have no fears on this head.

I now hurried back to my troop, and brought them
up to the very verge of the wood, bidding them
shelter themselves as best they could behind the
tree trunks from the shot both great and small that
was now coming from our Corvetto, for we were in
the direct line of fire, and not 100 yards distant from
the Pirates and their stranded ship. Going forward
again a little myself I perceived that my Lord's
men were crowding into the boats. Now, I considered that all would depend upon my timing my
action rightly, for unless I could in some way distract

the attention of the Corsairs from our boats when
they were close in, I should do little or nothing to
help my Lord, having so small a body of men at my
command. For I did not apprehend that either the
enemy's cannon or their musketeers, distracted as
they were by the continuous fire from the ship, would
do our people much harm till the boats that held
them should come within 200 yards, or our men
perhaps be actually in the water.

I waited patiently then till the boats approached,
which they did very swiftly and much helped by the
wind, which blew nearly aft (for my Lord had provided for this by going well to windward of the cove).
When the two guns had fired a shot apiece, and
the boats were almost in the shore surf, I drew my
men from the trees. I had bid them leave their
carbines in the wood, and carrying nothing but their
swords and pistols. The sand was deep for the first
fifty yards, and in the uproar our coming was
unheard; through this sand we kept our horses
well by the head and in hand, at a fair pace; then
coming to the hard wet sand we let them go, and
with a shout we charged right up to the gunners
while they were loading for the second shot, and
we sabred or pistolled every one of them. Then
breaking into twos and threes we rode here and
there among the groups of musketeers as they were
firing upon the boats, ensconced as they were in
nooks among the rocks and sand, sheltered on the
sea front, but quite open to attack from the rear.

In all my experience of surprises I have never seen one so complete, which I ascribe to the noise of the sea and the firing, and the favourable nature of the ground. It was not so much that we killed very many of the enemy before the Corvetto's crew came to help us, for I do not think we cut down, apart from the fourteen or fifteen gunners whom we slew at the first, more than some half dozen more of the others, but it was the confusion we put them into. There was the enemy from the sea who would be upon them in a moment, and whom they reckoned so surely upon accounting for, and then suddenly to be taken in the rear by an unexpected cavalry force: 'twas doubtless a most confounding circumstance to them. We had not fought for three minutes I believe when the boats' crews had jumped into the water, knee deep, eager to be at their enemy. So great had been the interruption our fellows had caused that I do not think six shots of a musket were fired at the boats after our coming among the enemy, and certainly no man on our side was hit on the passage from the sea to the land; so unsteady are men under a hot fire.

Doubtless our troopers would have very soon been hard put to it had there been any longer delay or time for the enemy to gather his senses, for our numbers were very contemptible among such a crowd of armed men and very hard fighters, but a new complexion was put on things when our people landed from the Corvetto. My Lord had brought nearly 150 men in his four boats, being all he could

spare from the ship, and these running in among the
Turks there was soon a pretty stiff and lively medley
in which the Infidels had greatly the superiority in
numbers; nevertheless victory inclined to our side
from the very first, partly by the sudden disconcerting
of the Turks in their scheme of attack (which the great
Maurice used to consider among the best fetches and
stratagems in War), and doubtless too by the admirable
activity of our troopers, who rode briskly among the
mêlée, swinging their great swords above their heads
and, distinguishing foes from friends by their Turkish
dress, bringing their weapons down whenever they
found a turban within reach of a cut, thwacking and
banging and slashing the Unbelievers in a most
potential manner.

But what chiefly caused us the victory was the
brave fighting of our sailors; and this to my thinking
was a marvellous thing, for but a few months ago
these very fellows could hardly have been persuaded
to deal a blow against the Corsairs; and I have heard
of a crowded shipful of Christians driven into captivity by a few of them, like sheep before a sheep
dog, so great was the terror of the Barbary Corsairs
in these seas and so invincible were they reported.
But now my Lord had inspired these poltroons with
the souls of brave men, informing their dull hearts
and leaden spirits with some of his own indomitable
courage and genius for enterprise. Nor was it
admiration and confidence only but love for him
which these rough fellows felt, of which they gave

many proofs afterwards, but one very signal one on this occasion of their first encounter with the Pirates. It happened in this wise, that in the sorest of the medley and when we were scattered all over the beach, fighting stiffly, every man carrying his life in his hand and knowing that a shrewd killing blow or a quick timely parry would be the making or marring of him, my Lord got with half a dozen of his sailors among as many of the Pirates, and, every one of his men falling killed or wounded by the chances of battle, he was left standing against the Turks alone. Presently Ralph received a pistol shot in his sword-arm and had to transfer his weapon to his left, and could make but a very poor defence with it against the Pirates that came hacking at him with their crooked scymetars and ataghans. Luckily some of the Christian sailors happened to perceive my Lord's sorry plight and imminent peril, and immediately a great cry rose among our fellows that the Pirates were killing their *Capitano* (for so the sailors would always call my Lord), and straightway some dozen of them ran together from all points to his rescue, and fell with such incredible fury upon his assailants that in a trice they had cut to pieces the five or six Turks who were round him and about to slay him. Seeing this, a body of the Pirates ran up to avenge their friends, and there was great stress and heat of battle all round my kinsman. The cry that my Lord was hurt had reached me through the din fifty or sixty yards away on the right, and I galloped up, some four or

five troopers following in my track as good soldiers
will always crowd up to their leader in a fight; but
when we came to where the struggle was we could do
little good, so closely engaged were they, friends and
foes together, many down on the ground and fighting
with shortened swords, daggers, and even great stones
picked up on the beach to pound and pummel each
other with, for the men had all discharged their
weapons, and there was no room to fight even with
their muskets clubbed.

I could not tell for a time whether my kinsman
was killed or no, for I could see nothing of him; he
having in truth, in his faintness and weakness with
loss of blood, been hustled down upon the slippery
rocks where the scuffle took place by the great
brawny fellows, his friends, coming all round him to
his succour; and they, no longer seeing him and
thinking he had been done to death by the Pirates,
smote them with such redoubled rage and animosity
as soon put the whole number round my Lord to the
sword. Then in their thirst for vengeance running out
from the heap of the slain they had made in this spot,
they fell with exceeding spite and fury upon all whom
they could meet, and in a very short time had routed
and dispersed the whole crew of Turks. A few,
perhaps two score of the enemy, ran towards the
wood and would have got there and hidden themselves, but my troopers galloped up and prevented
them; and as they stood there in a body back to
back loading their firelocks and pistols, I called upon

them to surrender and they should have quarter. They perceived that they were cut off from the wood, for our horsemen were drawn up on the way, while a body of our sailors were hastening up to them from the sea shore, biting their cartridges and ramming them into their firelocks, as they came along. Seeing themselves thus surrounded on all sides, and my troopers with drawn and bloody swords about to charge in upon them, the Turks threw their muskets on the ground with one accord and begged for quarter, which we very willingly accorded to them.

I left them in haste in my concern to know what had betided my kinsman, and galloped up to where the chief conflict had taken place. It will, I think, readily be conceived with what content and solace of mind and relief of my great disquietude I discerned my Lord rising out of the heap of dead and wounded, faint still and staggering, indeed, with his wounds and bruises, but no otherwise hurt than by a disabling wound in his arm.

So did this day end in the most complete defeat and discomfiture of the Turks, and we had no more to do than to bind the unhurt prisoners and to tend our own and their wounded. By the time we had accomplished this we perceived the other five vessels of the squadron in the offing, one of them having the disabled Corsair in tow. My Lord resolved to return to Syracuse, instead of proceeding with his cruise, having many prisoners and wounded, and a prize of war to deliver to the officers of the Port.

Though the fighting was so short, the losses were heavy on both sides, we having in killed and wounded some fourteen men of the Corvetto's crew, one killed of our men, a Spanish trooper, and two of our Englishmen wounded, but not mortally.

CHAPTER XV.

THAT afternoon our troop, numbering now but sixteen (for the lightly wounded of them had embarked in the squadron for Syracuse), rode on some six miles westward to where we had already set up a barrack for our use, which as yet stood empty, and loading our spare horses (of which we had five) with provisions and necessaries from the ships, we took our way thither with great contentment of mind and body.

Alas! war and fighting are but sad, senseless things in themselves, even if, in this wilful and wicked world, they are necessary, seeing that men will so seldom be led into the right way of thinking and acting but by compulsion; which indeed, as the vulgar might say, is as long as it is broad, when we consider how sectaries at home are for ever taking the sword into their wicked hands and compelling us silly, honest folk to do as much to save ourselves from conversion to their devilish ways and vile opinions.

So often as I fight, I have no thoughts—woe is

me!—of anything but the ardour and delight of
fighting ; but as soon as it is over, and I see some
who are my dear friends wounded and dying, and
others, the loss of whom would make every breath
and step of my after living a bitterness and regret to
me : when I see others, I say, saved but by the skin
of their teeth (as in the book of Job 'tis strangely and
strongly said), then I begin to lament myself and the
folly and wickedness of the world that forces us to
bring death and destruction to our fellows. Perhaps
I am in the wrong altogether to have entered so
particularly into this history of my Lord's campaign
against the Pirates by sea and land, even though it
was for the righteous cause of preventing these Infidel
robbers of their prey. It may be, and indeed I am
pretty sure is (I mean by entering into it so fully) a
form of the sin of intemperance now being committed
by myself (and by my Readers too, let me tell them)
to dwell at such length and with such gusto as we
are both doing upon these various stratagems of
War, these surprises, and these plots to assault, and
counter-plots to parry and defend. In all which this
same sin of intemperance appears (by the judgment
of the philosopher Plotinus and other grave moralists)
to consist in running too eagerly after any pursuit
on which our affections are immoderately set : which,
though to be sure it extends the peccability of man,
and his duty to refrain, almost beyond endurance of
ordinary mortality, is nevertheless a high and edifying doctrine. Inasmuch, however, as it is (by con-

consent of all but the over learned) easier to practise virtue in the pages of a book than in the daily walks of life, so shall this remembrance now stand in the way of my speaking more than very shortly in the future of my Lord's operations on shore and on the sea. The rather is this reticence due, as I have other matter of very deep import to convey to the Reader, and certain most strange adventures of my Lord to tell of, which I should fear to relate were I not well known to be a plain, simple man, whose judgment may not be widely respected (on which point it becomes me neither to insist nor deny), but whose word at least, in these troublous times, has never once been impugned. Were it not for this, I would in truth hardly dare to narrate what I am shortly going to put before the Reader.

I have used this flourish here because the things I have still to tell are indeed most strange, in good sooth almost marvellous; and I would not for the world have the smallest sentence of my writing called in question. I am indeed aware that those who have travelled beyond the seas are at times taxed by un-travelled and envious and ignorant men, I will not say with invention and falsehood, but with overlaying the plain truth with unsifted fables and unscrutinized reports. So Marcus Pelus the grave Venetian, Fernandus Mendes Pintus the Portuguese traveller, and our own Mandeville have not unfrequently been indicted of trespasses on the credulity of their readers, while all the time (as later and closer enquiry has

abundantly shown) they have been most heedful and
exact and modest narrators, often rather hinting at
than fully expounding the wonders of foreign lands
and peoples, as fearing that a complete lifting of the
veil from the naked truth might be too much for the
aforesaid envious and ignorant folk at home.

But to go back to my self-accusation of intemperance in the indulging of my love (and the Reader's)
for warlike themes, I will now hurry over the matter
in a very few words.

This first action of ours that I have described on
the south coast of Sicily was but the prelude and
exemplar of many other fights and many other
victories; not but what we ourselves suffered loss
at times, and some discouragement. One of our
galleys was attacked by two Corsairs and captured
by them before my own eyes, who was standing on
the shore, with forty of my soldiers, helpless to succour
them, though her crew came ashore in their boats,
the enemy sheering off with their prize before our
squadron could come up to the rescue.

Another of our ships, our third and smallest Corvetto,
was overpowered by a squadron of three Rovers, and
though she sank one of them, she was overcome by
the fire of the others all coming about her, then
boarded and captured with her crew. This defeat
indeed turned in the end greatly to our advantage,
for the fight against numbers made by our ship being
long, there was time for her consorts to come up, who
gave chase in force, and ran the Pirates and their

prize almost to Goletta in Tunis Bay before they came up and engaged the enemy. Our people could indeed do no more than rescue their Corvetto, seeing that we fought within actual sight and hearing of the Port of Tunis, and every moment apprehended the coming forth of the enemy in force, which to be sure happened, for they came buzzing out like angry hornets from their nest ; not so quickly however but that we got away with but little damage to ourselves, taking our captured ship and crew back with us, and so had all the honours of war ; and what was perhaps better than such barren honours, we carried off the prize crew of Turks put on board the Corvetto, numbering some thirty men. This action almost under the fortifications of Tunis, and which took place about three months after the commencement of our campaign against the Pirates, was much talked of, both in Sicily and along the Mediterranean coasts, and finally opened the eyes of the Africans to the valour and efficiency of my Lord ; for Tunis Bay, with Goletta which is an inlet therefrom, is the place of assembly of the ships of all the Moslem Robber Powers of Africa.

The Corsairs hail from the ports along the whole coast of Africa, many hundreds of miles in length, from Tripoli in the east to Morocco in the far west, and from very ignorance in them it was some time before all of them learnt to avoid the coasts of Sicily from fear of my Lord and his ships; so that for months every southerly or south-westerly wind would bring

some one or more of their Rovers, many of which fell
into our hands. In this way we made many prizes
and crowds of prisoners ; which great success of ours
put us into two altogether unexpected difficulties ;
one of which was that our sailors and soldiers (for the
proceeds and profits were divided equally among the
two services) got so much prize-money that they
were many of them more eager to enjoy and spend it
than keen to adventure their lives in making more.
This evil was, it is true, in course of remedying itself ;
for, first, the men spent a good deal of their gains in
carousing on shore during their frequent sojournings
in port. Secondly, though the prizes we took
from the Turks (many were Galleons, Brigantines,
Bricks, Snows, and of other Christian rigs) always
fetched good prices from traders and merchants, the
prices of the prisoners ran down to almost nothing,
so soon as our Sicilian Harbour galleys were fully
manned, and we had sold three or four hundred of
them to the chain-gangs used for road-making and
other State purposes ; for there is a law in this country
against the buying of slaves by private gentlemen.
And this *glut* of Turks, to use the merchants' term,
took place, although in every shipful of prisoners a
goodly proportion was by the law of the country
always got rid of summarily; namely, by being
hanged in chains on the hills and headlands looking
to the sea all round the Island : these being the
Christian Renegados of all nations, who were so served
for the comfort and encouragement of the Islanders.

and the warning of the evil disposed. Such a wanton
waste of prisoners was felt to be a hardship by our
poor fellows at first, and they complained bitterly
when they saw so many fine, strong, brawny Renegados
swinging idly on the gallows, whom they had been at
all the pains in the world to capture, and who might,
as slaves, they contended, have brought them several
good gold doubloons apiece; but as our captures of
Turks became more and their price fell almost to
nothing, our sailors learnt to bear this little hardship with more equanimity.

Still they did very well, what with the ransoms
paid by some of the richer prisoners and sometimes
the prize cargoes found in their ships' holds, and the
arms, jewels, carpets and hangings which the Turks
always carry about with them—all very rich and
marketable commodities—the prize dividends continued pretty high, though certainly not so rich as at
first. To meet this difficulty of the over-enrichment
of the men, my Lord proposed to the Council to
make a new Ordinance, that all ransoms of prisoners
should appertain to the State, and that all prisoners
should as far as possible be exchanged against Christian captives in the Pirates' hands; this traffic being
undertaken at all times by Jew brokers passing, no
one well knew how, from one country to the other;
and lastly that all prizes, except ships and prisoners,
should go to the Sicilian government, excepting one
fourth part thereof, to be divided in certain proportions
between officers and men.

Now this was no doubt a wise and equitable plan, and would have worked very well, but for the Council of Palermo. So soon as these Lords began to perceive that the service of my Lord St. Keyne against the Pirates was one of profit and great honour to those engaged in it, as well as of benefit to the country, they began to persuade themselves that it behoved them to be meddling therewith. Now of statesmen of the lesser kind—statemongers I would rather call them, being those upon whom authority has been thrust without any particular virtue in them to deserve it—of such I have observed three or four particularities, which I will hereunder set down. First, that when a thing goes well by the ordering of one who is set under them, they must needs order it anew, though the performance may be marred in the altering, lest the world think they are not themselves its first designers : Second, that if there be a place of profit and honour, well administered, they will be ever trying by plot and cabal to thrust out the holder thereof in order to thrust in a creature of their own : Third, that if there be repute to be gained or pelf or power to be acquired, they will move heaven and earth but it shall be their hand that is at the helm, and if there be lucre about, they will have it to stick to their own fingers and no one else's.

These three characteristics belong truly, I think, to whoever of the baser kind hold power; and this not in one country, or two or three, for I verily believe that no Kingdom whatever is free from such impro-

bities, save the Kingdom of Heaven itself, of which I
have as yet no experience. Therefore I say to the
Rulers of the earth, Beware of your instruments, and
see that their hands are clean and their hearts pure,
and that they be honourable gentlemen you employ,
who fear the reproach of a baseness as the reproach
of a blow ; and to the ruled I say, Keep your eyes
open upon these knaveries and backslidings, neither
consorting with their doers, nor countenancing or
conniving at the doings, but loudly denouncing them
till your voices reach the ears of the King himself.
But come ! I am preaching, which very ill becomes a
soldier, and is, to be sure, a sin I have not committed
before, nor will ever again, nor would now but for the
provocation roused in me, and the great indignation
that the conduct of these Lords of the Council of
Sicilia has worked in me and does still work in my
memory.

Now to the understanding of what next befell my
Lord in these most strange adventures that were soon
to follow, the Reader must know somewhat (though
I need tell him but a little part of the whole matter)
of the condition and way of government of this Island
of Sicily.

Know then, that though it is a dependency of the
Crown of Spain, it is one which the King of that
country is constrained to leave to itself in these
distracted times of wasting war by the Africans in all
these Mediterranean waters, content only if he can
draw his tribute once a year.   There is consequently

full scope for intrigues and for plots and counter-plots in the Council itself, and insurrections, tumults and outbreaks of the people, fomented by cunning fellows who have no interests but their own in their moving (one such insurrection, a very bloody one, had happened but a short time before our coming). All this, under a fair and peaceful seeming, we soon found to be lying under the surface in Sicily. Some of the Councillors would be caballing against the Viceroy himself, and it was understood that to gain their ends there were some who would as lief as not hire the stiletto of a bravo or resort to a secret poison dose. One of the Lord Councillors would set his heart upon ousting another a little higher placed than himself, hoping to get his place and pay, and he too would stick at nothing to accomplish his end ; so that envy and hatred of one another and of their Regent, and greed and ignoble avarice, distracted this Sicilian Council which contained, I will positively declare, no honest man but one, and he, good soul, one between fool and fanatic, and as such the tool unknowingly of cunninger men than himself; and this was the Lord High Inquisitor.

We had marvelled in the beginning to find so simple a youth as Don Diego de Camporeal Generalissimo of the Forces, seeing that all the security of the Viceroy's throne was based on his Grace's soldiery, Don Diego being a young nobleman of a very pleasing exterior indeed, but knowing nothing of the soldier's trade, never going among his regiments, and caring for any diversion in the world rather than to lead them against an enemy. He was however a very civil, pleasant and obliging gentleman, who sang very prettily to the touching of his own lute, and bore so great a regard to my Lord, that learning once that a favourite gyr falcon of his Lordship's had met with an accident to her feathers (for both my kinsmen and I were passionate lovers of the sport of falconry), Don Diego waited upon us to make his condolences, and nothing would serve him but he must *imp* the broken wing with his own hand ; which I will admit he accomplished with a cunning I have never seen surpassed by any trained falconer. He never spoke at the Council, save to agree with his uncle the Viceroy, nor stirred himself to think upon State affairs. At the first I will confess I apprehended that this carpet knight and soft-spoken gentleman would yet bear malice at the rivalry of my Lord so near his own domain, and so do us some under-hand injury, but it was in my simplicity that these fears were based, and afterwards I began to per-ceive wherein lay the craft of the Viceroy in this regard.

His nephew was a young Lord of vast wealth, being a Grandee of Spain, Lord of Seron in Almeria and of all the lands between the river Almanzora and the sea. His rightful place was at Madrid, where only, he averred, a gallant gentleman could consent to live, and where be held the noble hereditary office (if my memory serve) of Assistant Deputy Lord High

Chamberlain of the Infante's Bedroom, and he was still entitled to wear in virtue thereof the embroidered silver key of office on his shoulder. A scandal at Court had caused Don Diego's banishment for a time to his estates in Almeria, whence the Viceroy had called him to Sicily and made him General of his Forces, knowing well that he need fear neither ambition in one who was so idle, nor mercenary plotting in one so rich. So the Viceroy could sleep easily of nights in his Palace, unlike his precursor on the Sicilian throne, who never knew he should not wake to find the Palace Court-yard filled with his own soldiers in mutiny, and his own Generalissimo holding (to speak in metaphor) the stiletto to his throat.

But the Viceroy, though fain to keep his army and navy demoralized in order that he might have nothing to fear from soldiery swelled with successes, and officers accredited by doughty deeds, suffered greatly in his government and his revenues (public and private), as did likewise every statesman who sat with him in the Council Chamber, by the unhindered ravages of the Turks. Affairs had latterly grown from bad to very bad, for trade had dwindled to a tenth, and a breadth of land five miles deep or more all round the sea coast was lying bare of crops, and bare also of inhabitants, through fear of the constant invasions. The farm people who had not yet been captured had run into the woods starving, and many had turned brigands. So that the revenues of the land from taxes fell off greatly, and with them the incomes of the great Spanish Lords who came to Sicily but to feed upon the Sicilians.

It was in this condition of affairs that my Lord appeared in the Island, with the blush of his honourable exploits still upon him, and when the Viceroy offered him the office of repressing the Pirates, his Grace knew well he could trust a foreigner and an English gentleman not to raise a mutiny against him, and he was not unwilling too to have some sort of a trustworthy body-guard against his own troops, should they ever prove unruly. The Councillors were for once of the Viceroy's way of thinking, because they saw in this course the only way of restoring the ruined Island (and their own purses) to prosperity; and so for a time all went well. In about six months, my Lord and I not having once in that time rested a day, he had made the name of Sicily so terrible to the Corsairs that they would not in their expeditions even pass near it, and at last we could cruise in the seas round about for weeks without seeing a sail, and the beacon men strained their eyes over the blue waters but could never view a hostile ship. Then the people began to creep out of the woods to their deserted fields and their empty houses; the smoke went up again from the unused chimneys, forage was cut in the fields, fruit plucked from the orchards, the plough cut its furrows in the long fallowed fields, and seed was again committed to the ground.

After this began our trouble. Till this we had been left alone, but now that the work was accomplished, the Councillors persuaded themselves it had been easier than it was. They did not venture to propose my Lord's own removal, for they perceived him to be too much beloved by his soldiers and sailors for that to be safe; besides which they could not be sure of no further danger from the Pirate nations. They knew they could not do without his genius and his sword, but they took advantage of his asking for the aforesaid new ordinance on prize money to put forward a scheme of their own by which to administer the new services. First they accepted my Lord's counsel that the common soldiers and sailors should get but one fourth of the prize money from ships and prisoners, and the State the rest; second, they enacted that any treasure, cargo, or any articles found in the ships taken, or on the persons of the captives or anything of value, their property, or treasure trove, or other treasure found on shore (for they were very particular to leave out nothing) should become the sole, undisputed and undivided property of the commander of the ship effecting that capture or trover. Their third enactment explained the motive of their first and second; for each ship was to be in chief command of an officer to be appointed by the Viceroy in Council, with high pay and emoluments, my Lord remaining in command of the Flag Ship, as heretofore, and being continued in the supreme command of the new land and sea forces. As to the cavalry forces, they were to be divided into troops of 200, that is, into five troops ; and officers, also appointed by the State, were to be set over them, with rights to special shares of booty and prizes. This gave ten rich appointments into the hands of the Viceroy and his Lords. The ship commanders were to be called Vice-Admirals, and those at the head of the troops Colonels.

My Lord raised no further objection to the new decrees than to request leave to protest in Council against the commands of the several detachments at the several barracks being in other hands than in those of the lieutenants whom he had chosen himself for their fitness ; and against the command of the ships during their cruises being taken from those whom he had picked out from the others as most able to navigate and fight his ships and keep his sailors in subjection. The Spanish Lords, who desired nothing but to give honorary duties and substantial pay and emolument to their creatures, readily consented to my Lord's amendments, and so their project passed into law. There were to be vice-admirals who were not to go to sea, and colonels who were never to command in battle.

In truth, my Lord was now of opinion that all his real work in Sicily and all the fighting was over ; the Pirates were, he thought, cowed. The new ornamental vice-admirals might wear their uniforms in harbour, and the fine gentlemen colonels were soldiers enough to march at the head of the troopers through the city streets.

CHAPTER XVI

WHEN our squadron had made two or three cruises without finding any Pirates to fight or scare away, my Lord judged it useless for him to accompany the ships, and thereupon gave himself for a time to travelling inland from post to post, advising with me and perfecting the disposal of the stations, and rebuilding the beacons and barracks in more favourable places as occasion served ; for it was well, in view of the Pirates making further assaults upon the Island, that they should not be aware from repute of where each station was placed. Said he to the Council : " There is now but one thing I apprehend, and that is the appearance of the Pirates in force enough to overpower our squadron, when, if our ships should happen to be caught far away from the four fortified harbours of the Island, they will infallibly be conquered and captured." My Lord then repeated his project of the sea batteries, and offered to build them, now that he had more fully explored the circumstances of the coast, in such a manner, and employing the guns and gunners of the present useless fortresses, as should, with but little expense, afford harbours of safety from attack all round the Island, into which ships in stress of war could run, and each little port or bay secured and defended by a double battery ; and all this should cost the State but little. This, however, being the project which the Lord Treasurer had already condemned, he was equal to finding some very prevailing arguments, even if they were but weak, in opposition to my Lord.

" For a generation past," said he, " and I might perhaps be justified in saying for a much longer period, there has been no such incursion upon us as my Lord foresees ; and if he will permit me, who am an older man than he is and have no small experience of this country and these waters, to express my assurance, none will there be in time to come. When an invasion does come it will be time to take such measures as he recommends : *Quieta non movere*," added Don Pasquale, " when things are going well it is unwise to stir at all ; that is an axiom which statesmen can do no better than follow."

The Council was prevailed upon by these and a host of arguments of the like kind, and no batteries were built.

My Lord accepted these decisions with a stoical equanimity that somewhat astonished me, who am, I fear, more of a praiser than a practiser of the stoical virtues.

I may take occasion to observe here that during the time of my Lord's being under my tutelage, I

had never failed to impress upon him the advantages
of the Stoical Philosophy, causing him to study and
become impenetrated with the works of the great
Teachers of this system, as Seneca, Epictetus, and
Marcus Aurelius, and furnishing him with plentiful
examples from Plutarchus of great men who have in
adverse circumstances shown that Apathy or Noble
Indifference of mind to the troubles and crosses of
life which is taught by this Philosophy ; and the boy
was so impressed by the axiomata and practice of
the great men and writers aforesaid that though in
time he began to abandon, or rather, I should say, to
go beyond and leave behind the moral theories of
the Stoics, he never ceased to practise their leading
principles of living and conduct.   Indeed, I must say
it with self-reproach, he put me, his tutor and pre-
ceptor (as on this occasion), to shame by the contrast
of his fixity in these great principles to my own
inconstancy; for when I was almost beside myself
with indignation at the narrowness, bigotry in their
unreason, and utter forgetfulness of the good of the
State in their own self-seeking, of these ignoble Lords
of the Council (of which said resentment I have, if I
mistake not, already given a sample to the Reader),
my Lord, as I have said, preserved a perfect and
smiling equanimity, neither reproaching them at the
time nor expressing any adverse opinion afterwards ;
and to all my animosity he would go no further than
to say : " This, Humphrey, is but the nature of these
Lords ; we can no more change them (and be hanged

to them !) or the world, in a day, than we can take the stings from hornets or the poison-teeth from vipers ;" and he went on his way with no more outlet to his impatience than the little innocent imprecation above recorded, which I have set in a couple of *ancini*, or brackets.

My Lord now conceived that the time had arrived when he might properly rest after his hard labours of nearly a year, for so long (that is, for eleven months and a fortnight) had we now sojourned in the Island of Sicily, fighting or preparing to fight against the Turks ; in the course of which service he had been weakened by the receipt of several wounds, which had ill healed in the hurry of constant warfare and of so many journeys to and fro ; and for this reason too he required leisure, for ease and refreshment of his health. He had been very willing to borrow some one of the empty castles in the great mountains which overlook the town, belonging to the Sicilian nobles, who in these degenerate days find less delight in a country life than in the city and in nearness to the Court ; but the Viceroy besought him not to depart so far away, begging him to consider as his own a great habitation with courts and halls and gardens which forms part of the Royal Palace and is indeed a noble palace of itself.

This his Grace offered him for his lodging, and when my Lord still urged his desire to remove himself for study and recruitment of his strength farther from the city, his Grace frankly set forth his

P

politic reason for wishing my kinsman to live by
him, which was—to state it plainly—the troublous
and unquiet state of men's minds, who having so
lately passed through an insurrection might easily,
in their present temper, be cajoled or provoked into
a fresh one by designing men.   For the safety of
his throne therefore the Viceroy wished the presence
near him of troops and a leader whom he could freely
consult and on whom he could wholly rely.   My
Lord accordingly consented, and presently we and
a body of about 350, picked from the cavalry under
my Lord's orders, including our English troop (my
Lord's private body-guard), were quartered in the
habitation aforesaid and in barracks adjacent thereto.

The Royal Palace is a hamlet or assemblage of
palaces, situated in the outskirts of the city on very
rising ground, and which commands a great view of
the town and harbour and the sea beyond.   In the
Building given up to our use was a lofty hall richly
adorned with black silken hangings, a vast and
sombre chamber with vaulted and arcaded recesses
and alcoves, which my Lord reserved for a *studio*, as
the Italians have it, or place for meditation and
mental research.   "It rather seems fit," said he, "but
for its greatness, for the cell of a recluse philosopher
than the dwelling of a soldier, but I like it none
the less for that."

It was in truth the life of a philosopher and student
that my Lord now began to lead, and he set himself
to search for truth wheresoever he might find it :

in the starry skies ; in the inner burning white heat
of the crucible ; in the air ; in the earth's interior and
in the watery depths ; but chiefly in the minds of
living men, "For," said he, "books are helpful towards the truth, but they are mostly but dead men's
minds recorded, and I love best to turn over living
volumes ; namely, the thoughts and experience of wise
men, who, being questioned, will answer me again."
And this being known, all strangers in Sicily who had
seen foreign countries and had observed their wonders,
waited upon him, and he discoursed with them ;
welcoming knowledge and learning, and searching for
the hidden secret of life wherever he thought it might
be hid.

In his great room there soon had been gathered by
him many learned volumes, and presently it became
encumbered with the instruments and implements of
all the arts known to the learned ; as alchemical
crucibles and alembics, astronomic quadrants, astrolabes and armillary spheres ; and here were displayed
too, many strange creatures and objects from far-off
countries, as corals from the ocean's depths, the
Crocodile of the Nile, the horned Serpent of the
desert, and the crowned Basilisk of Arabia, the Sea
Lion's skull and tusks, and the great air-borne
Albatross of the Indian seas, whose bones are hollow
and whose wing-stretch is by thrice greater than the
greatest of eagles', and which lives in the air all its
days and nights, yea, sleeping upon it with outspread
wings, and whose female alone resorts to a rock, and

P 2

that but once a year, to hatch her eggs and rear her young.

In this chamber he would pass long hours by day and night, measuring his wits against those problems of nature that are still involved in their native darkness, and more deeply involved still by the obscurity of men's false questionings and false learning.

He had strange fancies, and yet, am I inclined to think, wise ones too, for he held that pure reasoning alone, the *lumen siccum* or dry unassisted light of the intellect by itself, was all too weak to force from unwilling Nature her secret fruit. She must be helped to delivery thereof by all the powers of the spirit. Chiefly must the imagination give wings to our reason and lift it from the earth and carry it afar into unexplored regions. 'Twas on this account, I think, that he had the somewhat fantastic notion of lighting during his watches of the night only one extremity of the great hall with the glare of wax tapers in silver sconces and tall candelabra, while the alcoves and vaulted recesses of the apartment outside the circle of light were deep in shadow. The room was thus itself an emblem of the world about him, where some few of the facts of life are clear and open as day, but the greater number hidden, as to their causes, in obscurity. So it was that this *chiaroscuro* (as the Italians say), this alternate light and darkness, stimulated him, as he fancied, to fresh and fuller thought.

There was a watch-tower to the flat roof, to which

a winding stair led from the great chamber where he passed his time in study; and on clear nights, the townspeople would observe him while he stood for long hours immovable against the star-lit sky; and stories gathered in the city around my Lord's name—his greatness in war, his generosity, and now these evidences of his learning moved the people to admiration ; and very strange reasons were given for his watching the stars, yet not in the manner that those learned in predictions are wont to regard them, namely, with help of astrolabes, quadrants, and the like instruments. It was said by many that his power over the mysteries of nature was greater than other men's, as was proved by his conquest of the Pirates, whom none before had overcome. Some said that he could predict the future from the movements of the heavenly bodies, not as common astrologers use, with common methods, but by some occult intuitive faculty known only to himself; and that now his learning had told him that some great catastrophe was hanging over the Island ; and they would have it he was watching the conjunctions of the skyey spheres to foretell the moment of its coming, and to learn how best to avert the misfortune. Then the people remembering what he had already done for them, blessed him in their hearts.

In truth he was but meditating on the problems he had set himself to solve. He was making no astronomer's reckoning nor astrologic calculations; he was but deeply pondering, in the presence of the stars thus rolling in their courses ; for in these southern regions they seem of nights, not as in our northerly clime, mere pin-heads and points of brightness set in the misty dark, but globes of fire, wheeling each in his harmonious appointed track through infinite space. A wonder to us of the north, and one that led him often to marvel greatly and to enquire whether Kepler were not in the right of it, and these harmonious motions of the stellar bodies are not indeed made to the accompaniment of symphonious tones, sweeter, and fuller, and diviner than any earthly music, but alas! inaudible to our gross mortal ears ; music, whose strains if we could but catch, and learn the subtle counterpoint that governs them, we doubtless should straightway gain the key of the deepest mysteries of heaven and earth. He was marvelling, too, whether, after all, these movements in the skyey vaults might not be, as the same Kepler maintains (with so many of the learned), in some sort harmonious and synchronic with the movements and actions of God's creatures on earth ; so that to know the government of the stars and predict their motions would lead to our seeing far deeper than we now can see into the lives and destinies of the human race.

I have hinted, if not said outright, that my kinsman had been not only instructed in the teachings and practices of the Stoics (that most noble and worthy of Philosophies, which being joined to the doctrines and commandments of our Holy Church, is surely the highest and most perfect noviciate, discipline,

and education which a man destined to a great part
in human affairs can undergo) but he had also been,
as I have not, I think, yet conveyed to my Readers,
somewhat impenetrated with and impressed by the
beauty and fitness of the religious doctrines of this
sect of thinkers. If I may, in this common parlance
of mine, employ a Greek word where an English one
is wanting, he had founded himself upon the *Ethical*
teaching of these Philosophers ; in that, namely, which
considers the laws underlying the right actions of
men, the subtle motives whence they spring, the
directions to which they run, and the effects in which
they end.

Yet, as he grew older, and from gathering his wisdom
at second hand from between the pages of books, he
began to turn over the leaves of life itself, and to
harvest a fuller and more authentic wisdom thereby ;
he soon perceived that the first practice and principles
of this ancient wisdom of the Stoics might be true and
just in essentials. To wit that there is through nature
a Providence that, on the whole, makes for goodness
and virtue, and which overcomes its opposite, evil ;
that man is of God's essence and immortal, and not
having been born from nothing, so he can never fall
into nothing, but, when he quits the regions lighted
by this sun and moon, will be absorbed into the
Divine Essence. So likewise did he find in their
notions of obedience to Duty as being obedience to
God, the highest concept of human righteousness, and
in their doctrine of the necessity of a possession by

man of an æquanimous soul in trouble, and his power
of rising by his will superior to Fate, the highest
fortitude. He held to all this as high and comfortable
doctrine, tending, if practised, to the highest life.
But then again, the teaching of the Stoic writers
seemed to him narrow in many points, unsatisfying
in others, and wholly wrong in some. He knew now,
by his wider knowledge of the world, that to affirm
with them that pain and pleasure have no concern
with the governance of the world is a tenet untenable.
To learn to grow as callous to pain as to pleasure
might seem noble in so far as a man's self was concerned, but such callousness was, in his view, not
far removed from insensibility and from stupidity.
The truer nobility seemed to him to lie far beyond
the Stoics' ideal ; it was to feel and yet to bear ; for
the martyr who feels not the flames is no true
martyr. And again, not to feel for ourselves was, by
the Stoics' doctrine, to extend to not feeling the griefs
of our friends and fellows : a palpable heresy to him, as
failing in the approach of our human nature to that of
an Omniscient and Omnibenevolent Deity, of whom
compatiscence with human joy and pity of human
misery was, in his eyes, a certain attribute. That,
however, which in the Stoic Philosophy most troubled
my kinsman at this period, and most inclined him to
branch off and travel into new regions of thought,
was the intellectual apathy and incuriosity of the
Stoic Philosophers, which, in his opinion, they had
forced themselves to arrive at by their own deliberate

action ; for while they thought to be relieving themselves of the burden of their emotions, their sensibilities, and their affections, they were in truth casting
away, in their guise, spurs to strong endeavour, shields
and armour against error, and keen weapons in the
chase after truth.

Yet let it not be supposed that Ralph St. Keyne,
while broadening and deepening the dogmas on which
his youth had been nourished, departed from them so
far as to err and stray into the pleasant, pernicious paths
of the Epicureans. I have shown (since *neque semper
arcum tendit Apollo*) that he knew how on fit occasion to relax, for he feared the narrowness of asceticism
and the peril of pedantry coming from an anchoritish
mortification of the flesh. "*Nihil humanum a me
alienum puto*," he would say, "all that is human is
in my domain while I am human too ; all the pursuits
of men, *quidquid agunt homines*, all that they do and
pursue, I must follow ; and loving my kind, I do
love their pursuits." Yet if he was so wise as not to
fall into the prevailing Puritan excesses of flesh and
spirit mortifying, he guessed that the soul, if she is to
take a high and strenuous flight, can accomplish it
but in one way ; for, as a falcon can only be trained
to stoop to the lordliest quarry by the sharp setting
and starving of her body, so too must he who would
have his soul to soar, thoroughly restrain and mortify
his material nature, yet at times only, not too constantly, lest he dull and weaken his nature to that of
the poor formal habitual ascetic, and, like him, lose in

stupid apathy his co-sensibility with his fellow-men.
For he would distinguish between those foolish and
ignorant ascetics of India or of Africa, who will sit
motionless for a life-time, remaining with uplifted
hands till they can never more reach them down, and,
losing the very form of humanity, lose its attributes
and emotions too ; or who stand for a life-time upon a
pillar, chained to it of their free will, crying aloud in
lunatic prayer or praise, abiding in sun, wind, rain,
storm or fair, and making (whether of purpose or no,
and in vanity and self-esteem or no) a show and
wonder to idle men. Between such as these he would
distinguish, and those wise Christian hermits who
mortify the flesh, but not so as to kill the spirit, but
only the rampant mortality of it, feeding on roots
indeed, and going scant-clothed, drinkers from the
spring or running brook, and, if their spiritual natures
were still in abeyance to the corporeal ones, beating
their bosoms with great stones (as Jerome), spurning
more food and sleep than is required to retain the
spirit in its tabernacle of clay (as Bernard), or rolling
to overcome their material nature, with a keen religious delight, naked, amid thorn bushes (as Benedict).
And all of them content to rest in their hermitages,
solitary, never courting the wonder of admiring
worldlings, for all the days of their lives, desiring for
only compensation a place to commune with God and
with Truth.   Yet would these holy men not hesitate
(being called) to betake themselves into the world
(as to a new penance) to lead it by example and

teaching to virtuous courses ; as did that same holy St. Benedict, and many other famous saints and sometime anchorites.

So did my kinsman, keeping to the nobler tenets of the Stoics and their most noble practice of fortitude and æquanimity, yet enlarge the boundaries of their doctrines ; for he saw that their concept of the perfect man, as one wholly self contained, was lower than of one who should not disdain touch of, or help from his fellow-men. His ideal of the most noble attainable state was of a being set apart by his own choice from his fellows, yet none the less a partaker with them at times in their pleasures and pursuits, and their joys and sorrows, with no Stoic restraint, so that he might be able to feel akin with them in all things. Yet for all that he would be one standing aloof, stronger than other men in thought and in action, for that he had in silence and watching and with fasting, and by taking deep thought, and in self-restraint, and by studying the laws and secrets of nature and of men, stored up and funded a mighty stock of energy and knowledge, and of ready-hand devices of right action and prevailing speech, to be used in times of emergency ; while other men wasted their power and used their thought upon the present commodities and frivolities of life, with hardly a care for the future, or of providence for the coming exigencies of destiny. That my Lord had already shown his great prevalence and supremacy in several various and most unaccustomed departments of war

is to be set down to this long habit in him of forethought and prevision and preparedness of himself,
all in accordance with his great scheme of life, as well
as to his native genius, of which things more anon ;
but such warlike triumphs were but of the smallest
account in his eyes; he hoped to extend these
triumphs in the domains of Peace as well.

He looked now (and to this end was he moiling
and toiling in patience), using all his endeavours to
arrive at some true conclusion and result, to obtain
ascendency over the hearts and minds of men, as well
as over their bodies by conquering and killing.

It cannot be denied by those who have studied the
actions and fame of great men, that no mere taking of
pains or self-preparation, or concentration of thought,
or restraint of the vulgar affections, will make a great
man of a mean fellow (even had he the strength to
train and incline his nature towards becoming one).
He must have the genius in him, as my Lord had,
and to become great he must mew his spirit and set
her sharp, as I have said above, and prepare her
courage and preen her for flight, as a falcon is trained
and treated ; for 'tis undoubted that none can become
great without these things, and I will for once warp a
wise Latin saying, one of the Poet Juvenal's, and put
it that *nemo repente fuit heroissimus*, no man ever
jumped from the ranks into a great general's place.

Now, if I could feel persuaded (as would indeed I
could be) that none but the grave and learned would
read these pages, I would willingly expatiate at

length on these great themes, well knowing that I
could do nothing for the greater profit and delectation
of the wise and curious Reader; but every writer
nowadays must make his account with the idle, the
incurious, or at best the cursory, who chiefly hate and
despise learning in anger at their own lack thereof.
Moreover he must not forget that in this impertinent
age there are those (whom my breeding forbids me to
name more particularly) who will for ever be aban-
doning their spinning-wheels, and their distaffs and
their samplers, and be for turning over the leaves of
grave works that were never meant for them who
look for entertainment rather than edification. Yet if
a poor writer should omit to give them their due, or if
he say but a rough or crabbed word of them, which
for my part I have hitherto, as the Reader knows,
cautiously forborne (save indeed once or perhaps
twice, under the stress of a necessary and righteous
indignation), he is like to meet the fate of the wretched
Pentheus at the hands of the infuriate horde of
Mænades. For all which reasons therefore I will
hasten my pace and somewhat abridge this matter of
my Lord's philosophy.

I cannot however forbear relating one circumstance
in connection with my Lord's searchings at this
present juncture after the hidden secret of Nature, for
it was upon this discovery of his, that all with him
now turned, and upon the motives or levers that
were most effective to lead men by: this same circumstance being a great discovery which he now

made into man's nature, and which he communicated
to a friend and correspondent then living in Paris,
Mr. Thomas Hobbes, formerly of Malmesbury, the
now noted Philosopher, who in his answer to my
Lord, approving his originality and subtlety (they
corresponded in the Latin tongue) speaks of my
Lord's hypothesis as *inventio*, implying its novelty,
and again as *excogitatio sublimis*, which I may fairly
claim to have somewhat under-translated by my
phrase of "great discovery." I would very gladly
cite this letter of my Lord in its original dress, if for
no other reason than to exhibit the beauty and correctness and pithiness of his Latinity, were it not
for the fear before my eyes of the before referred
to cursory and idle Readers and the fate of the
afore-mentioned Pentheus. I will therefore make a
translation of one part of the epistle.

I must premise, to make the matter clearer, that
my kinsman had previously expressed to his correspondent his confidence that while we are part of the
essence of the Deity it were idle to assert that, first,
each one of us has received an equal portion of
the Divine Essence, or, secondly, that the quality of
the said Essence is not more subtle and refined in
some cases, and in others grosser and less perfect ;
perhaps by coming to the ultimate recipient through
an unkindly medium, whereby some part is modified
or the whole dissipated, by the way. Which proposition,
when it is once stated, no one who looks around him
to survey the innate differences in human beings can

for a moment deny; and is a fact he may doubtless reconcile with the eternal justice and loving-kindness of our Creator by remembering the plain text, "to whom much is given, of him shall much be required." What here follows are my Lord's very words, in my English version of them.

"I would propose, Sir, to divide mankind into two kinds or species; a higher, a rarer, and by comparison almost a divine species, the individuals of which act by their own spontaneity; and a lower species which acts and moves and thinks and speaks from necessitation, and of blind impulse and instinct, unwitting and unaware. The first I would name *Spontaneists*, as being such as spontaneously give birth to and nourish primary concepts; and I would call the last *Automata* (rather than men at all) whose actions are the effects of causative faculties that are born with them and perhaps are no other than (as our lawyers phrase it) incorporeal hereditaments passing from father to son, or their action and these concepts are imitated unreasoningly from others, as we see plovers, parrots, marmots, apes and certain other animals mimic the actions of other creatures, a circumstance not assignable to any cause or reason, but because it would seem they have in themselves the innate faculty of imitation. Such men as these I call *Automaton men* (as being of the nature of those self-acting toys of which Aristotle speaks), they moving, thinking and acting in correspondence and accordance with a higher and forcordained intelligence that is wholly

outside and beyond them and above their compre-
hension. Whereas on the other hand, those rarer
men whom I have called *Spontaneists* have within
themselves, underived, the springs and nascence of
notions and of concepts and of ideas. Now, I would
have no such men to be puffed up with the conceit
that they are certainly not as the *Automaton men*, but
necessarily of a higher and more gifted fabric ; for it
is quite doubtful whether they be not greatly to be
pitied for having escaped into this higher region where
the air is thinner and harder to breathe, from the
easier lot enjoyed by the *Automaton men* below them.
For these several reasons ; first, that there are degrees
in the intelligence of the *Spontaneists*, and a man may
be of this kind, and ideas may spring in him and yet
be naught ; as plants do indeed spring up in an unkindly soil, but they are not wholesome wheat or rye,
but darnel, cockles and thistles : secondly, however
endowed the *Spontaneist* may be, he has need of infinite
care and labour to subdue and cultivate his soul,
having to deal such hardness and rigour to himself as
the *Automaton men* need never trouble to use, to whom
their ideas, opinions and notions (such as they are),
flow in at second hand with but little or no labour to
themselves : thirdly, the *Spontaneist* has all the pains
in the world to get acceptance from the *Automaton
men* for his notions, and must with infinite labour
coin the virgin gold of his thoughts into current
money that shall be accepted by the masses of
Automaton people ; and even then it is odds but he is

assessed as a madman, or condemned for a villain who is for spreading new, hurtful doctrine, when the world was quite contented with the old.

"Moreover it is to be remembered that the *Automaton men* are the prevailing party everywhere in Church and in State, in the land, in the army and at Court, pushed by their kind into all offices of trust or profit, and in numbers abounding, a thousand to one perhaps, wherever men congregate for pleasure or for business. If the *Spontaneist* would gather any harvest of fame and honour and reputation and fortune and titles, and all that the common run of men most signally covet, he must put off his higher nature and conform to the lower, and as the greater includes the less, and the higher the lower, so is this degradation very easy. To attain these baser ends (which indeed are not base at all except they be viewed from the very highest standpoint of perfectibility) a *Spontaneist man* must set himself to observe the *Automaton men* narrowly ; he must partake their nature and pursue their ways.

" Now, Sir, I would have you to know that an honest *Automaton man* is well enough, I am very willing to love and respect him ; and a good *Spontaneist* is well enough, and sometimes better than well ; but between the two is a pestilent creature bred with the sins of both and the virtues of neither, a self-willed, unreasoning, extravagant, crooked-witted and fantastical fellow. Of this race come fanatics, zealots, cruel bigots against good understanding, ever in rebellion against all authority of God and man, and therefore

Q

criminals, as bravoes, self-seeking politicians, plotters, assassins, and the like ; madmen for the mischief they do, but too cunning for the chain and strait waist-coat ; or idiots in wits, yet too harmful and cruel for any pity of them. For want of a better name I call these unfortunates *Border men*, as being betwixt and between the other categories of mankind. There is happily no great crowd of border men, but alas! some few of them still meet us at every turn of our lives."

These are but the conclusions drawn from a very elaborate chain of reasoning and inquisition into facts by my kinsman, and I cite them here for that they bear very consistently upon the ends he set himself to aspire to at this time, and interpret and illustrate certain subsequent dogmata and pretensions of his in regard to supernatural things, which have, then and since, made no little stir in the thinking world. He was at this time in correspondence with many learned men of different nations, sundry of whom, hearing the fame of his researches, had invited themselves into epistolary intimacy with him. I am the less ready to mention the names of these learned persons, for the disparagement I am here forced to allege against them, in remarking that my Lord gave much more than he got at this game of letter-writing; discovering too often (as he hinted to me) after he had entered into argument with some very learned gentleman, that he was only at prisals with an accomplished and plausible *Automaton man*, who would yield him no harvest for all the working and weeding that should be bestowed upon his intellect. Among them all he accounted the most profitable the aforesaid English gentleman Mr. Hobbes, who about this time had brought out a very pretty book entitled *Leviathan;* an entertaining but fantastical work dealing with matters of government in Church and State.

It will readily be agreed that my Lord was himself of the *Spontaneist* order, and that according to his own theory and belief it was due for him to enter sedulously and rigorously upon that difficult course of preparation and training which I have already signified.

He knew himself to be one set apart from among other men, and that while others might take their fill of the good things of this world he must ever be striving and resisting and girding himself in solitude for the encounter, and breathing himself for the race; and times were when the prospect saddened him, and the thought of long fasts and anxious vigils was sore for his human weakness, for he loved his kind, and took pleasure in all the refreshments, delights, and conveniences of life, having as little natural love of austerity in him as any man could have. Insomuch that there were some at this period, not looking very deeply into the causes of things, who reproached him somewhat with the charge of fantastical, as being at times merry, at others moody, now all for hunting or dancing or what not diversion with the Lords and Ladies of the Court, and himself the soul and centre of all wit and gaiety and entertainment; now silent,

pale with study and watching abstracted and caring
for no converse but on learning and philosophy ; but
these be the trials of the *Spontaneist*, not very easily
to be apprehended of *Automaton* men and women.

There happened at this time to touch at Palermo a
war ship of the Sultan of the Ottomans who had
given passage and safe convoy to an Embassy from
the Moslem King of India, namely, Shah Jehan, the
Grand Mogul of Delhi ; and the Ambassadors, who
travelled with extreme magnificence, carried in their
train (for they were passing from one to another of
the States of Europe) several Sages or Philosophers,
well knowing in all the learning and metaphysic
of the Indians.   With these Doctors and the
Ambassadors themselves, for they too were learned
men, my Lord enjoyed many discourses through an
Italian interpreter, and he enquired closely as to the
ancient learning of the Indian Philosophers, sundry
scraps and fragments of which had already reached
us and raised in my kinsman a mighty interest and
curiosity.

I cannot deal in this place with the many deep and
learned disquisitions held between us (for I myself
took some small part in these conversations), but
suffice it to say that these Indian doctors spoke much
of an ancient Philosophy or Religion, it seems to
have been something of both, that at one time prevailed over these countries (and is even yet, it seems,
much spread beyond their borders), but now lives
only in the memory and esteem of the Indian Sages.

My Lord was greatly impressed with finding many lines of convergence (though some of wide divergence) between the teaching of the Greek Stoics and that of the Indian Saint and Philosopher Gautama (called Buddha for his wisdom), such, for instance, as the pervading Essence of the Deity, the re-assumption into It of man's being, the sanctification and redemption of man from his utter misery coming of ignorance, his final perfectibility, by self-imposition of an ascetic training and the withdrawal of the soul within itself from all contact with the affective emotions of man's nature. So presented to him as a whole and suddenly, these notions seemed at once to excite and delight him with the thought of man having in these remote regions of the world travelled so far on a noble course of thinking, and at the same time to disappoint him at finding how poor and blind and ineffectual after all was man's most earnest endeavour after truth, and how short and limping a journey he made.

It was after this that my Lord began to be confirmed in opinions which, as I have just now hinted, had long been brooding within him; to wit, that upon higher natures there were imposed higher duties, as well as harder duties, than upon lower ones. It was not enough to mortify and restrain the sensibilities and raise the soul, only for the redemption and the salvation of itself; it was necessary for the higher nature to go beyond self and enter upon a new crusade for the redemption of the world from the tyranny of error, and the establishment in it of the truth, mercy, and

happiness of God. This doctrine had grown up in him
as a corollary and sequel to his great doctrine of the
Automaton and *Spontaneist* men. " To whom much
was given, from him much would be required," and the
reverse would hold ; the crowd of *Automaton* men and
women might take their ease in the world and enjoy in
moderation, with justice and mercy and charity one to
another, and gratitude to their Creator for comfortable
gifts greater than belonged to the other creatures of
God. It was their function to enjoy life and live in
contentment as the beasts of the field live and the
fowls of the air, but if they went beyond their own
domain they did mischief and must be restrained ; for
great evil arose from the ambition of busybodies of
the *Automaton* kind pushing out beyond their homes
and firesides, and their counters, their workshops and
their desks, their benches and bars of law, their pulpits
or their thrones, or wherever it might be that their
narrow lives were centred, and assuming to set the
great world beyond their ken to rights. In their
ignorance and littleness, their obstinacy and unwisdom,
—nay, their very folly and madness, they would do
inexpressible hurt to their fellow-men, seeking for
nothing, poor mistaken souls ! but to benefit them.
This business was beyond them altogether ; it was a
delegation and commission from on high charged upon
them that were higher in moral stature than the
crowd, and not idly to be undertaken even by them,
but only by rarely met with and rarely endowed
individuals among them, perhaps but one or two in an

age; and never by them save after long subdual of
the lower nature, long perlustration of the ways
of men and the tendencies of the age, and long
perfectioning of the soul.

I believe I have now sufficiently exposed the standpoint which my kinsman had reached in his short
repose, after the hardships and vicissitudes of our
campaign. I have been at some pains briefly to set
forth his most ingenious opinions, the like of which
have not been held by ancient or modern Philosophers,
but, studying brevity, as was incumbent upon me
with so much other matter to deal with, I shall
yet, I fear, fall under the reproach with metaphysical
and enquiring readers, of baldness and insufficiency.
Let these critical and learned gentlemen hold me excused, on the ground that I write not for them alone
but (as I have so often said) for the cursory crowd as
well, and that too much fulness on abstruse points is
a thing it will never forgive a poor author. However, to make amends for my shortness now, I will
make this undertaking with the learned: if any of
them find my arguments too light for their taste, or
my information as to my Lord's doctrines to fail in
fulness, let them address themselves to me (to the
care of the putters forth of this book) with the matter
stated on which they require fuller knowledge, and I
will expound thereon to them to their heart's content.
Note; if they be foreigners, let them address me in
the Latin tongue, in a hand as nearly resembling
print as they can make it (for my eyes, with age and

troubles, are weakening fast) ; if they be my countrymen, I pray them to write to me, as I will answer
them, in the vulgar English tongue, which is, to my
thinking (let the learned say what they will) as noble
and lucid an exponent of thought as any language
in the world, either dead or living.

CHAPTER XVII.

RALPH ST. KEYNE was now, as I have shown, set upon one thing, the preparation of himself for what may perhaps be called the moral conquest of mankind (though he himself in his modesty would have shrunk from such a fine phrase), though as yet he knew not clearly in what domain his campaign for this purpose would lie, but he guessed it might be in our distracted country, so soon as fit occasion should offer for his return thither. As he was thus, as I have said, set upon this great task of reaching the hearts and understandings of his fellow-men, so he left no stone unturned for its accomplishment; and he began to fear that he might be losing his right way too much with the refinements and pleasant subtleties of the philosophers—holding his head up in the clouds, as it were (with many another *doctor subtilissimus*), while the true way to victorious action might lie much nearer to earth, namely, in the very hearts of men and in studying how to set that to work that should move them.

This begot in him a questioning as to whether there might not lie in man himself, and especially in certain men gifted more adequately than others with some innate effluvial essence or potential emanation of energy, some power not as yet quite patent to the acknowledged senses, or named and recognized by the general, and yet existent and even known to the learned in all ages, but so overlaid with idle exaggeration and the gossip of the credulous (and especially of silly women) as to be a circumstance fought shy of, as it were, and avoided by the learned as savouring too much of superstition and a false intrusion of the supernatural into the domain of philosophy.

In this belief, which he had long entertained, he was confirmed not by his reading only, but by the perception that such a faculty lay in himself, though unused and perhaps impotent for lack of use ; and further, the truth of it was now brought very intimately to his perception by the experiences of the Indian gentlemen, who spoke of this very faculty (which my Lord had somewhat coyly and half-heartedly hinted at to them) as a thing of common knowledge and experience among themselves. They told him of men held entranced by the will of others ; of command wielded by some over persons so held in subjection, as in being ordered to lie motionless, to all seeming pale in death, and yet the soul never so active, travelling at its commander's will into strange unknown regions of earth and heaven, and seeing and knowing things unknowable by the common denizens of earth. That which was strangest of all and yet not irreconcilable with the wisdom and accumulated experiences of nearly all the great teachers and seers among the ancients and moderns, was these Indians' free confession that at times and when the will of the compelling master spirit was in great ascendency over that held in subjection, the *anima* (the soul or spirit) of the obeying person would take on a dim and adumbrated image of its bodily form, unseen to grosser sight, but not to those endowed with the inner keener sense, and would thus pass on its pilgrimage to its invoker; a being immaterial and yet material, not able altogether to disregard the laws of nature, but capable seemingly of enforcing its way against many obstacles that oppose the motions of gross corporeal beings.

Here now was confirmed most strangely, and by all the learning of the East, that very phenomenon of potential present transmigration which my kinsman had, if the Reader will recollect, so insisted upon in conversation with a certain sceptical Philosopher at Amsterdam, and so convincingly supported with the recorded learning of the Western world.

My kinsman likewise questioned the Indian doctors on the most strange reports that have for this long time past reached us in the West, and which indeed have seemed to many almost past belief for their marvellousness. I mean their essentializing and quintessentializing of drugs, in such potent form as that all fancies of our poets and playwrights are distanced by the wonders of these sages' inventions; for it seems that, by their arts, they can purge from drugs and simples, well known to us, all the qualities that in our less cunning hands are hurtful to man's constitution, and so combine them into elixirs with certain other substances corroborative of their good or subtractive of their evil properties, as that these drugs' sovereign power is multiplied a hundredfold and their nocuity avoided.

On this matter my kinsman could not but somewhat stick at and mistrust their declarations ; as for instance when they told him of their artful handling of the juice of the Indian poppy, which our apothecaries know so well for its dormitive faculty under its common name of *Opium Thebaicum*, but often fear to administer for the great harm and disturbance it causes to the bodies of patients, rending them almost like a devil entering therein, or filling them with a black and melancholy humour. But the subtle apothecaries of India have known so to handle this devil Opium as to render him a very good angel, most kindly ministering to man, calming and dwindling his pain to nothing in a sweet dreamful slumber, and corroborating his weakened energy. They effect this change in the drug by coction only and the sublimation of its evil properties, and so killing the remaining hurtfulness with acids and sweet essences, and so subtilizing the resulting compound that, said these Indian gentlemen, but as much as will lie on the point of a blade of grass will overcome the strongest man with a deep and pleasant sleep. Hearing this most marvellous relation, my Lord bowed his head courteously, refraining from those natural doubts

which he could not but entertain. Upon which the
Ambassador, guessing his mind, smiled, and taking
from the hands of an attendant a little case of chased
silver he opened it and showed a lump of a reddish
and shining substance, and with the point of a tiny
bodkin he separated from it two pieces of about the
bigness each of a grain of wheat, and, eating the larger
of the two himself, presented the other to my Lord.
"If," said his Excellency, "your Lordship will command one of your slaves" (he presumed that our
servants were no freer) "to swallow this smaller piece,
your Lordship will presently observe him to fall into
a heavy slumber, from which for twelve or fourteen
hours there will be no possibility of rousing him, but he
will then awake and arise in health of mind and body."

"And will it not," enquired my Lord, "have a like
effect upon your Excellency?"

"Nay," he answered, "for I am accustomed to its
use ; it will cause with me but a trifling exhilaration
of the spirits."

My cousin resolved to commit the experience of
this marvel to no one but himself, and when the
business of the day was over he administered to
himself the Ambassador's drug. He bade me remain
by him and he would endeavour to force his wakeful-
ness against the dormitive power of the poppy-juice ;
but it was wholly in vain, and my kinsman, overcome
by drowsiness, sank down upon a cushioned settee in
his chamber and fell into so profound a slumber as
nothing could wake him ; and it happened exactly as

the Ambassador had predicted, that in twelve hours afterwards my cousin woke up, refreshed, and with a feeling of a renewal of life and strength upon his spirit. The Indians further told him of other and greater wonders, as of that strange drug *Churrus*, compounded of a lowly Indian herb, which entangles the senses of men and holds them in an insane ecstasy, not unlike that madness caused by the juice of the renowned Hemlock, fatal to Socrates; but which is yet, it would seem, most kindly to man's nature and sovereign in many distempers. Again they told him of poisons so deadly that but to breathe their odour once will cause a man to fall suddenly to the ground, and yet, before he touches it, he will have died in all his members; of another so slow and subtle that if a man but swallow the bigness of a millet-seed of it he shall pine and languish day by day, week by week, and month by month, and in the end shall surely die. No physician can save him.

My kinsman pondered deeply upon these new wonders, and reasoned therefrom: " If so slight a thing as a drop of the juice of a humble plant, or a pinch of a powdered mineral, can have such power over man's nature as to command the most wakeful to sleep, the sanest to go mad, and the strongest to die, shall it not be that man's will, that has conquered all else in the interspace of heaven and earth, has power also to conquer and prevail over man's own nature ? " And he was confirmed in his hope that to him it might be given to overcome and lead captive to his will the wills of other men. He could never succeed in gaining the end he had set himself without power over the various hearts of men ; and one key to their hearts and to that power was knowledge, and he would procure it, yea, though he must pluck it down from the firmament above, or pick it up from out of the dust beneath his feet. The other key was the power to use this knowledge; for in his reformed scheme of life knowledge was nought if it were self-concentred and contained : it must be disseminated. This second key, then, was the art of disseminating truth, that is, eloquence. So highly did he esteem this faculty in man, that he was inclined to set the great preachers and evangelists of truth as high as, or higher than, the great seers ; for he ever held with Bruno, the Nolan Philosopher, that Philosophy itself is nought and a dead thing, unless it be joined by art to fancy and imagination and to poesy ; to the making faculty, as the Greeks held it to be. Plato, the disseminator and seer, therefore my kinsman set above Socrates the seer and disputant : Seneca as high, or nearly, as Zeno, and those highest of all who were seer and preacher too, as that same Plato and the greater poets. For reason, standing by itself, even though it lift truth from its well into the light of day, was a lower faculty, an earth-born one, subjectable to plain rules of logical formulæ—a mathematical process, as the working out of a mathematical calculation is mechanical, though still a wonderful and beautiful thing ; but when mortal men use eloquence, high

eloquence written or spoken, not mere rhetoric—they
touch the spear that God Himself might handle and
will allow none but His favoured ones to use. For, said
my kinsman, to use right eloquence a man must
in his soul have attributes and faculties that are
nothing less than God-given ; an imagination that can
project him into the hearts of his fellow-beings ; a
noble, tolerant sympathy of soul that can read their
inmost feelings and still not despise them ; understanding, with long-suffering, that can judge men and
not condemn them ; compassion and pity that can
enter into their hearts and exult with their joys, or
grieve with their sorrows. Now, to possess these
things is to reach as high as man can reach, for are
they not the attributes of God Himself?

I cannot, even I cannot, go to all the lengths that
my dear kinsman went in the praise and exaltation
of this mere faculty of expressing great thoughts in
great and heart-reaching words, and in truth I have
smiled at times and seen others do so (who yet
respected and admired him for a genius almost more,
to their seeming, than human) when I have heard
him hold up for this God-derived gift of eloquence
the poor player W. Shakespeare (then deceased some
twenty years or more) as one who in his esteem and
in respect of this great Heaven-derived quality, held
rank above the greatest of the earth. " When I open
his book," he would say, " I feel to be standing by the
shores of a great unfathomable sea, in whose depths
are hidden riches greater than all the treasures the

earth can hold (for they are riches of the heart and mind and soul of man, not commodities of his hands and for his eyes), whose surface, as I look upon it, is now fair and peaceful, and yet can be stirred by tempest into being as dark and gloomy as a thunder cloud."

I remember that when once he had so spoken, a learned English gentleman, who happened to be travelling in the Island, and was present at his *levée*, objected that this same Shakespeare had but little philosophy in his composition, or if he were a philosopher, had never troubled himself to so much as hint at a cosmogony, as befitted a true philosopher.

" Why," said my cousin, " I think you have read him amiss, or have forgot." Then he cited to us some lines which I can but ill remember and will not try to set down fully, but they began so :—

> " The cloud-capt towers, the gorgeous Palaces,
> The solemn Temples, the great Globe itself,
> Yea, all which it inherit shall dissolve."

And my kinsman uttered these great words and some others which follow them with such a feeling voice as stirred our souls, putting into them, methought, his very heart ; then breaking off into a lower and as it were more reflective and sadder tone, he begot, I do declare, almost an awe in us all who heard him, for he spoke as one telling of a new-solved mystery :—

> " We are such stuff
> As dreams are made on, and our little life
> Is rounded with a sleep."

R

CHAPTER XVIII.

WE had now lived in peace from the African Corsairs for a year and two months, and many in the Island could hardly bring themselves to believe that they had once been so harried and held down by these cruel rogues. After the wont of the unreflecting, they began to belittle our exploits in conquering the Pirate squadrons and capturing ships and crews. " It wanted far less of warlike array," they said, " of fleets, and of troops of horse, and of beacons and batteries, to daunt a few cowardly Infidels ; a little show of audacity at any time would have served to keep the coasts clear of such fellows : " and there were even grave Councillors of State to lend their voices to these arguments in the Council Chamber itself. But about the very time that these envious surmises and foolish contentions were being heard, there came to us rumours from abroad of a kind that caused the idle talkers very suddenly to change their note.

I need not observe that at this period there was no peaceful trading at all between us and the

Corsairs, nor, indeed, that I know, between any
Christian port in the Mediterranean and the coasts
of Africa ; yet, for all that, we were always kept
pretty well informed of what the Pirates were about.
Reports coming to us, as I take it, in a roundabout
course, very much as the riches of that coast, such
as gold, ivory, dates, and feathers of the ostrich and
marabou (which are found in no other known land) are
bought and sold, as I have daily seen, in the markets
of Palermo or Messina, but reach first some honest
Moslem port, as Smyrna, Acre, or Beyrout, and
thence get shipment to us. By this same slow route,
doubtless, came the rumours aforesaid, which were to
the effect that the Barbary Rovers, all along the coast
from Tripoli to Salee, were resolved to avenge their
many defeats in Sicilian waters, and were at that
very moment gathering a great fleet for our subdual,
in Tunis Bay, under the leadership of their Admiral,
El Saida, renowned in all these parts for his boldness, cunning, and ferocity, and who was reported to
be no Turk at all, but a renegade from Christianity,
either Greek or Albanian. The fleet was reported to
number already twenty great galleys, but El Saida
had declared he would not put to sea till he had full
thirty sail under his command.

It is inconceivable the commotion and terror this
rumour occasioned in Sicily. Nothing was now said
of daunting the Pirates ; on the other hand, com-
plaints were made that our squadron was too weak
in numbers, the ships undermanned, the old coast

batteries all but useless. One of the newly-appointed Admirals resigned his post; three others were very suddenly confined to their houses with illness. My Lord was commanded to appear at once before the Council (who were in a very distracted condition) and lay before them his scheme of action in this emergency. Several Lords spoke as to the great danger the whole community lay in, and called for immediate action ; but none of them pointed to any particular measures to be taken.

My Lord said that he considered they had about three weeks or a month before them, and that which could be done must, he said, be accomplished within that time. The forces at his disposal would not allow him to meet the enemy either by sea or on land in case they made an invasion upon the coast. He had several proposals to make : first, he would remove men and guns from all the existing coast batteries (which otherwise would certainly be captured at once by the enemy) into new earthworks which he proposed to build at once with the help of the peasants. He laid a plan before the Council, in which the positions of these batteries were set forth. They were to be set in pairs in every case, on the projecting headlands of small harbours or bays round the coast, and were to serve as harbours of refuge from a too powerful enemy, or, if you will, traps into which to inveigle him.

The Island of Sicily, as my little chart shows, has something of the shape of a triangle, with the north side the longest, the east side the shortest, and the south side between the two for length. On the north side we proposed to set two of the double batteries ; on the short eastern side none at all, for there are already armed ports there, namely, Messina, Taornina, Catania, and Syracuse, into which the Pirates would not dare to enter, and where our ships could always find refuge. On the south side of the Island we proposed to set but one pair of batteries ; we would have built more, but that on this inhospitable shore there is hardly any safe entry and lying for ships, save at Licata and Girgenti and one or two lesser places : but none of these, by reason of the lying of the coasts, suited us so well for our purpose of a double battery as the little bay of Port Niccolo, lying just east of Licata and under the great round Tower of Palu. Here, at Port Niccolo, we built the strongest of our double batteries, and armed them with the heaviest guns we had. My Lord's other proposal was to concentrate all his troops in the close neighbourhood of these three fortified ports. Thirdly, he recommended that the defences of the chief cities of the Island be looked to, and the gunners and armaments increased. As for the peasants along the coasts and within reach of the sea, he was for warning them either to retire forthwith from the more exposed situations, or, if further inland, still to be ready to make a run for it on the Pirates showing their faces.

To all these proposals the Lords of the Council

in the great panic they were in, hastened to agree, and that without any debate or question. This was all we proposed to do, except the manning and arming of two more of the ships last captured from the Turks, thereby bringing up the numbers of the Sicilian sea-going squadron, one being a powerful galley and the other a very fine Genoa-built Corvetto, for there were other ships armed, manned, and officered in each of the chief ports of the Island, but which had never made a cruise outside them, and which were, by general consent, wholly unfit to do so. Some of the best men from these useless hulks were drafted into the two newly-commissioned ships, and with some of their more serviceable cannon they were armed, and we had thus two very fair makeshift vessels of war to add to our fleet now numbering nine sail, all told, namely, five Corvettos (for though we had lost one, we had before this commissioned two others in its place), and the rest very powerful, fully-armed galleys; and this was all we could get to pit against a possible thirty of the enemy.

About this time there was blowing a pretty strong breeze from the north, and we knew that so long as it lasted, which was some five weeks, there was no likelihood of an attack from the Corsairs. This was a happy thing for us, for when the work of building the new batteries began, and the shifting the armaments from the old ones, and the providing of fresh barracks for the troops near the new batteries, we found that it would take longer than we had reckoned to accom-

plish all. However, we did our best, and as there
was no lack of hands to work, for the peasants trooped
in their hundreds, nor of money to pay them with, we
set on a night shift at each battery to work by the
light of torches ; and so before the good north wind
was blown away we had our batteries completed, each
one mounting from eighteen to twenty heavy guns, *en
barbette*, and so placed that every pair of batteries
could bring a converging fire of some forty guns to
bear on a vessel in the fairway of the coves or little
harbours they protected. What was more, we had
time to let the gunners practise a few days with their
pieces, my Lord giving them a floating target of a barrel
to fire upon. When they had got the range at between
a quarter and half a mile, which was the farthest he
designed them to shoot, he caused the distances to be
marked with fishermen's buoys. This he did with all
the six batteries. I mention these little particulars,
though to men of peace they may seem of but very
trifling importance, but 'tis forevision of these small
matters that wins the day or the forgetting of them
that loses it, when the emergency comes, as the sequel
of these events will show.

Now so soon as the wind shifted to a southerly
quarter, we knew it would bring the Corsair fleet, and
my Lord passed the word round the Island for the
men in their barracks to be in readiness for the enemy,
and betook himself to the harbour of Trapani, in the
extreme west of the Island, where the squadron were
already assembled. Here he expected to get the first

news of the enemy, which proved to be the case, for on the morning of the third day after the setting in of the south-west breeze, the beacon on the great mountain close behind the town of Trapani signalled the appearance in the south of a fleet of twenty-six sail of the enemy, sailing to the westward.

This was as good news as my Lord desired, and we put to sea without loss of time, slipping in between the islands and the coast and keeping our course, like the enemy, towards the west. So soon as we had rounded Cape Boco, some fifteen miles to the south, and where the coast line begins to trend wholly to the westward, we expected to view the enemy, but had run some twenty miles further, now getting the S.S.W. breeze smartly on our quarter, before they hove in sight, and we counted not twenty-six sail as we had been advised from Mount Julian, but twenty-nine ; showing that they must have been too far off when first sighted by our beacon men for the clear discernment of their number. They stretched in a long line across the horizon, bearing about S.S.W. of us.

So soon as we had sighted the fleet my Lord gave the signal to heave to, which doubtless led the enemy to suppose, as it was our intention it should, that we had a mind to run back to the protection of Trapani, which is not only a strong harbour but well garrisoned and strongly armed ; and there was indeed still plenty of time to do this, for as yet the Pirate vessels were hull under. As quickly as their Admiral perceived or thought he perceived our intention, he ordered (in his

great cunning), a dozen or so of his galleys to tack to
the north, and so cut us off from our earth; and my
Lord remaining hove to, as if irresolute, for some half
hour or more, these twelve vessels, fetching a long
board to the west, presently went quite out of sight,
while their seventeen consorts, keeping their course,
neared us every moment. We then continued our
westerly sailing, the pack of our enemies now stretch-
ing in a great semicircle some nine or ten miles right
astern of us. The wind was pretty strong, with the
sea running high, and our square rigged Corvettos,
with their topsails spread, made very good weather of
it, but the galleys in our little squadron had some ado
to keep up with them. As we were now making all
the speed we could, the Corsairs evidently feared we
should give them the slip after all, for though there is
not a single good port or place of arms all the length
of the southern coast of Sicily (so far as they knew),
still they clearly feared that if they continued their
cautious company sailing, and we could go on travelling at the rate we did, we might easily get round
Cape Passaro, the eastern corner of the Island, and
so into Syracuse or Catania harbour, and behind
friendly guns, before they should win within reach
of us.

Therefore they changed their tactics, and we perceived that the order passed to leave company sailing,
and for each captain to make his best speed to over-
take and engage us; for in about an hour's time some
of the slowest sailers had lagged behind and were hull

under, while the foremost four or five galleys with all sail set, goose-winged in the favouring breeze, were advanced to within four or five miles of us; but we noticed that they made as bad weather of it as our own galleys, for the wind freshened as the day went on, and they all, the galleys to wit (for our Corvettos were steady, being on their best sailing point) rolled nearly gunwale under with the press of canvas. By four o'clock in the evening we had travelled not far short of ninety miles, having left Trapani at dawn, and by this hour we at last sighted the great white Tower of Palu, which lies above Port Niccolo.

I do not think a single sailor on board our little fleet but guessed what my Lord's plan had been in setting sail from Trapani in presence of so great an Armada of the Corsairs, and in running down the coast before them. They had understood his manœuvre when he heaved to in the morning, and threw out a third of his enemies, and now when we sighted the Tower of Palu, and they perceived how near they were to their refuge, there passed a great cheer from ship to ship. The foremost galleys of the enemy were now crowding us pretty close, the nearest not above two miles astern, one of them being, as we judged, the Admiral's ship, for it was the largest and loftiest of them all, and contrary to their common usage, carried an ancient, and from her mizenmast we had observed signals to pass to the others. This great ship was some three miles ahead of the others, and a mile or more separated each of the next six, which came staggering on under all their canvas in a long straggling file, and beyond these six we could see no more of the fleet than some of their mast heads.

So soon as we had arrived abreast of Palu Tower my Lord signalled to the four galleys, which were in truth labouring somewhat heavily in the still rising wind and sea, to run in under shelter of the batteries. He himself in his flagship with the other four Corvettos remained outside. My Lord had hitherto kept me on board with him, but now giving me his last directions for the conduct of the operations on shore, he sent me on board one of the Corvettos, with which I entered into the shelter of the little harbour. We had built our pair of batteries in a little inlet or creek, called Port Niccolo, lying snugly encircled by a jutting headland on the east side, and by a tall hilly promontory on the west; on the extreme points of this hill and of this headland we had built our batteries, and on them we had disposed our heaviest guns and manned them with our most skilful gunners. The hill battery carried no fewer than twenty-three cannon and the headland battery but two less. We had so cunningly hidden the mouths of the cannon with branches and bushes, and disposed pieces of rock along the face of the parapets to deceive the eye, that the batteries where wholly masked from the sea. The entrance of the bay was not 600 yards in width, so that an enemy entering in mid-channel would be exposed to a converging point-blank fire from forty-four heavy guns. Inside the bay there was, it is true,

but little room for vessels in from three to six fathoms
of water, and shoal water on either side of the deep-
lying, but what room there was my Lord had taken care
to mark out with buoys and furnish with moorings.

When the boat which carried me to the Corvetto had
returned, the first two ships of the enemy were already
upon us, and began without delay to open fire upon
the four Corvettos without waiting for their friends to
come up, imagining as I suppose, that these heavier
vessels could not venture into the shallow waters of
the little bay.   Then, my Lord having already con-
certed his plan with his three Corvetto consorts, the
whole four of them advanced to the encounter of the
two foremost Pirates.   My Lord laid himself yard
arm and yard arm with the Admiral's ship, while one
of his consorts closed up on the other side of the
enemy, and the two fired into him with all the
quickness they could.   In the meantime the second
and third Corvettos executed the like manœuvre
upon the second Pirate, the whole four of our side
very busily plying their guns, and, as they did not roll
like the crank and narrow galleys, with so true an
aim, that in less than a quarter of an hour they had so
maltreated them that both galleys were disabled and
the crews (those that were left of them) had taken to
their boats and pulled for shore, many of them getting
swamped in the heavy sea.   My Lord put a prize
crew into the Admiral's ship, and affixed a tow rope
to her bows, to hale her into harbour.   The second
ship was served in like manner, but she had been

struck so often between wind and water that she sank while she was still at the entrance of the little bay.

My kinsman after so quickly conquering the two foremost Pirates was in a mind to turn upon three more that had come up just at the end of the fight and who added a few shots to their friends' last dying broadsides, but perceiving that the bulk of the enemy was nearing him and would be upon him before he could dispatch his business with the two or three leaders, he somewhat unwillingly gave the signal to his consorts to retreat, and himself towing the Admiral's ship at his stern, they passed in safety between our batteries into still water, all but the second prize, which, as I have said, had sunk and settled in the fairway.

Here all our galleys were already lying in a half circle, each anchored stem and stern, and all broadside on to the entrance of the Bay. The Corvettos now took their places in the line and waited for the attack of the enemy. It was now nearly six o'clock, and being then in the middle of the month of June could not have been far from the longest day of the year, we had therefore still some hours of daylight before us. The enemy had now come up and hove to opposite the entrance of the harbour, at no more than a mile or a mile and a quarter from our squadron; and now, for the first time, we ascertained that the threat of the Corsair Admiral, El Saida, that he would put to sea with no fewer than thirty galleys, was true to the letter,

for it appears we must have overlooked one in our
reckoning; for here were sixteen galleys drawn up
outside, which with twelve gone to cut us off from the
northern route, one we had captured and one sunk, made
thirty sail, not twenty-nine as we had supposed. One
more or less out of this huge armada may seem but a
trifle, but I have my reasons to be very particular,
seeing that the history of this action on the southern
coast of Sicily has been most strangely misconstrued ;
yea, even by Spanish writers ; by some exaggerated,
by some belittled, by all distorted.

We made sure the enemy would attack us forthwith, but all they did was to open fire upon our ships
as they lay at anchor ; and as their galleys rolled
exceedingly they made very poor practice, not one
shot in twenty or twenty-five striking, though we
made a fine target, lying as we did in a line a
furlong or more in length. We did not reply to
these compliments except now and then with a deliberate shot from the ships, but as we were lying
very steady in the still water, our aim, when we
did shoot, was good, and the enemy getting several
round shot into their hulls, began to get sick of the
unequal game and presently sheered off and left us in
peace. We were amazed at this slackness and lukewarmness of the Corsairs in attacking an enemy whom
they so greatly outnumbered, for their boldness is
usually beyond expression and they never use to count
the odds either way when their foe is a Christian ;
trusting, as I have heard say, to a sort of Nemesis or

Fate, that will not fail to carry them through if their enterprise be but bold and bloody enough to please (as they fancy) their savage God and licentious Prophet. This, to be sure, is but the idlest of superstitions to us who are Philosophers ; yet does this boldness and its oft success arise from a cause implanted in our human temperament : *Fortuna favet audacibus*, good luck is ever with the bold, said the ancient wisdom, fondly personifying the issue, Fortune, when 'twas the causes leading thereto men should have enquired into, not depending idly (as all so love to do) on a mere axiom.

Alas ! 'tis none of mine, this wisdom, but comes at second hand, for I only repeat, parrot-like, the sayings of my dear kinsman, who had in quiet and meditation enquired very carefully into the wherefore of this necessity, in all urgent affairs and emergency of business, of sudden audacity (to which indeed he was by nature apt), and he had resolved it so that his own action was ever, *rebus in arduis*, in trouble, conformable to the issue of his slow previous inquisition. Now let us, henceforward, no more, as the common run of idle onlookers do, ascribe all great and glorious action of heroic men to some possession of God-given genius in the doer, and so acquit ourselves (who are indolent in all honourable achievements) against an indictment for ignoble faineance, on the plea that we possess not this good gift. Know, vile and slavish sluggards ! that our Great Ruler does not drop this seed of great price save in fit and receptive soil,

and you have, be sure, been tried and found wanting ;
or if, of His bounty, the seed be too generously
bestowed and has fallen on stony ground (such as I
take your barren souls to be) it withers and decays.
For this same seed must be warmed into germination
with exceeding precaution, and lovingly watered and
fertilized with study and thought-taking into growth
and goodly expansion. Witness J. Cæsar, who nourished his youth and manhood on all the wisdom
of the earth, before he set about the performance of
his imperishable exploits ; and Alexander, son of
Philip of Macedon, who patiently sat at the feet of
the great master Aristotle (facile sovereign of all the
ancient arts and learning) before he went forth to conquer all the known kingdoms of the Eastern world.

Surely never was great Captain, even such as these,
in sorer straits than now my Lord in this adventure
of the Corsairs' invasion, seeing that with but nine
ships of war he had put to sea in face of a fleet of
thirty, all great ships, and every one armed and
manned as strongly or more strongly than his own
ships, and commanded by the most renowned sea-
leader that the atrocious African Pirates have had
for a hundred years, since their famous renegade
Admiral Barbarossa whom they called Hayraddin.

We marvelled somewhat, as I have said, at the
Corsairs not coming at us without more ado when
they had thus, as they must have thought, run us to
earth, but we presently learnt the cause from a wounded
sailor on board their captured flagship. It was that,

the Admiral having escaped on shore on the taking of his ship, their second or Vice-Admiral of the Fleet, was in command of the twelve galleys that had sailed to intercept us in our supposed flight to Trapani. It was clear that only the want of a commander had held them back for a time, and as the second division of the Fleet could not long delay their arrival, we foresaw that action against us would not be delayed either.

It fell out as we had expected, and before nightfall the twelve ships were in the offing. It was doubtful whether they would attack us that night or wait till morning. A prudent leader, other things being equal, would have delayed his attack, but these fellows are very reckless of danger, and the common expectation among our sailors was that they would brave the perils of a difficult navigation in the dark and fight us immediately. The more likely was this as the wind had not abated, and their crank galleys, riding more and more uneasily, ran no small danger of foundering on the lee shore, so that they must either, we conceived, sheer off and go to windward for safety, or find shelter by coming in upon us at our moorings. They did not guess how vastly to their advantage this course might be, knowing nothing of our batteries and that if they could but enter in the dark of night, they might slip in without peril of fire from them and so make their numbers tell at close quarters.

I will here observe, what they who live in northerly latitudes may not be acquainted with; namely, that

S

the midsummer nights are not so light as with us, but if there be clouds over the sky as there were this night, 'tis often pitchy dark at midnight. It was now past the full of the moon, though she was still pretty large, but we could get no help of her light till some hours later.

My Lord, foreseeing that a night attack, though it might lead to some disaster among the enemy by their stranding, could end in nothing but complete annihilation of our ships, as in the dark we should be quite unhelped by our batteries, hit upon a notable expedient to lessen the odds against us.

There happened to have been taken in as ships' stores at Trapani, and for the caulking of our ships and boats, about 150 barrels of tar, which commodity is furnished of great excellence by the pine forests in that part of the Island. My Lord caused some of these barrels to be got up from the holds of the different ships, and at nightfall carried in boats to the prize galley which had gone down by the stern in about three fathoms of water at the entrance of the bay, and lay with her bows and forepart well out of the water. He ordered the men to load their boats with a sort of resinous shrub that they call *Lentisco*, growing abundantly on the shore, and with this herb or bush to fill up the hatchways and forehold of the sunken vessel, tying great bunches of it in the rigging; then they started about ten of the barrels and sluiced the decks with the tar, drenching all the *Lentisco* shrub. As many more barrels, unstarted, were left lashed to the gunwales and the foremast, for the deck was all on a quick slant aft, and some six or eight more barrels were rolled down the fore-hatchway. A boat's crew with two officers were then left to watch for the in-coming of the Pirate fleet, with orders to fire the ship so soon as they perceived the enemy to be entering, which, though it was already dark, they could not fail to do through the dusk of the summer night.

My Lord had passed from ship to ship of the fleet, giving exact orders to the officers how to conduct the coming fight. I will here observe that, as I have often had occasion to notice on the eve of great emergencies, my kinsman was never stern, and silent, and wrapt and abstracted into his own meditations, after the manner of many commanders that I have known before an engagement, as if the cares and forethinking of the coming event were all they had a mind to; which behaviour in one whom all have their eyes upon is very apt to breed doubt and fearfulness among their people. My Lord was never so debonair as at such times, seeming to have already resolved all his action, and having a friendly word, a jest, and a laugh for all about him, so that the very sight of his face, or sound of his voice as he passed by (as I have heard many say since), would inspire the men with hope and confidence.

My Lord visited the batteries with me, and apprehending they might lack light to do their work with due expedition, ordered a couple of tar-barrels to be set in a convenient place at each of the works, with

orders to light them only when they perceived the
first gleaming of fire upon the sunken ship. He
enjoined them to have their guns laid upon the entrance,
a little pointing seaward, and in readiness to fire heavily
upon the first vessels that came in, and the gunners
were to stand by the guns with their linstocks in
their hands.

By the new marshalling of our land forces we had 340
troopers in barrack within half a mile of Port Niccolo,
and as the new batteries were altogether undefended,
except by a little ditch and low curtain wall, my Lord
caused 200 men to be dismounted, and 100 of these
kept at hand near to each battery, in shelter, to resist any
attack upon them by land. The rest of the cavalry, 140
in number, I took under my own command, and by my
Lord's orders posted them behind the western hill in
readiness to act against any body of the enemy landing
in their boats ; the shore, except the two hilly headlands aforesaid where the two batteries stand, being
a hard, sandy tract, interspersed with little rocks standing up here and there from the sand, and much growth
of the before-mentioned low scrubby *Lentisco*, but still,
such ground as horsemen could travel upon to advantage.   This western hill is but some 300 feet in height,
bare of trees, and with the ruins of an old fortification
at top. We had not used the old work, but built our
parapet on the very point of the headland some 200
feet below.   Here is a rough draft of the bay and batteries ; but 'tis from remembrance only, and perhaps
not to be trusted by navigators of this coast.

Plan Of Port Niccolo
showing the 2 fleets & our batteries.

High Mountains
1½ miles inland

Flat Sandy Beach

Hill whence
I watched

Here the
two others
stood

our squadron

Rocky
ground

This is where
the 3 galleys
were burned

The W. Battery

the East
Battery

The wind blew
It in us, about S.W.W.

The 28 Pirate galleys two being lost.

Note
The bay is some 700 yards in depth and,
as I judge, 3 furlongs (say 600 yds) across.

CHAPTER XIX

On the western hill-top I took my stand and kept
a look-out, with three or four of our troopers by me,
dismounted, for messengers in case of need. It was
a black and gloomy night, being then long past dark,
and I could hear more than I could see, the loudest
sounds being the roaring of the surf on the shore, and
the whistling of the strong wind through the shrouds
and rigging of our squadron in the bay, for though the
headland kept the waves off, 'twas too low for complete
shelter from the wind. I could hear too, every now
and then, the jingle of iron, as one of our horses just
below me would throw his head up or champ on
his bit, but from our fellows themselves, or from
the sailors or the gunners, not a sound came. All I
could discern seawards was the long line of breakers to
east and west, which somewhat glistened in the dark,
and I could make out, or thought I could make out,
the loom of the enemy's vessels in the offing, and the
waves breaking in spray against their hulls ; but in
the bay, under the shadow of the tall mountains
behind, all was black, and I could see nothing at all
of our ships.

I say I thought I could make out the loom of the galleys at sea, and still keeping my eyes fixed upon them through the dark, I perceived I was right, for the shapes I saw now began to move, first one, then another, following in single file towards the entrance of the bay. As soon as I was quite certain that my eyes had not misled me, I fired off my pistols, this being the signal agreed upon. A moment after, I perceived a little streak of light to creep slowly across the hull of the sunken galley, and while I was still fearing that the wind and spray might be too strong for the kindling of the fire, the light grew in bigness, and in a moment more leapt up to a great flame, which divided into tongues of fire and licked all the surface of the ship ; and these joining together, there went up, in less time than the telling takes, a huge column of fire and fiery smoke across the firmament, that lit up the land far and near and the mountains behind with their pine-trees as in daylight, and showed every little jutting point of rock and every little shrub on the beach, and our ships and the crowds of men in them all standing on their decks in readiness. The glare shone on the steel of our troopers behind the hill sitting on their horses, and their faces, reddened in the fiery glow, were turned up to me ; and so strong was the light that I could see their knit brows and the set, resolute, eager, angry look on their faces, impatient for the fight to begin ; and the glare shone far away over the waves of the sea, and we saw the whole fleet of great galleys, their sailors at the ropes, their gunners with linstocks in their hands, the gaping mouths of their cannon, the sails set, and the ships coming in upon us, heeling over under the pressure of the wind.

The two leading vessels were abreast, and just about to enter the harbour mouth, when a gun was fired from my Lord's ship at them. Before the echoes had come back from the hills, the fire was belching forth from over thirty great guns in the ships, and from the forty-four in the batteries. The distance was so short, our aim so steady, and the guns so heavy, that almost every shot seemed to tell. The leading ship staggered in her course, but still carried on a little ; then, hardly giving time for her crew to cut the lashing of their boats and enter them, she foundered on a level keel and went under water all but her masts before she had gone thirty yards inside the harbour. The second galley was to windward of the sunken ship that we had fired, and shots from the western battery must have struck her helm, or perhaps her rudder itself, for she lost steerage-way, and was carried by the wind, while still in the fairway, right upon the burning ship, and herself presently caught fire too and was in a blaze. Four more of the enemy were following in single file about two cables' lengths behind the two first, and so quickly did the gale fetch them in that our gunners had not loaded, nor were their guns laid, before the first had passed in. She therefore got off and into the harbour safely, but there presently she received the broadsides point blank of all our moored ships, and sank at once in deep water. The battery gunners served the second and third and fourth of this batch of four as they had the two first comers, riddling them with shot and disabling all three so completely that they drifted with the wind, water-logged, and with their sails and rigging hanging useless, one foundering in deep water, the others stranding in the shoal-water of the bay.

Thus in a very short time we had caught six great war-ships in our trap, and overcome them without the loss of a man, and the rest of the fleet for a time were daunted and hung back, and we hardly thought they would again venture in ; but we observed them to be signalling to each other, which they did (strangely enough) by the light of the lamps we had lighted (to wit, their own burning ships). Then presently they had formed a new and cunning plan, and followed it very boldly.

It is certain the Pirates very well knew the pilotage of Port Niccolo, as they know all these coasts and waters from their frequent hunting over them for their prey of ships and slaves ; and they must have been aware of there being deep water almost from point to point of the entrance, otherwise they would not have ventured upon the boldness of what they now projected. There were still twenty-two galleys outside, and of these they told off eight to run in and engage the batteries, four to each, which they presently did, with very great skill and courage; and while the guns therein

were thus rendered powerless against other enemies
their plan was for twelve of the remaining fourteen
to run boldly in upon our ships in the bay. But in
the meantime the remaining two galleys of the Pirates,
getting further away east, behind shelter of the eastern
headland, and where the surf was a little less strong,
began to land their crews, and it was very evident they
intended a land attack by the disembarked crews upon
the eastern battery. Now, my Lord had foreseen that
my troopers, who were on foot, could take some useful
part in the coming struggle by using their firelocks
upon the crowded decks of the vessels in harbour, and
as I had 100 men lying idle in shelter behind each
battery, I had at the beginning of the engagement
ordered these men to scatter themselves among the
rocks and natural escarpments and battlements of the
two headlands, and fire at their ease upon the gunners
in the enemies' ships below them. It is incredible how
galling and distracting the fire of even a few good
marksmen can be, themselves being unmolested, upon
men working their guns ; and our troops were now
from practice very fair shooters, even with the short
carbines they used. When I perceived the intention
of the enemy to land and assail our east battery, under
cover of the distraction of the fight, I considered with
myself whether it was wise in me to allow the men
told off for its defence to remain dispersed among the
rocks, while the enemy might be creeping up in their
rear, but so useful to our side did their sharpshooting
seem to me to be in this great juncture of our fortunes

that I resolved to let them continue this molestation
of the enemy, and to adventure my cavalry for the
defence of the eastern battery (for the western was
safe on account of the great surf that beat on the
point and all the coast west of it). So taking good
note of the lie of the land, I rode with my 140 troopers
quickly round the head of the bay, and got, un-
observed, among the bushes and rocks to within 100
yards of where the two galleys were landing their
crews.

Now there had already got ashore from the two
galleys which my Lord had worsted at sea earlier in
the evening, many more of their crews than we had
thought for. We had indeed observed at the time,
but confusedly in the hurry of the fight, most of their
boats to be swamped in the mighty surf that was
beating upon the shore. Yet many of the sailors had
escaped through the rush of water alive to land, for so
soon as the boats, to the number of eight, put off from
the two galleys, choosing a sheltered little creek that
lies some fifty yards eastward of the battery for their
disembarkation, as many as 130 or 150 of these ship-
wrecked men ran down from their concealment in the
woods, many having arms in their hands, and adventuring themselves into the surf, somewhat lighter
here from the shelter the cove enjoyed, laid hands
upon the bows and gunwales of their brother pirates'
boats, and pulled them safely in through the troubled
water.

I waited till the party had gathered in a crowd of

perhaps 350 men, of whom over 200 were the armed crews newly landed. Then I formed my troopers into line and galloped down upon the enemy. The sand here is hard and level, and allowed our charge to be fast and in good order. We struck them very heavily while they were thinking of anything but a charge of horse, and though with their pistols and scymetars they made a very pretty fight of it for a time, presently we had worsted them, having pistolled or cut down some sixty or seventy before we had felt any sensible loss ourselves. I do not remember in the annals of War to have read of so curious a skirmish as this, for our horses' hoofs all the time were wetted by the great waves that kept running in, and sometimes they were knee-deep in salt water, and the spray that the wind brought in beat hard against our faces. The roar of the sea and wind almost overcame the noise of battle, the shots, the clatter of sword upon sword, the shouts and curses of fighting men, and the neighing of our horses. We charged through them twice, and then, having broken them utterly, and the sailors from the woods beginning some of them to fly to this same refuge again, we strayed here and there dispersedly upon the beach in pursuit of the straggling enemy, but after a little while, there being no longer any array of them to charge into, we stayed our hands.

Thus, in less than five minutes by the clock, we had killed or wounded all who would stand, and the rest had fled by twos and threes, and by sixes and dozens, to the woods hard by. None had sought refuge by way of the sea, or thought of escaping back by the way they had come, for the breakers were too great, and the boats they had landed in lay grounded on their sides, beating to pieces with repeated strokes of the waves.

Perceiving that we had wholly overcome the intended attack upon the battery, and knowing we were wanted elsewhere, I quickly recalled my men, gave them a few moments to recover their breathing, and moved them towards the harbour side again, and halting behind the east headland dismounted four-fifths of the troops (that is, nearly 100, for some were wounded and a few killed outright). Then we left the horses in the shelter of the rocks in charge of the remainder, dispersed ourselves among the rocks, and were in good time to help in the great fight that was going on in the bay.

Now I had not seen the beginning of what I will call the second engagement, for none of the enemy had yet entered the bay when we began to ride round it to the eastward, only we had gathered their intentions by their movements. To speak by the card, I could not in this my narrative have spoken so plainly of that which had come to pass, had I not heard it since from the mouths of eye-witnesses.

When we got to the headland, which, though lower lying than that on the west side, stands still some thirty feet or so above the water, we marvelled at the turmoil that we saw below us, and more even at the great red light of the burning ships that lit all up ;

yea, even penetrated through the clouds of thick
smoke from the firing. Our troopers ran boldly to the
edge of the cliffs without needing to seek shelter or
concealment, for the smoke was now cover enough of
itself. They loaded and fired, loaded and fired, as
fast as they could, and as often as the smoke lifted
for a moment with the wind or there happened a little
rift in its thickness to show us the decks of the Turks.
All the water of the bay was covered with our own
and the enemy's ships, and with many of the boats of
the Corsairs, for four or five more of their vessels had
gone down or got aground in the confusion of coming
in so many together, some having fouled one another,
and some encountering discomfiture through an excellent stratagem of my Lord's. It was this, that
having heaped the Pirate Admiral's ship which we
had taken with brushwood, and poured some barrels of
tar upon that, he hauled her to the eastern extremity of
the bay, and pointing her head towards the entrance,
which was within about six, or six and a half, points
of the wind, upon the starboard tack, he made fast her
helm on that course ; then as the enemy came through
the fairway of the harbour, those on board cut her
cables, set fire to the tarred brushwood and went off
in their boat, leaving the ship to herself. This
happened while I was away with the cavalry, but
I heard its relation by our people, who likened the
putting to sea of this huge crewless ship (comparing
great things with small) to a child's sailing of his
paper boat on a pool of water, who will start it from

the bank and watch it as it goes forth on its uncertain course across the little water, helping it with
his wishes when he can no longer help it with his
hands ; so did our people watch this great galley set
forth on her voyage.

She started so near the wind that she went slow
and staggeringly, and the wind seemed like to take
her sails aback and blow her back to where she
started ; then a slant of wind coming more northerly,
or perhaps the ropes that held her helm fast growing
somewhat tauter with the wet, her helm went up
and she bore up and went on a better course ; at any
rate, said those who watched her, good luck steered
and sailed her to the best advantage for us (so that
the most cunning pilot could have served us no
better), right athwart the in-coming fleet of Corsairs,
who started to right and left to avoid her, for now she
was full of fire and very terrible ; and the necessity
for them to so suddenly shift their courses was the
cause of some of the enemy fouling each other, and of
some getting into shoal-water and stranding. Then
the fire ship seemed to be pointing to the galleys
which were beginning to attack the western battery,
and they, in the terror of this great tower of flame
coming upon them, sheered off very expeditiously,
using their sweeps in all haste, and let the battery
have leisure to ply the other galleys in the bay with
their shot, which they did very heartily and service-
ably. However, to go back to the fire-ship, she
passed very quickly through the water where the

galleys had been firing upon the battery, and just
then her sails caught fire, and straightway her voyage
was ended, for she was at the mercy of the wind, and
drifted towards the point she came from. Being
then in the fairway of the bay, she fell back upon
the two ships that were on fire there, stranded (or
rather, one was stranded and the other foul of her), so
these three great galleys were consumed together,
sending fragments of burning stuff into the air and
down the wind; and such fierceness of heat was
engendered as, coming to us, who were on the east
headland, with the wind, scorched our faces, and often,
with the blinding smoke, somewhat hindered us of our
aim in firing.

In the meantime, we knew little or nothing of
how the fight was going, so thick was the smoke
and so deafening loud was the cannonade on both
sides. Yet we hoped for the best, in spite of the
great numbers of the enemy and their skill and
courage; for first, by my Lord's disposition of
his squadron, as each vessel lay broadside on to
any attack, he could not have his own ships
enfiladed (or as sailors say, raked) by the enemy's
fire, who, coming of necessity bow on, must needs
himself submit to be searched by our fire from
bow to stern: secondly, with shoal-water behind
them, our ships lay in no danger of being served as
we had the Admiral's ship earlier in the day;
namely, of finding an enemy on either beam. Our
main danger was their boarding of us, to which

course it appears the enemy from the first committed himself, running right upon our line, fouling our ships and sending his men aboard in huge numbers. Now, but for the enemy's mishaps, this policy must needs have been our undoing, as he could put on our board two men to our one, but what with the fouling of some of their ships, the stranding of others, and the great injury done them by the heavy cannon fire that issued from our deck and land batteries, he had but about thirteen or fourteen vessels (counting in this number some that had engaged the batteries) to, as a soldier might say, charge with. With these, nevertheless, he executed, as we afterwards learnt, very bloody work, and had not our Admiral foreseen and provided for this event, assuredly the day had been lost to us. My Lord, however, had moored his ships so closely, the bow of one a little overlapping the stern of her neighbour, that it was easy for the crews to climb from one to the other ; and being moored in still water, and the guns on the lee-side of the ships not requiring to be worked, he had the greater part of the crews idle and ready for service. These fellows he kept armed with their weapons ; to wit, pistols, hatchets, or cutlasses, prepared to resist boarders of their own ship or of their neighbours'. Now, had the enemy attacked all at once or nearly at once, this scheme had failed, but it takes but little acquaintance with warfare to know that, with all the accidents and misadventures of so hot a conflict in so narrow a

T

space, such concurrence in attack is not to be accomplished. So it fell out, for first three of the enemy came upon our ships with orders to break in and board, and presently after two more ; and from the first three, after receiving our fire and some stray shots perhaps from the batteries, there ran aboard our Flagship and one other some 300 or 400 men, and were met by nearly as many of the crews of the vessels they were attacking, and almost immediately reinforcements of 200 men came leaping in from our ships' consorts on either side, and the Turks, seeing they were outnumbered by two or more to one, retreated to their own ships, leaving no few dead and wounded behind them.

Then followed the next two ships meaning to board, with no better success, and so with some six or seven other of the Pirates, and the last of their boarders had got back into their vessels, not a little discomfited, by the time my troopers came up to help in the fight. We perceived by the gaping mouths of our ships' guns, all of a row, now black, now fiery, which we could still plainly see through the fog of the smoke as the strong gusts of wind blew it aside, that our men were firing quickly and steadily upon the enemy. As to hearing the guns singly or particularly we could not ; it was one enduring thunderous peal of artillery. Just then, when every cannon on either side was being momentarily discharged, when every pistol and every firelock that could be levelled at an enemy from either side was being fired and loaded again in hottest haste, when the noise and confusion was at its height, and the light of the burning ships was at its very greatest and reddest, bright as daylight, but a more terrible angry glare than ever yet proceeded from the luminous sun; just then there arose above all the roar of this fearful artillery, drowning and subduing it at once, a mighty rush of sound, as loud as the report of a thousand cannon fired at once. In the next instant all noise of battle was hushed and all the air grew dark as pitch. This sound and wind proceeded from the blowing up of the powder-room of the sunken flag-ship which the fire had reached, and the force of the outburst had blown the two ships that had fouled and grappled with her likewise through the water, extinguishing all burning wood therein, so that first the very ground shook beneath our feet; then the water of the bay rose in a mighty fluctuation. When it fell again and the sparks and burning splinters of timbers had rained down upon the bay, such a darkness fell on us (for the tar-barrels near the batteries had by this burnt out) as that none could see his hand if he held it close to his face, and no man could fire gun or pistol or cannon, for he could not so much as find his ammunition to lay his hand upon it, far less see his enemy. After this great shock and ex-plosion and the darkness that followed, not another shot was fired nor was any sound heard,—nay, not so much as a shout or a cry of any man; only now again we could hear the noises of the tempest, the

T 2

whistling of the wind through the rigging of the ships, and the splash of the waves upon the shore.

Thus did we remain for a long space, no man in this chaos of darkness and uncertainty knowing what to do next, or what next might happen, or how far from or how near him stood his deadly enemy, and no officer could see his men nor any man his officer; each holding the gun or pistol, discharged or just loading, or the rope he grasped, or the linstock or rammer in his hand, just as he held it when the shock came and the darkness fell. And no man of us all knew whether we were beaten or had conquered in this terrible fight.

We stood fixed thus for a space of time; then suddenly, while we all waited in expectancy in this deep and stagnant darkness, up rose the full and radiant moon, and we all did so little look to her showing so soon, forgetting how quickly pass the minutes of a battle, that we were taken aback, and for a space neither friend nor foe would stir, but stared upon her stupidly, as her fair round face up-reared itself from the sea; nor till her disk was fully above the horizon, and hung, a great lamp, to show us our situation, did any man move. Then one or two fired the guns or pistols they held still loaded, and one of our fellows put the match that still burned in his hand to the touch-hole of a cannon and fired it, and the shot seemed to awaken our senses, but less to fight anew than to look about us first and see how the battle had gone.

It was pretty evident to us and to the enemy too, that we had overmastered the Pirates. There were lying no fewer than three of their galleys stranded on the lee shore of the bay; two more had got, I know not well how, on the western side, but perhaps had run thither, by mischance, for safety in the confusion of the night, thinking to escape through the harbour mouth. They lay there on their beam ends, wrecked and helpless. Four more had sunk, under the heavy fires of our guns, in the midst of the bay, and only their masts were above water. The bay was covered with floating wreckage and splinters of blackened wood, and above a dozen boats of the Corsairs were upon the water, carrying the crews of the disabled ships to those galleys that still were sound. On the decks of all the galleys, and on our ships as well, were lying stretched the bodies of scores of dead and dying men. Our ships were still in their line, as I had seen them the night before; yet all were struck and some grievously damaged, with great holes of round shot in their hulls, and some had lost masts and spars, but none had foundered. All this I took in at a very quick glance under the full light of the rising moon. Then in a moment was the battle renewed, but 'twas from our side chiefly that came the shooting of great and small arms now, and very soon we gathered that the Pirates had no mind for more fighting, but were each by common accord, as it would seem (since we saw no signalling), resolved upon flight from this bay of most fatal omen to them.

The wind had now moderated and the sea somewhat gone down, and the remnant of the enemy's
galleys, and of this remnant three or four much
hurt by our shot, began to use their sweeps
with all the expedition they could ; and presently,
taking advantage of the slant of wind that entered
the harbour, they got under way and made off
to sea with less hurt and loss at the last than the
fury and zeal of our gunners to hinder their going
had promised, for but one more of their galleys was
disabled. This one, however, could not carry away
all the shot we had given her, and the very last
ball from the battery striking her between wind
and water was the straw that, 'tis said, breaks the
camel's back, and she quickly filled and sank in the
very entrance channel. Her boats landed her crew
of over 200 men on the western shore of the bay
without molestation from us, and our cavalry, riding
round again, were in time to surround them at the
landing, and they, seeing our superiority, surrendered
at discretion.

Would that this had been the last of the battle, for
surely with all our losses and the disablement for the
time of several of our ships, our victory was a very
great and glorious one, and we might have rested
under the laurels we had won in this great deliverance ; but alas! my Lord, *nil actum reputans dum
quid superesset agendum*—never satisfied while aught
of glory was to be reaped—would not stay quietly
while still the enemy was in sight, but sallied forth in

his Flagship with three other of the Corvettos in pursuit of the retreating galleys.

They had made to windward toward Tunis Bay, and having apparently no stomach for further fighting, did not turn back, though they must have seen that but four ships were pursuing them, and so the chase lasted as far as we could see ; the galleys, being on their best sailing point, had the legs of our ships (except one or two that lagged), and presently we lost sight of enemies and friends as well.

It was not till eight hours afterwards, being then about noon, that three of the Corvettos returned, towing two of the enemy's galleys as prizes, and bearing marks in damaged hulls and tattered sails of a hard fight. They brought the grievous news that the Flagship was sunk by the enemy, and all her crew, my Lord with them, taken prisoners. Their account was that in the chase, the Flagship, being the fastest sailer, had outpaced the others, and had overhauled first one, then another, of the enemy's galleys, which were flying in no order but a long straggling line ; these two vessels, having both received some damage in Port Niccolo and fleeing the slower, our Flagship had engaged both vessels one after another, disabling both, and had then sailed on after the others, signalling to her consorts to put prize crews into the captures and turn their heads homewards. When the Corvettos, which had been delayed a little in their obedience to this order, had come up with the Flagship, they found the whole fleet of galleys round about her. They

surmised that my Lord's ship had first been disabled
by an unlucky shot in a third encounter with a single
lagging ship of the enemy, and that the Pirate's consorts, seeing my cousin hard put to it, had come
round him and overwhelmed him with numbers ; but
the Flagship was already hull under when the third
encounter had taken place, and they had seen the
occurrence but very confusedly. They however lost
no time in coming up and joining in the fight ; but in a
very little time the Flagship was sunk by the continual
cannonading of the Pirates, and her crew, escaping
into their boats, were immediately taken prisoners.
The Corvettos were near enough to observe that my
Lord was among the captives, and they believed he
was wounded, but they did not think the wound could
be severe, for though his hand or arm was tied up, he
stood up in the boat, as if to give orders. Seeing that
they were like to be themselves overwhelmed by the
superior numbers of the enemy, who were still as three
to one of them, and that they could render no further
service to my kinsman, they sheered off and went
down the wind toward the Sicilian coast. For a little
while the Pirates followed, firing a shot or two, but
as the Corvettos could outsail them before the wind,
the enemy presently gave up the chase.

CHAPTER XX.

I WILL hasten over the narration of what followed immediately upon this disastrous news of my Lord's being taken captive thus in the very midst of his great crowning victory. The reader will very readily apprehend the disquiet and solicitude which we, his nearer friends, and I, his nearest friend of all and kinsman, felt upon this emergency. For a while the tidings went far and near that my Lord had died of his wounds in the Pirates' hands, and the news came in such authentic shape, though roundabout, from the African coast, after about a month of waiting, that we could not but believe it; and I grieved for my dear kinsman as one that was lost and gone for ever. Then came a swift galley into Palermo harbour, bearing a herald's flag, to deliver a special message to the Viceroy, which was that my Lord was recovered of his wound, was being treated in accordance with his high rank and great exploits, and that he had listened favourably to overtures made to him to take service with the Bey of Tunis. I knew very well that this was a foul lie, knowing my Lord's honour and

his fealty to the Christian faith ; but to the Sicilian
Lords, say what I would, it seemed no improbable
circumstance or unreasonable belief (so low were they
sunk in their iniquitous schemes of life) that a Christian gentleman and a soldier of his King should
condescend to service with a Miscreant and a Pirate !
But in my sudden joy in knowing of my dear
kinsman's health and safety, I somewhat overlooked
this lying traducement of him, and that he was still a
captive in the hands of an inexorable and cruel
enemy, and the conclusion of the message, which was
that the Pirates were still willing to treat for the
ransom of their prisoner ; and the terms they offered
for his tradition were the restoration of the Corsair
Admiral El Saida, whom we had captured, and
of all the galleys taken by the Sicilians, with their
guns and crews, and in addition the sum of 500,000
gold doubloons. Now, when we considered the
worth to them of their own great Admiral, and
that this sum was more than could be raised by
the whole revenues of Sicily (nay, it is doubtful if
the Treasury of Spain itself could then have furnished
as much without great wringing and delay), we concluded that it was but another way of saying that
they had no mind to part with their captive for a
while. Either they hoped to convert him to their infamous faith and to use his genius for war on their side,
or they feared to have so terrible an enemy against
them, who, if he should extend his warfare beyond
Sicily, was like to close all the Mediterranean Sea to

their adventuring as completely as he already had the coasts and waters of Sicilia. This surmise we learnt afterwards was the true one, and they were resolved not to part with him on any terms ; no, not even to get back their own famous Admiral El Saida, whom the Sicilian Viceroy freely offered to deliver up as ransom, with every ship we had captured in the late engagement.

The mention of this reminds me that I have been in such haste to record this most tragic event of the capture of my Lord, that I have not related the ending of the fight, nor struck the true account of losses and gains, as a soldier chronicler must do after a battle, no less duly than a merchant after a trading adventure ended.

When the Pirates had fled and we began to look into our own lists of killed and wounded, we found fewer than we expected, 115 only between dead and hurt, and of these but 22 killed outright : this among the sailors only. Our troops had lost but 2 killed and 7 wounded, these losses being in the fight by the sea-shore. Of the enemy's loss in killed and wounded, we knew little or nothing, but the steady firing from our guns, batteries, and small arms must have told upon them heavily : over eighty dead and desperately wounded lay upon the sea-shore after the night skirmish. The lightly wounded had escaped into the woods, and the crews of several of the disabled and stranded galleys had likewise escaped ashore and hidden. Their haunts were revealed to us by the peasants as those of so many ravenous wild beasts ; and searching the coasts and shore forests, we picked up no fewer than 470 of these unhappy runaways,—among them their Admiral, who had escaped at the very first, when my Lord took his ship. This, with the 200 taken by my troops as already recounted, raised the number of our prisoners to between 600 or 700, in exact number to 687.

But it was in captured galleys that the fruits of our victory was so great. To begin with, we had utterly destroyed by burning three of the Pirates' Fleet. There were in all five galleys stranded which we got off after lightening them of their guns, and found them, with some patching, still seaworthy. Five more were sunk in the harbour, but as the water was not above a fathom deep over their decks, and the bottom hard, we raised them easily by filling and emptying of great barges lashed to their sides. Our Corvettos had likewise brought back the two prizes taken by my Lord on his last ill-fated cruise. This made fifteen vessels of which we had deprived the enemy, of which twelve were fit to take the sea. After staying some days in Port Niccolo, to repair the shot-holes in our own vessels and to raise and clean the sunken galleys, we put to sea, and brought our prizes and our prisoners safely into Messina Harbour. I will not speak of the elation of the people at this astounding victory over the Pirates, and the saving of them from the terror of a Pirates' invasion ; but 'twas a joy mingled with tribulation and with forebodings that, without his help who had gained them this great deliverance, their lot would shortly be as unhappy as before.

The Viceroy had, since the battle of Port Niccolo, graciously accorded me several private audiences, at which his Grace spoke very freely of the defence of the coasts and the affairs of the navy; no doubt as conceiving that I had been imbued with the ideas of my Lord, and might, therefore, carry on the campaign against the Rovers, as it were, by procuration. At length his Grace was pleased to speak out very openly.

"Captain St. Keyne," says he, "'tis very plain that, whatever happens in this Island, your illustrious kinsman will never again command the active forces of Sicily; it not being to be supposed that the Corsairs of the African Coast will set free a prisoner who has in these few months done them more harm, and caused their fame more disparagement, than has come to them within the last hundred years. They will either persuade him to conform to their own faith" ("That they will never do," quoth I), "and they will then," said his Grace, not noticing my interruption, "give him the command of their navies" ("He would die first, your Grace," I cried), "or," the Viceroy went on, smiling a little at my lack of courtliness, "should he refuse, imprison him for his life-time in one of their inland fortresses." ("'Tis very sad," said I, shaking my head.) "It is the most melancholy circumstance in the world," said the Viceroy, "but it

behoves me to think what I can do in this great misfortune that has come upon the Island. Now," says
he, " Captain St. Keyne, I have had evidence enough
of the ability, diligence, and loyalty you have displayed under your kinsman, and I do hereby offer to you
the same command over the land and sea forces of
this Island as was held by Lord St. Keyne, until such
time as his Lordship may happily return to us, of
which, however, I will say that I see at present not
the very slightest chance or prospect."

I bowed to his Grace, for in truth speech was denied
me for a time at the strangeness and greatness of this
offer ; but I hastened to give his Grace to understand,
after humbly thanking him for his condescension, that
though I trusted he had not over-estimated my
loyalty to him or my diligence in his service, both of
which, I declared, were second only to those I bore to
my King and my General, he had nevertheless vastly
over-rated my ability for such a high command. " I
am," said I, "a critic of war, and can perhaps (like
many another) make shift to follow where a good
lead has been given me ; but I would have your
Excellency to observe that in this campaign, as in all
well-conducted ones, the enemy have every time been
defeated because some wholly new-imagined stratagems had been executed against them, and in their
execution carried out with prevision of the smallest
particulars. Now," said I, " when once a stratagem of
war has been displayed and is known to the enemy, its
value is gone, and need is, in fresh operations, to

imagine and think out fresh devices and inventions, and to accomplish them and consummate them to the very last detail, anticipating every chance of their hindrance or of their prevention ; and this, your Excellency, is the secret of the art of war, and per-adventure of many other arts known to man ; and in this my kinsman was supreme, and I am in no sense worthy to take his place."

The Viceroy was pleased to smile, perhaps at my entering upon so uncourtierlike a tractation *de scientiâ militari.*

" I was fully prepared, Captain St. Keyne," said his Grace, " by your known modesty, for your refusal of my offer. I did not in truth the least count upon your acceptance of it, but I desired by offering you this command to show you how truly I value your services and confide in your loyalty to my person. You are already in command, under Lord St. Keyne as Generalissimo, of the land forces created for the defence of the Island. I desire that you now continue in this command, owning therein no superior officer except myself."

I kissed his Grace's hand upon my acceptance of his gracious offer.

CHAPTER XXI.

I HAVE now to enter upon a matter which, though it has been pressing upon me for some time back, I have deferred because it likes me not to touch upon it, or upon matters kindred thereto. The Reader, if he is of the way of thinking that some who suppose they know me are (though erroneously), and who consider me a churlish and ungallant person, may guess that here is to come some talk of women and their ways. Well, I would it were not! Not so much for any real antipathy I have to them and their practices, as for my great ignorance of both, and that I am so given to plain speaking on all occasions as I fear is exceedingly displeasing to themselves (why, I must leave the Reader to determine!). Moreover, so poor a hand am I at flattering as that the civilest woman must in her heart wish me at the devil fifty times in a day, had I the hardihood or desire to give her time and leisure enough to form so many as fifty wishes in my presence : which same hardihood and desire (again to avoid flattery) I am removed by an incredible distance from possessing.

The matter then, to come to the point, is that as women of all ages conceive that their chief business and interest in this world is that of marrying, being married, or giving in marriage (Lord! how well it would be if they would let us alone, but 'tis no matter), so my aunt, and my Lord's, the Lady Priscilla Scudamour, sister of the late Earl of Scudamour, and who is the lady that I have already mentioned in the beginning of this narrative as being the Abbess of the House of St. Scholastica, near the Groyne in Galicia of Spain, could not rest content till she had found a match for our little cousin Geraldine, whom we had confided to her charge.

It was about six weeks before the events of which I have now told, that my Lord received a letter from the aforesaid Lady Priscilla, in which, with as much formality as if she were a sovereign Prince treating for the cession of a town or Province with another Potentate, she informed us that a lady of high rank in Madrid, and of her acquaintance, naming a certain Duchess, had signified to her that His Grace the Viceroy of Sicily, cousin of the said Duchess, had, at her (the Duchess's) recommendation and instance, expressed his willingness to contract a matrimonial alliance with the distinguished family of Scudamour. His Grace was a widower and without a direct heir. Then did the reverend Lady Abbess consider which of her several marriageable nieces and cousins dispersed in several Convents in Spain, France, and the

Low Countries, was worthiest of an alliance with a
cavalier who belonged to one of the noblest families
of Spain, was a Grandee of the most distinguished
renown, and in the flower of his age (the Viceroy
being then not above fifty-eight years and ten
months). Finally she had fixed upon her niece the
Lady Geraldine Scudamour. All this she conveyed
at very wearisome length to my kinsman, and having
fully made up her own mind to the projected *con-
sorcium*, she now requested the formality of my Lord's
consent, as the young lady's sole guardian and nearest
male relative.

Now the first effect of this communication upon my
Lord had been to throw him into an unbounded rage,
in which unphilosophic state I found myself, to my
own no small surprise, likewise involved ; and together
we strode up and down the apartment, each of us
using expressions wholly improper to be applied to
the Head of a Religious House, and which therefore I
shall take the liberty not to record on this page. We
agreed that our little cousin Geraldine was still but a
child, in regard to whom to raise the question of
marriage was an absurdity ; further that our elder
kinswoman was a meddlesome and impertinent old
woman ; thirdly, we were of accord that even if our
cousin had been of an age to be married, it was a
monstrous extravagance to propose to marry a sweet,
innocent young English girl to a man of the Viceroy's
years and appearance. For though he was a man still
strong and hearty, he carried his age but heavily,

having neither in his carriage, which was slow and unwieldy, nor in his face, which was pale and care-worn, nor in his aspect anything to remind the observer that he had ever been young, and active, and lusty. Presently, however, we began to reckon the months which had passed since we had parted from our cousin Geraldine, then little over fifteen years old, and though tall and slim, still but a child ; and it was a surprise to us both to find how time had passed, and that the child of nearly three years ago was now a woman of eighteen. My kinsman fell into a study, and for a time said nothing.

"These matters, Cousin Humphrey," he said presently, "are women's politics, and it is not for us to resolve them ; but, I know not why I say it, 'twill be more than I can bear to see the child (so he would still call her) the wife of our Viceroy. Why is that, do you suppose ?"

"It is natural enough," I said ; "a young girl, unknowing of the ways of the world, should not be advised into marrying a man old enough nearly to be her grandfather, and it goes against the grain with you to let such a thing come to pass."

"That must be the reason," he said, "and I will refuse my consent. And yet the girl might wish it. 'Tis a grand marriage ; it is making her almost a queen. Consider, Humphrey, a girl rising from a Convent, at a bound, almost to a throne."

We spoke no more on the matter, but I could see it was deep in my cousin's thoughts.

A few days after this discourse of ours, my cousin received a letter from Geraldine herself. It was a sweet letter, and an artless one. She had been told, she said, of the marriage proposed for her; she had no wish to marry. She was not discontented with the Convent, where she had many friends, though it was in truth a trifle dull and doleful, and though she felt no calling towards a religious life. Her aunt had spoken to her of this marriage as of a thing which for her own sake, for her family's sake, and for her Convent's sake she ought not to refuse. She did not know how to decide. Her kinsman had always been her truest and dearest friend, as well as her nearest relative : " What you tell me to do, Ralph," wrote the child, " I will do. I will obey you in this as in everything, and I will obey no one else, for I love no one else in the world but only you. Advise me what I am to do, for I trust only in you, but if you can advise me not to consent to this marriage I shall be very glad. If you tell me I am not to marry any one at all, you will make me very happy."

My kinsman said nothing as to this letter, but he thought upon it very earnestly, and was troubled. After pondering for two or three days, which was a thing uncommon in him, for he was used to resolve all questions swiftly, he answered his kinswoman, and showed me the letter.

I thought it cold, and less kind than I should have expected in him. He told her that he desired her happiness before everything, but that in the matter of

a woman's marrying or not marrying he did not see
that it was possible for him to advise her one way or
the other. From him especially, advice could not
come with any wisdom, for the subject was one apart
from his meditations. From one who had considered
marriage in a single aspect only, which was that he
was resolutely set on avoiding it for himself, no sound
counsel could issue. She must resolve the matter in
accordance with her own inclinations, and the opinions
she had been brought up to form. It was some years
since he had seen and known her; she was then a
child, she was now a woman. The child he had
known and still knew well, and loved: the woman,
her present self, was wholly unknown to him. He
could not judge for her. In one respect only could
he help her; he could tell her what he knew of the
Viceroy. He had served under him, and he could
say that he was a man to be respected for his ex-
pertness and moderation in affairs of State. His
manners were courtly and gentle, befitting his birth,
which was very high: his wealth was great; his present office in Sicily gave him almost kingly state, and
power, and rank. His age was over fifty-eight, his
health and strength were seemingly good, but his
figure was bent and his gait slow, as of an even older
man. To most women wifehood with such a man
might well be beyond all their dreams of wealth and
splendour; to others, not so: it was for her to make
her election. This was how the letter ran.

Remembering how Ralph had loved the child in

former days, how tender and pitiful his fondness had been for her, she being an orphan ; how between these two cousins and nearest relatives (they having none nearer in parentage than each other), she a child, he not much more than a boy, and that in their equal forlornness a very uncommon affection had grown up between them, I marvelled at the coldness of his letter. It seemed to me that he must have used some constraint over himself to write so hardly to one whose memory, as I well knew, from many small casual mentionings of her, was still so green and fresh with him.

This letter-writing had come in an idle time, some weeks before the news of the intended invasion of us by the Moors. That urgent business put the matter out of my thoughts, but not (as I had imagined it had) out of my Lord's, for on the very day we were sailing along the Sicilian coast to Port Niccolo, chased by the Pirates' fleet, he said to me, " Humphrey, this will be the sharpest affair we have yet had, and after it I purpose to leave Sicily ; that is, if—" He delayed a little with his speech.

" If ? " said I, resuming his last word, " If what ? "

" If Geraldine marries the Viceroy. If she were to become his wife, I should not desire to live here."

" Why not ? " I asked him.

He hesitated a little over his reason, and finally gave none.

" Why," he said, " if she were living here in the Palace, the Viceroy's wife, I should not desire to be in Sicily also."

He said no more, and these words were all that passed between us in the matter.

Then occurred the great fight at Port Niccolo, my kinsman's pursuit of the enemy, and his capture by the Pirate Fleet.

During the first month or so after this, and before we got the message from the African coast, it was, as I have noticed before, very confidently noised abroad that my Lord was dead ; and this news reaching Spain, as I had afterwards occasion to know it did, decided my young kinswoman to give way to the insistence of her aunt, there having been no advice against it in her guardian's letter. So now I learnt from the Viceroy himself that the Lady Geraldine had agreed to become his wife, and that on his proceeding to Madrid in about a year's time the wedding would there take place. A little while after, a letter from Geraldine reached me, confirming this news. She lamented her cousin's melancholy fate ; but the letter was short and very sad (I thought) and spiritless, unlike her who was by nature always light of heart, both in spoken and in written speech.

So far then had this matter gone when we got the happy announcement of my kinsman's safety and of his health, but, alas ! he was a close prisoner.

Ever after this I gave myself no rest in devising and rejecting and devising again plans and plots to procure his release ! but no invention that I could hit upon seemed even to myself to have any possibility in it of good issue. I inquired of some who had

themselves been captives of the Turks, and afterwards
ransomed, to tell me of any scheme by which, either
through boldness, cunning, or the profuse spending
among them of gold in subornation of his keepers
and castellans, it might be possible to win him his
freedom. They said they could hardly remember of
a prisoner escaping from the Pirates of Tunis, so close
was the custody and so contrary to the interests and
avarice of all the people was it to wink upon an
escaping prisoner, and so far too from their cruel
nature to pity a Christian captive. But as for my
Lord, who was worth to them a King's ransom, it was
not conceivable but that he should be guarded with
uncommon vigilance and wariness, in some high-
walled, deep-moated castle, of which the Tunisians
had many score in their country. I asked if they
knew where such a prisoner as my kinsman would in
most likelihood be impounded. They said they knew
not. There were gaols and dungeons for prisoners
new taken at a certain town named Bizerta where
the ships' arsenals were, which town lay some few
leagues north of the great city of Tunis ; but they
agreed that for so esteemed a captive it was more
likely the Bey would find a securer imprisonment in
the city itself, and in some gaol or castle near his
Palace, where he might, no doubt, touch with his
prisoner upon the matter of his conversion to the
Moslem Faith, and his entry into the service of the
Pirates, and where the prisoner would constantly be
under the eyes of the officers of the Bey's own body-

guard. This was a very heavy discouragement to me, and I had perforce to give up all hopes of attempting any rescue of my kinsman by force or by guile ; but I nevertheless did not wholly abandon my projects, though I could never put them into any practicable shape. Then did the months go slowly forward ; very gloomily to me, no sign or token ever coming from my kinsman ; and I saw myself obliged to yield up my last expectations of doing somewhat for his help.

It was five months after his being taken, and three months and three weeks after our receipt of news that he was alive and well, that one day as I was passing through the town of Messina with a part of my troop, the corporal who rode behind me was accosted by one in the habit of a seafaring man, who asked if I were not Captain St. Keyne, and being told I was, the fellow begged to have speech of me on a matter of importance. Now it had ever been my Lord's custom to be easy of access to all kinds and conditions of men, as often being able to gather from the lowly some whisper of things going amiss and some hint as to a reform of them ; so, desiring to follow him in this as in everything, I pulled up my horse, and, " Well, Sir," said I, in Italian, " in what can I serve you ? " The fellow looked about him, and seeing none within earshot (for our men had fallen back to let him come to my horse's bridle rein), " Captain St. Keyne," said he, in good broad English, but dropping his voice almost to a whisper, " I come direct from your kinsman, Lord St. Keyne, and I have a message for you."

Now, I do not pretend to have a stronger command over my behaviour in public than another; still when a man is a seasoned soldier and has been through fire and slaughter, he counts upon some proper restraint of himself, and in truth I have no reason in general to complain of myself on this score. This sudden speech of the stranger however so took me aback that I protest I turned dizzy and had some ado to sit steady on my horse; but I commanded myself and thought what I would do next, and then I spoke, calmly enough.

"Walk by my horse's side, Sir, I pray you; a hundred yards from this are the barracks, where we intend an hour's halt." Then I put the troop in motion again, and carried the stranger with me through the barrack gates. He was a black-bearded man of forty or so, his face roughened by sun and wind; he was dressed like an Italian sailor, and wore a little red peaked cap, in the mode of the southern Italians; but for all his darkness, his beard and his garb, there was Englishman written in his looks as plainly as I could hear it in his speech. As soon as we were in private, I questioned the English sailor, for so I fancied him to be, and this is what he told me.

"I am an Englishman from Poole in Dorsetshire, and I was brought up to the trade of shipbuilding. Business being slack at home, I was offered work in the arsenal of Antwerp and after that at Trieste, where I worked profitably as master shipwright five years and married a wife. I was then offered employment at Naples, and travelling to this latter city by sea, was captured by a Corsair in the Adriatic some two years ago and carried to Tunis. There I have worked at shipbuilding in the Bey's arsenal, and my ransom being fixed at only thirty gold doubloons (for I took care to hide from them that I had any particular skill), I procured this sum through my Italian wife and some friends at Trieste, and became a free man. A little before my going I heard of the capture of the famous Sicilian Admiral, Lord St. Keyne, and his crew. The crew are already sold for slaves and dispersed, and I know no more of them, but the Lord was kept prisoner first at Bizerta and latterly in the Castle at Tunis. The Pirates guard him closely, and yet for reasons of their own, give him some considerable liberty, as of examining the city, and the ships, and conversing through an Italian interpreter with the people ; for 'tis well known they have no will to allow his ransom for any sum whatever, and they hope in time he will consent to take service with them. I had some occasions to have speech with his Lordship, who, knowing that I was about to regain my liberty, confided to me the coming hither and the communicating to you of a scheme he had formed for his escape, with some five or six of his fellow captives of all nations."

" Stay, Sir !" cried I, " let me understand this

matter a little better. Am I to take it from you
that my Lord by direct word of mouth to you has
conveyed a message to me ? "

"He has, Sir, no longer than ten days since, for
there happened to be in Tunis Port an aviso ship
from the Knights Hospitallers of Malta, treating of
the ransom and release of certain prisoners, and
by them I was carried with some fourscore other
ransomed prisoners to the Island of Malta, which is,
as your Honour knows, not two days' sail from
hence."

Now, desirous as I was to believe this good news
of the stranger, I could not hide from myself that
there was room here for treachery of a kind to which
these perfidious Miscreants of Africa are but too prone ;
and so it behoved me not to be entrapped into doing
what might bring trouble to my Lord, and destruction
or captivity to those who might seek to give him mistaken help.

"My friend," said I to the Englishman, "I believe
in my heart you are an honest man, but you are too
well acquainted with the Turks not to know that it
behoves all those who have dealings with them to
be wary——"

The stranger interrupted me here with "Sir, I am
expecting a question from you which you have not
yet put, and which, being answered by me, should set
your reasonable doubts at rest." He smiled upon me
as he said these words.

"Ha !" cried I, "I had forgot. Do I see you come

to that? Then show me the token that you are a true man indeed, and the faithful ambassador of my cousin."

On this he opened his shirt and took in his hand a little round package made of leather neatly sewn round and hanging from his neck by a thong of the same piece of leather. He had a great clasp knife hanging by a yarn round his middle after the fashion of sailors, and setting the edge of the blade against the seam of the little package, he cut through threads and all and laid bare a silver coin of nearly the bigness of an English crown, which, without a word, he handed to me.

It was a silver ducat of Venice, and worn pretty smooth. I took it in my hand and carried it to the window to look closely at some marks scratched upon its surface, but the rather, I will honestly confess it, to hide from the stranger, while my back was turned upon him, the signs of the perturbation of my spirits into which this matter of the coin had thrown me.

Holding the coin so that the light shone slantingly upon it, I could very plainly see, scratched thereon with the point of a knife or dagger, a shape of an escutcheon, and drawn across that a band or belt with three little diamonds thereon depicted.

Now, that the reader may understand the meaning of all this, I must tell him of an understanding between my cousin and myself so long ago that it was before ever my cousin had seen a sword drawn in anger. It

was in England, and when he and I were riding through
the western counties to join the Royalists then in
Cornwall under Sir Bevil Greenvil. The boy was
jesting with me after his wont (his humour being ever
sprightly and merry) and his head being then filled with
the extravagance of the tales of Knights Errant and
the like, and set upon considering only the glory and
magnificence and romance of war, little recking how
dreary is the reality ;—" If ever we are parted, Cousin
Humphrey," said the child (for in truth he was little
more), "and you are taken captive by the enemy and
desire to send word to me where you be, how shall I
make sure that your messenger is a true man and to
be trusted ? "

"Why, Ralph," said I, " I cannot tell."

" Well," said the boy very seriously, "your messenger must bring from you a sign or token that he is
a true man, as you will remember was done by Arnaldo
in the tale of Garvin de Montglane, who, being taken
prisoner by the infidel Soldan of Lombardy, the
messenger was known to be no traitor because he
brought Arnaldo's cross-handled dagger, with seven
notches made by him on the blade. Now, Humphrey,
should you ever be taken prisoner and desire to have
word with me, do you send me either a smooth pebble,
or a coin, or a shell, or any like thing, on which you
have emblazoned with the point of your dagger the
charges on our shield ; and by that token shall I know
the messenger to be the messenger of truth, and I
swear to you, Humphrey," cried the boy, lifting his

hand to Heaven, "that, after getting that token, I will die, but I will work your release."

I had, I will confess, forgotten this idle talk, but Ralph reminded me of it on that very last day before the fight at Port Niccolo, as we were running down the coast with the enemy in hot pursuit. In our flight we purposely kept our Corvetto hindmost of our squadron and nearest the enemy; my kinsman and I sitting together on the taffrail through this long and idle day, from early dawn to near sunset, devising of many things that had befallen us in our late busy life, for seldom had we had in the thick of our doings and our many separations so full leisure for talk as we had that day while we sat there waiting for the white tower of Palu to show over our bows. Be sure I often went over afterwards everything that happened that last day. I remember how the white and grey sea-birds flew in circles above our heads and we watched them, and Ralph ever and anon, in the lightness of his humour, would throw pieces of biscuit into the waves, and laughed to see the birds swoop down and plunge, and struggle together for their prize. "Humphrey," said he to me all of a sudden, "do you remember when we rid together to the wars across Dartmoor in Devonshire, and that which we agreed upon then?" and he reminded me of what I have said above. "Remember," said he, "if you are taken by the Turks, you are to send to me the tracing with a dagger-point of our arms, and that will be a token that there is no Turkish deceit in the thing." Now the blazon of the St. Keyne arms is *argent on a fess azure three fusils of the first;* and this is what I found very plainly inscribed upon the coin.

I turned round to the stranger, and took him by the hand : " Friend," said I, "give me my cousin's message."

CHAPTER XXII.

"MY Lord St. Keyne," said John Fowler (for that was this honest fellow's name) "besought me to go straight to you in Sicily, to tell you freely who I was and whence I came, and if you should show any suspicions of me (as my Lord said you would, Sir). I was to deliver to you this coin. He bid me tell you this ; that he is not so well guarded in Tunis city but that he has very good hopes of giving those about him the slip, and that he has entered into a plot with some other Christian captives for their escape on a particular night in the coming month of December, namely, on Christmas Eve. His Lordship wishes you to procure a swift galley, man it with a crew of trustworthy men, disguising them in the dress of Moroccans, and run boldly on the afternoon of that day into the strait or channel, named Goletta, which leads from the Bay of Tunis into the great lake whereon is situate the city itself. Now, you are so to time your visit as to be running up the aforesaid Strait of Goletta a little before sunset, and to drop your anchor about a mile from the great fortress which

X

lies on its north shore. If you advance farther, you
will be boarded and examined by the officers of the
Port, and should that threaten, you will immediately
put to sea again and escape ; but if not, you will bide
where you are till dawn, and nothing happening by
then, depart for the time ; but if all goes well, my
Lord will that night give his keepers the slip, and at
a little past midnight come aboard you in a boat."

He added to this some further instructions for our
conduct which I need not here set down.

" It is well," said I, "all this can I do very easily,
save in one matter I fear a mistake. Who shall pilot
us in these waters which no Christian navigator ever
goes into to come out again ? "

" My Lord," said Mr. Fowler, " has provided for
this, and has undertaken with a pilot who will be
waiting for you at the end of the great Bay an hour
or so before sunset on Christmas Eve. He will
show a small white flag as he nears you, and to
your questions will give you the watchword ' *Sicilia*.'
He will then board your galley and show you exactly
where you are to drop your anchor in the Goletta
channel to wait for my Lord."

It was now the 20th of November, and we had
therefore a month and more to get ready in. It
happened that we had taken from the Corsairs some
time before a small galley, so fine in the lines of
her hull, and therefore so swift, that had the wind
been moderate, we should never have overhauled her ;
but we chanced to come upon her in that great Bight

wherein lies Catania, where we had the weather gauge
of her, and the wind blowing almost a gale from
S.S.E., she could not escape from us, and we took her
without a shot fired. This vessel, from her crankness
and lightness, my Lord would not commission to be
part of our squadron, but had a mind to re-fit her
some day for his private use, and so bought her back
from the Treasury, but for some reason nothing was
done with her, and she now lay idle in the Harbour
of Palermo.

Repairing thither, I laid the whole matter before
the Viceroy, and begged him to allow me to put a
crew of our best men into this little galley, and with
them endeavour at the rescue of my kinsman. His
Grace was very willing, but advised me to let no word
get abroad of our purpose until we were about to sail ;
" For," said he, " the Corsairs have spies here, as we
well know, and you are to bear in mind that with a
fair wind a boat can reach the African shore in three
or four days, and you might find the Tunisians
prepared to counterplot you."

I therefore set about all my preparations with due
caution and secrecy. I fresh rigged and victualled
the galley entirely at our own expense, furnishing
her with sweeps as well as sails. I christened her
the *Golondrina*, which is Spanish for *Swallow*, a name
that might typify the little vessel's lightness and
swiftness. We then drafted into her, with his Grace's
leave, some 150 of the smartest and best of the sailors
of the fleet, this being a very large crew, seeing that

we meant no fighting, but my purpose was to man the sweeps very strongly in the case arising of our finding ourselves becalmed or with a contrary wind in Tunis Bay.

On the 6th of December, all being in readiness, I put to sea for a cruise, to practise the crew and to see how the galley behaved. We ran round the coast from Palermo and in and out of the harbours of Messina, Catania, and Syracuse, one after the other, for I designed to make the crew as handy and smart as I could in this sort of work ; and I had reason to be well pleased with both men and ship.

Five days before Christmas-tide we put to sea from Syracuse, having, as I calculated, a voyage of between 300 and 350 miles to Goletta, but the wind was favourable ; namely, a five-knot breeze from nearly due east. So soon as we were out of harbour, I shortened sail and calling the men together told them shortly whither we were bound. I had as yet taken none into my confidence but the Captain of the ship, a very honest Genoese, and his Lieutenant, who happened to be his own brother. Jan Loots was of the crew, being a very cool-headed man not likely to fail me in a sudden strait, and him likewise I had told what voyage we were upon. None of these three had made any cavil at the enterprise, but I feared it might appear to the men but a desperate business, as I was expounding its nature to them, though the Captain had told me not to fear they would hang back, for the confidence they had in any scheme of their *Capitano* (meaning my Lord), and because the hatred they had of the cruel Corsairs would ever over-power their terror of them. In spite of the Captain's telling me this, I say, I was a little half-hearted about their consent. " My lads," said I, addressing them, " I am aware 'tis a desperate venture we are upon, for we are going to put our heads into the lion's mouth ; but 'tis to save your *Capitano* from these black-hearted devils of Corsairs, and it is his own commands you will be following if you continue upon this voyage, for it is he who has ordered beforehand every step we are to take." Then I told them of all we were to do ; how we were to disguise ourselves as Turks, stain our arms and faces, how we were to meet a Pilot and where, and all the rest of it. I then said :—" It is a perilous service, and if any of you think the danger too great, there is a boat here that will serve to carry back to land any who fear to go on with us." But looking closely on their faces and seeing no signs of flinching, " *Per Dio!* " cried I (which is a little oath for ever in their own mouths) smiling upon them, " I perceive that for this service a very little boat will suffice ! "

In truth, no man thought of holding back ; so I ordered full sail to be put on the ship, and, with some little variations of the wind and weather, we made Cape Bon on the morning of the third day of our voyage, and lay off the Cape till very early on the morning of Christmas Eve ; having then still, as I imagined, some 60 miles to travel, with a favouring breeze on our beam.

I had provided red skull-caps for the men, such as the Moroccans wear, and such clothes as are in common use by all the sailors of the Barbary Coast, to wit, loose trousers, gathered at the ankle, and such like, we having great store of such apparel captured in the Turkish galleys. I had likewise provided a stain of an infusion of walnuts, wherewith we every one of us (except some half-a-dozen of the Italians, whom nature and the wind and sun had already stained as dark as any blackamoor), every one of us, I say, washed our hands, arms and faces with this brown juice, and we came out, what with our baggy breeches and red caps, and the great crimson sashes wound about our middles, with pistols stuck therein, such villainous-looking rogues as our very mothers would not have known for Christian men. At all which doings our lighthearted sailors laughed and jested, despising and forgetting (like brave men) the imminent peril they were running into.

Tunis is, as I believe I have mentioned before, a gathering place of all the Barbary Pirates, from Tangiers in the far west to Tripoli in the east; and in that circumstance we hoped to find our safety, for any Turks who should see us would judge us from a distance to be of a kindred nation to their own. In the Bay we passed not a few Corsair galleys, some at anchor, some standing out to sea; and we were not afraid to pass quite close to them or even to answer their hail, for we had one or two on board who could speak their tongue; one in especial.

a Spaniard of Malaga, who had passed eighteen years of his youth and manhood in captivity at Tetuan in Morocco, and spoke their dialect as well as or better than his own. This fellow, who had a present wit, answered the hail of one great galley that passed us outward bound, and he told us afterwards what their talk had been. " Where from, and what luck ? " cried the Pirates. " From the Sicily coast," answered our disguised Spaniard, " and very good luck we have met with. We have 150 Christians on board at this moment." " Allah is great ! " cried the stranger, " and you were wise to go there now that we have got their great *Capitano* (whom may Sheitan confound !) a prisoner in our hands." " Ha ! " cried our Spaniard, " but they say he is about to return ! " " Never fear ! " cried they, " the Bey is too wise for that."

I was glad when the galley passed out of hearing, and learning our interpreter's raillery, desired him to be more chary of his tongue for the future.

The wind was variable from light to almost nothing, and as we had plenty of time to get to the head of the Bay before nightfall, I went forward with as little spread of canvas as might be ; fearing to anchor and wait, lest some inquisitive boatman or fisherman should board us. We conjectured a storm to be brooding, for there was a blackness in the sky toward the south, and the heat was great for the time of year. We went on thus in a very leisurely manner, to time our coming to the Goletta Channel to nearly sunset.

As we came to the head of the bay we kept a sharp

look-out for the pilot-boat that was to show us the signal flag. Several crossed our bows and hailed us, but each time our Spaniard, by my ordering, put them off, and we carried on till presently one fellow ran across very close, and as my eye was upon him, I saw he showed a little bit of a white rag for a moment between the gunwale of his boat and the water. I immediately stopped the way of the galley, and he hailed us. I bid the Spaniard ask him if he had any business with us, and one of the two men in the boat stood up looking hard at us for a bit as if he were doubtful of us, but presently he sang out " *Sicilia.*" Then we took him and his boat-mate on board, and towed their boat. Neither of the two would say much; and I, doubting still how far they were to be trusted, ordered the crew to go forward, and the Spaniard to interpret for me with the head man of the two.

"Ask him," said I, "what orders he has."

" To pilot the galley into the Goletta, and show the right anchoring ground."

"Where is that ?" I asked.

"About a mile this side of the fort," said he.

"Will the officers come aboard this evening?"

"Not if we get to our moorings at nightfall."

"Should we shorten sail?"

He nodded. It was then less than an hour of sundown,and we had got into the narrow channel they call Goletta.

He stood on the roundhouse with the Captain, myself, and the man at the helm, giving his directions very quietly, after the manner of pilots, with a motion of his hand this way and that. Presently he pointed to the fort now three miles away : it was already falling dark, the blackness of the sky somewhat advancing the time of dusk, the wind being gusty at times, and then calm again, presaging with the blackness overhead a thunderstorm. At our pilot's direction we dropped our anchor opposite the fort, and at the same moment the clouds were cloven asunder with a lightning flash. It thundered very quickly upon the flash, and the rain began to come down thick and steady. It was so dark already, what with storm and rain and nightfall, that we could not see the shore on either side. Thought I, this could not happen better. The little boats about us now began to run for shore, fearing the gusts of wind, and I saw there was little danger of any officers boarding us while this weather lasted.

We waited patiently till midnight, listening in the lulls of the tempest for any sounds of a boat putting off from shore. The storm continued, and the wind got so heavy that I feared at one time for our moorings, and at another that in so wild a night no boat could pass across the water. Of this, though, there was the less peril, as the wind, which was chiefly westerly, was partly off the north shore of the channel, which here runs about east and west, and we under its shelter; therefore, though we felt the wind strong, there was no room for any heavy sea to get up. I had let the men have their supper and turn in, for I knew not what work might not lie before them ; but an hour before midnight I had all hands piped on deck.

It was a little past midnight, and our eyes were now fixed most earnestly upon the shore, whence we expected the first signs of a boat putting off, when we saw lights glancing hurriedly to and fro on land just below the Fort. This made us uneasy, for it was from thence, as John Fowler had warned us, that my Lord's boat would come, and we thought it strange he should let lights show at so momentous a time, and the Fort and soldiers so close. Presently after, we saw lanterns carried here and there in the Fort itself, and a gun was fired after that, seemingly as a signal. Then came the rattle of musketry fire, but against whom they were firing we could only guess, for it was so dark we could see nothing save the flash from the muzzle of the guns, and we heard nothing but their faint report. Now we knew at once that the alarm must have been given, and my Lord's escape discovered. While we were wondering what would happen next we heard the splash of oars rowed towards us with a very quick stroke, but the splash only, the oars being seemingly muffled in their rowlocks.

We were showing no lights, by my Lord's orders through John Fowler, and for signals we had done nothing but this ; when it was exactly an hour after sunset we had shown a light three times, for thirty seconds by the watch, and with the like space of time between the showings. This was to warn those on shore of our having come. We knew now that the boat was escaping towards us, and but for my Lord's positive orders to let no light or lantern be seen, lying as we were under the very guns of the Fortress, I would have done so now, fearing his missing us in the dark.

Listening as well as we could through the noises of the storm for the coming boat, we presently could make out other sounds of rowing oars and these not muffled, and we knew thereby that my Lord was being chased. Our two pilots, who had kept so cool hitherto, now began to be very unquiet, shouting out to us this and that in their language, and pointing to the sails, and again making signs as if they would shoot at something in the water. I called the Spaniard to interpret for me, and learned they were bidding us put up sail to be ready to make off before the guns of the Fort should blow us out of the water, and that we were to be ready to resist the soldiers who were pursuing the fugitives in their boat, and would assuredly, they said, board us and cut all our throats. This was good advice, and I bid the captain get as much sail on the ship as he dared, without dragging our anchors (for we had two down, the wind blowing hard now from the west), which he did, but she could carry but little breadth of canvas in the great wind that blew : only as much as showed like a lady's kerchief. I told off forty of our men to stand by with muskets in their hands, and set Jan Loots and another to hold axes ready to cut the anchor cables at a word from me. By this time we plainly heard the regular oar-beat of boats racing very swiftly towards us, and now and then the sound of a shot, which we guessed to be the soldiers in their boat firing on the runaway. The shore being over a mile away and the sea bad for travelling in, we had had full time for getting in readiness, and now we peered into the night for the first signs of the boats. We could just see about thirty yards or so from us, and that only dimly, beyond that was like a wall of darkness and rain drizzle. Presently the nose of my Lord's skiff shot swiftly through from the darkness into our sight, and immediately after a great wherry of the soldiers, pulling twelve oars. Seeing their prey so near escaping them, two of the soldiers in her stood up, and levelling their pieces, let fly, while my Lord's boat was within a few yards of us (we could now plainly see Ralph with the helm in his hand and we could hear him cheering on his men). At the shots a gentleman sitting by his side in the stern sheets, started up, lifted both his arms with a loud cry and immediately fell forward wounded. Seeing this cruel act, our fellows with the muskets could not forbear their indignation, and without waiting for an order fired a volley upon the soldiers. It was a very unfortunate thing for us that they did so, for it served to mark our position to the gunners on shore, who must have been waiting for a sign of us, and before the smoke of our muskets had cleared away we saw the flashes of over a hundred great guns from the fortress. Two round shots came on the instant crashing through our side and fifty others ploughed up the water all round us, while others went whistling over our heads. By this time, however, the little skiff was alongside and made fast, and my Lord, springing on deck, called out to cut the cables, which was immediately done. The ship, which had been straining at her moorings, started forward into the night like a greyhound from the slips. We were still in great peril and imminent danger from the cannon fire, for the shots came all about us, but in three or four minutes the great force of the wind had driven us beyond the range of the guns ; yet its great violence, though it saved us from the gun fire, brought us in great peril in another way, for we were now scudding before a tempest in the black of night along a narrow channel, with sunken rocks and sandbanks on either side, and in which we had by daylight seen some half dozen ships at anchor. Only ever and again in the departing storm came the last few flashes of lightning and lit up the whole firmament far and near, and the unquiet waves, and the fortress with its puffs of smoke, and the channel studded with ships at anchor ; and these short lightings up helped us to steer our course ; indeed, but for them I know not into what hidden dangers we should have run in our flight.

So we managed somehow to keep in mid-channel. Once, in the darkness, we were like to have stumbled on and run down a great war galley of the Corsairs, but seeing her loom just in time to clear her, we went flying by and only grazed her quarter with something of a bump, but with no great harm done, save the oversetting the most of her crew of over 200, who had swarmed up on deck at the fearful noise of the cannon-nade from the fort. So swiftly did we rush by them that they had no time to do us any hurt (sprawl-as they all were on the decks) either to shoot upon us or grapple with us, only we heard a great shouting out of (as we supposed) pagan curses, in their foul and filthy lingo.

When after a little of this quick travelling we guessed we must have got out of the Goletta Channel into the great Bay, we had no means of assuring ourselves of it, with no landmarks visible and the lightning now ended, and we should not have known but for our pilots, who bid us let down a bucket over the side. When they looked at what came up they told us we were already in the Bay, for the water in Goletta, coming from the city lagoon, is green and ill-smelling, and that in the Bay clean sea water. Thereupon we altered our course to northerly, and felt at last that we had given our enemies the slip. Presently, the rain having quite abated or we sailed out of it, a little waxing moon arose, and our pilot could see his land-marks and set our course aright to drop him and his boat-mate off a little village (whose name I have forgot) at the entrance of the Bay, to which they belonged. This we did, my Lord giving the two a bag of gold coins between them ; so they departed rejoicing, and we sped on our way, rejoicing too.

Now at last we could look into each other's faces

and give welcome to my Lord and question him of
his great escape, and how it came so near of failing,
which it seemed was owing to one of the gentlemen
he brought off with him. My kinsman had rescued with
himself six sailors of the crew of his Flagship and
three Spanish gentlemen, two being officers of the
King's army, and the third a rich merchant living at
Syracuse, in Sicily. It seems that the whole of them,
under my Lord's management, had safely and secretly
broken from the castle near the Bey's Palace in Tunis,
and come by divers ways to gather together before
midnight in the broken, rocky ground under the
Fortress, where, under its very guns, my Lord justly
thought, if they were missed, they would never be
looked for. It was the unfortunate gentleman from
Syracuse who, coming in the dark upon a sentry
near the Fortress, took him for one of his own companions and made I know not what foolish speech
to him, whereupon the sentry, scenting the project
in hand, very naturally levelled his piece at the poor
Spaniard, and would have shot him through the head
had not my Lord knocked the barrel up in time, and
so saved the gentleman's brains. The alarm, however,
was given, and though the two Spanish officers very
expeditiously knocked the soldier on the head, the
garrison began to buzz out like bees from a hive, with
torches and lanterns, these being the moving lights
we had seen. Upon this, our party ran helter-skelter
down the rocks and entered their boat, getting by their
haste some little start of the soldiers, who, however,

in their great wherry could row more swiftly than they, and yet just missed of catching them up. It was this Syracuse gentleman (who seemed born to be unlucky) whom, with the last shot, the soldiers wounded with a bullet : it passed from behind between and through his shoulders, by a little only missing the spine, and so right through his lungs ; yet the man recovered when he got among his friends at home.

With the diversion of recounting this hairbreadth escape, and other the like pleasant occurrences of my Lord's captivity (since all's well that ends well), we passed the time very agreeably till we reached Syracuse again, late on the evening of the Feast of St. John the Evangelist, so swiftly did the strong west wind bear us from Tunis Bay.

The secret of the purpose of our departure had not been so well kept but that, through some hint given or guess made, it was noised abroad among the people after our sailing that we had gone to fetch them back their great Admiral and preserver from the Turks ; insomuch that we learnt afterwards that they had kept watch for our return, counting the hours till our galley might re-enter the harbour and confirm their hopes or dash them. She was first sighted from the heights, about noon, and as our Italian crew had run up all the flags and pendants and ancients in the *Golondrina*, and decked all her rigging with every bit of coloured stuff we had on board, the townspeople knew the good news so soon as the galley was sighted. Then straightway such a clamour of gladness was heard in Syracuse, and such demonstration of rejoicing made, as, I suppose, never before or since has been witnessed in that city ; the bells in all the churches rang out, rockets went up, music was everywhere in the air when we landed, and crowds of citizens flocked down to the water's edge to catch the first sight of his face whom they had mourned for, as lost to them for ever.

Y

I WOULD very gladly have left the politics of the Island of Sicilia alone, and with the politics the politicians, for I greatly mislike the one and the other, as being (both here and elsewhere) for the most part, the latter base, self-seeking men, and the former base and ignoble courses which these ignoble men employ towards their private ends : I say, I would very gladly leave all this alone, but that my Lord's fortunes now became very intimately bound up with the affairs of the Island, as thus, briefly ;

I have said the statesmen, councillors, magistrates, and captains, with others in authority, were all seekers after their own honour, interest and profit, who cared nothing for the good of their country : "After me, let the deluge come" (as Monsieur Scarron has it) was their maxim. Yet they were not all so ; the Viceroy might have been (nay, as we gathered afterwards, in heart he was) as evil-minded as the rest, but he well knew that the safety and prosperity of the Island conduced to his own prosperity and honour, and he endeavoured to rule place and people well, so far as his instruments and the ever tumultuous *mobile* would let him. So again was that good man (for so I still can honestly call him) the Chief or Grand Inquisitor of Sicily, the Italian Jesuit priest whom I have already once named, Monsignore Distorri. Now this to me is a very delicate subject, for as good Catholics, my Lord and I could not but approve the good Father's zeal and godliness, but as diligent seekers after truth along the path of enquiry as well as along that of authority, we could not but very strongly condemn this priest's narrowness and bigotry. His learning was indeed incredible, but more incredible and marvellous still was so learned a man's unwillingness to let godliness or wisdom take any form but blind faith and obedience to the orthodox teaching of the Church. His charity to all his fellow creatures was boundless as the sun's light, but it ever stopped short at the souls of men ; their bodies it utterly despised ; and he racked, tortured, and burnt them as often as their owners seemed to him to stray by a hair's breadth into heretical paths. He did this with a zeal, and unction, and delight which, I am willing to believe, arose quite as much from truest kindliness and affection to his victims (who were thus by fire, or other salutary torment to be purified, delivered from the Evil One, and restored to salvation), as for any edificatory and deterrent effect the spectacle might have upon the faith and compliance to the Church of the outer world.

It may readily be conceived that the common idle

talk, among the citizens to which I have already adverted, of my Lord's necromantic power stirred in this devout ecclesiastic no small perturbation of mind. He listened to many who, for reasons I shall presently allege, were ill disposed to my Lord's continual ascendency in the Island. The Grand Inquisitor having heard from them a very twisted and malignant account of the matter, he touched upon it with my Lord himself, who, esteeming him a learned man, very freely and innocently replied to his questionings with no disguise of his own opinions. The good priest, who had grown out of all understanding of deep matters or metaphysical reasoning, and had come, through prejudice and preconception, into as bigoted a condition of superstition as ever possessed a poor benighted peasant or fishwife, was by this conversation confirmed in his worst fears of the peril my Lord's soul stood in through his manifest tamperings with the Black Art, and clear communion (so he would have it) with Satan himself.

Lest any in the future (as some through folly or malignity have done in the past) should charge my Lord or me, his humble historian, either with such communion with the Enemy of mankind as was imputed by Monsignore Distorri, or, on the other hand, with an entire denial of the possibility of any such communion, or the sin of it (if the thing be possible), I will here very shortly express the opinions of my Lord, many times communicated to me, on this matter of resort to the Father of Evil.

My Lord held that there is no reasonable doubt whatever that the Creator does, on rare occasions, allow non-natural and unreal apparitions or phantasmata of things and bodies, perhaps to exhibit to such as are (by affliction of unreason) wanting in faith in the unseen world, some true token that there is a power beyond their own. Furthermore, Ralph could not fail to observe that in the common affairs of life, God but very seldom intervenes directly, else would there be justification for such as sit idly expecting of God's providence, and waiting for signs thereof in their behalf. Nevertheless He hath established in His omnipotent science of all things, certain well-known laws whereby certain resultants follow whenever certain causes set them in motion. So likewise certain other more hidden, and, so to speak, esoteric laws do exist unknown to and unseen by the common run of mankind, which laws are set to work by certain rare, yet none the less previsionable and determinable causes. Of such an order of laws are those which govern some at leas of the aforesaid appearances ; namely, the passage before the eyes of men of ghosts and spirits of the dead, and certain phantasmagoric apparitions of the living. Now, it may be affirmed (and herein my Lord was in full agreement with that great man, Mr. Thomas Hobbes, late of Malmesbury and now of Paris) that our Creator and Ruler hath so willed and determined it, that no law of His is so subtle and obscure but that He has granted to His favoured creature man the power to resolve and declare it ; and this being so, it follows that men exist, though perhaps rarely, who possess this deep science and can set in motion those laws whereby the aforesaid ghosts of the dead can be called up, or souls of the living conjured, and even spirits other than mortal ones under the human dispensation and of power greater than men's, can be invoked and convoked at pleasure. Now, to do this reverently and for the honour of God and the good of His cause, which is that of Right and Justice, were no sin. But who can say that a man shall exercise this power and not be doing it for his own selfish ends and private greed, or to revenge his injuries, or gratify his sinful desires? Surely none shall arrogate this privilege but he who should know himself placed above the temptations of common men.

Therefore my Lord was in full agreement with the aforesaid Mr. Hobbes in considering that both the Church and the Law do proceed lawfully and righteously and expediently in condemning the above practices, under the general name of Magic, as harmful both to Religion and to the State, and indeed as nothing less than instituting a new Religion and Laws beyond the ken and practice of the judges of the land. Wherefore witches and warlocks, often indeed only thoughtless or pretending and ignorant persons (yet not so ignorant but that they are often skilled in the black and devilish art of bargaining with the Fiend over the price of their own souls) are justly punished by all tribunals. My Lord, however, would often say he hated the cruelty of it, and would have some measure used in punishing these criminals, as by reproving and admonishing them of their folly and wickedness, when their guilt was not very black, and in not incontinently condemning them to tortures and flames (poor wretches!) as is now the custom. Even in cases of obstinate impenitence and recalcitrancy he would execute the offended law upon the bodies of criminals mercifully, and, so to speak, kindly and lovingly, as by hanging of them by the neck, or submerging of them, till they be drowned, in some neighbouring River, or Lake, or in the Sea.

But to go back : The state of parties now in Sicily was ticklish, and, briefly put, it stood thus ; the Viceroy, trying to make a stand for the honour of his post against the exactions and robbery of the great officers, was for ever crossed by them, while the people, angered by the cruelties, injustices and extortions of their Spanish masters, were preparing for a new revolt. The Viceroy, who saw his safety, in all these troubles and tangles of State, to lie chiefly in the good discipline which we had established in his troops and their love and loyalty to my Lord, was very willing to uphold my Lord's designs in everything against the High Officers of State, while these latter opposed us for several reasons : first, that they could plot to no purpose against the Viceroy while we and our troops stood by him ; second, that my Lord was an honest and honourable man who would never wink at their doings or tacitly approve them, and that rogues have ever this of conscience about them that

they most cordially hate a disapprover of their
roguery ; third, that he was a foreigner among them ;
fourth, that he had raised himself to a greater eminence than any man in Sicily by his exploits and
through the love and esteem which the common
people bore him ; and the Lords Councillors, being
ignoble men, they envied him.   Any one of these
four reasons would have made them willing to undo
any man, but all four together put them in a fury of
animosity against my kinsman.

Apart from all these causes of mischance, and
mingling with them for greater mischief and misdoing,
was the polity of the Grand Inquisitor, who being
neither a Spaniard nor a Sicilian, but an Italian
Jesuit, and an honest man into the bargain, cared
not a rush for honours or pelf, regarding nothing
gained unless the Church gained (no matter by what
means) and desiring nothing but to foster religious
zeal and suppress religious heresy.   To him all parties
in the State were fain to pay court, for in his single
person he held, as it were, by procuration all the
powers of the Holy Catholic Religion itself, which in
Sicily doth, or did at that time, mightily sway, through
fear chiefly, all hearts and minds.   The Lords Councillors in their opposition to us were not slow to perceive
his Reverence's estrangement from my Lord, and
used, as I have hinted, all their efforts to foment the
suspicions of the Churchman as to his Lordship's
supposed heretical opinions and conduct.   With this
view they spread (or rather further extended, for it

had already begun to spread) among the common herd, the repute of my Lord's dealings with forbidden Powers. Now, these stories coming exaggerated to his Reverence's ears through his Inquisitorial emissaries and familiars, together with reports of the esteem and gratitude the people held my kinsman in, the Grand Inquisitor began to fear the Faith itself in danger when one so favoured by high and low could venture openly to deal with magic arts. It behoved him therefore to stir in the matter and make some examples, and assuredly my Lord would himself have run no little peril of a trial by the Holy Office, and of the fate of the great Nolan Philosopher Bruno, whose honesty and genius and virtue and piety could not save him from the cruelty of the Italian Inquisitors, and who perished at the stake some two score years before. My kinsman however stood too high in favour with the whole people and with the Viceroy, and was too sure of a very faithful support from his soldiers and sailors, and they thought it wisest to let him be.

The Grand Inquisitor indeed was a man who feared little or nothing, yet was his boldness too politic to strike at my kinsman except indirectly; and he therefore caused his Familiars to use their diligence among the people, so that several poor fellows, on one pretence or another, were dragged into the dungeons of the Inquisition, and, under pressure of I know not what infernal torments, confessed to I know not what uncommitted crimes, some dying under the stress of their torturings, and some being brought to open and shameful deaths in the streets and Piazzas of Palermo City.

My kinsman did his utmost to prevent this iniquity as he deemed it, and scandal to the Church, and fearing to fail to bring conviction to the Lords Councillors if he alleged the ferity or injustice of the act he inveighed in Council against it on the score of its impolicy; urging that it would move the citizens' spirits in their present inquietude against Spanish rule in Church and State. Many agreed with him publicly and more in private, but the influence of the Inquisition was strong enough to pass this inhuman measure in Council, and the prisoners were burnt.

I will note in passing that, strange as it may appear in my countrymen's ears, the Grand Inquisitor had both a voice and a vote in the Council of State ; not indeed in the Lesser or Inner and Privy Council, which consisted of but five members and did not even include my kinsman, but as in this body the Viceroy could command but two votes, his own and his nephew's, the Generalissimo, so it was seldom or never convoked by him. I am speaking now of the greater Council where twenty-three Councillors sat, or had a right to sit, and in which (being a sort of little Parliament) nearly all measures of State were debated and passed. The Grand Inquisitor feeling his power and seeing his success so far, was emboldened to go still further. In this, however, he went too far ; for, that the people might not doubt that their favourite had come under the heavy displeasure of

the Church and was powerless in her hands, and even
that my Lord's very soldiers were not safe from her
chastisements, he caused to be arrested three of our
troopers (one being an English Corporal of the name
of Cappers in the Viceroy's own body guard, and
the other two Spaniards of good army standing).
These three were taken up on I know not what idle
pretence of a charge trumped up by the priestly
delators, and immediately lodged in the prison of
the Inquisition.

The Council was sitting, and my Lord, having no
intention that day of attending it, was busy in my
company with affairs of his command, when Lieutenant Brown (late Corporal in my Lord's English
troop) ran pale-faced into the room where we were
sitting to give us the news of our fellows being taken.
My Lord having enquired closely as to the facts, spoke
no further word, but buckling on his sword which
lay upon the table, and catching up his hat, strode
hastily through the Palace to where the Council were
sitting.

I followed as far as I could go, that is, to the ante-
chamber of the Council Chamber, where our own men
of the Viceroy's body guard were on duty, and it was
pretty clear by their troubled faces that they too had
learnt of the arrest of their fellows, and would not
take it calmly. They easily gathered from my
Lord's knitted brows and hasty stride through the
room, what was his purpose in now attending the
Council.

What took place at the session leaked out through several there present, for the proceedings that day caused a great stir in the Island, and were, in truth, the beginning of great changes.   My Lord told me somewhat afterwards of what took place, but I learnt most from the telling of others.

It appears that there was that day a large attendance of some twenty or twenty-one Councillors, and his Reverence the Grand Inquisitor was in the act of speaking on the question of the arrest of the soldiers as my Lord entered.   Now, I must remark that my Lord had always observed a very ceremonious deference in addressing the Councillors.   He spoke no oftener than he absolutely needed to, never using passion or vehemence, but often, if the subject allowed, as much lightness and restrained raillery as was decent, being thereby willing to attest that, as a foreigner, it did not beseem him to concern himself too earnestly with the affairs of a country which was not his own ; and this modest bearing and his wit and soundness in debate gained him friendly hearing even from his enemies.   What then was the surprise and even consternation of the gentlemen of the Council Board when my Lord burst into the Great Hall with knit brows and a terrible face, his long sword clanking along the pavement as he advanced, his right hand clapped upon his dagger, his left clenched in anger.

He saluted the Viceroy on his throne, but none other of the Lords, and they were fluttered by his belligerent attitude, and there fell a sudden silence at the Board; the Lord Inquisitor, on whom my Lord fixed his eyes, stammering out a few confused sentences of his speech and then ending it tamely.

My Lord did not interrupt him, as the Churchman's supporters afterwards alleged, but when no one spoke he addressed the Viceroy in these words :

" I have learned," said he, " that the agents of the Holy Office, contrary to the laws of this Island and in contempt of the privileges of your Grace, have arrested three of your Lordship's Body Guard under my command."

None answered him, but presently the Viceroy said, "I refer your Lordship to the Grand Inquisitor."

My Lord turned to the Priest with, "Is it as I say ? "

" The soldiers have been arrested by my orders," said the Grand Inquisitor, and he was proceeding to an explanation when my Lord, in a voice which over-sounded his own, cried, "I demand their immediate release under the Grand Inquisitor's hand."

In a moment a majority of the Lords rose to clamour against so unusual, and, as they said, unbecoming a demand, but my Lord still standing at the table in a threatening attitude opposite the Grand Inquisitor, and in a voice which over-bore those of the Councillors, called out :

" In the name of my master the Viceroy, and of

the offended laws of this land, I demand on the moment an order of release, signed by the Grand Inquisitor!"

When no sign of compliance was made, he stepped nearer to the table, and pushing a sheet of paper towards the Churchman pointed to it with a menacing gesture.

"Your Reverence," said he in a very firm voice, "will do well to sign the order, for in a few minutes 'twill be too late, and my soldiers will have broken open your prisons for themselves."

At the boldness of this speech (for in all the worst tumults in the Island none had dared to lay hands on the officers or the prisons of the Inquisition) the Churchman exclaimed and raised his hands, as if in horror of such a threatened desecration, but my Lord stood unmoved before him, with a fixed, stern countenance, still pointing to the blank paper. Some of the waverers, seeing my cousin so very masterful, stood away from the Grand Inquisitor, and though none in this crisis spoke, they made manifest by their attitude and movement towards my Lord that they were rather with him, who was gaining power, than with the Priest, who was losing it.

The Grand Inquisitor appealed to the Viceroy—"Your Highness!" he cried, but the Viceroy shook his head as if to imply that the debate lay between him who shadowed the Church and him who had the soldiery at his back.

For a space there was silence anew in the Council,

and the strain of will against will. Then the Grand Inquisitor, daunted and overcome, taking up a pen, wrote slowly upon the paper before him the order for the prisoners' release and signed it with his name and cross.

My Lord took it, read it in silence, inclined his head to the Grand Inquisitor, bowed low to the Viceroy, saluted the Councillors with a lesser formality, and passed out to the ante-chamber where I stood. From his going in to his coming out not eight minutes had passed by the clock.

"Take this order of his Reverence the Grand Inquisitor," said he to me in hearing of the guard, "with two files of your musketeers to the Prison of the Holy Office, and claim the delivery to you of my three soldiers, wrongfully arrested and imprisoned."

CHAPTER XXIV.

IT may very easily be imagined the stir that this event made among the people of all classes, who, though they never had dared to murmur against the cruel tyranny of the Inquisition, lived in daily terror of it, and in their heart of hearts hated and abhorred it. As for our soldiers and sailors, my kinsman's rescue of their fellows served but to cause a renewal and redintegration in them of the love, esteem, and trust they already had towards him.

Though my Lord gained by this boldness some voices in the Council, namely, of the weak-kneed, who ever array themselves on the side of the resolute ; the Viceroy, though still acknowledging to himself the necessity of my Lord's support in the troubled state of the Island, began to be a little fluttered and frightened by and mistrustful of my kinsman's in-dependence and over-riding of forms. This at least is how I now read his Grace's mind, with the help and by the light of after events.

Very soon after this affair of the three soldiers there arose another question, which was a second trial of strength between my Lord on the one side and the Grand Inquisitor and his following on the other, and which I doubt not was designed by the Churchman to give him a chance of recovering his influence. As this matter led to a very singular sequence and had an extraordinary great influence upon the fortunes of my Lord and his house, I shall dwell upon it a little, though not at greater length, I hope, than the fastidious Reader will find endurable.

It will be remembered how, at the crowning victory of Port Niccolo, we had taken the Corsair Renegado Admiral of the Fleet, by name El Saida, whom we had considered, with the rest of the Christian world (into which his fame had gone out far and wide), to be either a Greek or an Albanian (a Greek for his cunning and an Albanian for his ferocity). It turned out, however, he was nothing of the kind, but one Ronald Campbell, a Highland gentleman of good birth and parentage, being related to the Campbells of Lochaw, a very potent clan and of some repute and great possessions in the north-western parts of Britain. I have mentioned before that to fellows of his inconstant persuasion in matters of faith it was customary in Sicily to give a short shrift and as short a rope. This famous Renegado Admiral however was spared from this fate, because it was supposed he might help us in procuring the ransom of my Lord, and on my Lord's happy return he was still alive and in the prisons of the state.

The Grand Inquisitor had not been so set upon

making an example of this arch-apostate of an
Admiral, but that he had seen the policy of saving
him from the rope which was his due while the
ransom of my Lord was still in treaty, for at that
time the Priest was among our warmest well-wishers.
Perhaps after my Lord's return he might still have
overlooked the captive Admiral, which he indeed did
for a whole month ; but then came his suspicions of
my Lord's orthodoxy, the clashing of their opinions
and wills in the matter of the arrested soldiers, with
my Lord's victory over him in the Council. After
that the Grand Inquisitor cast about for means to
re-establish the tottering faith and orthodoxy of the
people, and he resolved upon a grand ceremonial or
function of the Church, or, as the Holy Office terms
it, an *auto da fé*, at which the execution of the
Corsair Admiral at the stake should be exhibited to
the people with all possible pomp and gala of pro-
cessions, solemn music, and bravery of banners, flags,
flowers, streamers, and so forth.

Now, I am much afeared that if I say that it went
very heavily against my Lord's heart and conscience
(and against mine too) that this thing should be
done, many pious, heavenward-stepping men will
charge him with lukewarmness to the faith ; and it is
to clear him of any such infamous imputation that
I must beg the Reader to let me state my Lord's
opinions on this important matter a little fully. So
far from his, or my objecting to the mere execution
of Renegados, I will remind the Reader how, a little

back in this narrative, I mentioned with approval the practice of stringing up these scoundrelly apostates by the dozen or score, as a most laudable custom. Therefore it can hardly be necessary for me to protest very strongly on my Lord's behalf against that pernicious doctrine advanced in these latter days by one section of General Cromwell's followers (his too, of all men!) of the wickedness of taking life under any circumstances whatever. So far from holding which, I will declare boldly that it has never appeared to me (nor, I believe, to my Lord) to be more than a venial sin to kill a man. I mean not, of course, the foul sin of murder, nor the honest killing of soldiers by each other, offensively or defensively, for that is so far from being a sin that it is a virtue. I speak now of the merciful ending of those lives which the owners have forfeited to the laws, for surely this is a virtuous and salutary action. I say merciful, for sometimes I ask myself if soldiers, who are accounted such cruel wretches, are not of their natures more merciful than Lawyers and Statesmen and Churchmen, who are so mighty fond of condemning the poor rogues that fall into their hands to torments of every kind, as the rack, the wheel, and the stake; things that make my blood (a soldier's, too!) to run icy cold even to write down, and presently after set my heart on fire to avenge these barbarities on the authors thereof.

To be sure, we soldiers may be (what Bishop Jeremy Taylor reproaches us for being) fathers of great misery, through wounds, death, arson, and what not ; still, that is our trade, and 'tis not we who command in this, but Rulers and Statesmen, and sure no good soldier but will rather kill outright than wound ; and as for arson, what honest soldier will set fire to so much as a haycock but for some good reason of policy—to strike a terror, and thus, maybe, save life in the end ? As for this matter of killing, we know more of that matter than those who stay at home and preach on the terror of it, and if they will take my word, it is a thing neither so terrible as they are apt to contend, nor, I am sure, otherwise than a salutary one for many most pestilent rogues and scoundrels, who greatly better the world by leaving it. As for the killing of honest men (soldiers themselves, for the most part, who expect no kinder treatment), why, what is it after all but expediting by a little what must come to us all some day ?

I have thus, I believe, purged myself of any possible charge of undue leniency in the lawful taking of life, and *a fortiori*, in the rightful doing of malefactors to death. I have said enough, too, I believe, to show why my cousin and I set our faces against the torturing of the Corsair Admiral. It was less the killing than the manner of it that we objected to ; but my Lord went some way further than this, and would have the prisoner spared from death altogether. If his reasons seemed over subtle to some in Sicily, they seem to me (as they will to the Reader) most clear and conclusive.

"Had you hanged the prisoner at once," said my

Lord, in Council, " there would have been nothing to say in the matter ; but as you kept him alive to serve your own purposes, it were base to slay him now, when your ends can no longer be served. You have kept him between hope of life and fear of death for all these months, and therefore he has undergone already punishment far more bitter than death ; and now to add to this the sentence of death is clear injustice. Why is he to be punished by this so much more cruel a sentence than any of his fellows have got in past times ? Is it as a recompense for his own iniquity, and that he may serve as a warning to others ? No ; it is not to satisfy justice at all, but that the people may be persuaded that the Church is strong. Why, gentlemen !" cries he, very indignant, " I tell you that to do this man to death, however you accomplish it, is a base and dishonouring act, and if it come to pass as the Grand Inquisitor purposes, I for one will shake from my feet the dust of that land where so shameful a deed has been committed !"

These words, hard as they were, went home to the bosoms of the Lords of the Council, of whom, though I have in no respect held back the tale of their many wrong doings and perversions, yet were they all Spanish cavaliers of old lineage and good blood, coming of a stock of soldier gentlemen who had, in days gone by, followed chivalric courses, and spurned all dishonour; and now this true blood in them rose conscious to their faces, and they remembered their high pedigree and ancient worth, and suddenly perceived the baseness of the course to which the Churchman was leading them. After this, rage as the Grand Inquisitor would (who had himself seemingly no lively sense whatever of honour and dishonour), they gave all their voices to our side, and the Corsair Admiral was thus saved from a cruel death.

So did my Lord, in regard to these Spanish Lords, to apply the fine verse of my friend the late William Habington of Hindlip—

"Keep
Strayed honour in the true magnificke way."

This is not all that my Lord did for his now dis-comfited enemy, the Renegado Admiral. He had procured the gift of his life, and considering now that he was expurgated and freed of the great crime of apostacy by his long sojourning in prison, and the humiliation of his shameful fall from highest state to cruel captivity (since, sure, to those placed high, dis-comfiture in this kind brings penalties and torments of the soul the meaner sort of men can never apprehend), my Lord, partly because he would ameliorate the prisoner's lot, whom he knew to be suffering sore sickness as well as captivity, begged of the Viceroy that he might have the custody of the Admiral in his own Palace which his Grace had bestowed upon him, and under guard of his own soldiery. This he asked too as a precaution against any sudden re-arrest of the Corsair's person by the Inquisitor, which my kinsman was not without apprehending.

So soon as my Lord and I saw the prisoner, a deep pity fell upon us for him ; for we had expected this terrible fierce and famous Captain of the Pirate Turks to be of rough aspect, and complexion conformable to his repute, whereas he was a man but a few years older than my kinsman, with a wan face, now worn very thin with sickness, and his manners and carriage were gentle, and his speech smooth, bespeaking gentle birth and breeding. There are some whose fortune is far lower than their power to rise, and whom the evil counsellor that abides in a man's own heart tempts to leave their lowness behind, and leap to unconditioned eminence, across bounds that conscience sets in vain to restrain them. Of such was this great fallen soldier of fortune, and such had been his life's history ; though we never questioned him of his past doings, or of the temptations that had led him to fall so low and thereby rise to the ill-savoured honours he had got.

My Lord, seeing that he needed only salve for his unquiet conscience, and solace for his remorseful soul, gave him no words but of comfort ; and perceiving how great was his disorder, called in a surgeon to him. Then we learned that he was sickening unto near death, for a decline that long since he had been in was hastened by his doings the night of the fight of Port Niccolo, when he with others saved themselves from their captured ships, and their boats were beaten to pieces on that sea-tormented shore, and many perished drenched and drowned in the surf, or wounded by the jagged, jutting rocks. Among the

wounded was the Admiral, who being struck insensible
on the stones would certainly have been drowned by
the waves, but his sailors pulled him inshore, and he
remained all that night, through the pelting storm
and the loudness of the fight, without sense, lying on
the sand till next morning, when my troopers took
him prisoner. This exposure, his wounds, and his
bitter captivity, had made his disorder mortal, and
even now he lay on the point of death.

He remained in my Lord's house above a fortnight
before his death, solemnly recanting from his wicked
apostacy from our faith, and obtaining due absolution
by his repentance. On the last day, being then very
weak and feeling his end to be approaching, he asked
to have private speech of my Lord and myself. We
thereupon sent those who were in waiting upon him
from the room, and my Lord seeing him unwilling to
speak, took the dying man by the hand, and very
earnestly assured him that any wish he might have to
communicate his last words or desires to friends or
relatives at home would be fulfilled by him, and therefore to speak his mind freely ; but, " No," said the
dying man, " I have none near me in friendship anywhere whom I would remember dying, nor have I any
near relation living, nor any one to whom I wish a
message sent."

Then he spoke of that which lay at his heart, and
on which he had not yet opened to us at all ; which
was that, as he lay in prison, word had been brought
to him of the near danger he ran of an infamous

death through the designs of the Grand Inquisitor, and how it had become known to him (indeed the whole city could speak of nothing else), that my Lord alone had stood between him and this cruel public sacrifice of his life, and of the vehement contention my cousin had made for him and for mercy before the Council. Here his voice, which had sunk very low, trembled and failed him, and yet I think less with weakness of his disorder than a disablement coming from some deep emotion in him. We turned away our eyes from his face, guessing yet not willing to see that he wept, for, sure, it becomes not a soldier to look upon the infirmity of one, who has never been unmanned in stress of battle, brought low by sickness and unmanned by that.

So we waited ; and when he had recovered himself he spoke thus, with a firmer voice :

"To you, my Lord St. Keyne, I owe much more than life, which God indeed had already in His justice seen fit to make forfeit of to me : I am a soldier, and you have saved me from disgrace, a gentleman, and you have stood between me and everlasting dishonour." Then again he fell to a silence.

Presently he said, "Will your Lordship grant me a favour, the first I have asked for long years, the last I shall ask of man ? "

"I will," said my kinsman very heartily, "whatever it be."

"I desire," said the dying man, "to make you my heir."

Here we began to think the poor man was wandering in his mind, and the mists of coming death to be already clouding over his senses, for of what legacy could he, a death-stricken captive, have the bequeathing?

Then he told us a very marvellous tale; and but that strange things happened in these unquiet times, and in these lands beyond the seas, it was a story over marvellous for belief.

He told us that he had in his beginnings with the Pirates served under his uncle, himself a famous Renegado Captain, from all he told us a bold and bad man who lived red-handed in denial of his Redeemer, and died red-handed still denying Him, and who was unfaithful not to his Christian fellows alone, but to his Infidel masters. This uncle of our prisoner had served first the Corsair Dey of Algiers, and then, when war had threatened to break out between the Mussulmans of Algiers and them of Tunis, he had gone over to the Tunisians, and given them information of a great gift or bribe that the Algerines were intending to send, with strong convoy, by sea to the Grand Turk at Constantinople, the Suzerain of both States, to incline him to their side. This ship and convoy the Tunisians had intercepted, and in a fight the Algerines had been worsted near the little Island of Ustica, north of Sicily, and the Algerine treasure-ship had gone down and all on board her had perished, except the Emissary, bearer of the treasure to Constantinople, who had escaped in a boat to land, carrying with him in a little leaden coffer, or casket, the very heart of the great treasure. "My uncle," said the dying man, "having some suspicion of this, pursued the Emissary, slew him and those with him, and became secretly possessed of the casket. None but he took any account of it or knew of its contents, or their inestimable value ; for while, in the hold of the ship was great wealth destined for the Sultan, rich stuffs, carpets of Ispahan, embroidered silks of Broussa, many chests full of gold and silver work from Persia and India, and arms from Damascus, together with great weight of bullion, and coined money besides, enough altogether to load and fill a great galley, in the little casket was stowed that which out-valued all this rich cargo a hundredfold, for it contained great diamonds, seventy-two in number, each the size of a wren's egg ; all white stones, sharp cut and perfect, and each one gleaming with inner fires of green, and blue, and red.

"Sure his mind is wandering," whispered I to my Lord, but my cousin put his hand on my shoulder as we stood together at the bedside, in sign I should let the dying man speak on.

"But this was little," the Renegado continued, "for in the coffer, which was hardly bigger than a man might enclose in his two hands, was contained that which is the wonder of all the world, namely, the famed Amulet of Sultan Solyman the Magnificent, which is made of three chains of gold interlinked together, each chain holding in golden circlets three great Rubies of equal shape, each a smooth, flat, trans-

lucent gem, nine in all (but one is missing), the like of
any one of which for blood-red tint and greatness the
the world possesses not, for they are in size of round
equal to the eye-circle of a tiger or a lion ; and each
one bears on one side engraved a verse of the Koran,
and on the other the name of the Hebrew King
Solomon, whom the Moslems hold the father of all
enchantments, and with his name a sign or token is
inscribed, which no man can read ; on each stone a
different sign. These stones were in collecting a
hundred years by the Sultans of Turkey, and the
great Sultan Selim in his long life found only one, the
eighth stone. His son, the mightiest of the Sultans,
Solyman the Magnificent, procured the ninth ruby and
completed the Amulet. Now with this Amulet was held
to lie the great good fortune of this Sultan, who overcame Moslem and Christian alike, and never suffered
defeat till the Amulet, a hundred years ago, was
stolen from him by the Renegado Barbarossa ; and
him too it strangely befriended, it is said, till the
ninth stone of the Amulet was lost (which is still
missing), when he died miserably. Since then the
Amulet has lain in the Treasury of the Dey of
Algiers till it was sent in the treasure-ship to Constantinople with other gifts to bribe the Turk, whereupon it fell into the hands of my uncle in the Island
of Ustica. There it has remained, buried in that
island ever since, for he feared to bring it home, lest
rumour should fetch to light how it had been saved
from the Algerine ship and taken by my uncle. This

little Island is peopled by a few fishermen and shepherds only, but they had fled and hidden at the coming of the ships, and after the fight the Tunisians staying for a space in the Island to repair their ships, and my uncle being encamped on the shore, he buried the casket as deep as his arm could reach in the loose sand under his tent.

"My uncle lived in great honour and fame with the Tunisians for many years after, commanding their frigates in many adventures, but never having their whole fleet under him, so that never being in chief command he never was able to revisit privily the Island and recover the jewels. Then he died, leaving to me the secret of their burial-place, which I, too, in three years that I have been Admiral-in-Chief of their fleet, have never been able to come at, though always endeavouring to do so. Once I was driven away by a great storm, and once by your ships; but I had resolved when I brought my great fleet of thirty vessels hither, to proceed to Ustica after defeat of the Sicilians, to dig up the casket, leave the service of Tunis, and live ever after in my own country, richer and more powerful, through the great treasure in the casket, than the greatest in all the land."

Thus spoke the dying Renegado Corsair, and we listened incredulous, being sure that in the delirium of his disorder he had dreamed a dream of that fabled lost Amulet of Sultan Solyman, of which all have heard, whose presence brought that great Emperor of the Turks victory, and its loss defeat. Still, not willing to disabuse him in his dying moments of the belief that he was conferring a vast benefit upon his benefactor, and to humour him, I enquired by what signs and tokens we should find the place of the buried casket ; but he had fallen again into a stupor, overcome by his long speaking, and my words did not rouse him.

" We will let him be," said my kinsman.

But my words had reached through the numbness of the dying man's senses, and presently again he spoke, but very weakly and slow :

" On the easternmost point of Ustica, a little north of the only harbour, is a tall, black rock standing upright to the height of the mainmast of a frigate, with its foot washed by the sea at high water ; its peak is very narrow, and the shadow of it, exactly an hour after sunrise, fell upon my uncle's tent ; it was then the 125th day, counting from the winter solstice. There look for the casket—take it—it is yours."

No more words spoke the Renegado, nor once did he recover his senses ; and that night he died.

CHAPTER XXV

MY cousin Ralph was not of my incredulous mind as to the testament of the Renegado Admiral. He never doubted that the casket had indeed been buried on Ustica Island as the Admiral had told us, but he greatly suspected (knowing the many lies, villanies, and deceits of the Infidels) that it might contain none or but few of the priceless treasures imputed to it ; also he was doubtful if the casket could be found again on the sand of the sea-shore, with so fallible a description of its whereabouts as we had got.

It was now mid April, and therefore near the time appointed for the determining of the hiding place of the casket by the falling of the shadow of the rock ; and our united squadron being about to proceed upon its monthly cruise, my Lord, on the 24th day of the month, put to sea and steered for Ustica, which lies some seventy miles due north of Palermo, and on the evening of the 25th anchored off the Island, with his whole fleet, in a little cove on its eastern side. So out of the track of all commerce and its conveniences is this

Islet, that there is no quay or other mode of landing, and as on account of the pointed nature of the shore rocks and the unruly movement of the waters around them, it is ill disembarking here in boats, we waited for the people of the Island to come and carry us ashore, as is the usage ; but not a soul appeared, all having fled, as we afterwards heard, into a great rocky recess of the mountains, taking our ships for Corsairs, so remote and ignorant are the inhabitants of this Islet. We therefore approached as near as was possible in our long boat, and made shift to wade to land as best we could. Then by means of a line of our men from boat to shore, standing in water to their middle, a little tent was passed over dry from one to the other, together with picks and tools to pitch it, and with food and other necessaries, for my Lord designed to pass that night and the next on shore, which we did ; and next day, which was the 26th, being as we calculated it, the 124th after the winter solstice, we wandered along the shore and pretty soon discovered a tall, mast-shaped rock. We easily guessed it was the one intended, for there was none other of its bigness or shape near about, and it had its base washed by the sea.

We rose at dawn on the 27th, which was the appointed day, and waited for the rising of the sun and the falling of the shadow of the rock. When the rock's shadow began to shorten and, in an hour's time, fell on just such a level bit of sand as would be suitable for a tent to be pitched upon, we marked the very spot, but did not dig at once, for the sailors having landed in numbers, had dispersed themselves for pastime about the shore ; but we ordered our tent to be immediately pitched anew over the spot, which we had marked with a large stone. Then, in our impatience, hardly waiting for the men to have done, we pricked the sand deeply with our swords inside the tent, and thinking we encountered somewhat in one place, we dug down upon it with a spade, and presently, at about three and a half or four feet down, came upon a hardish lump of something, but it was no casket at all, only a great, heavy, pudding-shaped lump of hard sand. Note, that here the sand is black and heavy and sharp, more like iron filings than any sand I ever saw elsewhere. Holding this great round lump in both my hands, I cast it, in my grievous disappointment, upon the ground, when lo ! there broke away and crumbled from it about a half or two-thirds of the sand in powder, still leaving something of a central part or core which did not, like the rest, fall to pieces. As I spurned it with my foot in my vexation, my Lord, who had laughed at this baulking of our hopes, and at, I suppose, my dumbfoundered, angry aspect, looking attentively upon this central portion as it lay on the ground, took it in his hand, and weighing it therein, " Why ! Humphrey," he cries, " I believe this lump of stuff is nothing less than the casket itself."

With that, he pulled his dagger from its sheath and putting the point between the interstices of the sand,

presently reached to something that resisted the steel,
but not much, for he easily ripped open that which
was in truth the leaden casket buried by the
Renegade ; only the lead thereof was eaten away, and
had turned, by corrosion of the salt water and the
eager nature of the sand, to a softish film no thicker
nor much tougher than paper. Still holding the
coffer in his hand, in a moment he had opened it fully
and laid bare the contents ; and we looked upon them
speechless, and then upon one another in amaze ; for
here were scores of huge diamonds that sparkled in
the morning light, and, mingled with them, lay the
great blood-red gems of the famous lost Amulet of
Sultan Solyman the Magnificent.

There could be no doubt that we held in our hands
a vast treasure, whose twentieth part even would
furnish the ransom of the greatest King in
Christendom. We picked out the gems, finding the
great rubies in the Amulet to be, as we had been
forewarned, eight in number, all flattish stones, blood-
red, perfect, translucent, most beautiful ; all equal in
size to a hair's breadth, all alike in tint of redness,
and all, as the Renegade had told us, of the bigness, or
as I should judge, a little more, of a tiger's or a lion's
eye : such marvels as I had never conjectured the
world could hold. Of the diamonds, two score and
ten were, as we had been told, of the size of a wren's
egg ; that is, of the width, in their greatest diameter
of an English silver groat, but there were twelve
(for the tale of them we had got was right, namely

seventy-two in all) that bulked larger and might attain to half as much again in carats' weight; I should equal them very nearly as to size, to the egg of a robin or goldfinch. Of the value of the twelve larger diamonds I would not give a guess, fearing to say too little (as knowing how rare such great stones are) but as to the smaller diamonds (if small they can be called which were themselves of monstrous bigness) I believe I might hazard the assessing of them, for we soldiers of many campaigns get to have some experience in judging of valuables, as gems, jewels, gold plate and the like, coming to us in the way of spoil. These diamonds, then, I priced in my mind at 1,000 gold doubloons of Spain apiece, (or about £3,500 of our money) but I did not reckon the purity of their "water," as the jewellers call it, and the first two that I offered a week later to a jeweller of Venice, travelling through Sicily, he took without a word at my first price, which was 3,000 doubloons for the pair; the old man's hands trembling with eagerness as his fingers closed on the stones and he pushed me the price I asked in gold. I saw thereby that I had been over-reached, but the fellow had my word and I said no more ; only I made my Lord laugh heartily when I told him of the poorness of my first bargain in jewel trading, and at only getting 3,000 doubloons for what I thought worth 2,000.

I the more rejoiced in this wonderful fortune that had befallen my Lord because from the first, feeling upon him the pride of an English gentleman, the

servant of the greatest of Kings (though now eclipsed
in exile), he had, with perhaps undue generosity and
magnificence, refused to receive for himself any *salarium*
or salary from the Viceroy of Sicily, though insisting
that his men, soldiers and sailors, should all be lodged,
paid and boarded with unusual munificence. Now
my Lord's own state had ever been princely, and his
outlay for retinue, liveries, and the entertainment by
sumptuous banquets, by masques, by music and
otherwise, of the Lords and Ladies of the Vice-regal
Court, was, beyond experience of the Palermitans,
magnificent.

I would not call this pomp by the hard word
prodigal, for it suited with the great revenues of my
kinsman's estates, comported with his eminent station
in Sicily, and was in congruence with his own
generous and openhanded humour (and if a man
check and thwart his true humour in this line 'tis
not unknown what ill may follow). Of a truth,
however, I had latterly feared somewhat for the
ending of it all, for the Fanatics had now laid
embargoes upon as many of the St. Keyne lands as
they could come at, and though privily he still derived
rents from the loyal holders of them, who well knew
that the rule of Cromwell was for a time only, still my
Lord's revenues had within the past year or two very
sensibly diminished,—by a half perhaps, or even two-
thirds. It may be gathered then how contented I
was at having this great windfall and vast addition
of means to meet the outgoings of my kinsman's

establishment. But this is but base, money-bag talk : let us pass on.

Our purpose in coming to Ustica having been so fully accomplished, we had no further reason to stay in the Island. We therefore divided the jewels into two parts and folding them into napkins, disposed them about the persons of each of us, after which we returned the remnants of the casket to their grave, filled it up, smoothed down the sand, and caused our tent to be struck. Then we went on board as we had come, leaving no trace behind us, and no man knew either then or thereafter—nay, no man has ever known or ever had cause to guess until now, and until this my telling of it, that we bore with us from the Island of Ustica a store of great diamonds more precious than any King's Treasury in the world could show, and that which was far beyond them still in price, eight rubies of the renowned lost Amulet of Sultan Solyman the Magnificent.

CHAPTER XXVI.

WE made at once towards Trapani, but were no sooner arrived there than we were recalled by a letter from the Viceroy, bidding us assemble the Squadron at Palermo and prepare to set sail with a part of it for so far off a destination as Cadiz, in Spain, which lies outside the Mediterranean Sea, ten leagues beyond the Pillars of Hercules. There we were to await the arrival of the Lady Geraldine by sea in a frigate of war, from the Groyne of Galicia, in the far north of Spain.

For some time past, that is since the knowledge had reached the Island of my Lord's safety, the Viceroy had been in communication with the Lady Geraldine's friends, and had at length induced them to shorten the time before the marriage ; and in view of the unsettled condition of the Island, to dispense with the presence of the bridegroom in Spain, and to consent that the marriage should take place, not at Madrid, but in Sicilia. My Lord himself had put no obstacle to the consummation of the Viceroy's wishes in this regard ; and as there could be no reasonable objection thereto from any one else, the plan had been carried through. The assent of Lady Geraldine's friends and her own had been made known by letters arrived during our absence in Ustica Island.

My Lord resolved that in the then unquiet state of Sicily it was impolitic to remove the whole of the Fleet to so great a distance; less, however, from apprehension of trouble from the Pirates than of dissensions and revolt both among the troops and the citizens of the great cities, who were now growing incensed against the ill-rule, tyranny, and corruption of their masters. He laid the matter very freely before the Viceroy, who, following his counsel, despatched my Lord himself to Cadiz with two of the Corvettos only, and named me to the command, in his absence, of the squadron that was left.

It was intended that my Lord should sail from Palermo some weeks before Lady Geraldine's ship departed from the Groyne, so that he might have time to visit the King of Spain at Madrid, in New Castile, and report to him of the condition of Sicilia. This was by command of His Majesty himself, who desired to have word of mouth with one who had made such a stir in the great world.

While my Lord was away I took occasion to set his affairs in some order, and with this end I disposed of some six or seven of the smaller gems among the jewellers of Messina and Palermo; the large ones I reserved, not desiring that our possession of such huge stones should get bruited abroad. But even the

sale of the smaller diamonds caused a great commotion, and the goldsmiths to buy them were forced
to join in companies to make up the price of a single
pair of the diamonds, for I had now arrived at some
just appraisement of their value. With their proceeds
my Lord's treasury was amply replenished, and I
could carry out his last orders, which were to prepare
a wing of his palace against the coming of our cousin,
in which, with her suite of ladies, she could dwell under
our guardianship, who were her relatives, in the
interval between her coming to the Island and the
ceremonial of her wedding with the Viceroy. To this
end I was to spare no expense in labour of the best
artificers from Genoa and Naples, or in rich furniture
of hangings, tapestries, and carpets, from the East ;
all which I set about and accomplished in good time.

We lived at this time in one portion of that assemblage of palaces at Palermo, which taken together
are called the Royal Palace. The buildings are set
round a great piazza or courtyard that a small army
might parade in, and the Viceroy and his suite were
very finely lodged over against our palace across the
open square ; my Lord being placed so near the
Viceroy's person that his Grace could readily send for
him or come to him (as he would at times do) familiarly
for converse and counsel on affairs of State. The Lady
Geraldine's dwelling was to be a range of apartments
that lie just beyond my Lord's, and forming part of them,
and that we had held too dainty for a man's and a
soldier's quarters, and so had never used. Here had

formerly been the state residence-house of the Norman
kings of Sicily, and the adornment of the halls,
chambers, and corridors is, for marvellous richness
and fineness, such as mine eyes, in all that I have seen
of the magnificences of the greatest Kings and Princes,
have never yet looked upon ; for the doorways and
windows, all with round-headed arches over them,
and deep set with strange devices and mouldings, are
not cut and carved in common stone, but of rare,
rich marbles, green and yellow or red, polished.
Interspersed with these precious marbles are in-
crustations of gold mosaic, with which the very walls
and the vaulted roofs are everywhere set thick, so
that a torch or lamp being held aloft in these halls
or corridors, its light is cast from ten thousand points
of burnished gold and colour till the place seems on
fire, so great is its glory. This strange work is, I
have heard, not of the Normans, whom the world long
has known for plain, rough, honest, fighting men,
unskilled in such matters, but of the Saracens of the
Island, enslaved by these Northern warriors. The
dwelling-rooms and halls intended for the Viceroy's
bride being thus already so fair to see, I had but little
trouble, with the rich stuffs and hangings aforesaid, to
fit the abode for a great lady's residence.

I may observe for the curious in these matters, that
all these palaces being built in the Moorish fashion,
no such thing as an honest door and door-fastening
is to be found, this being contrary to the lazy habits of
the Moslems, only in their places are hung great

curtains of some rich stuff, silk or embroidered velvet. In my cousin's apartments I ordered these door-curtains to be fashioned of Genoese velvet, very rich, of a delicate dark green hue, and embroidered here and there with black and gold. Ha! It makes me laugh to think how I, a plain grizzled old soldier, had come to this employment of tricking out a lady's bower with satins and velvets; and how I would stand, with a severe, frowning, ignorant face, feeling the substance of a rich hanging, and pretending to know more about it than the seller thereof; or giving an inexorable judgment, with no appeal therefrom allowed, on the value of a Venetian mirror or a carpet from Teheran!

Note, also, that so great is the roguery and so infinite the subtlety of these Sicilians, that I would trust none of them with so much as the victualling of my Lord's palace; as not wishing to deliver over my kinsman to the robbing and reiving of the citizen purveyors of the Island; but I caused the whole provisioning and supplying of our palace to be done by Corporals and Sergeants of our troops, Spaniards or Italians, honest fellows as day, but mighty simple in the hands of these foxish Italians of Sicily.

Good lack! what a state it was we lived in : not a morning but a hundred beggars at the gates waited for the largesse of broken meat of the day before. My Lord's retinue of servants in livery was indeed kingly, and when we passed through the corridors and outer halls, their standing up to salute us was the rising of a multitude. My Lord chose to ration the men of his

Body-Guard with meat, bread, and wine, at his private
cost, not esteeming the treatment in this kind of the
Sicilians worthy of such approved and valiant troops ;
and to every two of the Viceroy's soldiers (whom he
ennobled with the title of *Gentlemen of the Viceregal
Guard*) he appointed a servant to wait upon them.
There were besides these soldiers' servants, a vast body
of servants of his own, of whose numbers I have now
but a confused and doubtful memory, and fearing to
set down a greater number than the truth, will forbear
from any record. I can however well remember that
for victualling of our own Palace and our own guard I
gave orders that the daily purveyance should never be
less than, of wine one and a half *salma* (that is, about
sixty gallons English), of fat beeves two, of sheep
seven (but the Sicilian sheep are small, seldom reaching to seven stone by our West of England computa-
tion ; to wit, between fifty and sixty pounds), of flour
and meal of various corns four *salmas* (dry measure).
Besides these necessaries, there were fixed quantities,
which my memory has let slip, of hams and lard from
Trapani, olives and oil from about Catania, poultry,
fruit of every kind in season, fish *ad libitum* from the
three Seas of the Island, and beasts of the chase and
warren in autumn and winter, to wit, wild boar, deer,
hares, and coneys ; besides game and wild fowl, as
cranes, partridges, frankolins ; together with all manner
of swamp birds, such as snipe, dunlins, ducks, and
didappers ; the whole in very great variety and
abundance.

My Lord was away fifty-seven days before I received a letter from him, so slow and difficult are communications through these Pirate-scourged waters. He had prosperously and quickly reached Cadiz and there, receiving news of the busy doings of the Rovers on all the Spanish Coasts, had sent his ships round to Lisbon in Portugal, having got word that our cousin's ship would touch at that Port on her voyage south, and resolving to convoy the Spanish Frigate in which she travelled through the perils of the southern seas. My Lord's letter was expressed in a private book-cypher we used between us, and he told me how King Philip had received him graciously at Madrid (whence he then wrote), and had made him a surprising offer, which was no less than to take the command of a Fleet for the recapture of the two great sea cities of Portugal, to wit, Lisbon and Oporto, which had been, with the Kingdom of Portugal itself, lost to Spain about twelve years before, Portugal having then happily recovered its ancient independence, after having lost it for some sixty years. My cousin Ralph had refused this offer, he told me, not being willing to fight against the liberties of a free people. I cannot hear that any further attempt was ever made by Spain, either by way of Fleet or Army, to recover the Kingdom of Portugal. Her independence was however not fully acknowledged by her great neighbour for many years. I imagine therefore that my kinsman's opinion of the King's and his Councillors' project, which he probably was pressed for and propounded (though he forgot or forbore to speak on the subject to me afterwards, in the press of more important topics) may have dissuaded them from any committal of themselves to a foolhardy and indeed an infamous undertaking.

As my cousin Ralph at his writing was on the eve of leaving Madrid for Lisbon, and would again depart from that city for Sicily so soon as the Lady Geraldine should arrive, I was not without expectation of seeing them very soon, there being then a favouring wind from the west ; and this happy event took place in less than ten days afterwards.

I am informed that in Spain the Court ceremonial is excessive beyond all example in other countries, and tedious to those persons that care nothing for such empty formal observances, among whom I name myself. Chiefly long and tedious are they, and beyond belief absurd, when any women's affairs are in hand, such as a wedding, or the birth of an Infante or Infanta; circumstances these in which the women about the Court, chiefly the old women (of both sexes —the females being known as Dueñas or, as we say, Duennas) claim to have a voice, and getting it, carry their follies to more unconscionable lengths than usual. As the Court of Sicily never fails to repeat to the echo every observance of the mother Court of Spain, and as the commotion from a falling stone is greater in a horse-pond than in the sea, so it may be imagined the stir which the Viceroy's projected marriage, and the arrival of his bride, made in the capital city of this Island. Indeed I will ask the forbearing Reader to imagine it rather than to ask me, a plain soldier of my King, and with such brains as he possesses set on the grave affairs of life, to chronicle such preposterous nothings as now took place at Palermo on the coming of the Lady Geraldine. Suffice it to say that on the arrival of the Spanish Frigate and my Lord's Corvettos, Lady Geraldine and her four demure Duennas, all ladies of great birth (and age to match), had been transferred at Lisbon to my cousin's Flag Ship. On the arrival of the vessels a salute of seventeen guns was fired, neither more nor less, and the city (by command) hung with flags. The Court then betook itself to a Pavilion set up in a Piazza near the quay, the streets being lined with troops, and horse and foot patrolling everywhere, for it was well known the people were ripe for insurrection.

To this place came the Viceroy on horseback, encircled by his body guard of troopers under my orders. Arrived at the Pavilion his Grace dismounted and the troop closed in upon him. Thereupon the foot-guards, under me too, for I now had sole command of all the palace and city troops, stood around him as he sat upon a gilt throne, each man with his musquetoon so close to his neighbour that never an assassin among the mutineers could get an opening for a snap shot at his Grace betwixt our ranks. I mention this, for we had warning that several discontented citizens with stilettos or horse pistols were to be in the crowd that day. It is to be observed too that, for all the show of holiday bravery of gold lace on our fellows' doublets and scarves, and their white buckskin gauntlets, all flashing bright in the sun, each man of my cavalry had had his sword fresh ground and set that morning, and his great horse-pistols were loaded with ball and fresh primed ; and the foot soldiers too had their musquetoons loaded with slugs and all in readiness for a fight.

However, the crowd were daunted, and no worse weapons or missiles than scowls and curses reached the Viceroy and his little Court, as he sat with his Councillors, while the great crowd of discontented Sicilian citizens swayed and surged all about, outside our swords and muskets.

From the Pavilion to the quay is a distance of about 100 paces or less along the Piazza and through a short straight street, all which way was laid down with a crimson cloth, and along either side thereof were planted high poles bearing banners, and from pole to pole were hung, in great garlands, all manner of sweet-scented blossoms and green leaves, for it was now the middle of the floral month of July, when all the gardens of Sicily are at their richest and fairest. Along this flowery and sweetly odorous lane was the bride to pass, so soon as she had disembarked from the Viceregal barge which should fetch her from the ship ; not afoot though, but borne in a gilt litter fantastically carved and carried by twelve turbaned negroes in the Moorish dress, very rich and brave ; six

others of the same swart complexion, bearing aloft a
canopy of gold-embroidered purple silk over the
maiden's head.

All this came about as it had been ordered, and my
first view of the newly arrived bride was now, for I
had not dared to leave my men and their ordering to
go and greet her on board the ship in the Harbour, so
critical and momentous did the state of things among
the citizens seem to us all.

Ralph St. Keyne walked by the side of his cousin's
litter, and the first knowledge we had of their coming
upon the quay was the cheers and joyful clamour of
the multitude, the first in that kind we had heard this
day, for the Sicilians ever looked upon my Lord as
their friend. Presently the bride was arrived to where
we stood, and alighting from her litter with my Lord's
hand given to her, she was led by him up the two or
three steps of the *daïs* under the Pavilion to where the
Viceroy bridegroom was sitting. He, such was the
obligation upon him of his state, could do no more in
his courtesy to welcome her than to rise from his
throne and advance two paces to meet his bride, taking
her hand in his and bending over it with some spoken
words of salutation which the shouting of the crowd
did not let me hear.

I had taken some pains to prefigure to myself the
transformation that must needs have taken place from
my little child cousin to a grown woman, but good
lack ! how far was I from expecting to see such a tall,
fair and comely maiden as this, with the sweetest,

softest face and eyes, poor child ! that ever, I think,
woman possessed. I say "poor child," for now when
all was done, and she was here in Sicily and in a few
days to become the wife of a husband so unfit for a
young girl, I said to myself, even as I stood there
among my soldiers, "What have I and Ralph done to
let things come to this ? We have between us betrayed
our cousin ; " and my blood ran hot through my veins.

She came forward, modest and wondering and
dazed, seemingly, by the crowd, and the noise of
shouting, and the clash of cymbal music that had filled
the air from her landing ; and yet very graciously and
gracefully, for the maiden had a most noble presence
and a carriage that fitted her birth and breeding, and
with some show of courage too through all her
modesty, for I watched her closely with the above
thoughts running strongly in my head. Then when
she caught sight of her husband that was to be, her
countenance fell, and she went suddenly paler and
looked enquiringly at her cousin, as if to ask, "Can
this be he ? "

The Viceroy was very gallant in his dress and
bearing that day ; his vest and doublet so heavy with
gold embroidery on green velvet, his sword hilt and
laced baldrick and belt so sparkling with diamonds,
that it was easy to see even by this bravery, and
apart from his alone wearing the red jewelled cross
and collar of the Order of Calatrava, that he was the
chief of all who stood there. He made his advance
to the Lady Geraldine very courteously, and, bowing

B B

low, his periwig (which he and his courtiers wore in the fashion of the Court of France) fell straight down on either side of his face like a great curly fleece of wool, and almost hid it for the moment. Yet it was impossible for this perruque, abundantly as it was furnished and much as it advanced on either side of his face, to hide the wrinkles and sallowness, the heavy jowl and the dull and careful eyes of age.

I cannot say whether any Reader of mine is lenient enough to my many shortcomings to accept my opinion on a woman, and certainly I would counsel none to do this hastily, not because, as has been very falsely alleged of me, I am a misogynist ; I am indeed no woman hater, but I will frankly acknowledge that I have always been indifferent to and unobservant of the sex. Because I am indifferent no doubt I am wholly ignorant ; and 'tis probably my ignorance only that has made me ever so extremely mistrustful of them. It is therefore perhaps either this ignorance and inexperience of mine that is now speaking, or that I naturally favour one of my own nation and so near myself in blood ; but I do now protest that this sweet English maiden seemed to me to show here in Sicily like a swan among crows. Instead of being formally muffled up in black, like the Spanish ladies about her, whose fashion is to wear their very ears and napes covered with a mantilla, she was attired after the latest mode, which our King's Dutch painter, Sir Peter Lely, has since then put upon his canvases ; to wit, with a wild but studied disorder in her gown-folds, which gown to-day was of pale blue satin with a little white about it. Her neck was bare, though it was midday, her hair cut down short over her forehead and combed into little delicate ringlets at the temples ; in the bosom of her dress, to set off the blue satin, a twist of great orient peals, set there with an artful, artless grace. Her arms like her neck were bare, to the astonishment and envy of the Sicilian ladies, only on her little hands, which bore her fan, she wore white gloves reaching half way to the elbow and embroidered with seed pearl, and with great round pearls for buttons. Her skin was indeed incredibly white, and as smooth, methought, as cream, her eyes blue and gentle, and her young, innocent, simple face set among the swart, sharp-featured, hawk-nosed Sicilian dames, —did I liken her to a swan among crows? I would rather say to an angel come among devils (though, I admit, comely and seductive ones) but after all, I am the maiden's cousin and countryman, and some allowance is to be made for me, if I show a preference.

Well, I have got as far as I can bring myself to go in the reporting of the Court ceremonies that now took place ; but let no one suppose what I have told was all, or nearly all. It was but the beginning, for indeed there was no room in the Pavilion for the deploying and manœuvring of all the forces of Courtiers and Court ladies. The grand Parade and Field Day was therefore put off till it could take place in the Viceroy's Palace. And we were all, Courtiers and

Officers alike, drilled beforehand, like recruits, and had to learn each of us his movements in the "Function" (as they called it) from a written paper. *Ex ungue leonem :* here is a bit of my own lesson ; *Captain St. Keyne will thereupon slowly advance to the Viceregal Throne, and at about six paces from it bow three times very low to the Viceroy, carrying his hand the while lightly to his sword-hilt in token of fidelity to his Grace's person : then will he remove his hand from his sword and bow once, but rather less low, to the Lord President and the Councillors of State on the right of the Throne, and to the Lords Lieutenants of the Island, the Judges and great officers on the left ; and upon recovering from the last of these reverences, he will advance and kiss hands, first that of the Viceroy, then that of the Lady Geraldine Scudamour."* Enough of these futilities ! Let us come to more urgent matters.

My Lord had returned from Spain in a very changed humour, which I was at first inclined to suppose might arise from discontent with his service here with the Viceroy of Sicily, since he could not but perceive after his journeying to Spain that a genius for war and for affairs like his might find scope for flight worthier of him, and a quarry nobler than any to be started in this remote Island of the Mediterranean Sea. But when I questioned him, he told me plainly this was not so : That he was here and bound to the Viceroy, was a matter of no concern to him at all ; he and I, he said, had given as good as or indeed better than we had got in Sicily, and he felt so little irked by his bond that he would take leave, if he were in a mind to do so, to break it at a moment's notice. Indeed he had so resolved long before, and but for his cousin's marriage intervening, and the threatening of an insurrection, and his unwillingness to leave the Viceroy in the lurch, he would not now be in the Island.

"Why then, Ralph, in the Devil's name" (for at times, if I happened to lose patience, I used some of my old tutor's freedom with my cousin) "in the Devil's name, man," said I, "what ails you to be so glum and moody?"

He was pleased to smile a little, but presently resumed his old sad look and knitted brow.

"Is it our cousin's marriage that troubles you?" I asked him.

He said it was; but vouchsafed no further interpretation of his solicitude.

"Would to God!" I cried, "I could clap her and you and myself aboard the *Golondrina*" (this was the swift galley we had got him out of Tunis with) "and sail for Bristol city, and so get us all to St. Keyne Castle, out of this nest of ceremonious foreign rogues and civil-spoken, posture-mongering thieves."

He shook his head: "I would 'twere possible!" he muttered.

"Why not?" cried I. "Say the word and I do it to-morrow!"

"Why, Humphrey," said he, "what is this you

say? You know as well as I do what stands in the
way—that 'tis her honour and her plighted word,
my honour and yours."

Truly enough, I knew it and had only spoke thus
idly in my anger at this turn of ill fortune that had
come upon us. "Poor Geraldine!" quoth I, with
something liker to a sigh than anything I had uttered
in my life before, I think. "'Tis a melancholy fate we
have prepared for thee."

I have so often said that I know nothing of women
and their ways, and yet have so often made bold to
pass my opinion upon both, that the most forbearing
reader will peradventure begin to be impatient with
me if I now say that the very best and wisest of them
(and I take my cousin Geraldine to be both) have but
the very sorriest notion in the world of foreseeing the
future, and are by nature so little provident of their
own welfare that if they are advised to any course
or if only they tell themselves it is one that others
follow, they will pursue it as one sheep follows the
flock, unthinking, and as if they were imperilling
some other life and body than their own. They only
begin to be dismayed and to cry out for help when
help can no longer come to them, and when they
have slipped or leapt (and be hanged to them!) over
the precipice and see the rocks below which shall
presently (poor wretches) rend and destroy their
tender bodies.

Chiefly, as I think, are women thus simple when
marriage is concerned, and though we men are no

better than fools for the shutting of our eyes to what
all but we can see, and will bind ourselves for
life to a scold that we love for her sweetness, or to
a fool for her wisdom, a slattern for her discreet
carefulness, or to some other disguised imp of Satan
that we take for a better kind of angel ; yet in this
matter of pure blind, insane foolhardiness, our male
foolishness is as nothing to the madness of women
Only one ground have I for not calling my sweet
cousin Geraldine by a stronger name than fool, if
stronger name there be in the direction of foolishness ;
and that is that the child was not heart-whole, and
being forlorn and hopeless and desperate, recked less
than nothing of what became of her, and so had
taken ∤this devil-possessed leap in the dark. I did
not indeed know this for certain till afterwards, and
perhaps have no right even now and here to hint at
the matter, but already I had reason to guess something of how the matter lay.

I was never, all my life long, much of a courtier,
having found my knees of a most unaccommodating
stiffness when I have come to bend them before any
alien Sovereign. Indeed they refuse any pliancy at
all at such times but on compulsion of my will. Nor
will they ever willingly ply but in presence of my
own revered Sovereign, to whom to feel love and
offer allegiance is sure sweeter and nobler than
Independence itself. So it was that when I
endeavoured to treat my girl cousin with some
of the respect and observance owing to her coming

state and dignity, I found it a hardish matter to accomplish. The more so as she would in no wise help me : indeed I believe it was as much the maiden's kindly nature as my own churlish one that was in fault, she not being willing to endure to be so stiffly treated by one she had loved as a child, and who she knew loved her too (for I must make free confession here of that weakness in me). Be it how it might ; if I but said " Madam " to her she would laugh. If we were at Court and in observation of the Courtiers, and I made her an obeisance, she would whisper as I came near her, " How can you, dear Humphrey ? " If I reproved her, as I would in private, and pretty sternly too, for not forgetting our kinship and for not being more haughty with me, her countenance would fall and the tears stand in her eyes. So it came to be that when the Courtiers or Duennas were not present to observe us, she and I would often fall into our old way of talking, and speak of old times with us, when I was guardian and tutor to my Lord at St. Keyne and in a fashion to her as well, and my two young pupils were companions and in a way playmates, though there was a difference of between seven and eight years between them. She dearly loved now to hear of all that had happened to her kinsman since our parting with her at St. Keyne Castle. "Ah!" she said, " if I could but have come with you as I had desired."

" Why, Mrs. Geraldine," said I, "thou wert surely never in earnest to propose thyself for a Bellario ? "

" Yes indeed, Humphrey, I was quite in earnest."

" I warrant now you never thought of your poor cousin Ralph again after our parting," said I, willing to droll a little with her.

" Ah ! " cried she, " you little know! You should have let me come with you to take care of you both, Humphrey."

" Why, poor child, thou wouldest have had but a rough service, what with fighting our way through our enemies in England, and our hard days of travelling through Germany, and then again the snows and the frost and the lofty hills to climb, and the robbers to fend off in the Tyrolean Alps."

" Nay ! " she cried, for she was ever tender of heart, " I saw it all in thought, and you never put foot in stirrup or marched a step on your way but I was with you in heart. Alas ! " cried she, " I had like to have died a hundred times for fright of his—of your fate," and she cited from Dr. Donne' poem, clasping her little hands and looking up, in the fashion of the players :—

> " I saw him go
> O'er the white Alps alone : I saw him, I,
> Assailed, fight, taken, stabbed, bleed, fall and die."

And it was the prettiest thing to see and hear her, for she had got, or put on ('twas the mode then) an odd sort of a little lisp in her speech ; she dragged her words out slowly, just as the play-actors do, and with such a feeling and sadness in them that it seemed not possible but she must weep outright ere she could end the line and come to, "bleed, fall and die."

"And would you in truth, Geraldine, knowing all the dangers we have run, have been willing to accompany us?"

"Ay! with all my heart."

"Why then, Mrs. Geraldine," said I, still drolling with her, "how would you have fared in the sea-fight off this city, when we were so hard pressed? You could not have skulked below; being in man's dress and so near my Lord it would have behoved you for example's sake to stay, and face wounds and death itself."

She trembled a little and turned red, "And do you think, Humphrey, I would have feared wounds or death by his side?" Then in lower, muttered voice to herself, which I could not be sure I rightly caught "Besides, I was sorely wounded, all the time, before."

CHAPTER XXVII

I HAD never known my cousin Ralph in so brooding and unhappy a humour as at this time. He was in truth divided between his duty on the one side to his master, the Viceregent of Sicily, which behoved him to stand between the Throne and the insane murderous turbulence of the citizens, while on the other there was his hatred for the tyranny and oppression of the Sicilian Rulers, against which the people had justification enough to protest and murmur, and even, as we conceived, to rise in arms; for the Spaniards are in Sicily by no right but of conquest, and as such, are more than other Rulers, bound to justice and mercy towards their subjects.

About five years before this, Spanish oppression had so overborne the fears of the people in Palermo, that they had run desperately against their rulers; and their desperation being sharpened by a famine that was then pinching them, and which they believed arose from the cruel taxings and exactions of their foreign masters, their mutiny was so fierce and sudden that the Spaniards were overborne and the city of Palermo had no doubt been burned to the ground, and every head man and magistrate murdered by the enraged multitude, had not the moderate counsels of some monks and others, who were neither against the lower people nor exactly of them, prevailed ; but this only after fire had been set to some Palaces and many of the Spaniards had lost their lives. The Viceroy's troops were quite daunted, and hid or fled, and he himself with his Court and chief officers (not this present Viceregent, but a precursor of his) sought refuge ignominiously in his ships, and thus saved his neck. In the meantime the people acclaimed for their leader one Alessio, an honest, well meaning fellow, with his mouth full of high talk of equity, and mercy, and reformation of wrongs ; but poor Alessio soon found, as others have, that the Throne is an uneasy seat, and the Sceptre a heavy instrument for a weak, unused hand to bear. For all his talk of justice and mercy, he began his reign by hanging a brother insurgent ringleader who he fancied was creeping too near his throne, with a mind to oust himself. Then he went on from bad to worse ; ruling too mercifully for some, too hardly for others, letting some of his followers get too rich, and keeping others too poor. He increased his enemies daily, and his friends not at all, was wrongly accused of treachery by the first, and coldly defended by the last ; insomuch that after a few weeks of wretched rule, in a rising of his new subjects the unhappy Alessio was by them torn cruelly to pieces and his head kicked like a football through the streets of Palermo.

Over the ruins of Alessio's short empire the Spaniards crept again into their places, and as soon as they felt securely seated therein they began to scourge the city with exceeding malevolence for its mutiny; using the barbarous cruelty of repression which the weak and the cowardly ever employ. They established their government again upon the terror they inspired, and again lived and prospered upon the wrongs and oppressions of the unfortunate Sicilians.

This had taken place five years before, and since then my Lord's victories over the Pirates by increasing the labours and profits of the farming and fisher people in the Island had bestowed prosperity with peace upon all alike and so had staved off for a time that famine which ever follows upon oppression.

Now, had the Spaniards been but moderate in their exactions, all had yet gone well, but so soon as they perceived the yield of the fields and markets to rise, and the gains of country folk, city folk and fisher folk to increase, they must needs lay their greedy hands upon these gains in their haste to grow rich at the people's cost, and again starvation and famine threatened the people of Sicily.

These then were the horns of the dilemma we were fixed on : for my cousin argued, " If in my impatience of the Spaniards' tyranny I leave them to the anger of the people, the revenge the insurgents will take

will be bloody and without bounds, and no improved government of this wretched country can
ensue; for the Spaniards, with all the power of
King Philip behind them, are strong enough to re-
conquer the Island ten times over, with suffering to
the poor ignorant people beyond words. If on the
other hand I stay, I countenance the tyranny and
cause it to continue."

This it was that troubled him greatly; and he could
see no way of escape for him but to stay on and endeavour to temper the severity of the governors while
he persuaded the governed to more patience.

So it was that while the preparations for the
wedding were taking place, Ralph was busy almost
daily, either at the Council or with the Viceroy, or
with the secretaries, the consuls (as they are called
here) and other rulers of the city and people; warning
them of the imminent peril of over-severity, prevailing
upon them to mingle lenity with justice, and generally
interceding for the people. The governors were not
so blind to the future or forgetful of the recent past
as not greatly to fear an insurrection; and when he
so warned them and pleaded with them, 'tis acknowledged he persuaded them to his way of thinking; and
so an insurrection that we knew was just then actually
kindling to a mighty flame and blaze, was, for the
time, stifled and stayed.

It was upon this great and imminent business that
my cousin was engaged immediately upon his return
from Spain to the excluding of all other affairs,

insomuch that he for days together abstained from appearing at Court, and even withdrew himself from the society of the Lady Geraldine, though she was residing under his very roof.

I now fully understand his reason for this restraint of his cousinly and friendly intercourse with and interest in the girl, but at the time I did not even suspect there was anything in the matter beyond the great urgency of State affairs, being myself of a very un-regarding habit, and never apt to look below the surface of my friends' and companions' minds for motives and purposes which they themselves refrain from informing me of. So soon as he had despatched this aforesaid great business, and so soon as he could assure himself that he had warded off the peril of a sudden movement of the populace, and he had his leisure again, I expected from my cousin a return to the comity and companionableness of life, in which he had till now ever been the first to delight, in times of freedom from affairs. Yet he still held aloof, and so far from helping me to reconcile myself to the lot which lay before our girl cousin, he avoided mention of the subject as he still avoided the maiden herself.

CHAPTER XXVIII.

As I am chronicling the opinions as well as the life-story of my cousin, I must endeavour to make clear in this place that one of all his concepts which has roused the most questioning and curiosity among the learned. The more bound am I to do this, inasmuch as his arriving at this opinion was a sort of turning point in his own life, from and after which a change was upon him. Not that he ever turned his back upon his former way of thinking or of action, or altered either in essentials; but the river of his life, so to say, hereafter flowed with a stronger and swifter current : it had in its course broken down and passed through a great obstructive weir, which till now had dammed back the waters of his being into stagnation. This turning point, this eventful passage in his life, has been spoken of since, but too vaguely, as his acceptance (I would myself rather call it his discovery) of the Doctrine of the " World Spirit." This phrase, " World Spirit," I will use for lack of a better, and because it was he who first coined it, but he was never quite pleased therewith.

That my cousin should have chosen, as he did, the

short lull in affairs that now occurred, as a time for abstracting his thoughts from the world of men, and for thinking out this new doctrine of his philosophy, would seem as strange a circumstance to me as I am persuaded it does to the Reader, did I not know that the cause of it lay in that power acquired by him (of which I have already spoken) of transporting and abstracting himself, for duty's sake, from pursuing after that which his soul might love. I alone could guess what it now cost him to seek solitude and to convey his thoughts upon the cold, solitary heights of philosophy when the valleys below tempted him, whence came up to him confusedly the sounds of life and comfortable hum of men and women's voices.

There are times in all our lives of such heavy dreariness, and bitter disappointment and hopelessness of all attainment, that we are driven thereby into deeper melancholy, which I am persuaded could end in nothing else than madness, were we not able to work out a salvation from our misery by our own energy, and through the workings of that same mysterious *World Spirit* in regard to which I will now speak of my cousin's doctrine and opinions.

When we passed through the Low Countries Ralph had been greatly disappointed to have come too late to have word of mouth with that greatest among thinkers of our day and most generous among men and soldiers, Monsieur René Descartes, who had for many years found in these civil regions a refuge

C C

from ignorant spite and persecution ; but this famous Philosopher had passed away from the living only a few months before our arrival, and that not in the land of his adoption but in Sweden, whither the rage of his enemies had at length driven him.

In Monsieur Descartes's exposition of the problem of life my kinsman had once thought to find safe mooring for his own questionings, so cunningly did the French philosopher steer his way among the shoals and rocks which had wrecked others, and so honestly refuse to seek or enforce conviction but where his foundation was sure.

Ralph St. Keyne could go some way in his company. He could say with him, " *Cogito ergo sum ;*" because I can think, I know that I exist—not otherwise. I could not think were I not a being holding of God ; were I, that is, bereft of certain innate and connate ideas, and chief of them that there is a perfect God, who was, and is, and will be ; and that as perfection includes omnipotence, so must God be not the Creator only of the material universe, but its Informer, whose infinite perfection is reflected in me in the aforesaid innate ideas of Justice, Mercy, Truth, and even of Limitation and Doubt ; for that I doubt itself implies that I look to a certitude beyond myself, and that Certitude is God.   Thus was the Cartesian Principle reflected in the mirror of my kinsman's intelligence, a faint image, though not a distorted one ; but hereabouts he began to differ and his path to diverge from his who was in a sense and in his beginnings (chiefly for the great admiration he had for this master's understanding and honesty) his guide and teacher in philosophy. For in my cousin's esteem, the Cartesian God was too abstract and metaphysical a Deity for his own acceptance ; it being a positive profanity in Ralph's eyes to contemplate the great Creator of the Universe otherwise than as its Preserver too, and as the Perfect and Infinite God who was all in all, was present in every creature and in every act of that creature; " So that," said he, "it is not I who think, but God within me who thinks." So too was it that when Monsieur Descartes insisted upon an essential difference in spiritual and material things, in thought and extended substance, my kinsman insisted upon all phenomena and all created beings, all their acts, all thought, volition and emotion, being forms of extension emanating from the Divine Essence. That some of these phenomena are evil was no stumbling block, for evil was in his eyes perhaps not a positive thing at all, but a negative one, the absence of good—as cold is not a positive thing but the absence of heat ; or it was a perversion of the good, and being so, might in time be changed and perfected to good. Thus we could obtain the comfortable assurance that the reign of evil would not tend to permanent ascendency, but that there was that of Divine implanted in all societies of men which ever made for goodness.

So wandering in the maze with all of us who are not content to sit in idle and indifferent thought-

lessness, Ralph St. Keyne soon let go from his hand
the clue that Monsieur Descartes had held out to him.
He had pondered very deeply upon the problem
of life and death and the ordering of the world, and
in turn had walked with all the great masters of
thought, both of old and of these later days, and
with all in turn had come before the locked Portal
which might not be passed. Each would offer him a
key to the lock, but no key would open it to his hand
and show the promised shining land beyond : and he
was grievously discouraged to observe how each
thinker was for opening this ultimate Portal with a
key of his own designing ; how each Philosophy contained nothing of a description of the further land but
only of the key to the Portal, its wards and figurings,
and how, rightly used, it could not fail to thrust back
the bolts and bars of the Portal gate. Beyond
promising this, none went. None even could tell what
this lock was, that so obstinately shut out the inner
world from man's inspection ; of the lock they said
nothing ; of the Portal, nothing ; of the land beyond,
nothing ; of their key, too much. Now it was this
very consideration of the great divergence of thinkers
and the as great divergence in their solution of the
problem, that first shed some little ray of light upon
Lord St. Keyne in the darkness of his groping ; for
he began to ask himself the reason, and whether it
might not be that man's self, man's own mind and
heart, his intelligence, that is, as influenced by his
emotions, were not themselves the locked door which

barred him from the truth ; or, to put it more clearly, whether his own imagination, habits, prepossesions, and prejudices did not so grow up in him as to cloud and bedim his own intelligence, that only spyglass wherewith to view the far-off spiritual world.

This set him upon thinking how infinitely different are men's minds, and how impossible for any two to see quite alike. Again, as that is not confirmed truth for the world, or even for the seer himself, which but one can see and shall fail to persuade others to see, so perhaps will the truth of ultimate things never be revealed to the world because of this Babel of diverse intelligences, of which doubtless the failure to reach to heaven by the confusion of tongues in the old Babel builders is but a fabled fore-image.

After perceiving this he began to enquire whether there might not be some attribute common to all men, some universal faculty or quality, untouched, or at least not eradicated by habit, passion, emotion or prejudice, whereby they and perhaps all creatures of God could be (as the arithmeticians say) brought into some common denomination together, and so perhaps the resolution of the great problem attained.

" Yes ! " he cried, " *Eureka !* I have found it— there is one thing in common so strong that it can overcome or nearly overcome all passion, habit, emotion or prejudice." It was the endeavour in all created beings after the heightening and enhancement of their existences, the unreasoning delight in the living functions even when life is no longer

delightful, which is implanted in all living creatures:
the desire not to live only but to increase and extend
the mere delight of continuing to breathe this vital air
This something, this mysterious and unreasoning force
he would christen " *The World Spirit*," as being an
incarnation in all life upon the earth, in all living
creatures, from man to the fly and worm and meanest
creeping thing, of the very soul of God Himself; and
as being that which beyond all else informs and
dominates the world we live in, its soul and spirit in
manifest shape. It is an attribute, an energy, mean
and limited in the meaner creatures, but rising with
increasing glory in those of higher endowment till it
reaches its earthly altitude and meridian in man
himself, and comprehends all that raises him towards
Heaven, as love, and charity, and the energy to
employ every high faculty of the soul ; but yet is still
imperfect and unaccomplished, and must needs attain
its final culmination only in the Creator and Informer
and Preserver of the world Himself. By means of the
reverent contemplation of this universal " World
Spirit " in all its so various and varying phases, we
could, my kinsman hoped, consider and contemplate
God Himself, and reach to a nearer knowledge of His
nature and the working of His Spirit in ourselves.

I have thus but indicated my cousin's doctrine of
the " World Spirit," giving here but a foretaste and
ample of that which I shall hereafter fully lay before
the world in my still unfinished work on my Lord St.
Keyne's Philosophic System, to be entitled " *Nobilis-*

simi Domini Sancti Keynii Doctrinæ Expositio."
Enough to say now that the Doctrine widened his
Philosophy at once and softened the asperity and
austerity of his long-held stoical convictions.

I have said that he perceived this aforesaid "World
Spirit" in all that was endowed with life. I should
have limited this last word perhaps to sentient life,
but I was and still am unwilling to make this reserva-
tion in his name, for he was inclined and all but consented to extend the existence of the "World Spirit"
into inanimate beings, so that he loved in fancy at
least to read its manifestation in all the nature of this
fair and favoured Island; in the leaves of trees, turning their green and glistening surfaces under the
breeze with a hundred changing shapes of beauty towards the radiant sun; in the flowers heavy with
odorous wealth with which in their bounty they en-
riched the surrounding air, that already did not lack
the accompaniment of music, namely the treble song
of woodland birds, and humming of innumerable bees
to make an harmonic bass in this symphony of things
and beings, all creatures and obeissant lieges of
God.

There is a retired valley high up in the mountains
behind the city of Palermo and within the reach of it
in an hour's riding, and therein stands a little country
house set in a goodly garden adorned with many
smooth-lipped fountains and conduits and runnels for
the flowing water, all of polished white marble. Here
in spring and early summer, the song of throstles and

nightingales is ever heard, and the plane and orange trees, thickset, with jasmine and roses in their inter-spaces, make a green dusk and refreshing odorous coolness in the heats of noontide.

To this solitary place, which had no owner but himself, my kinsman had lately resorted daily, and here when I wanted him for advice or orders, I sought him. I would find him ever, now against his former wont, idle, having abandoned books, with all researches into the nature of things, and all conference with the learned; living now only in reverie and meditation here in this retired and hidden nook, where silence reigned, but for the summer hum of insects, the rustle of leaves, the twitter of hidden birds, and the sound of ever falling and flowing water.

Here he sought and found the rest he needed, for in truth my kinsman was at this season of his life somewhat worn and wasted with the vicissitudes of our busy campaigns and weakened with the fever fol-lowing upon sundry grievous wounds gotten therein ; and he sorely needed the rest that now he was taking. I have observed that they who are of such fine and eager spirit as his are less able to bear wounds and fatigue and the hard betidings of war, than men of coarser grain and rougher fibre, such as my own ; as the humble cruse or crock will endure usage that shall break in pieces the vessel of more artful workmanship, and as Mr. Dryden has well said, the souls of great men over inform their bodies and waste them to decay.

It was in this secluded pleasance that he discoursed to me after the tenour of what I have now been setting down. It was in such a spot as this, if in any, and in this season, if in any, that the fatigues of constant warfare might easily have seemed to him vain, fond and foolish; that he might have cried, "A truce with war, *sat militavi*, I have fought enough, and again, *Deus nobis hæc otia fecit*, Providence has surely prepared for me this retreat and repose now that I have so laboured through the heat and burden of the day;" but far from him was any such faineance. If he paused, it was only that his philosophy was enlarging its bounds, and that he rested a while before he should take a loftier flight; "for," said he, with this new doctrine of the "*world spirit*" forcing itself upon his convictions, "am I not in the wrong if I think, by myself alone and with unaided strength, to force myself along the path to truth when I should take all Nature into my confidence and enter into hers, and so," he waved his hand round about him on all within this fair garden, "take my own part in this eternally entoned symphony of the creatures of God?"

Thinking I saw in all this some lessening of that ascetic spirit which had as yet caused him to measure out the future fate of our cousin Geraldine in a path as hard to tread as his own; and guessing that this would be a favourable moment to confer with him on the lot that was before her, I came full upon the matter with him one day that I had ridden out to his retreat among the mountains.

"Cousin Ralph," said I, "they have fixed the marriage for this day se'nnight. Now I am for this, that we cannot let it be at all."

He looked at me with a face full of amazement at my offhandedness.

" On what account or reason ?" asked he.

" On account first that to marry a young girl to an old man is a sin."

" 'Tis too late to refrain from committing it," he said.

" Secondly, on account that we who are grown men and know the world have taken advantage of the weak will of a child who knows it not, and the spoiling of all her life will be our doing, not hers, who has had but a poor half-knowledge of things in the nebulosities of a Convent close."

" Will she not, being a woman, and young and unset in opinion and habit, fall into the ways of her new life, and conform to it and find her happiness in it ?"

" By Heaven ! Ralph," cried I, losing patience with him, "if she learn to conform to the ways of an old Spanish Courtier husband, and to love their formality and hypocrisy, 'twill be the spoiling of the sweetest, tenderest, truest maiden that ever breathed our English air."

Ralph St. Keyne was dashed a little by my boldness and impatience with him, and held his peace, as perhaps not finding an immediate answer to a plea he knew so sound.

Now, Reader, thou thinkest doubtless I am as

simple a man in certain matters as some idle, shrewish talk of mine throughout this narration has evidenced. Well, perhaps I have a little misled thee of set purpose. Perhaps I have a shrewder knowledge of men and women than I have cared to betray. I will make no boast however, and indeed I will not say another word on the subject, except that I have not read the writings of Messer Niccolo Macchiavelli without some profit therein. This subtle Italian is of opinion that if we have a mind to gain our will of one of a noble nature we must take him by some noble quality he possesses, as pity, or gratitude or generosity or what not ; contrariwise, if we have to do with a mean man, we can surely turn him through some mean attribute in him, as envy, vanity, self-love—the numbering of them is but too easy.

Perhaps if I were as simple as thou, Reader (in thine own possible simplicity) hast taken me to be, I would have blurted out to my cousin a thing that, by this, after long suspicion, I had come to know very surely ; to wit, that Ralph's boy-liking for his cousin had deepened into a strong abiding love. Now a man has no need of being a Philosopher to know that the love of one of my kinsman's kind is not as the trivial love of common men, but may be likened to a tempest that tosses a great sea ; and that, once so possessed, such a man is made or marred by the possession ; made, if things go well and he loves and is loved again worthily ; marred, if they go awry, or his love fall on stony ground.

Therefore in this is my afore-claimed shrewdness shown, that I would not for all the world put into plain words, for his pride and nobleness of soul to split upon, what he himself hardly guessed or did certainly not dare to formulate to himself, and say to him, " Ralph, thou lovest thy cousin, therefore suffer her not to bestow herself on another." That would have been to appeal to the lower side of him, and straightway have warned and armed him to resist himself; but I knew that, though he was a philosopher and a sound logician, armed with all the weapons of the Scholastics, there was in him that most unreasoning and unphilosophic quality of pity, which, being moved, would scatter all his metaphysics to the winds ; and by this I was going to take him.

" It is meet, Ralph," said I, coming upon him as it were from afar, " it is meet you should know that if our cousin enters upon this marriage, it will be the more cruel a thing in this, that the poor child has already bestowed her heart on another."

He broke in upon me at once with, " Has she told you that ? "

" Come ! " said I, " Ralph, look at me well, and tell me if a young maiden would be apt to choose as curst and crabbed a fellow as myself for her confidant ? "

" Why," said he, looking on me curiously, " I will swear, Humphrey, she might do worse."

" No," said I, " Geraldine has told me not a word of her love, but, as I am informed, there are many ways of judging of such affairs by other means, as by looks, tones of voice, sighs, the gossip of other women and the like."

"And by one of these methods you are assured that our cousin has——"

"Yes," said I, "'tis sure enough she has given her heart for good and ever to this gentleman."

"Who is the man?" setting his face a little, though he had been forcing himself till now to smile pleasantly on the matter.

"Why, it would appear that she met the gentleman in Spain, passing through from her Convent" (Heaven forgive me, if this was more of a lie than an evasion!) "or maybe 'twas in Portugal; I am not truly informed."

"But," said my cousin, studying the matter deeply, "I was with her all the days in both countries, and I cannot bring to my mind that Geraldine seemed to regard—to prefer any one, Spanish or Portuguese, courtier or other gentleman. No," he said, "most positively she distinguished none of them."

"I have never heard," said I, "that a Philosopher was any good at women's politics, Ralph, and thou art still but a Philosopher, and knowest no more than a child the way to read a woman's thoughts. Be sure she beguiled thee."

"Well," said he, "even taking it to be as you say, she is young, she will forget; time and distance, I have heard say, cure heart wounds."

"It is a very foolish saying, and never meant for Geraldine. Weak women may be as changing as the moon or the ocean water, as in your verse you once rhymed it, but they of the nobler kind love once and love for ever ; yea, through all changes of their lives and through death itself. Of such is Geraldine, and as she lacks something of your stoical philosophy, Ralph, so the wound she has got will rankle and be the sorer the longer it is borne and the further it is carried. She will not complain, but the poor child, in the sad yearning of unaccomplished desire, ever setting what might have been against the cold and bitterness of what will be, will quickly lose her youth, her happiness, her health, her trust in God's goodness, and finally her life itself (for no so tender nature as hers can long bear up against the negation of all that her good star intended for her). So she will die, and the last breath she draws will still be her happiest, for thereafter she will know shall come her release. And this fate will be not of her own contriving, nor mine, nor any one's in all the world but yours alone, Ralph."

He answered me nothing, but my words had touched his heart, and troubled him.

I had this day brought him word of some slight apprehended trouble in the city ; and presently he and I, with our little cavalry escort, rode back to the Palace. On the way citywards he came back from time to time to the matter of our discourse, but I judged it best to let my last speech work in him and add nothing thereto, barely answering his questions as he asked them.

" Is this gentleman," he asked me, " by his manners and his age, and his birth, the equal of our cousin, and worthy of her . . . ."

I cut him short with " He is a gentleman of ancient lineage, high rank, a very honourable man, and by his sword already made famous abroad and at home."

" What may his age be ? "

" His age I judge from all accounts to be near your own, neither more nor less ;—but Ralph," said I, " I came out to confer with you on the state of the citizens' minds in Messina, and the eastern parts of the Island . . . ."

" Has this gentleman, who must needs know of the Lady Geraldine's engagement to marry the Viceroy, ventured to speak of his love to her ? "

" He has not—would that he had !—and your mention of the Viceroy reminds me to tell you his Grace's particular injunctions to me to inform you that . . . ."

" Come ! " said my kinsman, " I must be certified of this. Have you any knowledge of how this gentleman is inclined to my cousin ? "

" He loves her ; of that I am assured. For her love he shuns his friends, his business, the studies that he used to love, and all pleasure of his life. If he miss getting her, he is a lost man."

" But he knows she loves him ? "

" Nay, he does not remotely guess it."

" Then why does he not set his fate on the hazard

of an avowal? Why, in Heaven's name, does he not speak out, like a man?"

"Why 'tis just because he is a man, because he is an honourable man, who, knowing of the maiden's bond, will do nothing to persuade her to break it."

"This is a noble fellow," said my kinsman, after musing a little, "and one after my own heart."

"Indeed," said I, "he is after mine too."

"And you are persuaded she loves this gentleman?"

"With all her soul; if she miss getting him she weds misery."

"Alas!" said my poor kinsman, "this is a very pitiful affair. You do not know, Humphrey, all the pity of it."

"I believe," I said, "I know more about the matter than you do."

He considered a little: "Were I fully assured that our cousin's heart was set in earnest upon this, and that to continue in her present engagement was to bring this great life-long unhappiness upon her, I could almost resolve to forfeit my promise and break my plighted word with the Viceroy."

"What!" said I (willing to prove him), "and give her to this stranger, whom she loves?"

"Ay!" setting his face hard, "and give her to this stranger."

"Cousin Ralph," said I, "I believe I never loved you till now."

He seemed not to hear my words, but falling into

deep thought we rode on silently till we neared the
Palace gates ; then he said :

" I must have some assurance from Geraldine her-
self that you have read her heart and mind aright.
As she has said nothing, you may have mistaken.
How am I to make sure ? "

"Why, man, question her yourself closely, and I
warrant you force all the truth from her. You are
in your rights, being her guardian."

" No," said he, " I will not question her, nor shall
any other : I will not have the girl shamed before us.
And yet it is a matter too momentous in her life for
me not to arrive at the truth, and I will know it otherwise. I will question her, and she shall confess all
that is in her soul before you and before me, who will
never betray her, and she shall never even guess she
has spoken a word."

" To do that," said I, " seems to me a wholly impossible thing. How will you perform it ? "

" Can you not guess ? " he said. " Do you suppose
I cannot, if I choose, call her spirit before me as she
sleeps, and question that ? What passes thus will be
as an unremembered dream to her ; or, if she recall it,
she will recall it only as a dream, a vision, a fantasy
of her own creation."

Now, I will honestly admit that I then had but an
infirm faith in this faculty which my dear cousin was
used to arrogate to himself ; not indeed that I would
at this time, even, have denied the possibility of a
thing which could be supported by him with such

D D

wealth of argument and of authority, but I suspended
my judgment upon the feasibility of this seeming
miracle in modern days; in short, I conceived of it
rather as a pious opinion, for which much could be
advanced, than as a vital article of belief. The more
so as Ralph allowed that he had not succeeded, or but
seldom and imperfectly during his captivity among
the Turks, in calling my own spirit into his presence,
which he had endeavoured on several occasions to do.
Once or twice he had supposed my *imago*, or rather,
I suppose, the *imago* of my spirit, was actually in his
presence, but so faintly adumbrated and responding
so imperfectly to questions and suggestions from himself, that he was fain to believe in the end that what
he thought he perceived, he would not say what he
saw, was perceived by his mental vision only, and was
something projected upon the background of his perceptions by his own vivid imagination and by the
strong desire he had for communion with me, but was
in truth no real spirit form at all—only an illusion.
The great distance between Sicily and Tunis may
doubtless have had something to do with this failure,
as my Lord was ready to admit; for, as distance
attenuates and weakens all material bonds and con-
necting *vincula* whatever, so it cannot but weaken this
link between man and man, which he would not for
worlds pretend to be other than as material a thing as
the calling voice or beckoning hand of a friend. I
am, however, willing to believe that the chief difficulty
in my case was my own temperament, who am in

truth of a very obdurate and insensitive nature, and moreover the soundest sleeper in the world; so that I doubt if any invocation less audible than a cannonade or less moving than an earthquake would, while I sleep, persuade any portion of my spirit to travel abroad.

CHAPTER XXIX

By the time we reached the Palace it was late, and
had got to be dusk, and Lieutenant Brown, knowing
of our coming, had sent a small body of troopers to
meet us, as a guard through the city streets, for there
were at this time flying rumours of insurrection among
the citizens. We indeed little needed it, seeing that
my Lord and his troops and sailors were at this time
much liked by the common people; still, it was good
policy for us military not to traverse the streets of a
disturbed city save in imposing numbers. However,
nothing occurred of note, save perhaps that our presence called forth more than the usual voices of the
mobile in our favour, and more than the ordinary cries
against the Viceroy and the Spanish Lords.

So soon as we had reached the Palace, and my Lord
had despatched his immediate business, which was to
hold audience with sundry magistrates of the city and
Captains of the Guard in its various quarters, all of
whom were awaiting his arrival, he sent in his usual
report to the Viceroy, not considering that the urgency
of affairs at this juncture required an immediate

personal conference with his Grace. Lord St. Keyne
received in reply a message from his master, through
the confidential secretary who passed between them,
requesting his presence at an early hour in the morning for conference, and further repeating an injunction
which the Viceroy had already laid stress upon, that
his Lordship for the present should on no account
show himself about the city or elsewhere without a
strong guard of his troopers.

I desire to be very particular in recounting the
events of this night, even the most trifling ones, for
'twas of all nights in Ralph St. Keyne's life the
most eventful, and the most pregnant with his after
fate.

There had been this evening at the Viceroy's Palace
a great banquet, given to the courtiers and chief
nobles of the Island, from which and other recent
festivities of the kind my Lord had obtained the
Viceroy's leave to absent himself, on the ground of his
retirement into his country-house for the recruitment
of his health. By the time we had concluded our
last business, it was within an hour of midnight, and
we had knowledge of the departure of the Palace
guests, for one of them, a young Castilian Lord, Don
Pedro de Moroña, hearing by chance of my Lord's
return, waited upon him in his apartments. Don Pedro
was a newly made Member of the Council, not long
arrived from Spain, a gentleman very constant in his
admiration of my Lord and in friendship to his
person.

With this gentleman we removed into the dining-hall, and sat down to a light repast—I can hardly call it a supper—of bread, botargo, dried fruits and Tuscan wine. The young Spanish Lord, coming straight from Court, entertained us, with his accustomed liveliness of wit, by a recital of the various humours of the Sicilian noblemen and noblewomen's manners, which ever seem strange and uncouth, and indeed most ridiculous, to the Spaniards of Castile, who are, I need hardly say, very staid and ceremonious in their behaviour. Though my kinsman had, as I knew, such particular cause for dejection, being indeed in as anxious a mood as a man could well be, he did not let his guest perceive it, it being ever his wont, by principle and by habit of courtesy, to subdue his private humour to that of those who sat with him, or conferred with him.

Don Pedro de Moroña, who was one upon whose judgment Ralph greatly relied (and as to whose loyalty to his person he justly felt sure), had, as I learned afterwards, made this night visit to us from no idle desire to beguile us with the humours of the Sicilian Court, but to inform us of some current rumour at Court of new designs on the part of the Holy Office. As Don Pedro took his leave, which was upon the stroke of the half after eleven, leaving his merry humour (for till then he had touched upon no affairs of State), he informed us that the talk of the assembly he had just quitted had run upon this matter, and in view of the late opposition to the work of the Inquisition having originated with my Lord, it was currently supposed that it would be against my Lord or his friends that the first activity of the Grand Inquisitor would be directed. To Englishmen, among whom happily the Holy Office has never had authority, it is not possible to convey a notion of the uneasiness, nay terror, which its secret action and all but unopposable power inspire among the people of countries where it holds sway, both the high-placed and the lowly; for none is so humble but that he may be haled up by it on a charge of heresy, none so pious but he may be accused (by some hidden enemy) of impiety, and be cast into the terrible, torture-haunted prisons of the Inquisition. Even powerful statesmen, wielding the might of a nation's treasuries and armies, have trembled before a power that is greater than their own; nay, kings themselves have felt their thrones shake under them and their sceptre tremble in their hands, if but the shadow of the Holy Office has fallen upon the Throne Chamber. It was on this account that the Viceroy, as we well knew, though no word touching the Holy Office had been uttered by his Grace, had warned my Lord to go ever guarded, and to beware. My kinsman, not bred up in this universal terror, and having twice already set his wits and his strength against the Grand Inquisitor without defeat, was inclined to disregard these warn ings and to rely upon his own resources, upon the citizens' friendliness, his officers' watchfulness, and his soldiers' fidelity. We had better reasons for our security even than these, and which Don Pedro, as a very recent comer, could scarcely estimate. First, there was the fear and hatred which the Grand Inquisitor had inspired among our soldiery by his arbitrary arrest of three of their number ; so that they felt their *Capitano*, who had stood up for them, was their champion, for whom they would stand up in their turn. It was to be observed too that whoever else dreaded the mysterious, abhorred Inquisition, our reckless, dare-devil soldiers felt no religious terror for it whatever, and would, the chance given, have clouted the masked and hooded Familiars of the Holy Office over the head with the greatest pleasure in life. Again, we knew that, though the power of the Holy Office was still great, it was somewhat decadent and declining of late years, and that the order had gone out from Head-quarters to temper zeal with a discretion that in old times it had been unnecessary to employ. Above all else, we knew that while the Viceroy saw it politic to stand our friend, we had no cause to fear the worst the Inquisition could do.

Upon Don Pedro's taking his leave of us, my kinsman returned to the great hall which I have already had occasion to mention, and where he had till lately been used to follow his various studies. He then ordered all the servants to retire, and informed them that he would need their services no more that night.

The hall was lighted, as usual, with many great waxen tapers in silver candelabra standing upon the floor, but from the apartment's great height and size, and the walls being hung with black tapestries and with tall curtains of the same dark stuff before the doorways, the hall, with its several deep vaulted alcoves, was still obscure and sombre, save just where the candles burned. Many of these my kinsman now extinguished, leaving but ten or a dozen burning, so that, when this was done, there was far more of obscurity than of light in the room.

Ralph had fallen into silence again when Don Pedro had gone ; but presently he turned to me abruptly and spoke of our cousin Geraldine.

" It is now," said he, " within a few minutes of midnight, and I intend to call her spirit hither. I do not know whether you will see or hear anything except my voice, but assuredly before the chimes of the great clock in the Palace Courtyard have rung out for midnight, Geraldine's spirit will be standing here and speaking to my questions."

There stood ready placed near the centre of the floor a metal tripod, knee high, of Eastern damascened work, and upon it Ralph St. Keyne now laid a heap of Turkish incense. He set light to this, and when it had well kindled, he unlocked a little casket and took therefrom a portion of the herb *Pechauri* given to him by the Indian Ambassadors, and which the Indians hold precious beyond all their drugs and essences, it being sovereign to many ends ; but, beyond all other virtues which it possesses, it is famous for its potency over the spirits of man. He heaped the *Pechauri* over the burning incense, and presently it kindled too. Then there went up so full a cloud of smoke into the room as was marvellous to behold, less for the volume of it, though that was very great, than for its appearance and properties. Though the *Pechauri* would seem to be nothing but the parched and rolled up leaves of some unknown Indian flower,—not unlike the dried rose-leaves of our Apothecaries, and it has no scent till it be burnt —its smoke gives forth a most potent, penetrating odour, yet incomparably sweet, and, as it were, vernal, as if all the scents that an odorous garden of the Indies breathes out upon the morning air in springtime, had been imprisoned in these dry leaves and now were released; and this aroma so takes the senses that they are rapt and intoxicated therewith.

Now I must hasten to absolve my cousin in the use of this strange drug, at this invoking by him of Geraldine's spirit, of any vulgar, superstitious, magical notion of *correspondences*, as the Alchemists and they who exercise the Black Art (or pretend to) use to say. He employed it only because the fumes of the drug *Pechauri* have, as the Indians who gave it to him maintain, a faculty of inducing recipiency in those who breathe it ; or, to put it more plainly, they throw the human senses into such a rapt and subtle state as enables them more easily to recognize and perceive the fine and tenuous lineaments of spiritual forms.

More strange, almost, even than the odorous influence of the drug was the behaviour, if I may so call it, of the smoke thereof, for it not only came forth with exceeding abundance, but it seemed almost to possess a kind of vitality in itself (though I know well this is an idle fancy) so lively were its motions. I aver that, though there was never a current of air in the hall to carry it hither or thither (the tapers burning all the time with a steady upward flame) yet the smoke, rising first in a great column, presently dispersed itself here and there in the vaulted hall in wreaths, and circlets, and spirals, with a causeless, ceaseless nimbleness of motion, like a thing endowed with life, so that I could not but watch it with a deep expectancy upon me, entranced too by the breathing of the odorous vapour, while I waited for some strange thing to be begot of this great curiosity of nature.

Ralph had been standing near the burning incense, but now he retired from it towards me with slow, backward steps, his lips moving, and now and then a low word escaping from them, but it was no incantation or magical charm he was uttering; he was but calling upon, praying, beseeching, throwing all his soul and will and heart into the entreaty to his cousin, the Lady Geraldine, that she would appear before him in visible spirit shape.

As he stepped back, his hands extended towards that part of the Palace where our cousin lay, though far off, the vapour, as if it had been a sentient thing, followed him, hovering above him, and now and then a part thereof, like an arm reaching out, descended suddenly to touch him.

At this moment the great clock in the tower outside began its double stroke, four times repeated for the four quarters ; then the deeper-toned bell began to toll out the strokes of midnight. As the strokes went on slowly, the vapour began to creep from various points through the air from the dark corners where some still had hung, even moving along the floor, snake-like, towards the portal entrance. Here it gathered before the tall black hanging, hiding it partly from our view, and I now could see that this smoke from the still burning *Pechauri* was rather a vapour than a smoke for its extreme tenuity, and was of a strange silvery whiteness that gave out a certain sheen or light in the half-darkened room. Yet was it not so tenuous but that it obscured what lay behind it, except the tapers, but they showed dim through it and burned with a greenish flame.

Now, as I looked upon the smoke before the doorway, there seemed to me to come a new motion into it, and the ever-moving wreaths and circlets that it kept forming itself into took fresh shapes, so that, verily, to my enthralled fancy, it seemed at one moment possible to disentangle from the curving and waving of the vaporous cloud, the lineaments of a white-draped human figure, but the moment after I could perceive nothing save the white, ever-moving vapour.

I turend to my cousin, and, looking upon him, I

knew immediately by his face that he was aware of
some presence that I could not see. Then I returned
my eyes again to the place whereon he was gazing,
and lo! there stood the form or appearance of my
sweet cousin Geraldine, revealed plainly to my eyes,
yet the figure's outline mingling and moving with
and melting into the white vaporous cloud that still
moved about the portal. The shape stood there for
the space of some moments, in front of the dark
doorway curtain, with out-held hands and pitiful,
uncertain, wide-opened eyes, gazing not at us but
at the vacant air before her. Then it advanced a
little towards us with gliding steps, and stood again.
The figure was clad as we knew Geraldine had been clad
at the Viceroy's banquet, with satin draperies of a
creamy white, that trailed to her feet. The neck and
arms of the appearance were bare, and the arms
unclasped by the bracelets that my cousin was wont
to have on, but still she seemed to wear, hanging by
a little chain round her neck, that which her cousin
Ralph had given her ; namely, one of the Rubies from
the recovered Amulet, a round, blood-red stone, large
and fiery as a tiger's eye. Her hair, deep gold, was
unfastened, and fell in waves and soft ripplets upon
her shoulders.

As the presentment of Geraldine stood thus, the
thin vapour still partly enveloping her, I looked
earnestly upon her, and a doubt came to me whether
this were, after all, only the unreal simulacrum of our
cousin Geraldine, and not herself in her true bodily

presence ; yet she did not stir, seeming only to be
swayed gently with the motion of the vapour, and
standing there so still, so dim and diaphanous in the
dimly lighted hall, all so white and shining against
the black hangings (since but for the red stone on her
breast, and the ruddy gold of her golden hair, she was
altogether white), I supposed it must indeed be nothing
but a spirit.   Then a sudden awe came upon me, but
not for that I looked for the first time upon a spiritual
being, only because of the passing beauty that was in
her face, cleared thus of all earthly taint ; and yet a
pity fell upon me too, greater than this awe, for the
deep sadness of her look ; and a sense of her mortality
grew upon me again from that, for sure, thought I, no
spirit ever yet could be so sorrowful.

I turned to Ralph, who stood enwrapped in thought,
his gaze fixed upon the apparition, and I whispered
to him :

" Is this the spirit of our cousin, or her mortal body
that we see before us ? "

I tried to speak in a low whisper, but my words
came from me harsh and loud with the reverberation
of the high vaulted chamber, and I expected to see
the vision fade and dissolve into air as my voice broke
the silence, but it remained, heeding me not.

Then Ralph answered, standing close to my side,
but not dropping his voice, as if assured that, unless
he so willed it, his words would not reach the spectre's
spiritual sense ; but he mistook, for, at the first word
he spoke, the figure thrilled and shivered, and raised

its hands to its brow. Yet none could, I think, have recognized the voice for Ralph St. Keyne's, so altered was it, so hollow and constrained by his deep emotion.

"This," said he in answer to my question, "is but Geraldine's spirit, and that which you perceive is not here at all in any material sense; for were we not prepared to receive this vision on the retina of our mind's eye, we should perceive nothing."

"Look, Ralph!" cried I, pointing, "it is surely she herself in bodily form—look how piteously she bends her eyes on us and wrings her hands! Sure it is no vision, but Geraldine herself,—I will go to her and comfort her."

"Stay," he said, laying his hand on mine, "you are misled. This is no living being, but the creature of our imagination and our will; just such a phantasm as bewildered men see at times in desert places, or by night along the lonely sea-shore, which their terror or their yearning for those they love projects upon empty space, near by or far away from them, if only it happen that another human thought coincides in time is willing to project its energy towards them. This apparition is only thin air; and that place where stands the image of Geraldine is but the point in space where her and our energies have met—ours to call her, hers to respond."

"But look again! I could never conjure up so true an image of her as that; my memory or my fancy could never contrive a beauty like that in her face, or, upon it, so deep a sadness."

"Nay," said he, "that is none of your doing ; it is her spirit that brings with it this portraiture of her mortal body, and of the emotion of which it is sentient. This it is which so misleads your eyes ; and as they are beguiled by an appearance, so will your ears be presently deceived when she speaks with a voice as unreal as this visible spectre of her earthly form."

Then he steadfastly regarded the apparition for a moment or two ; and as he did so, it swayed somewhat, and glided softly a little nearer us, again holding out its hands, as if it felt it was governed by his will and was wishful to grope its way towards him through darkness.

"Geraldine!" he said, and his voice dropped now to a tone as low as of one who speaks by the bedside of a sick child.

The vision seemed to shiver through all its members at the new voice, and stood still suddenly, listening, with wide-opened eyes, but that certainly saw us not.

"Geraldine!" he said, "they tell me you have given your heart away. Answer me!"

The spectral form of Geraldine dropped her hands, crossed them before her, bent her head towards the ground, and her lips moved, but no speech came from them.

"Gather all your thought, and answer this : Is there one, Geraldine, whom in your soul, and with every yearning of your heart, you love ?"

The answer came in a sound softer than any

spoken sound I ever heard, and as if from very far away :

" There is."

For a space of time no question came from Ralph. Then he spoke again.

" But will time never dull the edge of this your love and longing ? "

" Never ! " The voice was as of one dreaming, when but half the dreamer's understanding wakes, and who is compelled to speak to some dream-conjured questioner.

" But, Geraldine, he whom you love loves you not again."

" Alas ! no."

" Will that not help you to forego your love for him ? "

" I never can forego my love for him."

Again Ralph waited a while ere he renewed his questioning.

" This marriage of yours with the Viceroy, which will be so soon, does it seem terrible and most grievous to you ? "

This time there came no answer but a sob.

" Alas, poor Geraldine ! " cried Ralph.

Till then his voice had been so restrained that it ounded most unlike his own, but when he spoke these last true pitying words from his very heart, they came from him in his own natural voice, and the tone seemed to reach through the half-numbed senses of the spectre, for it raised its head and listened

E E

earnestly, and there came a quick radiant look through all its sorrow.

Again the visionary form began to glide towards us, but Ralph raising his hand, seemed to bid it stay, and again it stood fixed to one spot.

"Listen, Geraldine," he said, again speaking with his first, restrained voice, "you are mistaken if you have thought this man, whom you love, loves you not again. He yearns for you with a passion stronger even than your own."

There came a sharp cry from the figure : it raised its arms and we thought it would fall to the earth, so did it tremble, reel and sway in its place.

Ralph, forgetting that it was but a thing of air con-jured hither by our fancy, advanced ,quickly towards it, but remembering in time he stopped, being now but a step or two removed from where the spectre stood.

"Listen again, Geraldine, to what you are to learn. They who promised you in marriage did not consider that they were dooming a woman to a life in death : they have learnt to see more truly now, and rather than break your woman's heart, they are resolved to break their own plighted word, even though they suffer the penalty of dishonour thereby."

The spirit figure looked wonderingly : and as if bewildered by so strangely sudden a reprieve to the heavy sentence of unhappiness it had lain under, and Ralph spoke on, seeking to come nearer to its intelli-gence with plainer words.

"You are free, Geraldine, to give yourself to him you love, and who loves you so dearly."

She looked up quickly, and I swear that the sudden joy that was in her eyes, and the smile that came upon her face was not of mortal kind; it was such as only disembodied spirits can show when first they feel their freedom from earthly bonds, and see the white, shining plains of Heaven open to their view. Nothing so holy, nothing so beautiful, have I yet seen on mortal face.

We stood thus for some moments, neither of us speaking, but as I watched Geraldine's spirit (for so I must needs call it, if it still was indeed no tangible being that we looked upon) I thought I saw its lineaments grow slowly dim as if it owed what shape it had of life only to Ralph's will, were sustained into existence thereby, and as if that will were now failing it. I looked to his face, and saw the blackness of his despair thereon, but behind that lay the strength of a great resolution to bear this heavy strain upon his fortitude.

He watched the waning life in the apparition, and willed it to return to sentience.

"Gather your thoughts once more, Geraldine," and still he subdued his voice into the low, even tone of one who wishes to suggest a dream-thought to a fevered, sleeping child, "gather your thoughts and tell me this one further thing that I must know before I dismiss your spirit."

The spectral form seemed, at his bidding—or it

may have been my fancy—to grow less shadowy and become again distinct to my sight, and the intelligence to come again into the look that just before had been returning to that which the unexpressive face of a sleeper wears.

"One thing only need I know more; his name who has won your love?"

The spirit form moved uneasily at the asking of this question, as if it were troubled by the unexpectedness thereof.

Ralph repeated his demand very slowly and distinctly.

Still the apparition seemed uneasy, and its trouble showed in its silence, and in a look of sorrowful doubt, as if it were beginning to question the truth and reality of all that had passed. Then slowly, and as if doubtingly, it spoke, fixing its vision seemingly on Ralph's face, but in truth seeing him not.

"You, who spoke to me, who have told me of him, who know everything, and who have given me the tidings of this great happiness to be,—I thought just now I saw your face like a bright angel from Heaven and now I can see nothing before me but darkness." Her thoughts had wandered from the point he would fix her to, and again he spoke his question.

"Tell me, Geraldine, the name of him you love."

"Yes, that is the voice I have heard, and would hear again."

"Tell it me!" he repeated.

She answered at last, but it seemed that his desire

had hardly prevailed against her unwillingness, and that she was now contending against a lethargy that nearly benumbed her senses, for the words came so low,—hardly above a whisper,—that I had to strain my ears to catch them.

"You know well,—you must know well,—it is my cousin Ralph whom I love with all my soul, and have always loved."

A groan came from Ralph St. Keyne, but no spoken words. I looked quickly at him : he had gone as pale as death.

For some long moments there was silence unbroken in the room, and now there came a wonder so great that even at this distance of time I hardly like to tell of it. When I looked again at the spectral form (and I am sure that I had not taken my eyes from it for the space of a second) the place where it had stood had become encompassed with the vapour of the burning herb, which till then had been chiefly dispersed through the room, and I saw nothing there, only thick rising spirals of smoke, enveloping and hiding the space wherein the intangible shape of Geraldine had lately stood. Then the vapour passed away, and the air was clear, and I could again perceive the dark curtain hanging before the portal where first the apparition of Geraldine had showed ; and in that place there stood now no filmy spirit-figure, diaphanous, and with its outlines mingling with the tenuous vapour —wreaths, but the true living, bodily, flesh and blood form of Geraldine herself. She held her hands upraised and pressed to her temples, her eyes were widely opened, and not gazing now at vacancy, un-seeing real objects, like eyes of one who walks still dreaming ; but wakeful eyes, wondering and confused, but with all their human sense expressed in them.

How came she thus ?   How came the spirit, which had so lately flitted at Ralph's will, to be re-embodied in Geraldine's mortal shape ?   Was it the human joy so suddenly engendered in the spirit that had woke the sleeping body to be rejoined with its soul in a rapture that had commingled the spiritual with the material nature ?   I do not know ; I cannot explain ; I only testify that Geraldine herself was now present with us.

It was upon me that her first mortal look fell, and my face was to her, I think, as the face of a friend in the strange country of dreams she had newly returned from.

" Humphrey ! " she cried, coming to me, " why am I here ?   What has happened ? "   Her countenance was still radiant with the joy that had so lately filled her soul, but suddenly the sight and touch of dull material things around her awoke a fear in her.   " Ah, tell me ! " she cried, touching my arm as if to assure herself that she was not still dreaming, " Is it true ?   Is it all a vision, or true ? "

" It is all true.   Look ! there is Ralph ; ask him."

She turned to him.   She took his hand, as she used to do when she was his child friend, in the gardens of St. Keyne.   He held it for a while clasped in his.

"No, Geraldine, it is not true, it is all a dream. Forget it. Forget what you have said, forget what you have been told; it is all false together, a foolish dream that can have no continuance."

She dropped the hand she held, covered her face with both her own, and wept. Then slowly she began to go from our presence, dejectedly, with no spoken word.

"Stay, Geraldine!" I said; "be comforted, for it is no dream you have dreamt, or untruth you have heard. The man you love, loves you again : he stands there ; and you are free to be his wife."

Ralph looked at me with a reproachful aspect, but did not speak, and Geraldine turned towards him with a most earnest, pleading face.

"Dear Ralph . . . ." she began, but she proceeded no further.

Her softness, and her sadness, and her beauty, touched him through his fortitude to resist. He was not weak, but he could not help being human. He went up to where she stood and, taking her two hands in his, spoke to her thus, amid her weeping.

"Dearest Geraldine, it is true I love you, but not true that you are free. Far dearer are you to me than the life-blood in my veins, but dearer still are your honour and my own. You can never be my wife. Go from me, Geraldine, and let us never see each other again upon this earth !"

At this moment the curtain across the chief portal of the hall was lifted aside, and there stood, in the entrance, his Grace the Viceroy ; his coming having been, as it often was, for consultation on some affair of State with my Lord

The Viceroy remained thus for a little space regarding us, none moving or speaking, and he still holding the curtain uplifted with his hand ; then Geraldine, seeing him, cried out, and shrinking from him with a visible horror, laid herself close to her cousin, and clung to him as if for refuge from a hated and hateful presence.

It was the Viceroy who broke the silence that held us all for some space of time.

" Madam," said his Grace very slowly and deliberately, " I hereby release you from the engagement you have taken to become my wife."

He retired, the curtain closed upon him, and we saw him no more.

Ralph St. Keyne spoke no word, but he took Geraldine's head between his two hands and kissed her, first upon her eyes, hot and wet with her weeping, and then upon her mouth ; drawing her to himself, into his arms ; comforting her.

I, in my shortsightedness, rejoiced exceedingly, seeing in this sudden and so unexpected event, the solution of a great entanglement of the ties of honour with the bonds of love, to which solution, to say truth, I had seen no right way of arriving ; but I knew not, I could not guess, the revengeful spirit and the devilish guile of this Spanish nobleman, and all that was to come of these things.

CHAPTER XXX

THE following morning there was a sitting of the Council, which my Lord attended, having to lay certain schemes for the quieting of the outlying suburbs of Palermo before the Lords.   This business being got through, the Viceroy announced his intention of proceeding in state to Messina that afternoon, and, as a matter of necessity and of course, I received directions to attend him with the larger portion of the Viceregal Body-guard.   The time of the Council was mostly occupied by an address from the Grand Inquisitor referring to the condition of irreligion prevailing in the City of Palermo.   He had long desired to make some wholesome examples of certain leading and most pestilent heretics, and would ere now, he said, have done so, but for the opposition he had met with in the Council itself.   He had now, he informed the Councillors, received his instructions from Rome to proceed with more zeal, and was resolved no longer to defer some very strict preventive and punitive measures.

When none spoke to this discourse, my Lord stood up and replied to the effect that the severities of the

Holy Office in recent times had so moved the spirits of the citizens, who were to all common seeming as God-fearing a set of people as existed, that it was within his own knowledge, whose duty led him to inquire particularly into their disposition, that hardly any cause had so inflamed them latterly with an indignant, mutinous spirit as the knowledge that each man and woman in the city lay at the mercy of private enemies, who had no more difficult task before them if they wished to undo their man, than to carry a secret, baseless, infamous charge against him to an Office ever greedy for malignant accusations, and never careful to sift them. A fresh move in the direction of severity would, at this juncture, certainly have very disastrous consequences.

When this came from my Lord very calmly, the Council was visibly persuaded by his arguments; his warning no doubt reaching the fears and cupidity of the Spanish Lords quicker than it did their reason. My kinsman wound up his speech with an observation which angered the Churchman exceedingly. He said :

His Reverence had spoken of instructions from Rome, but no member of the Council was without knowing that the power of the Inquisition in Sicily derived in no way from Rome, but solely from our Master the King of Spain : that the Inquisition in Spain was a Spanish Tribunal, wholly subservient to the Spanish Crown, and that no Sicilian subject owed the smallest allegiance or obedience to any authority save that which came direct from His Catholic Majesty himself.

When the Grand Inquisitor had replied to this, with more passion and perturbation than logic, the Viceroy himself intervened to moderate the debate; and he inclined to the views of my Lord. As Governor of the Island, he said, it was his duty to consider no authority paramount to his Master's, and he was resolved to sanction no new measures of religious compulsion at this particular crisis in the affairs of the Island, when the passions and fears of the people were already so riotously stirred.

This discourse of His Grace's seemed and indeed was, so agreeable to justice, policy, reason and expediency, that my Lord, in his own loyalty and uprightness, never for a moment suspected that it covered the most dark and devil-hearted designs; but he was wofully deceived, and so fell into the trap wherein he was to get his undoing.

The Viceroy, before the breaking up of the Council, detained the Lords to make a further communication to them; which was to the effect that the project of espousals between himself and the Lady Geraldine Scudamour had unhappily come to an end; certain events having now occurred which had rendered those espousals, to his own extreme regret and sorrow, impossible. These events were no cause for animadversion to the friends of the Lady Geraldine, still less to that lady herself, and he believed he might claim to be held equally free from reproach in the matter. Here he ended, bowed to the Lords, and declared the Session concluded, having spoken, as I was informed, in this delicate affair, with a restraint, courtesy and high breeding that comported well with his noble birth and rank ; and which manner also perfectly dissembled the dark purpose of his soul.

That afternoon the Viceroy proceeded in state towards Messina ; I myself accompanying him with a troop of his Body-guard, a second troop having preceded the Viceregal procession by some six hours, and a third of equal number, receiving my orders to follow that evening : it being His Grace's desire to make his progress through the north of the Island with considerable state and show of force, this part of Sicily then being in a very disturbed and discontented condition.

As the weather was hot and roads bad, our traveling was slow, and we got no further than Termini, about twenty miles away, where we found the first despatched troop already arrived. I sent the detachment at once eastward, and we ourselves and the Viceroy lay that night at Termini. The next morning the third troop arrived and took our place, we ourselves travelling on by short stages, the reason of this breaking of our party in detachments being, as will be easily gathered, the lack of suitable lodging along the road for larger bodies of troops.

Travelling in this leisurely manner, on the third night after leaving Palermo we reached the town of

Naso, and were very miserably entertained in this small and poverty-stricken place; my Lord Duke finding a better lodging in the country house of a Sicilian nobleman beyond the town.

It was here that I began to be rendered somewhat uneasy by reason of a circumstance which I could not understand. It is in the knowledge of the reader that a mutinous spirit was at this time abroad in Palermo, and as often as I received my instructions in the lesser matter of ordering the movements of the troops, I usually took my orders either directly from his Grace or from him through an officer of his household. I was anticipated in my fear that we might be laying the city too bare of troops by the Viceroy himself, who observed that he must needs leave troops enough with his Lordship to keep the city in awe. For all this, he proposed to take with him no fewer than four-fifths of the only trustworthy soldiers in Palermo. When, after getting my orders, I thereafter communicated them to my kinsman, with some hesitation as to their wisdom, he disregarded my objections, saying that the citizens would be far easier when his Grace and the Spanish Lords were out of the place, and that he would undertake himself to keep order with a single company of his troopers, or even without any soldiers at all. Ralph was right in so thinking, for of the citizens those few who did not love him feared him, and his very name by this time was enough to appease the orderly and overawe the turbulent; but his and my foresight was baffled by a plot in a quarter in which we never thought to find malice arise.

It was nevertheless arranged between my cousin and myself that he should keep me informed of the state of things in Palermo by mounted messengers despatched from the Palace at punctual intervals of twelve hours. This was indeed an obvious measure of precaution, seeing that I was now in command of nearly all the available city forces, only half a troop being left in the Palace Barracks under my Lord's orders, the remainder having been spread abroad in the different outlying parts of the city and its suburbs.

Now, when, on the evening of the third day, we arrived at Naso (this making forty-eight hours since our setting forth), and no messenger had come, I began to wonder, and to be very uneasy. I was sure my Lord had not forgotten his promise to me. Had his messengers then lagged by the way? There was time both for the first and second to have reached me : had they been stopped on the road, and if so by whose orders, and why? All that night I was very uneasy, conjecturing every manner of disaster to have happened ; and falling into uneasy slumber towards morning, I was startled suddenly out of my sleep, for it seemed to me that my kinsman stood at my bed-side. It was only a dream, but for a minute or two I could not believe it was that, so vivid had been the presentment before me of Ralph, and so piteous his aspect. When I saw it was nothing but a dream, I

composed myself again to sleep; and again my kinsman stood before me, and this time his face was very
wan and there was, methought, a red gash upon his
forehead. Again I awoke, fearful, but presently I felt
sure it was no more than a dreaming fancy that my
waking thoughts had taken, and after a time I slept
again. Then I dreamed for the third time, and now
there rang in my ears a dream-voice that cried,
"Help me, Humphrey! Help me in my sore
distress," and then I seemed to wake, but in reality I
did not wake, but was dreaming on, only with a more
vivid ecstasy of the sleeping imagination; and I
looked, methought, into the gloom of night, and
slowly a luminous place grew before my sleeping
senses, and shaped itself into what seemed a vaulted
dungeon wherein stood my cousin Ralph, still very
wan and with a piteous and beseeching aspect, and on
his brow the red gash I had seen before; but this
time he spoke not, only looked upon me very
entreatingly.

After that I slept no more but rose, and though I
reasoned with myself that surely it was but a dream,
and I was not, like an ignorant peasant, to be guided
in my action by such conjurings of the distempered
fancy; yet I could not prevail upon my judgment to
let the matter go by. Thought I, if Ralph were truly
in trouble and distress of mind or body, would he not,
using that power which he had so clearly shown he
possessed, call upon me to come to him as he had
done? And again, I argued, assuming that it is

nothing but a dream, may it not be that my spirit
in sleep, freed from its material earthly shackles of
prejudice and misconception, has reasoned out a true
conclusion that Ralph is even now imprisoned,
wounded, and entreating me to succour him? Then
I began to marshal with my waking understanding all
the thin lines of thought that for these last three days
had passed across my mind, and still as I marshalled
them they pointed to and converged upon some
possible disaster to my cousin ; nay, they shadowed
even this very imprisonment and danger to his life
which had been figured to me in my dream ; for, I
bethought me, how strange is this non-coming of the
messengers ! How strange the Viceroy's sudden
journey, and his bidding such an unnecessary force
of us to accompany him, leaving Ralph all undefended
if he should be assailed. How strange, too, that the
Viceroy should have shown no resentment for that
very action against himself, against his self-love,
though so unconsciously committed by Ralph, which
of all other injuries men are apt to resent the most.
Could he have dissembled so profoundly unless he had
some fell and secret purpose ? When I had set together this string of improbabilities and inconsistencies
in one who till now had never shown himself in-
consistent, I marvelled that I had been so free from
suspicion. Then suddenly a great impatience and indignation seized me, for that I too perhaps had been
entangled in the plot that was undoing my cousin ;
that I too was blindly helping to hold the net that

perhaps at that moment was enmeshing him in its toils.

When once this notion had taken possession of my mind, I thought upon it again neither twice nor thrice, but I caused the *Reveille* to be sounded, though it was not yet dawn, and ordered the troop to saddle up. In a short space of time we were upon a very quick march back to Palermo : I having in the meantime sent an orderly to the troop ahead of us to bid them fall back and serve as the Viceroy's immediate Body-guard and convoy.

Now, if any soldier who, upon reading of this summary abandonment by me of the Viceroy upon his journey, shall charge me with indiscipline and a dereliction of my strict duty, I fear I have no answer to give him or apology to make, save to refer him to all that has gone before in this narrative, and to all that shall presently follow after.

By noon that day I had got as far as our first station, Termini, but had rid so quickly that only six of my troop were with me. Here we met the last detachment, who as we had agreed, had left Palermo the afternoon before. They brought with them no news from the city : it was quiet, they said, and their commanding officer reported that the mounted messengers to myself had departed at the appointed times. Now we had neither received messages at Naso, nor met any bearers of them upon the road, neither had the last arrived troop seen anything of them.

F F

I left half a score of troopers at Termini with orders to wait for the troop I had outridden, and with them follow us to Palermo. Then, exchanging my tired horse for a fresh one, I turned the heads of the troop back to Palermo, and we pushed on to the city, but not too quickly, for I had to keep men and horses fresh and brisk and all together against our reaching the streets of the city.

We got to the suburbs of Palermo that afternoon, and here we got the first hint that something was amiss, for we met first three or four bodies of citizens flying from the city, then a stream of men and women with children, all escaping for their lives, some afoot, some on horse or muleback, the sick, the old, or infirm in coaches and carts, or borne in mule litters. They were all of the wealthier sort of people. They would hardly stay to tell us more than that the people were up, but they knew not why nor wherefore. As we got nearer the strings of fugitives ceased, and we gathered from this circumstance either that the people held the streets and broad places and so had stopped escape, or that the troubles were already overpast. We entered the city in its busiest part, near the quays, and almost immediately found ourselves in a great crowd swaying hither and hither. The people did not run from the troops as they will mostly do when a mutinous spirit is on them, but standing back on either side to make a lane for us, cheered us, throwing up their hats and caps. Many seditious cries came from their ranks too, and some that were not too plain to me : " Down with the Traitors," cried they, "Death to the Spaniards!" "Death to the Viceroy!" "Give us back our Friend!" and I wondered to see these mutinous fellows standing so close to our passage that our horses all but trod upon them; but I pushed on, taking no notice, only willing to get to Head-quarters as quickly as might be. As we went on the crowds increased, and I saw many of the worthier kind of citizens among the people. Presently, recognising a tradesman with whom I was acquainted, I pulled up my horse and beckoning to him to come near, begged him to inform me how he came to take part in such an assembly, and what all the pother was about.

"Why, Sir," he says, "I apprehend you know a great deal more of the matter than I do."

When I assured him that we had but just entered the city from Termini, and that he was the first person I had had word of mouth with, he said,

"Then it is true they stopped the messengers to you?"

"At any rate we got none," said I.

"How should you, Captain St. Keyne?" said the citizen, "seeing that all travelling on the roads has been stopped these two days. Only at noon to-day has the guard outside the city been removed."

"Now, Sir," said I, "a word more with you and I have done. What is the Treachery these poor people complain of, and who is the Friend they are clamouring for?"

He stared upon me in surprise, then he broke out : " Do you not know, then, how that Lord St. Keyne was taken treacherously before dawn this morning by the Familiars of the Inquisition, and is now set fast in their prisons? We have no other cause for rising, and the people make sure you are come back to save him, if it be not already too late."

CHAPTER XXXI

I CLAPPED spurs to my horse's side, and we went through the streets of Palermo, crowded as they were, at a hand gallop, the people breaking to right and left of us as we rode to the Palace, and, knowing the purpose of our haste, cheering and shouting their " God speeds," as we passed them like the wind.

We found the great gateway, leading into the piazza or quadrangle that is formed by the four sides of the buildings (namely, of Palaces, Barracks, and the Prison of the Inquisition), barred, bolted and barricaded as we rode up to it, and entrance was denied to us. I got speech of the Officer of the Sicilian Army in command, not one of our people but of the old-established army of which I have already spoken, and which did garrison duty both here and in other cities of Sicily, but which had done no fighting against either a foreign or a civil enemy now for over twenty years. This gentleman told me that his regiment was in occupation of the Barracks. Where was the troop under my Lord's command? I asked. It had marched to Partimeo (naming a distant village) the day before. Had my Lord taken

command in person? He had not, there being no
expectation of actual fighting. Where was my Lord
at this moment? On that point the officer could not
answer. I asked for the gates to be opened and my
men admitted to their quarters. The officer replied
that he had orders to admit no one. I asked from
whom had he received such orders, seeing that I
myself came straight from the Viceroy with whom
was Don Diego, Generalissimo of the forces, neither
of whom had said a word of the Viceregal Body-
guard being shut out from their quarters. He said
that in the absence of these higher authorities the
army took their orders from the Council. The officer,
who held the rank of Colonel and had informed me
he was in command, was very civil spoken, and so
was I, but presently I had to speak plainly to him.

"Hark'ee, Sir," said I, "I cannot go tamely away
from here at the command of any but my lawfully
constituted commanding officers, whom I take to be
the Viceroy and my Lord St. Keyne, and failing
these, the Generalissimo. No one else in this Island
has authority by military law over me, or over yourself. Now therefore, I will beg you to admit me
peaceably through these gates, or to see me force
my way in, in spite of you."

The Colonel smiled as he pointed to the cannons
in the embrasures of the towers that flanked the gateway: there were twelve pieces, on one of which his
hand was resting while he spoke to me. "We have
a garrison of 500 men here," said he.

The Sicilian Colonel was quite right in supposing that his position was impregnable against any attack or assault in front that was not supported by a train of siege artillery.

"Well, Sir," said I, willing to humour this notion I saw he had in his head, "if you are prepared to stand a siege, 'tis very well. I promise you it shall be no longer delayed than till to-morrow."

"We have our orders to do that very thing," says he; and I pulled my hat off and saluting him rode away to make my preparations for forcing our way into our Head-quarters.

We had at this time, in Palermo, two corvettos (one the Flagship) two galleys, and besides these my Lord's private galley, the *Golondrina*; and from the crews of these vessels I could easily count upon a contingent of nearly 500 men that I could use on shore. I immediately called a council of superior officers on board the Flagship, and laid the state of affairs before them, but touched not of how far I believed the Viceroy to be implicated in the plot against his own General and his own Guard. It is hardly necessary for me to say that the Captains, my kinsman's own trusted officers, were for immediate action for his succour. I promised them they should not have long to wait.

By my instructions, a body of picked men was told off from each vessel, who were to hold themselves in readiness to land at a preconcerted signal from me on shore. By this time it was evening, and the second body of 120 troopers, that namely which I had outridden from Termini, had arrived, and we had thus, with our sailors, a body of 730 or 740 men ; not enough, even if armed with artillery, to take the Palace Buildings by direct assault, but sufficient, I believed, for the kind of attack I meditated.

I had with my parting words promised the Sicilian Colonel that my assault upon him should not be delayed beyond the morrow : I meant to be better than my word, and to commence my siege of him that very night.

The buildings that surround the great Piazza, though not designed to serve as a citadel or strong-hold, are yet so built, with an armed tower set here and there in the outer wall, as to defy any ordinary attack, even by a disciplined force ; but as every place of arms has its weakest point, so this place had so extraordinarily weak a one that 'tis a marvel to me yet that it was suffered to remain. My Lord and I had more than once remarked that the *glacis* or open space outside the *enceinte* (as the engineers call it) had been encroached upon in one place by a store-house built from the outside against the outer wall. Here I resolved to make my assault, and for that purpose so soon as the night had fallen quite dark I called out my men, and having already dismounted all my troopers, save a few to serve as orderlies, I marched the whole body from the Quays to the

Palace, taking with us four ships' cannon with ammunition on trucks or rough tumbrils ; on another similar truck we carried a good stock of gunpowder. made up in strong bags weighing some half hundred-weight each. A body of twenty sailors from the ships were armed with heavy axes and sledge hammers.

Now, I protest, as I was marching through the streets upon this expedition at the head of my men, it did not a little go against the grain with me and positively hurt my conscience as a soldier, that I should be setting my wits and about to use all the resources and stratagems and fetches of glorious War against a poor simple fellow like this Sicilian Colonel, who clearly was ignorant of them all, and indeed had nothing of the soldier about him but the uniform on his back and the sword by his side. However, as I was minded for this once to effect my purpose without bloodshed, and catch the Colonel and his garrison in my net without hurting him or them, I salved my conscience a little with the humanity of my intention.

There is in front of the principal gate of the great Palace quadrangle a broad stretch of open ground, and a similar but lesser space, also free of houses, in front of the two side gates of the Piazza. In front of these three gates I drove my four tumbrils with a gun apiece on them, two guns before the chief gate, and one before each of the smaller approaches, but retired back as far as the nature of the ground would allow.

Then dismounting the guns and their ship-carriage with no little deliberation and noise, the gunners loaded their pieces and fired, and loaded and fired again in hot haste upon the gates, before each of which I had already ordered a bundle of lighted torches to be thrown to show them off and dazzle the eyes of the garrison. I did not expect that this cannonade would prove very harmful to the garrison, or that they would return the fire with any particular hurt to our people, for I knew the Sicilian troops were unskilled cannoneers, and moreover I was aware from former observation that the guns were only laid to give a cross fire upon an enemy actually entering the gate itself, and their gunners would be some time endeavouring after an aim upon our pieces; which proved the case, and their shot never came near us at all.

When I had set this feigned attack going, for I meant nothing else by it than a feint, designing only to alarm the garrison into running (poor simpletons!) to their strongest points, and into leaving their weakest to my attack, I rode quickly round to the afore-mentioned storehouse, where the main body of our sailors and dismounted troopers were already gathered, under cover of the night and the noise that the cannon-fire within and without was making. We easily broke open the doors of the building, and I caused a heavy mine of powder to be laid inside it against the very wall of the *enceinte*, and retiring my men blew it in and down, with a terrible noise and much smoke. Before the smoke had well cleared away, our men had

all run in through the breach, and as there was not
a soul to oppose us inside we passed through at our
leisure, and deployed in good order inside the Piazza.
I had expected to find all dark here, and so had caused
every seventh man of our force to provide himself with
a torch, a novel armament truly for men storming a
citadel, and an imprudent one, as some may think,
had I not rather designed to fright than to fight the
garrison ; but we found the garrison had already lit a
great bonfire in the middle of the courtyard to light
them to their work; so I bid the men douse their
torches, but not throw them away.

I had bidden my gunners outside to cease their fire
at the rising up of the mine, and as the blast likewise
frightened away the gunners of the enemy (if I can
by that word dignify this crowd of wretched fellows)
there was a silence in the place broken only by the
tread of our men marching in line towards the chief
gate, where I could see, in the half darkness, a crowd
of the garrison running from their guns in confusion
and endeavouring after a fashion to form into line.
Three or four of these undisciplined Sicilians now
discharged their firelocks upon us, and I began to be
terribly afraid,—if I may venture upon so ill-omened
a word,—I began, I say, to be afraid that if any of
our men were hit, their fellows would open fire in
spite of me (for the most disciplined soldiers are but
men) and then would commence a senseless slaughter
of the whole garrison. So halting our line, I went
forward alone some two score paces and called upon

the garrison to lay down their arms and they should
have quarter. They gave me no answer for a bit,
but when they looked upon the array of our men, we
having the great fire at our back with its swaying
flames, that cast moving shadows upon the ground,
and gleamed very terribly upon the barrels of our
fellows' arms, the Sicilians were utterly daunted, and
presently began to fling down their firelocks on the
ground and to hold up their unarmed hands for
quarter. I advanced towards them, leaving my men
still at halt, and called upon their commander by
name to cause his men to do the like. He did so,
and handed me his sword, which I took and immediately restored to him, in presence of his people
and ours.

"Sir," said I to him, "let us proceed to business
at once and waive ceremony. I pray you to order
the gates to be opened, and your people may file out
and go their ways for me."

He did as I required, and when the garrison had
departed, our gunners from outside brought their
cannon in by the chief gate. While this was doing,
I asked the Colonel, whom I kept by me, of my
cousin Geraldine and of Ralph. The Lady Geraldine,
he told me, and her suite had not stirred from their
lodging in the Palace. "And Lord St. Keyne?" I
asked. The Colonel faltered, and his face grew dark.

"Sir," he said, "you are aware that his Lordship
has come into the hands of those against whom a
soldier's power does not prevail."

"I will find means to prevail very shortly," said I, and I gave orders for all the gates to be closed, and set my men to marching to the eastern corner of the Piazza, where the Halls and Dungeons of the Inquisition lie, keeping the Sicilian Colonel, the while, by my side.

"I greatly fear you may arrive too late, Captain St. Keyne."

"Surely," cried I, "they have not carried off my Lord by sea?"

"Nay," he said, "there was no occasion. I fear there is no longer need for any further doing by the Inquisition. But I pray you not to bring me into this matter; I hold not at all with the severities of the Holy Office. Neither I nor my men have had a hand in this deed."

"Why!" said I, a sudden fear coming on me. "What is it?—what has happened? What have they done with my Lord?"

"He was arrested between midnight and dawn this day by the officers of the Inquisition."

"Arrested!" cried I, "but did his people not resist? Did his soldiers make no stand?"

"Nay," said the Colonel, "there were no soldiers about him; they were on duty in the city."

"'Twas treachery—black, devilish treachery, that laid him bare and undefended to his enemies' spite! Speak, Sir, what you know, and quickly!"

"One who related the matter to me told me that when a body of armed Familiars of the Holy Office seized his person, he ran upon them with sword and dagger, his servants coming about him to his rescue, but they were mostly unarmed men and soon beaten down, and he himself wounded."

" Wounded ? "

" Ay, on the head, with a sword-cut."

" And then ? "

"Then they carried him to the Tribunal of the Holy Office, and put him straightway upon his trial."

"Trial!" I called out in the agony of my soul, " but their trial begins with the question,—it begins with the torture of the accused to force a false confession! Do you know that ? "

" Sir, I fear it is as you say. 'Tis a most cruel thing and a most grievous tyranny upon us here in Sicily."

While I thus spoke with the Sicilian Colonel, we were advancing rapidly to the Palace of the Inquisition, which contains Courts, and a Judgment Seat, and many cells, dungeons, and places of punishment for its prisoners. I quickly surrounded the building with my men, and we smote loudly upon the great door for admission, but there came no acknowledgment from within. Seeing that the windows all were barred with cross bars of iron and all were lightless, I gave orders for the men carrying axes and sledge-hammers to ply them on the main door, and for them who had torches to light them. When the door was down I entered at the head of fifty of my own dismounted troopers and with a dozen men bearing lighted torches aloft. Passing through the doorway, we found ourselves in a corridor, dark but for the light thrown by us: following it, we reached a vaulted chamber so vast that the flare of our torches barely reached to its extremities. As yet no one had answered my summons and no inmate had showed, but opening from the great chamber, which I took to be the Judgment Hall itself, was a lower chamber, reached by a passage at a slope with steps along it. This lower chamber had a low-pitched roof held up by many stone pillars. This kind of crypt ran back a long way, and at its far end I perceived the red embers of a fire still smouldering in its ashes, and about it some scores of moving lights looking dim in the distance and no larger than glowworms. Advancing towards them, we perceived the fire to have been kindled on a sort of altar-like square of built up stones, open on all sides, and the lights to be held in the hands of over two score armed officers and Familiars of the Inquisition. We could have no doubt of the horrid purpose of this fire and the uses of the crypt, for into the walls were let great iron rings with chains depending, and on the pillars were hung sundry devilish instruments of iron, which sent a shiver and a shudder through our veins but to glance at them.

The Familiars, masked and hooded men, and mostly bearing partizans in their hands and swords by their sides, stood in a kind of military order, not giving

way as my soldiers came near; and suddenly their
ranks opened and the Grand Inquisitor himself and
two brother Inquisitors, clad in their black garbs and
caps of office, stood forth.

"What do you here?" he cried out in an angry,
solemn voice, "desecrating these Halls of the Holy
Office? On your souls lies this sin against the
privileges of our Church!"

His boldness and the solemn array of silent hooded
men with hidden faces, daunted my soldiers for a little,
but they recovered their assurance with their indignation and resentment when I spoke.

"Your Reverence has arrested our General by a vile
trick," cried I, "contrary to the laws of Spain, and
you have tried him without evidence and condemned
him to these damnable cruelties," I pointed to the
cursed implements upon the walls, "without justice
or the fear of our merciful God before your eyes.
Now," I called out, in a voice that fluttered all their
ranks, "deliver him to me immediately or, by the
Heaven above us all, you die the death!"

The Familiars shrank back, and the three Inquisitors themselves, seeing that their spiritual terrors
had no effect upon us, stood dismayed.

"Disarm these fellows!" I called out, and at my
order the spell was off our troopers, and in a moment
they had run in upon the Familiars, jerked their
weapons from their hands, and tearing off the cloth
hoods which hid all but their eyes, discovered to view
some of the most villainous-visaged cut-throats 'twas

ever my misfortune to gaze upon. Our men, when
once they had their hands in, were not very content
with a bare obedience to my orders, but hustled the
Familiars of the Holy Office, cuffing and buffeting
them with their clenched fists, and pummelling
them most unmercifully with the butt ends of their
muskets.

The Grand Inquisitor alone retained some little
courage, but his voice, methought, trembled as he
said, " Sir, this is Sacrilege, which the Most High will
revenge upon you. He whom you seek is already
beyond human seeking, or human succour."

" Old man!" cried I, "sure you are lying to me,
and are less inhuman than your words. You have
hidden your prisoner. Where is he ?"

I was over lenient in my thoughts of them, for
in truth even now they had come from their cruel
work, having only desisted at the noise of our
assault.

Some of the fellows who were being roughly used
by the soldiers now in their own terror cried out
that my Lord was there—pointing to a particular
door near where the Inquisitors and Familiars had
been standing. I ran to it, and catching up a sledge-
hammer, and one or two who carried axes and
hammers joining with their blows upon the door, it
presently flew open and I entered.

Dear Father of all Pity! What a sight met my
eyes! Never may I blot from my memory the horror
and grief of this moment! For there was Ralph, my

dearest cousin Ralph, lying stretched upon a low truckle-bed in this vile dungeon, a great wound upon his forehead, his white shirt dabbled with his blood, his long hair soaked and matted therewith, and his poor hands and bare feet torn and wounded with cruel torturing and all their white skin streaked with his blood. I knelt by his side and laid my hand upon his heart, my lips upon his face. Alas! Alas! the pulses moved not and his cheek was ice-cold. Dead! Dead! cut down in his prime and pride of youth by these inhuman villains! The fairest soul, and sweetest, bravest, noblest nature that ever came to brighten this earth!

"O foul murderers!" cried I, turning towards the villains and lifting my hands to Heaven, "O bloody, cruel and most damnable crime! Bind them fast," cried I to my soldiers, "sure the sentence of Heaven upon them cannot long be delayed; but hold! bind them fast, for its execution is decreed to us—bind them fast till I can think how I shall tear their black hearts from their vile bodies with torments as horrible as they have used to him!"

I raved, I wept, I cried aloud, I know not what words I used, nor could I perhaps have intended their meaning truly, but in that moment I was distracted by my agony: I was mad.

There had accompanied the troop, as is customary, our surgeon, an Italian gentleman of great skill, and while I, making sure that Ralph was indeed dead, was giving vent to the ecstasy of my grief and anger, he was busying himself with my cousin's lifeless body.

"Stay, Captain St. Keyne!" cried he suddenly; and, looking quickly round, I perceived he was holding one of those little mirrors our soldier doctors use to carry on the field of battle with them, to my cousin's mouth. "There is still life here, the soul is not wholly fled. Bear him quickly from this close dungeon air," he called out, and four of our English troopers that stood nearest lifted the low bed and carried it and him to the crypt, and laid him down where the air was freer. We gathered in a great circle about, while the surgeon raised Ralph's fallen head, and touched his lips with some essence from a phial he carried with him, and with his hand upon Ralph's heart, watched for the coming back of the little remnant spark of life.

Thus we stood, and none spoke or whispered even, or stirred, or hardly breathed; but we all looked from the pale dead face of him we loved for a sign of the life's return, to the surgeon's for a sign of hopefulness, —most earnestly praying and beseeching our Maker to show His mercy to us:

Almighty God! thou Dear and Loving Befriender of us Thy children! Sure Thou art All-Merciful even before Thou art All-Powerful, and wilt let Thine own Dread Decrees bend before the higher Law of Thy great Love and Pity for the creatures Thou hast made! And didst Thou not, this night, recall the Death Sentence that had already gone forth from Thy

Judgment Seat, in answer to the urgent, instant entreaties that reached Thee from our Souls ?

The first herald that came to us of returning life was the surgeon's sudden looking to us, with tidings of Hope in his face, for he had felt the first weak stroke of the awakening heart ; then the brow that had lain so smooth and calm in the death that had already begun to relax all the members, gathered a little, and a faint glow of red tinged the wan face, but vanished again immediately, and first a long breath came, liker though to a sigh, then, alas ! a moan, for the life that awoke in him awoke to the suffering that his torturers had caused, and which only the merciful swoon of his exhaustion had set to sleep.

When his soldiers saw the first breath of their General, they drew their own more freely, but at his groaning they looked again upon their prisoners (whom they had forgotten) with most revengeful eyes, and as if they burned at once to take a full and bloody vengeance upon those wolfish men.

I have now to tell of a most strange thing that befell ; which was this, that while we had imagined my Lord to be in a swoon, nay, even already passed away from the living, but assuredly in a deep trance, and bereft of all sense and apprehension of outer things, it would appear that though he was indeed beyond every faculty of motion, he was not so bereft of apprehension but that my mad words against the Familiars had been perceived and were known to him.

'Tis certain that in the very stupor of his trance he could judge and decide with his old accustomed rightness ; for we now saw his lips moving as if in speech, and when I leant down my ear I caught his whispered words : " Humphrey, we are to spare these ignorant fellows ; hurt them not and let them go their ways in peace." So strangely conscious can the recipient soul become when all the bodily senses still are sleeping !

I delivered the order aloud to the men, and sent a body of them to escort the Inquisition men in safety through our people in the Piazza and through the outer gate. Then, upon the advice of our surgeon, my Lord was borne on the bed as he lay, by some of his English troopers from the crypt out into the great court-yard and to his own lodging hard by.

As our men, soldiers and sailors, had now fully established themselves in the *enceinte* of the place, their battalia, or array, had been broken by their officers and they had been allowed to disperse themselves about the place. Still, however, they remained waiting about the entrance of the Inquisition Prison, having learnt from the fellows who had escorted the Familiars the news of their General's distressful condition, and of his lying between life and death, and now they would not go about their private business till they had learnt the fate of him who was so near the hearts of them all.

So we found our men when we issued from the doors in a crowd of some 700, who, as slowly we moved along carrying the entranced body of our

leader, formed themselves in a lane to let the bearers
pass, and some of them as we came out having quickly
lighted the torches we had brought, now held them
aloft against the darkness of the night. When the
men saw their Lord's death-pale face, and body without life or motion, they feared he was already passed
away from them, and a reverence and an awe was
begot in them, as for the dead ; and they uncovered
their heads and looked downwards solemnly in their
sorrow. When he passed near to them, and they saw
the piteous sight of his wound, of his torn and bleeding
hands and feet, these rough, ignorant, uncouth men
were stirred to tears. Yea, I protest that with my
own eyes I saw it ; they wept.

We brought him into the great Hall where he had
been used to study, and let him still lie stretched as
we had found him upon the little truckle-bed ; the
surgeon not daring as yet, in the pain and weakness
which beset him, to do aught to his wounds.

It was perhaps the moving him in his weakened,
half-deathly state, or perhaps some baneful influence
of the night air he passed through, that caused him
to go back into his stupor, and his heart-beat to flutter
first, and then grow still. He lay again quite entranced, and again the surgeon brought him to his
senses with the fumes of the subtle essence he had
used before, and again he breathed, and his heart went
on a little, and he moaned heavily in his pain ; but
presently he fell back into lifelessness.

" What I fear," said the surgeon, " is that when his

senses come fully to him, the agony of his limbs, racked and twisted by the torments he has suffered, will be so great, it will extinguish the little flame of life that yet flickers."

We watched on, hoping a little, but fearing far more, he never advancing to any recovery, but his strength seeming to wane and ebb with the minutes, and we being quite helpless to save him.

Then it was that the surgeon spoke to me thus :—

"Sir, your Lord has enlarged to me more than once upon the virtues of a certain Indian herb, like that which our apothecaries name *Opium Thebaicum*, and which as the Indians prepare it has strange dormitive and corroborant qualities. It first excites and rouses the spirits, then sets sense and feeling gradually asleep, so that all pain is stilled and all sorrow forgotten, and the body gets such refreshment by the drug, that it sleeps on, corroborating itself in rest, and needing neither drink nor food. Could we but administer this medicine, 'tis true we cannot hope to save the life—the tenement which holds it is too broken and subdued—but we should allay the suffering that will otherwise make death an agony."

Looking on Ralph, I wondered if he had heard these words also, and, willing to refer so great an issue to his own arbitrament, I asked him whether we should administer the drug, and leaning down my ear to his lips, I caught the faint whisper, "Yes."

Thereupon we procured a portion of the Indian Opium, and dissolving it in *aqua vitæ* gave him to drink of it.

How strange is the potency of this medicament! In a few minutes his eyes opened, and though the gathering of his brow betokened that he still suffered, the anodyne already began to work, and he moaned no longer.   He spoke, and it was no longer in a whisper, though the voice was still weak :

"Cousin Humphrey, I have heard the surgeon's words, and he judges rightly ; I must die.   I cannot pass through what I have undergone and live.   Let me therefore see Geraldine, while the drug still gives me this strength to speak; but tell her first I must surely die."

While the surgeon departed to procure his bandages and dressings for the wounds, I went to the Lady Geraldine's apartments and brought her hastily with me, telling her by the way of what had happened. She, among her women and the Palace servants, had heard but a confused account of her cousin's seizure by the Inquisition, of his having been subjected to the question, and his being rescued by us with some remains of life still lingering in him ; and now I told her that, though we were able to subdue the pain he suffered, he yet must surely die.

When she came to his bedside and stood weeping at his most piteous condition, he tried to take her hand in his, but his wounds were too sore, and his strength availed not.   Then said he to her,

" Kiss me, Geraldine, my own true wife, before I go away from you in death."

So she bent down her face upon his, and her lips

were upon his, and in her kiss strong pity was yet no stronger than strongest love. So she kissed his languid eyes, and then again fixed her lips upon his weak and trembling ones, murmuring womanly words of love and comfort, which, standing back, I heard but confusedly. Her two hands she laid upon his breast, but so tenderly that he felt nothing but the solace of her touch upon him; and as I looked on, lo! there was a wonder, yea, almost a miracle! For it was apparent to me that the maiden was instilling a new vitality into Ralph's inanimate body and, by her presence and bodily communion with him, she sustained and bore up the little fainting vitality still left, while with the mighty energy of her woman's love she breathed upon and fanned the dying fire of life, so near to extinguishment, till it grew again into a flame. Yea, I looked and saw the life come back into his face, the eyes brighten, the cheeks recover their colour, the lips grow red again from death's own wanness, and again he smiled upon us. The surgeon, coming hastily back at that moment, stared, wondering upon the late dying man.

"He is saved!" he cried, "and" (looking upon the Lady Geraldine) "not by my art. Such a marvel have I read in books," he muttered to himself, "but never yet have looked upon."

We waited, watching this miracle in silence; then Ralph spoke again, and it was no longer the broken, dying voice that we had heard before, but had hope in it and assurance of life.

"Geraldine!" he said, "my beloved, you have called me back to you, from the dark land that I was just entering, and now I shall live, to stay with you here, to love you!"

Now the dormitive drug began to have its influence, and his eyelids closed, but the colour of returned life was still visible upon his countenance.

"Let me rest," he said, "I am weary."

He slept with a long, deep sleep. It was forty-eight hours before he opened his eyes again, and the sleep so held all his senses that the surgeon bandaged the limbs that had been so cruelly be-racked, and Ralph knew it not, and bound up all his wounds, dressing them with smooth, lenitive ointments, and Ralph felt not he was handled by us. All this while his cousin Geraldine stayed by him, by day and by night, and it seemed that some unseen influence, some emanation of her love for him and loving resolve that she would conquer death and keep her lover with her, was ever passing from her to him. Nay, I will not say it seemed; it was so; for if she, in her anxious care for him, rose for a moment to adjust a covering or to help the surgeon or me in our ministrations, and if she happened to remove her hand from touching him but for an instant, he would move uneasily, and his face immediately lost its calmness. Our handling of his grievous wounds, our binding his strained limbs never stirred him in his slumbering, only if he lost the contact of Geraldine he knew it; and when she laid her hand upon him again, he was soothed afresh. By this I knew he was wandering with her he loved amid the pleasant fields and woods of the Dream Realm, and even through the thick envelope of his deep-drugged sleep, would not forego his communion and bodily touch of her. So was Ralph recalled to life by love.

What little more of this narrative I have to set down, I will tell in very few words.

When my Lord St. Keyne's long sleep had ended, he was past all danger, and needed but a few days' rest to recover his health, but alas! not all his strength. The cruelty of the Inquisition had robbed him for ever of his full heritage in this great gift of nature, and he ever after bore on his brow the cicatrice of the deep sword-cut he had received when they assaulted him, and overpowered him, and cruelly wounded him. Was this the bleeding wound I had seen in my dream of him?

Ralph never drew sword again in battle; so was his hope that he should one day draw it in his country's cause frustrated.

Even before my cousin had awoke from his first sleep, I had established beyond doubt how deep the Viceroy himself was in the plot which had betrayed Ralph to his merciless enemies. This high-placed, disloyal Spaniard indeed was the Judas on whose guilty head chiefly lay the innocent blood of Ralph that had been shed; for the Viceroy's cruelty was base revenge, the Inquisitor's only mistaken zeal. So

therefore we were disengaged of our loyalty to the
Viceroy by his broken faith with us, and we removed
ourselves from the Sicilian service, and took out of it
with us, as the terms of our engagement allowed, all
our English troop. Embarking them all in our little
galley, the *Golondrina*, we sailed for Naples, where
the happy marriage of Ralph and Geraldine took
place. But this departure was delayed for over a
month, less to await the recovery of my Lord, for in
a fortnight he had got strength enough to be moved,
than because he was loth to leave the City of Palermo
in the commotion into which the recent events had
thrown it. In truth the city was in a sort of tacit
insurrection against the Viceroy, and would have
broken out into a flame of avowed rebellion, but for the
people's love and respect for my Lord. The Viceroy
did not dare to return from Messina, with his Body-
guard now inflamed against him, and because he
knew the Sicilian troops to be untrustworthy, and
feared too to face the man against whom he had
schemed so foul a treason ; but my Lord composed
the matter for the sake of the Palermitan citizens,
and the guard we had formed consented to serve the
Viceroy again.

We ever afterwards rejoiced to think we had done
the Sicilians two good services. We had broken the
tyranny of the Inquisition. After the great shaking
their power got that night, when their Officers, including
the three Head Inquisitors themselves, were bundled
ignominiously into the street among the crowd that

had gathered (with perhaps a few more parting cuffs
and kicks from our troopers and sailors than it was
in my strict orders to bestow), the Holy Office never
could hold its head up again in Sicily. Another
grievous tyranny we had broken was that of the
Barbary Corsairs. They never thereafter so harried the
Sicilian coasts. Perhaps they would have begun again
after a time, but shortly after we left the Island, our
famous English Admiral Blake (a rough sea-dog of a
fellow and a Cromwellian, but, I am willing to concede, a great commander) gave them a most terrible
trouncing in Tunis Bay ; yet it must not be overlooked that Blake had all the might of England's navy
at his back, and that 'twas my Lord who first taught
these Infidels to run from an Englishman.

My two cousins were fated never again to see
England. Six years of happy life they passed in the
several chief cities of Italy ; then, on the joyful
restoration of our rightful king to his throne, they set
sail for Bristol and their English home at St. Keyne,
whither I was to follow with the Englishmen and the
two Dutchmen of the troop, who now no longer were
soldiers, but lived as honoured dependants in the
household of my Lord.

Ralph and Geraldine took ship for Bristol from the
Port of Leghorn, in Tuscany ; and I watched the ship
sail out of harbour one May evening, and lost sight
of her at last in the glow and glory of the setting sun.
Alas ! I was never to set eyes on my dear Lord and
Geraldine again, for their ship went down among the

Biscay waves, and none from her ever won to land.

For this their death I have only lately ceased to mourn and sorrow; but now I grieve no longer, seeing that the time is at last come so near for my meeting again with these two, whom I have loved beyond everything in this world. In truth I have reproached myself in that I ever wept their loss at all, for I should have remembered Ralph's opinion and declaration touching death; namely, that, as it behoves us all, sooner or later, to make this passage from darkness here to unknown light beyond, so is it to be desired and prayed for that we may be stricken down in the pride and fulness of our youth, and in our contentment and joy of life, rather than later, when the bitterness of age and sickness shall have arrived ; and this wish he had obtained for himself and for her whom he loved better than himself.

FINIS.

www.ingramcontent.com/pod-product-compliance
Lightning Source LLC
Chambersburg PA
CBHW022010110726
47901CB00006B/1472